JEANIE IN A BOTTLE

SHEAR MAGIC

Donna LaPointe

Hope you enjoy!

[illegible]

Jeanie in a Bottle

Shear Magic

TWO NOVELS BY

LORI AVOCATO

METROPOLIS INK

ISBN 0-9579528-0-5

METROPOLIS INK
USA / Australia

web: www.metropolisink.com

email: inquiries@metropolisink.com

I want to thank my family for all their support throughout my career. Thanks to my sister, Margaret Braddon, and cousins, Barbara Nawrocki and Alice Meattey, for all their encouragement. Also, a big thanks to my co-writer friends at CTRWA.

Jeanie in a Bottle

Chapter One

Capricorn: A member of the opposite sex will seek your advice and company. Being shrewdly intuitive, you will know whether to accept or reject.

"Yeah, I'll accept the company of the opposite sex, if I remember what to do with it," Harrison Rainford said as he ripped the fool horoscope up into hundreds of pieces. If his sister didn't stop sending him these stupid things, he'd...well he wasn't thinking clearly right now—because of her. He jammed down the call button for his secretary, "Margaret, find my sister."

Margaret's motherly, yet always-stern voice came back, "We've been through this before, boss. She's hightailed it out of the country and even Scotland Yard couldn't find her. An old woman like me has no hopes."

He groaned. "Did you try her friends?"

"Does she have any that stay awake during the day, eat meat, or answer their phones by picking them up and actually talking into the receiver? If not, I'm not great at channeling."

He sighed this time. Too much groaning, no matter how much he wanted to, would make Margaret think he'd gone nuts, and worse of all, Leo might hear. "Is... Leo all right?"

"Immersed in the wonderful world of video wrestling. My grandkids will have a fit that I opened that video game for your nephew when it was one of their Christmas presents."

"I'll replace it. Christmas is in three months, Margaret. Besides, your grandchildren aren't due to visit for a few more weeks..."

"Don't you even dare. You know my family policy on kids, boss. The grandkids, whom I love dearly, can come for short visits. Two days tops. I don't do babysitting any longer than that, and if you're not blood—as poor darling Leo—you don't even get to come for a short visit."

He heard her stick her hand over the intercom and cheer Leo on.

"The kid's a doll, too introverted though, but still, I paid my dues with five of my own. Sorry. You keep forgetting, I'm a swinging single now."

"But, Margaret, I'll double your salary…"

"I think I hear a call coming on line one, boss."

"Leave the clairvoyant and woo-woo stuff up to my sister. Make that triple, no quadruple your salary. It's only temporary until she—God help me, this month she calls herself Tabitha—gets back from wherever in the world she is."

"You can barely afford me now. No. And no again since I know you were going to press the issue. I'll try the rest of the nanny services in the phone book just to make you feel better. But, I don't have to tell you, none of them do temporary jobs. It's the start of the school year and they're up to their—alphabets—in calls. But, I'll try."

He sank into his red leather chair and looked out the window. The trolley clanged along Saint Charles Avenue, passersby walked in the brisk fall air, most likely thankful that the New Orleans humidity had let up for now, and a lone bird—some kind of blue thing—flew past his window, landing on the sign hanging from the wrought iron post. *Rainford Advertising*. The bird took off in flight—and pooped on the sign.

"Margaret, I'm going out to lunch," he said into the intercom.

A pause. "Er… it's only ten-thirty."

"I need… lunch." A martini.

"Okay."

He grabbed his jacket and shoved it on, not caring if it were inside out. What a day. First Tabitha sends her kid over in a cab, suitcase and horoscope in hand, with a note saying she'll be out of the country, finding her soul, for a few weeks. She'd done this sort of thing so many times; this was the last straw. He shoved open the door to Margaret's office and paused.

Leo vigorously jammed his fingers on the controls of the Sony PlayStation Harrison had put in for Margaret's grandchildren. She wasn't opposed to them "visiting" here for a few hours at a time. He didn't much care since there wasn't a better secretary or friend in the world. Actually, all thirty-five of his employees were fantastic. That's why he had to get the biggest account of his career signed tonight.

He ran his fingers across Leo's head. "Hey, buddy, how's it going?"

The boy never took his eyes off the television. "Fine, Uncle Harry."

"Hungry?"

"Mom gave me a tofu salad before I came here."

"Uck," Margaret murmured.

Harrison raised an eyebrow at her. "That doesn't sound like something that would fill a guy's stomach up. How about a Big Mac?"

Margaret came over and adjusted the blinds so the morning sun wouldn't reflect on the television. "Since when did you start eating at McDonalds?"

"Never, but what do you say, buddy? Big Mac and fries?"

"I don't eat meat anymore. 'Member?"

Harrison sucked in a breath. Tabitha needed a good shaking and a few lessons on parenting. Not that he was qualified to give them though. "Well, I'll bring you back something. Veggies all right?"

"Sure." He leaned forward as if that would help his player knock some sense into the opponent dressed as Dracula.

Harrison debated about questioning that kind of game for an eight-year-old, but didn't have the heart—or the energy right now. If his sister were here....

He pushed at the door and mumbled, "I wish someone would give me strength to get through this."

"Whoa boy!" a woman yelled as the door slammed into her.

"Excuse me, ma'am!" Harrison said, reaching out to grab the woman as she started to topple to the carpeted entryway. "I didn't see you, the door opened so fast." Where'd she come from? He hadn't seen her, then as if out of thin air, there she was smack dab in the doorway. "Are you all right? I can get my secretary to call 9-1-1 if you are…"

"If you need anyone called, your wish is my command, Master," she said in a perfect English accent.

Master? Oh, great. This day couldn't get any worse. Did she hit her head? Actually she landed against the wall never making it to the floor. No way could she have hit her head. Besides, not one red hair was out of place. It all remained neatly tucked into a ponytail with some kind of black velvet hat-thing on the top of her head. Kind of like a yarmulke, he thought. But on her it looked Asian. It actually matched the black velvet skirt she wore and the silken number, which hugged her slender rather flat chest, pretending to be a top. And her darn feet were bare.

She sure didn't look like one of his clients.

"Do I know you?"

She glanced at him and gave him a smile that nearly had him forgetting about his sister. Then she shook her head. "I'm here to…"

"I have a secretary for making my calls, but if you need something she is inside."

She pulled herself up despite his outstretched hand and gave him a serious look. "I am here to serve you."

Serve him! His felt his eyes widen. "I… er… no thank you. If you are sure you're all right, there is nothing I can do for you, then I must run." He turned to go.

"Ummmmmm."

"What the heck…" He swung around to see her eyes closed,

her hands folded in front of her chest and she was humming—or ummming—much like some yoga person would do. Oh Lord, couldn't he get away from these metaphysical quacks? First his sister Elizabeth changes her name to Tabitha, this month that is, and heads off to find her soul. Now this woman stumbles into his office to… what? Um? "Excuse me."

"Ummmmmmmmmm."

"Excuse me!"

Her eyes flew open. "Yes, Master?"

"I don't know who you think you are, what you are doing here, or what you are selling if that's the case. But I'm going to lunch."

"But you summoned me, Master." She settled herself in the waiting room's brocade covered couch, folding her legs into a position he'd only seen a contortionist do on a rerun of the old Ed Sullivan Show.

"Summoned? What are you talking about?" And why am I standing here even asking you that?

She blinked. Did her chin wiggle? Yes, he was certain, her chin wiggled as she blinked. She looked at him as if waiting for him to say something.

He grabbed one of the French doors to the outside of the Victorian house that doubled as his office and pulled. But he didn't walk out. "What?"

She bent her legs further together. He winced, yet his eyes were drawn to her midriff. The skin looked so soft, creamy as she tensed with movement.

"I was looking to see if your wish had come true." She bent forward. "Do you feel any stronger?"

He blew out a breath. "No."

"Oh, dear. I'm new at this… er… you're my first."

He sucked in enough air to swim across the Mississippi, then blew it out with such force a strand of her hair yanked loose.

"Oh," she murmured, tucking it back.

"Look, lady…"

"Jeanie."

"Whatever... Oh, I get it. Genie." He shook his head and looked up to the sky. "Okay. Good joke. My planets must be way out of whack to be causing such a spectacular day. I'm a Capricorn, but self-confessed idiot when it comes to zodiac signs. The way I like it. But, I give up. Strike me with lightening now."

She unwrapped her legs and stood. A 60s kind of scent wafted from her, reminding him of what the hippies must have smelled like, flower children. He thought of when the last time a woman's scent had him notice.

"It hasn't been *that* long. Has it? You've only broken up with Laura..." he reminded himself.

"Six months, two days ago," the genie finished.

"Yeah, but who's count..." He grabbed her by the shoulders. Fragile. She felt as if she'd break. Without a thought he released her but caught her attention by leaning near. "What did you say?"

"You broke up with your fiancée..."

"You know Laura?"

She took a step back. Was that fear in her purple eyes? Purple? Had to be contacts. No one except Liz Taylor had eyes that color. "Of course I don't know Laura Dupre. Genies know *of* people, things. We don't have to know them personally to know when they are selfish, money-hungry liars..."

She'd described Laura perfectly! This time he grabbed her and held on. "I don't know what kind of game you are playing, lady..."

"Jeanie." She didn't try to pull away.

"*Genie*, but..."

"You're pronouncing it like 'genie' with a *G*, but it really is 'Jeanie.' *J-E-A-* only one *N-I*..."

"*E*. I know how to spell." He ran a hand through his hair, not caring if it stuck out in a million places. "Why doesn't someone just come and shoot me today? Put me out of my misery. At least horses get that much consideration when they're injured."

Her eyes widened like gems. "Are you hurt, master? I shall care for you if you..."

"No, Jeanie, I am not hurt physically, but mentally I'm a waste. My day has stunk since my sister dropped her kid..."

"Leo. Darling Leo."

He froze. "Yeah." Logic said he should be concerned this nutcase knew his nephew's name. It wouldn't be impossible that she came to kidnap him to get Harrison to pay the ransom. But there was something about her, and not just her appearance, that made him hesitate about calling the police.

She was weird, but he didn't see her as a threat—yet. Maybe Laura had sent her here for revenge? Hm. He didn't think Laura would know an oddball like this one. Then again, this was New Orleans. He reminded himself that a woman author who wrote about vampires lived down the street. The French Quarter boasted the Voodoo Museum, the locals had their beliefs in spells, and spiritual weirdness was an everyday occurrence in the Big Easy.

This wacko fit right in, but not in his orderly life.

She had to go.

"I'm starving. I have no idea how you know so much about me, but any PI worth his salt could dredge up stuff like that. Tell whoever put you up to this—maybe even Laura herself—that he or she is wasting their time and money. If blackmail, kidnapping or whatever is your game. I'm not playing."

She looked genuinely hurt.

"You ever do any acting?" he asked. "If not, Casting Central needs to take a look at you, Jeanie."

She sighed. "I was warned this wouldn't be easy."

He opened the door and stepped out. Over his shoulder he said, "Nothing is, sweetheart. Didn't your mamma ever tell you nothing in life is free or easy?"

"Helping others is."

He stopped on the top step and watched the trolley approaching. "Yeah, well. Help yourself to a ride. The trolley will take you toward the French Quarter. You'll find your kind there."

"My kind?" She followed him out, stood on the landing of the porch.

"Genies with a *G*. That is, women who think they are genies. Also you'll most likely find, vampires, witches, maybe even a leprechaun come next March."

She shook her head. "I knew this was going to be difficult. Harrison Rainford…" She laughed. "Hey, you know that your name is similar to…"

He cursed. "No. What is it similar to?"

"That actor. I loved his Indiana Jones movies. You look a lot like him, too, and your voice is like his."

He leaned against the wrought iron gate. "Imagine that. I'll bet my mother was a fan of his or something. Wait, that's right. She saw "American Graffiti back in '73. Oh, yeah. She named me after him. How could I forget such earth shattering news? It's not as if I'm reminded of it every time I meet someone. He's a few years older than I am though. Well, we'll have to chalk up Harrison Rainford and Harrison Ford—two hunks, I'm sure you'll agree—to coincidence."

"Oh, my."

"Oh, my is right. I'm not usually so sarcastic, but I've had a rotten day and more coincidences than I care to." He stepped up toward her and said, "Wait, I know, we can add having a genie drop into my office. No wait. Make that *appear* in my office as coincidence, too. The day I coincidentally need…"

"A babysitter for Leo."

"You don't even look old enough to take care of yourself."

She pulled her shoulders straight, making her what? Five feet? "My age is of no consequence. But for the record, I was born in Baghdad enough years ago to make me an adult."

"And you don't look a day over, what? a thousand?"

She smiled. No one past twenty-five had a complexion like that.

"Oh, I get it," he said, before she could interrupt. "This is some sort of joke. "Candid Camera" is back on the air, isn't it?"

"'Candid Camera?'"

"Television show?" Her mouth started to open. For a second, he lost his train of thought. "You… don't watch television," he mumbled.

She shook her head. "Don't own one."

"Look, I have very little time left. If I don't get lunch, my world might just end…"

"It's only morning…"

He took her arm firmly. "I missed breakfast. Lack of appetite since…"

"Since you broke up with Laura."

"Of course, you already knew that."

She wiggled her arm free, and rubbed it with her other hand. "That one I guessed."

"Sorry about your arm."

She shrugged. "Don't let me keep you from eating, Mr. Rainford."

"What happened to Master?"

"If you don't believe, then I can't grant you any wishes." She leaned against the railing.

He should go. He should turn and go, eat anything the waiter set in front of him and get a Big Mac for Leo whether he ate meat or not. Leo. He'd almost forgot about him. He ran his hand across his chin and sighed.

"The fact remains that you need help watching, Leo. I can help you, Mast…" She clamped down her words and glared at him—could a genie be so defiant to her master?

"Okay, Genie. Make me believe. Here's my first wish." He turned, walked down three steps, and yelled for all of Saint Charles Avenue to hear: "Disappear!"

With a chuckle that was the best thing that he'd felt all day, he turned around to gloat.

She was gone.

Chapter Two

Capricorn: Improvement in business opportunities brings a smile to your face and a boost to your wallet early this week.

Jeanie watched Harrison stomp down the stairs. No one noticed her, thank goodness. She couldn't help but keep watching him as he walked with a determined pace down the street. She wondered if he knew where he was going at eleven in the morning to find a martini. It made her smile. She reappeared on the landing near the foot of the porch, slung her purse over her shoulder, and walked down the steps.

And followed him.

This job had to be done right. She had a lot at stake here. After all, she laughed out loud, a new genie was merely on probation.

She was going to complete this job so well, that she would bring tears of joy to her mother.

She'd shed far too many other kinds of tears lately.

At the corner, she watched Harrison turn down the street and into a beautiful old French-provincial house. The sign said it was a restaurant. Open for lunch.

"But do they serve martinis?" she said, then laughed again. Being a genie made her happy.

She waited until he went in, then paused a few minutes and looked at herself in the window of an upscale boutique behind the fence. Her outfit might be okay, but she didn't have on shoes. They probably wouldn't let her into such a nice restaurant like that. Well, who would look at her feet if she gave them something more interesting to look at? She turned into the boutique, mentally calculating her expenses. Genies had money problems, too, it seemed.

"May I… help you," the clerk asked, although Jeanie was quite certain the snob didn't really want to help her.

"Nope. I'll just browse." She did, looking for that special something that would catch her eye. The woman's gaze followed her around like a visual security guard. When she lifted up a tortoise comb and looked at the price, she nearly dropped it to the floor. Talk about highway robbery. These prices were—

There it was on the glass counter across the room. She shut her eyes and made a wish. Maybe genies could make their own wishes come true. Just in case, she said a silent prayer that she could afford it.

She walked slowly, purposely toward the counter, lifted up the necklace, and held it to her chest, without looking at the price tag.

"Oh, my," the clerk said. She came near, making Jeanie think she was going to rip it out of her hands. But she had nearly sighed her words as if she, too, thought it looked perfect for Jeanie.

"It spoke to me from across the room…"

The woman smiled. "As well it should." She fingered the tiny figures on the necklace. Jeanie watched as her bony fingers gently touched each silver figurine with great care—as if they were real. "They are special, you know. Tiny fairies dancing across your chest. You look like a spiritual kind of woman."

You don't know the half of it, Jeanie thought.

"It's right for you."

With a deep breath, Jeanie reached down and lifted the white sales tag. "Oh."

At first the woman paused. Jeanie readied for her sales pitch, trying to talk her into something she couldn't afford. Darn it all. The necklace would have been perfect. It gave her class along with the mystique every genie should have. And it'd take the maitre d's eyes off her feet.

"Look, sugar," the woman's voice sweetened. She looked around the shop and leaned near. "You look like a nice kid, a bit flamboyant in the dress department. But I can see into your soul. And you have a good soul. Give me half now and it's yours."

"Oh gosh, yes, of course. I'll take it then."

"And give me the other half in one month."

Jeanie watched her jaw drop in the mirror. Damn. The old witch.

The woman went to unhook the clasp. Jeanie turned before she could touch it. She looked in the mirror, touched the necklace, and said, "I'll keep it on."

After putting half of the exorbitant price on her already maxed-out charge card, Jeanie hurried out of the shop. Surely Harrison hadn't had time to finish his martini yet. She walked down the steps leading to the huge wooden door of the restaurant. Jasmine filled the air, and a soft saxophone wailed on inside. Her kind of music.

Maybe she shouldn't admit that. Saxophones didn't exactly give off a Middle Eastern atmosphere.

So she'd keep another secret from her master.

He sat on the other side of the room, alone she noted, as she walked in. What had she expected? To find him snuggled up in some corner with a leggy blonde? Actually that scene would be befitting of the guy, the restaurant, and the sax. She could swear there was a mist of fog curling amongst the potted palms along the brick wall.

The poor dear looked exhausted though.

If only she'd been able to convince him to let her help him grant his wishes, she thought. Well, she wasn't going to fail at being a genie. No way. She had absolutely no desire to go back to her old position. Harrison would probably accuse her of having been one of Ali Baba's thieves. She held her head high, determined to convince this guy to let her help.

He went to take a sip of his martini, and looked at her above the rim of the glass. "I hope you're an alcohol-induced hallucination." He set the glass down and blinked several times, then stood. "Damn it."

She pulled out a chair and sat across from him. "Perhaps you should have something to eat?"

"Why? I didn't slur my speech, yet." He picked up the glass and a took a huge gulp. Redness worked its way up his neck, along his squared jaw line, and to his cheeks. She smiled to herself.

"You'd better cough or you might choke after taking such a large drink."

He glared at her, then coughed. "What… do you want anyway? And don't start that genie stuff…"

"May I get something for the lovely…" the waiter started to ask. His gaze froze on her necklace. Harrison hadn't even mentioned it. "Oh my, that is lovely, *mademoiselle*."

Harrison snorted. "You whip that up yourself?"

The waiter gave him a surprised look. "Mr. Rainford, may I bring your lunch now?"

"Bring me a seltzer with a twist of lemon." He looked at her. "Make that a martini. What exactly do genies drink?"

The waiter's gaze shifted back and forth between them like he was watching a tennis ball at Wimbledon. At least he didn't look at her feet.

"Water with lemon is fine, sir." She smiled at the waiter as he excused himself—swiftly.

"Water? I should have guessed. Do you actually eat food too, or wait, this must be your first time in a restaurant. What need would a genie have to *buy* food?"

She leaned near, picked up a linen napkin, and dabbed it on his chin. "A droplet of martini. You know," she continued. "You don't have to be so sarcastic. The alcohol must have loosened your tongue."

"I know. I know. Sorry. You only came to help." He grabbed a breadstick, and broke it in half with a force that it had her jump. "What do you want to eat?"

"What are you having?"

"Seafood jambalaya."

"Oh my." She took a breadstick, lifted his knife since the waiter hadn't given her a set of silverware yet, and ran a slice of butter across the stick. "I didn't realize how hungry I was before. Everything smells wonderful."

"Then jambalaya for two…"

She bit the stick, chewed quickly and said, "I'm a vegetarian…"

"No kidding. Hm, I never would have guessed." He leaned forward and touched her arm. "Solid," he whispered.

She couldn't help but stare at the spot he'd touched. Damn; she could still feel his touch, even though he'd taken back his hand.

"I half expected you to be made of air." *But you sure feel real,* Harrison thought. *Too real.* This woman was too much. He should call the police. Now, he thought, since she actually believed herself to be a genie. She needed medical attention, although she still didn't seem a threat to him or herself. Still, he'd keep a close eye on her and Tulane Hospital's phone number on hand.

She was easy to keep an eye on.

The waiter was right about her damn necklace. It did something for her. No, to her. Made her look more mystical. Much like Tabitha in her silken scarves and caftans the size of tents. Spirits must have a ball flitting around under those things.

"I'm quite solid all over, Mr. Rainford," she said.

He bit off half the breadstick and looked at her. "What happened to 'Master'?"

"I think it is better not to refer to you as such, in public."

He chuckled. "Good thinking. Make it Harrison then."

"Harrison."

In that proper King's English, his name rolled off her tongue. She sounded much like a royal nanny. Nanny. Babysitter. Leo! He had to get back and do something about the child. Poor kid. Well, if Margaret was Margaret, she'd have his problem solved by now.

The woman was a saint.

★

"I'm sorry, boss. No luck," Margaret said as he walked into the office.

The martini on an empty stomach had him a bit unclear. Surely Margaret wasn't saying... "No luck?"

"I believe she means about a babysitter for Leo, Master."

He spun around, more embarrassed than surprised that she called him that in front of Margaret. He turned to his secretary. She sat there grinning.

"Hey, you can play whatever game you want with your... beautiful friend. About time. Besides, boss, I'm no prude." She had the audacity to chuckle as she reached into the file cabinet and pretended to work.

"I... she's not my..." He hurried into his office.

"Slave?" Margaret offered, getting up and following him. She set a stack of phone messages on his desk.

"Genie," he corrected. "Cripes. What the hell am I talking about?" He slumped into his chair. "Sit down, Jeanie, or better yet, leave if you have someplace to go."

"If you need me, I'll be in my office, boss." On the way out, her shoulders shook, and he swore he heard her say, "But, then again, why would you need a secretary when you have your very own genie?"

"That'll cost you your Christmas bonus," he called out.

She howled.

"And, expect to work on Mardi Gras!"

Jeanie stared at him.

"No one in New Orleans wants to work on Mardi Gras. It's more important than all the other holidays rolled into one..."

He ran a hand through his hair. Obviously he had the deep chocolate hair styled. When she first saw him, she'd noticed that. Now that he ran his hand through it though, in obvious disgust she guessed, strands stuck out in various places. He mustn't care how he looked.

He looked adorable.

"Look, Jeanie, you seem like a nice woman. If you need money, I'll give you some if you sign something to the effect that you won't ever come back for more..."

She stood, and glared down at him. She looked as if she grew taller from this angle. He expected her to rise up to the ceiling in a cloud of smoke like a real genie growing out of a lantern. Real genie? One martini was way too much for him to handle these days.

"Harrison Rainford, I have been sent here to help you. I don't need your handout. I've never accepted charity in my life. I will help you with Leo until his mother returns." With that she turned and walked to the door. She yanked the handle, opened the door, and slammed it with a force that had the beveled glass nearly shattering.

His teeth, too.

How'd she know about his mother? Lucky guess, obviously. "Give me strength," he muttered, quickly looking at the door, half expecting her to fly in and announce he was the new middleweight champion of the world.

Well, that wasn't the kind of strength he was wishing for right now.

Chapter Three

Capricorn: Someone new enters your life. They may not be trustworthy. You would be wise to do a background check before letting this person further into your life.

Jeanie paused on the other side of Harrison's office door. The secretary continued to work, but not until she looked at Jeanie from the corner of her eye.

"It's not what you think, ma'am," Jeanie said.

"He doesn't pay me to think. Name's Margaret, sugar. What's yours?"

"Jeanie. Nice to meet you." Force of habit had her extending her hand. Margaret took it and gave her a warm smile. Jeanie's gaze was drawn to Leo. Engrossed in the video game, he was adorable.

"Leo, this is Jeanie," Margaret said.

Never taking his eyes off the screen, he said, "Hey."

"Hey." Jeanie nodded toward Margaret and walked to Leo. "Mind if I watch?"

"Go ahead." He leaned back and forth with the actions of the wrestlers as if he really were in control of them. With every turn, every throw of one body then another, he kept his focus on the screen.

"Yikes!" Jeanie sunk down on the floor next to the kid, folding her legs one over the other. "Get em! Ouch! That's got to hurt!"

Leo laughed a child's laugh, but it didn't reach deep enough into his soul, she thought.

This boy needed her.

"Hey, Leo, mind if I give it a try?" Behind her, Margaret stopped clicking on her computer keyboard. Jeanie didn't turn around lest the secretary tell her that she had to leave. If she didn't look, she didn't have to face whatever Margaret was thinking. Too bad genies couldn't read minds.

"Well, let me finish this one…" *Game Over* flashed across the screen. "Okay." He handed her the controls.

"What do I need to beat you?"

He gave her a "yeah, right" look. "Eleven thousand."

"Now don't be thinking a woman like me can't beat the wresting pants off an eight-year-old." She pressed *Start*. The game materialized. Her first wrestler appeared.

"How'd you know…"

Oops. "You… look eight. First I was gonna— Get em!" She leaned way over much like Leo had been doing. Her fingers clicked wildly on the controls. "I think this helps, kid. Anyway. Jerk! Not you, Leo. That's Dracula who's the jerk. I was first gonna say nine cause you look older, but something told me eight." *Game Over* appeared. "Get out of here!"

Leo laughed. In the background, Margaret chuckled. Then she buzzed her intercom and said, "Your business dinner's at seven instead of eight. Good old boy from Texas. Likes punctuality. You should be a shoo-in."

"Ten thousand five hundred. Too bad." He took the controls as she handed them toward him. "You really think I look eight?"

She folded her legs further together. "And a half."

"Perhaps genies can read minds?" Harrison said.

"Nope…" Shoot! She unfolded herself and sprung up. He stood in the doorway glowering. Margaret typed away, although Jeanie knew whatever the secretary wrote wasn't the cause of her grinning.

Leo paused his game and turned. "Genies? Why'd Uncle Harry say…"

Harrison hurried forward. "Private joke, kid. You have those with your friends, don't you?"

Leo's expression remained firm. "Don't have many friends. Tabitha moves us around so much…"

Harrison growled. Fear crossed the kid's face, and Jeanie touched his shoulder. "I don't think your uncle's guttural sound was meant for you."

"Yeah?" He smiled at her.

Harrison stood speechless. Leo didn't smile much. Actually, he couldn't remember seeing him ever smile except as a baby when he didn't know what real life was like. When the years passed, and his sister had gotten weirder, she'd divorced her husband and—Leo had stopped smiling.

Jeanie had gotten him to smile after just meeting him.

Don't go there, he ordered himself.

Margaret, the evil person, interrupted his thoughts with, "Hey, boss, I have an idea that will solve your babysitting prob..." She glanced at Leo while Harrison wildly waved his hands at her to shut up. "Situation."

"Time for your lunch, Margaret."

"I ate. Anyway, Jeanie seems the perfect..."

Leo jumped up. "Way cool! She's my babysitter, Uncle Harry?"

Harrison sucked in a breath, shut his eyes so he wouldn't have to see Jeanie and Margaret staring at him—nor the ecstatic look on Leo's face and said, "I don't think..."

"Do you want me to be, Leo?" Jeanie asked.

Harrison grabbed her arm. "Excuse us a minute." He pulled her back into his office and shut the door. Margaret's muffled voice said she must be comforting Leo, or digging Harrison deeper into this mess.

"You had no right..."

"You saw the look on his face. He likes me. Kids and animals always do."

"Great. If I get a dog, I'll call you. In the meantime..."

"In the meantime that boy has no one to watch him while you attend your fancy dinner and do business..."

He stared at her.

"I heard Margaret reminding you about that one. So, let me

watch Leo—just for tonight. If I screw up—and I won't—you can fire me."

Harrison let her go. He walked to his window and looked out. She doubted if he saw the sun's rays glistening on the bougainvillea or three bluebirds drinking from the birdbath nearly covered in ivy or the moss swaying in the welcomed breeze. Nope. Harrison probably saw a black and white still picture of trees and birds.

"I know nothing about you…"

"I'm good, trustworthy, considerate, and make a mean pizza that wows every kid I meet."

"Ever been arrested?"

She paused. He swung around. "Of course not."

"You hesitated…"

"Who would arrest a genie…"

"You know, I'd have hired you on the spot if you presented yourself as a woman, a plain ordinary woman…" Ordinary? What was he saying? Jeanie was not plain or ordinary with her fiery hair, her pert breasts beneath the flimsily material of her top—most likely no bra. His insides did a little dance that had him grab onto the back of his chair. The chair swiveled, he nearly tipped over.

She reached out and grabbed onto his arm. Damn but she had a firm grip for such a tiny spitfire of a woman. Something told him Jeanie could handle herself, and more than likely Leo, too.

But what Harrison wondered was, could *he* handle himself where she was concerned?

"I don't even know your last name," he said, easing free of her grasp. If he didn't, he couldn't concentrate.

"Merriday."

"Merriday? I should have guessed."

She sat in his chair, swiveled back and forth much like Leo had done the many times he'd been in here. She was child-like enough to get along great with the kid.

"How could you guess…"

"What I meant was, the name suits you."

"Actually my family's name used to be Barrow. Mother thought it too stuffy. She had it legally changed for her and myself after the divorce."

"Genies get divorces?"

She hesitated, then laughed. "We have to blend in."

He sat on the edge of the desk. "My sister changes her name on a monthly basis."

She chuckled. "A rose is a rose." She touched his knee and looked up.

He wished she hadn't done that. He gulped, looked down on black nails dotted with silver stars. Cripes. Visions of Tabitha.

"Give me a chance, Harry. Please."

Harry. She'd said it so matter of fact as if they'd known each other for years. Been friends. Not many were allowed to call him that. Actually, Leo since he was a kid and Harrison thought the less formal name would make a better relationship with his nephew, and occasionally Margaret with the deepest endearment, were the only two. His nanny never called him Harry nor had his parents. "Promise you won't mention that you are a genie to Leo."

She, thank goodness, removed her hand and crossed her fingers over her chest. "Cross my heart. Yes, genies do have hearts. No mentioning it to Leo."

He reached out his hand to hers. She took it, shook more firmly than he would have expected. "Temporary deal," he said. He let her go and finished with, "But I will be running a check on you, purely routine for all my employees..."

"Did you do a criminal check on Margaret?"

"No, but..."

She waved her hand and stood. "Fine. Whatever." On her way to the door, she turned, smiled a killer smile, and said, "I'll be upstairs at five to feed Leo supper."

"Good." His eyebrows rose. "How'd you know that I lived upstairs..."

She shook her head. "Harry, you're going to have to accept me as is." She stood on tiptoes and looked him in the eye. "You know what, Harry? Earlier you'd said, 'promise you won't mention that you *are* a genie to Leo.'"

"Yeah, so?"

She grinned. "Instead of saying, promise you won't mention that you *think* you are a genie."

He turned toward the window to hide his obviously reddened face. The woman was not only a nutcase, but frustrating as well. He turned back to explain what he'd meant—

She was gone, again.

He debated about wishing her back.

★

"Now, Leo, if you need me..." Harrison straightened his tie and reached into the pocket of his tux. "I'll have my phone right here. I wrote down the number..."

Leo slumped across Harrison's bed. "Doesn't Jeanie have it?"

This is in case you need me because of Jeanie, Harrison thought. But he didn't want to scare the kid, so he said, "I'll give it to her also. But, I'm giving you my beeper number, too. If you can't get me on the phone, beep me."

"Yeah. What would I need you for anyway?"

The genie might act weird—weirder. "I don't think you will, but you know me, kid, I'm a stickler for certain things."

"That's not what mom calls you." He jammed his finger on the remote and surfed through hundreds of stations.

This was the most activity his satellite dish had gotten, ever. "I can just guess what she calls me." He walked to the mirror, checked his hair and tie again, and leaned near. A new wrinkle had formed near his left eye since this morning.

The doorbell rang.

Leo jumped up. "Must be Jeanie!"

Harrison felt another wrinkle form.

"Let her in. I'll be right out." He walked to the full-length mirror and looked at himself again. Cripes. He'd never been this concerned about his looks. Shaking his head, he walked to the door, shutting off the television on his way out. Leo would have to use the one in the living room now that Jeanie was here. No way did he want her in his bedroom. Too sensual a thought.

Where'd that come from?

Again he shook his head, told himself he was acting weird and went out to the living room.

She sat on the floor in one of her pretzel positions, Leo trying to copy her. She laughing and instructing. Leo giggling like a typical eight-year-old. Again, a sight Harrison had never observed.

He swallowed. "Seems like you two will be fine…"

She turned to him, a sparkle in her eyes. *Gems*. He thought of gems. Didn't Mother have an amethyst bracelet? With a shake to his mind, he finished, "I left the number where I'll be on the counter. There is food in the frig…"

"We'll be fine. Bye," she said, bending her leg into a position that might require surgery to undo.

"Yes, of course, but I thought Leo might get hungry soon. He hasn't eaten dinner…"

"Kids eat supper not dinner, Harry. We'll be fine. Bye," she said much louder. "Keep your toes pointed out," she said to the kid.

"Bye, Uncle. I'm not hungry yet." He looked at Jeanie. "Like this?"

Harrison stood and watched, not certain why he couldn't tear himself away. The mantel clock chimed six-thirty. Half an hour to get across town. The traffic on the interstate could be a bear at this hour, but he stood and watched anyway.

She leaned forward. Her breasts weren't as flat as he originally had thought, since she did have some cleavage.

What are you thinking? he screamed in his head. *And* where *are you looking?*

"Fine. Bye, y'all. Eat whatever." Again he swallowed despite the fact that there was nothing in his mouth. Barely any saliva. He grabbed the door handle and turned. "I…" They were laughing hysterically as both collapsed into a puddle of limbs.

I won't be late, he thought.

★

Harrison stuck his fork into his mouth, but the food merely sat on the tip of his tongue. He couldn't swallow. He couldn't concentrate on the biggest client his agency had ever had, and he couldn't help but wonder what Jeanie and Leo were up to.

Jeanie that is.

No, he really wanted to make sure Leo was safe. "Please excuse me, sir. I need to go make a phone call." Mr. Renée, the client, glared at him. He hadn't been the best company all night.

"Don't you own a cell phone, son?"

Harrison stood. "Yes, of course, but I…" *I don't want you to hear me talking to my genie.* "I don't want to disturb your dinner. I won't be long."

"Nothing to disturb. Food's fine, but the company is lousy."

He knew Mr. Renée didn't mean for him to hear that, but he had. *Great. This business deal could be going down the tubes.* Maybe he could wish the contract signed, and it would be. Perfect. She had him thinking in "genie" terms. In the hallway he asked the maitre d' where the pay phone was. Despite the man giving him an upscale-restaurants-don't-have-payphones look, he did allow him to use the restaurant's business phone.

Ring. Ring. Ring. Ring.

With every annoying *ring*, Harrison's heart started to beat a little faster. She should have answered by now. He let it go four more times. Maybe the television was too loud and they couldn't—"Hello, you've reached the Rainford residence," his own voice said to him. Damn it all. No way was he going to leave himself a message. Where were they? Should he call the police?

And tell them what? His genie kidnapped his nephew whose mother was off in some foreign land trying to find her soul?

A pounding headache reminded that him he hadn't eaten, and his client, not-all-too-understanding client that is, was waiting at the table.

He shoved down the receiver so hard, the maitre d's reservation book sailed off the end of the podium. It landed on the floor. Harrison bent to pick it up, and watched a pair of black eel skin boots kick it toward him.

"Son, I've never been treated like this by someone who I'm fixin' to pay millions in advertising fees to. Ain't no way..."

Cripes! "Mr. Renée, please except my apology. I have a family emergency, and no, I am not usually like this."

The man ran his hand across his goatee. "Why didn't you say so. Word is you are a crackerjack businessman, but you coulda fooled me. Emergency?"

"My nephew..."

"Boy ill?"

"I..." *Have no idea if he is even in New Orleans any longer.* "I... no. Not ill. Nonetheless, I need to rush home." He yanked his wallet from his pocket, dropping it and the money he'd started to take out on top of the book. He thought better than to curse out loud. Rifling through the bills, he grabbed one, stuck the others in his pocket like some vaudeville act, and shoved a hundred-dollar bill at a passing waiter. He turned to Mr. Renée and said, "I'll have my secretary call yours and set up another meeting. Please forgive..."

The man waved his hand. "Get out of here and take care of the boy."

"Thanks!" Harrison called as he ran out the door and flagged down the valet parking attendant. "Hurry!"

Once in his car, he sped along the interstate with one eye on the road, and one on the rearview mirror looking for blinking lights of a state trooper. It wouldn't surprise him if he got pulled over for speeding—hell, for just being out tonight by the way things were going.

Tabitha's horoscopes, that she'd sent him on a regular basis, were beginning to be all too real. He didn't believe in that stuff, especially in genies, witches, or vampires, but what he did believe in was fate.

Hopefully fate wasn't going to throw another curveball into his orderly life.

He hurried into his driveway, not bothering to open the garage door. He might need to rush out and debated about leaving the car running. No, not a good idea in New Orleans. Surely it'd be gone when he came back out.

The chandeliers Margaret had installed because she said they went along with the "flavor" of the Victorian, burned brightly on the second floor. Good sign. Then again, Jeanie didn't seem the type to worry if she wasted electricity—especially someone else's.

He jumped out. It dawned on him that he didn't know what kind of car she drove. There were three parked along the front of the house and a van. An old van several houses down. Man. He didn't even know if one of the cars was hers.

"Then again, genies can get around on magic carpets so why would she..." He'd pulled in too close to the fence and struggled to get past the car. A tearing sound filled the air. "—need a stupid car," he finished, looking down at his tuxedo pocket clutched in the mouth of the wrought iron gargoyle at the top of his fence. He grabbed it out of the creature's mouth. "Oh no you don't! You are not going to add to this hellatious day!"

"Evening, sir."

"What?" Harrison looked up to see one of New Orleans' finest standing at the end of his driveway—just in time to have seen him talking to the gargoyle. Cripes. "Evening, officer."

"That your car?" He motioned toward Harrison's white Lexus.

"Yes, sir." *Who else's car would be in my driveway, you jerk.* "Yes, it is." He waved his hand in the air. "And this is my house. My business. My, well the house part is upstairs, the business..." Oh God. The man was glaring at him with a "yeah sure" kind of look. "I'm in a bit of a hurry. Good night." He turned toward the entry walkway.

A large hand grabbed his arm. Now he knew what they meant by "ham bone of an arm."

"Mind if I take a look at your license?"

Just what he needed. Well, at least the lights were on so Jeanie and Leo must still be here, he tried to convince himself. "No." He reached into his pocket to pull out his wallet.

All creatures of habit keep their wallets in the left breast pocket—always.

So why wasn't his wallet there? The cop glared at him. The fool was thinking he was lying. He'd show him. Wait! When he'd dropped his money and picked it up, he'd shoved it into his outside tuxedo pocket. The wallet had to be there, too.

He pulled out a handful of hundreds. Margaret always chided him for carrying so much cash, but he liked to be prepared.

Prepared wasn't the look the cop gave him. Thief was more like it. "Now where abouts did you get a handful like that?"

"The bank, you fool..." Oh, great. That should have remained a thought.

"Oh, so it's going to be like that, Mister. Huh?" It dawned on Harrison that the man had a thick Irish accent. Officer Muldoon, his nametag read. Harrison blew out a breath. The cop glared at him, wiped his face. Of course, this was perfect. Not only did his life stink right now, but he felt as if he was caught up in some scene from Dick Tracy.

The genie had to have her slender hand in on this one.

"What was that officer?"

"I didn't say anything, buddy. You wouldn't be hearing the likes of voices, now would you?"

"Only in my head."

The man looked at him. "How much champagne have you had tonight, Mister?"

Harrison readied to spout off his one-glass-per-social-function, five-functions-a-month routine, but thought better. "One Dixie beer, sir."

The cop's eyes sparkled. He licked his lips. Harrison was glad he'd mentioned the local delicacy. He doubted if the mention of donuts would have gotten such a reaction from this policeman.

"Sir, I seem to have left my wallet at the restaurant I just dinned at. This is my house. If you care to come in, I'll prove it."

The man gave him a dubious look, then looked at his watch. His shift must be over soon. Surly he didn't want the hassle of dragging Harrison down to the precinct and booking him and doing all sorts of paperwork.

He fiddled in his pocket and wished for his keys. "See, here are my keys to prove this place is mine." Suddenly his gaze was drawn to the upstairs window, his bedroom to be exact.

Jeanie stood there—smiling.

★

Muldoon saw her, too. Thank goodness. For a second, Harrison wondered if genies were visible in the night.

Genies!

That's what started this horrible day along with Tabitha's little surprise. He looked up to see that Jeanie was gone.

"Your wife?" Muldoon asked.

"I'm not married."

The man's fuzzy red eyebrows drew together. "Doesn't look like any daughter."

"I don't have children." He looked down and rubbed at his ripped tuxedo. "She's the babysitter."

The man stepped closer. "Babysitter?"

Harrison sighed. "Yes, that is what I…"

"Now what would the likes of you be doing with a babysitter—and no kids?"

Oh, great. "My… nephew is staying with me for a few days." *Weeks. Months. Until my nutty sister returns all metaphysically healed.*

"I think we better have a little talk with the 'babysitter.'" He stood aside and waited for Harrison to lead the way.

"Fine." *But don't be surprised if you find yourself facing some hungry alligator when I wish you away to the bayous.*

Harrison unlocked the door and turned toward the elegant stairwell that led to his home. Margaret had hired the best designers to make the tiny entryway both classy and opulent. She said it made for better business and wouldn't hurt when he brought a date home. *Date? What the heck was that?*

"Right this way, sir," he said as Muldoon took in the entryway and hesitated at the bottom of the stairs.

Maybe he was going to say forget it, he made a mistake. Harrison Rainford was a fine upstanding citizen.

"What's your name?" the cop asked.

"Harrison Rainford..."

Muldoon leaned near and chuckled. "No kidding! You know you look a bit like that..."

"I'm several inches taller. This way." He hurried up the stairs, hoping Leo was asleep. He didn't want the child to see him bringing a policeman into his home.

"You're home early, Master," Jeanie said from the top of the stairway.

Master! Maybe Muldoon missed that part—

His eyebrows looked as if they'd permanently grown together.

Harrison attempted a laugh. It squeaked out. "Stop kidding, Jeanie. Can call me Mr. Rainford as I'd instructed."

She looked at the policeman. "Hello. Is my Master in trouble?"

Harrison debated about jumping off the landing, but knew the height wouldn't kill him. The best he could hope for was a few broken bones and facing Margaret's wrath if he got the Aubusson carpet below stained with blood.

Chapter Four

Capricorn: You will be put into a situation where you wish you had said "No way." Listen to and understand children better. At least make the attempt.

Jeanie stepped closer to Lieutenant Muldoon. Obviously seeing the error of her ways, she corrected herself. "I love to tease him." She hooked her arm through the man's and led him into the living room. Harrison stayed in the doorway, debating about turning and running.

He had no idea where he'd go.

"He's so straight-laced, officer," she continued, then leaned forward and laughed as if she and the cop were sharing a joke. He laughed, too, thank goodness. "So stiff, you know the kind." She looked around his apartment.

Muldoon followed her gaze and nodded. Great. She's mesmerized him into thinking Harrison was some "kind." By the way his day was going, he really didn't want to know what kind. He shut his eyes and wished that Jeanie would get him out of this mess.

He opened them. She wiggled her chin, blinked her eyes, and smiled.

"I guess you're right, Missy. Anyone who lives in a place like this is allowed a few eccentricities. I mean, with neighbors who write about vampires, I guess talking to wrought iron gargoyles isn't that far off base." He turned toward Harrison, who now clutched onto the doorframe. "Find that wallet and don't drive without your license.

He nodded. "I will. I mean, I won't."

It was his turn to blink as Jeanie showed Lieutenant Muldoon out the door.

Had she really just granted his wish?

★

"Good night, sir." Jeanie smiled, shut the door, and leaned against the wooden frame. Poor Harry. Hopefully she'd been right about reading his expression, and he had wished that the cop would get lost. If so, she'd earn points for credibility—and she sure as heck needed them where Harrison was concerned.

Nearly floating up the stairs, she took two at a time and stopped in the doorway. He'd helped himself to a glass of something—Pinch scotch she guessed by the nearby bottle.

Poor dear must need it.

"So, are you going to tell me why the fuzz had to bring you home?"

He looked at her over the rim of the crystal glass. Wedgwood she guessed. "He didn't bring me home. He found me outside. I left my wallet at the restaurant..."

"Oh, yeah. They called and said they had it so I told them to drop it off here later."

"I could have used you outside earlier with that information..."

She hurried over, took his hand, and held it. With her eyes, she locked their gazes. "I did help."

He wanted to pull back, knew he should but didn't want to be rude. *Rude?* He should be throwing her out lock, stock, and barrel. She'd caused him nothing but trouble since this morning!

"By the way, I called earlier..."

"Oh, that was you? We were playing hide and seek, and by the time I reached for the phone, the recorder had turned on."

"Where's Leo?" He pulled free and headed down the hallway.

"Sh. He's asleep. Nodded off during my story. I carried him to bed."

Harrison stopped and turned. "You carried him? You're no bigger than an eight-year-old yourself."

She held up her arm, flexed a muscle. "I carried him."

He curled his lip and turned. The way things were going, he wasn't about to take her word for anything. The door creaked as he opened it, flooding a stream of light onto a snoring Leo. The kid stirred, covered his eyes. "Tabitha?"

"No, kid, it's me, Uncle Harry. Go back to bed."

Leo sat up, rubbed his eyes. "Hi, Uncle. Is Jeanie still here?"

"She's about to leave..."

"No!" He jumped out of bed and ran past Harrison into the arms of Jeanie. "Don't send her off. She'd got nowhere to go..."

Jeanie forced a laugh. "Kids. That was just a story, sweetie. I'll be fine." She brushed his hair from his forehead. "You go to sleep."

She let him go and turned down the hallway.

Harrison tucked Leo back into bed. "What did you mean about her not having anyplace to go? I'm sure she must have an apartment or..."

Sleep had taken Leo but he managed, "Van. Jeanie lives in a VW..."

Harrison turned and ran out of the room. "What kinds of stories..." The hallway was empty. "Jeanie!" He didn't want to reawaken Leo, but by the looks of the kid he was a sound sleeper. "Jeanie, what kind of..."

She wasn't in the living room, the kitchen, dining room, and he didn't waste his time looking in his room. He looked around, ran to the window. The rusty brown VW was headed down Saint Charles as if he'd traveled back to the 60s.

*

"No, I didn't get a license number, Margaret," Harrison said as he held the ice bag onto his forehead.

"Then how do you expect me to chase down an old VW in all of New Orleans? I don't have the power to do that. You keep getting me mixed up with your sister, boss."

"She's years younger." He sat without thinking. "Oh God, Margaret, I'm sorry. I didn't mean to be hurtful."

She got up and headed to the door, sticking the ice bag back on his head with a *swoosh*. "She *is* years younger, you're a fool to have chased off the only babysitter this side of the Mississippi, and Mr. Renée said he'll meet you for coffee today at one. Café Du Monde. Apparently he didn't think you could sit through an entire meal. Don't be late."

"Thank you. Margaret?"

She stuck her head in the doorway. "I aim to please."

"We need that account. Do you think there's hope?"

"There's always hope, boss. Right now, though, there isn't a babysitter past five. I have a crawfish boil tonight with a single guy from La Place that I don't intend to miss. You're on for taking care of Leo."

Harrison nodded. Hopefully he'd be done by five. "Where is he?"

"Outside."

"Fine." He shoved the ice closer to his right temple. Problem was, both sides pounded at the same time. It was a pain to have to switch the ice from side to side. Wait a minute. Outside? Leo? He never knew the kid played outside. Whenever he came over, he only glued himself to the television, which was fine with Harrison. Kept the kid occupied. More than he could do for his nephew. He didn't even know what eight-year-olds did outside.

Looked for vans!

He jumped up. "Aye!" The pain shot straight across, temple to temple.

"You all…" Margaret ran in. "Shall I call 911?"

"No. I don't need an ambulance for a headache." He pushed past her. "How'd you ever deal with the ills of five kids?"

She followed him to the door. "My kids never had 'ills.' They puked, barfed, got temps or broke bones. We weren't classy enough for 'ills.'"

"Sorry. A thought occurred to me and I…"

Margaret's hazel eyes lit up. "Right! She might have told him where she parks her van."

"Actually I though he'd just be out in the yard looking for her to drive by..."

She pushed him toward the door. "Get out there and start thinking like an eight-year-old—unless that's too farfetched an idea for you."

He grabbed her into his arms and kissed her on the forehead. "It is, but I'm living dangerously and giving it a shot."

She pushed him away and clucked her tongue at him. "I'm proud of you, boss. You are coming out of your stuffy shell. Don't forget coffee at one!"

Harrison waved at her as he hurried down his steps. The front yard was empty. Shielding his eyes from the morning sun, he looked as far down Saint Charles Avenue as he could see. Giant trees dripping moss blocked his view, keeping him from seeing very far, but Leo wasn't in sight. Harrison hurried to the backyard. Several birds occupied the birdbath. He thought of his sign yesterday and clapped his hands until they flew off.

If he were eight and looking for a genie... make that a babysitter with a dimple in her right cheek—whoa! Eight-year-olds didn't notice things like that. Least he didn't when he was eight. Where would Leo think to look for Jeanie?

This was all so nerve-wracking. He was a businessman, for crying out loud—not a father. And definitely not father material.

"Leo!" Since he had not an inkling of an idea, he did the next best thing, he yelled out and looked down the side street. Leo didn't know this neighborhood and wouldn't go far—he hoped—so Harrison started to walk around the block.

Two elderly woman nodded a hello to him. They acted as if they knew him. He looked to see his house bordered theirs on the back. They were his neighbors—he never even knew them. "Morning."

When he looked down the block, he saw a mailman pulling a

cart, like his own golf cart, with a sack of mail on it. So that's how he made it around this neighborhood.

The sound of children caught his ear. Must be a school around. Hm, shouldn't Leo be in school if that were the case? Tabitha should be tarred and feathered. He'd have to see about enrolling Leo in school even if temporarily. Otherwise he'd get too far behind.

At the end of the block he saw it.

The brown van was parked in a restaurant's lot. No other cars were there since it wasn't open this early in the morning. He wasn't sure if he was glad that he must have found Leo—or that he'd found Jeanie.

Hurrying across the street, he ignored the beep of a Mercedes and slowed when he got near the van. It felt as if he was invading her space, her home. Surely she didn't live in this… piece of metal. On closer inspection he noted an old peace sign from the 60s on the side door. A red flag of sorts hung from the antennae. And music—saxophone music—came from the interior.

He inhaled, half expecting to smell pot.

Pot! He ran to the side and yanked open the door.

Leo lay on a mattress, reading. Jeanie sat folded up in the rear of the van, ummming and who knows what else. Her eyes were shut. The only scent in the van was Jeanie's.

"Leo?"

The boy put his finger on the page so as not to lose his place and turned. "Hey, Uncle Harry. We were wondering when you'd come."

"Wondering?"

He looked at Jeanie who now opened her eyes and unfolded part of herself. Today she wore a white outfit, so very different than yesterday's. Angelic. Her fairy necklace danced across her chest as she breathed. Harrison had to swallow—and blink—several times.

The top was still a midriff though, and he hoped Leo was too young to notice a woman's skin. How soft it would feel to touch. How sweet it must smell. How warm to rest your cheek next to—

Cripes! Leo shouldn't be here in this den of sensuality!

"Time to go, kid." He reached in and took Leo's arm.

"Go where?"

"Home. My home. My place... let's go."

"It's boring at your place. No offense."

"Boring?" He leaned in and sat on the side of the van. The door slide back, he caught himself. Jeanie chuckled.

"Yeah. There's nothing ever to do except play video games or watch television. Jeanie says that ain't good for kids."

"Isn't good for kids," he corrected.

"That's what I said. Anyway, she's teaching me stuff."

Harrison sat up. Stuff? He wished he knew what kind of stuff a gorgeous genie could teach a kid! His insides tightened. No he didn't wish any sort of thing.

She scooted forward, pushed the hair from Leo's eyes. "Stuff like geography. I've traveled a bit in my time and have collected many books."

"What's the copyright? Eighteen ninety-nine?"

She smiled. "No, Harry, they are more current. Leo tells me he's been home-schooled by your sister..."

"Oh, great."

"Not exactly. She's behind in his lessons."

"Why am I not surprised?"

Jeanie grabbed his arm, yanked him out of the van.

"What? What are you doing?"

"You can think what you want about your sister, Harrison. And I won't argue that most is probably true, but not in front of Leo. She is his mother..."

"Man. I hadn't thought about that. Thanks." He looked at her before she turned back to the van. The midriff top had a transparent, rather wispy cover over it. When she stood it draped down to her knees. Beneath, though, she wore some skintight leggings of sorts. Provocative to the male adult—yet covering her enough to be decent. Except in his thoughts.

Cripes!

He had to stop this. A wish to find her unattractive sat on the tip of his tongue. He looked up. She stared at him as if waiting. Waiting for him to make the wish?

"So, thanks for helping Leo with geography," he said lamely while swallowing back the wish. He looked at his watch. Noon. He'd spend so much time with his headache and now finding the kid that he'd have to hustle to get to the Café du Monde on time.

"Look, Jeanie. Margaret is worried about Leo," he lied. "Why don't you bring him back..." He looked at the van. "Er... walk him back to my place. You can stay with him today. I have a meeting that might run past five when she has to leave."

Leo turned and grinned.

"Well, if that is what you want..."

Harrison took her hands into his. "Wish," he corrected.

"Then, master, I have no choice."

He couldn't believe that a genie could sound so sexy. Look so sensual. Smell spicy yet womanly and sweet all at once.

What happened to booming males that blazed out of old lanterns in a mist of genie magic?

Chapter Five

Capricorn: Meeting an attractive stranger throws you into a romantic dilemma, but what the heck. Go for it.

Harrison slumped onto his couch, Pinch in hand. Slowly, with purpose, he held the glass to his forehead. He didn't need the scotch, merely wanted the cold against his head. With Margaret long gone, he had no one to baby him or fix him an ice bag.

He lifted the remote and clicked on the CD player. Harry Connick Jr.'s mellifluous voice helped relax his frazzled nerves.

He propped his feet on the couch and thought that at least the long, drawn-out meeting went well with Mr. Renée. Harrison might be closer now than ever to getting the offices moved from the high-rent district off Canal Street to a building he'd had his eye on a few blocks from here.

The move would assure his employees of keeping their jobs. He couldn't afford to keep the offices where they were, and if he didn't invest in the building and rent out the other suites, that would more than cover his own rent, he was at a loss as what to do. Competition in advertising had skyrocketed over the past three years, and his business had been affected. Thirty-five people would be out of work if he couldn't move them. People who he'd trained, cared about, and even attended everyone's kid's graduations, birthdays, and weddings.

He made a mental note to remind Margaret that Lillie in accounting's son was due to graduate college this semester. With a chuckle, he told himself Margaret more than likely already had a card and gift in mind for the kid. A warm feeling sped throughout him at the thought of such good employees. His family life could never compare.

This deal had to go through.

He'd promised Mr. Renée that he himself would work on the advertisement although he had a fabulous staff and had done only management lately. Now all he had to do was come up with a clever, nationally appealing slogan that would have kids from nine to nineteen buying Mr. Renée's clothing. Oh, great. He'd seen the clothing line. Didn't these kids know their own parents and some grandparents wore those style years ago in the 60s?

The mantel clock chimed. Six thirty. He was getting hungry after eating only three bignéts with his coffee. The pillow-shaped donuts were a staple of every New Orleans native and a must for tourists to the French Quarter, but they didn't fill up a guy. If Jeanie didn't bring Leo home from their trip to the zoo soon, he'd order takeout. He didn't have the energy to cook. Zoo? He sat upright. What time did the zoo close? Maybe he shouldn't have let Leo talk him into letting Jeanie take him out of the house.

Setting his glass down so it didn't splash onto his glass coffee table's top, he stood to get the phonebook. They should have been home. Did he make an error in judgment that could hurt Leo? Should he have let a woman who thought she was a genie take him out of the house? Lord, he wished they'd taken the trolley and not her van.

Paranoia was not a pleasant feeling.

A noise in the foyer startled him.

"Uncle Harry?"

He blew out a sigh. "In here, kid." No response. "Kid? Leo? Where are you?" He hurried to the entry door and stopped. Now what had happened? "Leo…"

"Raaaarah!"

A giant monkey bounded around the doorway, landing Harrison on the floor, the stuffed toy on top, glassy monkey eyes staring at him.

"Cripes."

Jeanie and Leo stumbled in, supporting each other in their fits of hysteria. With her slender hand, she wiped at the tears streaming down her face in between gulps. Leo used his sleeve.

"Very lady-like," Harrison muttered.

"She's no lady," Leo said.

Harrison clutched the monkey and sat upright. "No?" He leaned near the kid. "What… is she then?" His gaze traveled to Jeanie. She'd promised she wouldn't fill the kid's head with her baloney. He would have her hide and his sister's too for this mess.

Why couldn't he get back to his everyday, dull—yeah sure, he wouldn't deny it was dull—kind of life. Just the way he liked it.

"She's my teacher, Uncle Harry."

He felt his face reddened. He forced a laugh. "Teacher. Yeah."

Jeanie stared at him. "I'll bet Uncle Harry is hungry, sweetie. How about taking Zazu into the kitchen and starting the salad?"

Leo grabbed the monkey from Harrison. "Come on, Zaz. I'll fix you something too." He leaned near the monkey's mouth. "Bananas? You bet."

Harrison and Jeanie looked at each other and laughed. "I'm guessing the zoo trip went well?" It was good to see the kid happy.

She settled on the leather chair across from him. Both legs tucked under her. Her head bent back and she seemed to stare at the ceiling.

He caught himself looking up, then pulled his gaze back to her. "I hope his salad doesn't include tofu."

"I'm sure his mother only has his best interest in mind."

"Obviously you've never met my sister on one of your celestial planes."

She looked at him and hesitated. "It's good for you, you know. Tofu that is."

"That's what they used to say about liver. I'm not fond of organ meats or white jelled stuff that comes from a bean."

She shook her head and looked at his glass of scotch. "It wouldn't hurt for you to be more health-food conscious."

A chill chased up his spine. Tabitha had said as much many

times. He didn't want to compare the two, but Jeanie could be a carbon copy of his sister where *woo-woo* was concerned.

Maybe she wasn't good for Leo.

Tabitha's habit of leaving the kid made Harrison furious. Would Jeanie follow in the same footsteps?

"Did you know Leo has never been to the zoo before, Harry?"

"Hm? Never been?" He should have guessed something like that, but the words still took him by surprise. "You're kidding."

"Nope." She untwisted her legs, stretched them out, and hooked one over the side of the chair.

Not the most lady-like position, Harrison thought, but then again, as Leo said, she's no lady. She was, however, darn attractive, sitting so casually in his living room. As if she belonged there.

Whoa, boy. Get those kinds of thoughts out of your head.

"I think you should have a long talk with his mother. You know, he is looking forward to going to school here." She folded her hands behind her back, taking the ponytail she always wore into one, and pulling out some kind of hair clip.

Waterfalls of auburn cascaded down her shoulders.

Oh, Lord. Harrison had to swallow, very deeply.

"That's... good. The school thing. He needs..." *What? He needs what?* he asked himself. The thought zapped out of his brain. No wonder. Now she undid the top several buttons of her flimsy, silken blouse. Oh, no cleavage showed—yet—and he guessed she must be warm in the outfit and tired, too, but... damn if he couldn't concentrate.

Earlier he was starving.

Right now he couldn't eat a bite.

She pulled her leg off the arm of the chair and stood. Slowly she came toward him. *Please don't touch me,* he thought. But it really wasn't a wish.

One very warm, very soft hand gently felt at his forehead. "You feel all right?"

His earlier headache had vanished. Maybe she had some healing power in the tips of her fingers along with the power to grant wishes?

Wishes? Here we go again. He eased free. "I'm fine. I was going to say Leo needs friends." He backed up a step.

She leaned near, paused. "I like your choice in music, by the way, Harry."

"Don't you think they do?"

"Think?"

"Music... er... kids. All kids need friends." Two steps more and the backs of his knees touched the couch.

Her steps were much shorter than his, but he calculated she took four because her face was so near, he noticed the violet of her eyes caught the light, and sparkled at him. Or was it a wink!

"We all need friends, Harry."

Had her voice gotten deeper? Sexier? More whisper-in-your-ear quieter?

He stumbled back, landing on the couch. She glanced at him and grinned. He looked at his glass to see if he'd had too much to drink and that's why he'd been making a royal fool of himself. Man. Even her accent had affected him.

He hadn't taken a sip.

"Yes, of course we need friends. I'll take Leo over to that school on Monday." He straightened himself up on the couch, grabbed a black brocade pillow.

She sat herself down on the coffee table, looking directly at him. Normally he'd freak out if someone even put his or her feet on the glass top, but she was so slender. So petite. Surely she would do no harm.

He could hear Margaret howling in the back of his mind.

"Harry, that's a great idea..."

"Thanks. Well, shall we go eat?"

She reached out and touched his arm before he could get up. In a whisper, she said, "You haven't thought this through."

He dropped the pillow and looked down at her hand on his arm. "What? The... eating?"

She laughed, but kept her hand in place. Did she just tighten her hold?

Oh, Lord.

"No, silly. The school thing. You can't waltz in there..." She looked up and smiled. "You are the waltzing type, aren't you?"

"Two left feet," he mumbled. Damn, he hoped she'd let him go, but she seemed to need the physical contact to make her point.

Obviously genies were touchy-feely types.

She chuckled. "Figures. Anyway. You can't take Leo to a school you know nothing about. He doesn't actually live here, and, you don't have his shot records."

"To my knowledge, Leo's never been shot," he muttered.

She laughed. Now her hand definitely tightened. "Medical shot records. They won't let a child into school without them."

"How do genies know so much about kids and school?" He heard himself ask it, but still didn't believe a stupid question like that had come out of his mouth. He'd graduated magna cum laude from Tulane University for crying out loud!

Before she could answer, he hurriedly added, "Could you please... not touch me, Jeanie?"

★

Jeanie smiled to herself. She hadn't touched him to make him feel uncomfortable; it was only her natural way. Still, his reaction was adorable. She'd love to lean over and kiss the tiny dimple that formed to the side of his lips when he smiled.

No, she couldn't do that.

She had to stay professional about all of this, even if the kid's uncle was a real looker. Professional? Was being a genie considered a profession? She looked up to see Harrison rubbing at his arm where she'd touched. She chuckled. He looked at her.

"So, what do you suggest about Leo?" He stood and walked to the fireplace. Without saying a word, he bent and turned a knob, sending a blue flame dancing between the logs. When he turned, he wore a business-as-usual look on his face. "I can't believe I'm asking the advice of a... stranger for my nephew."

That hurt. Well, she told herself, it shouldn't, knowing the kind of keep-to-himself, rather stuffy man she was dealing with. She'd been warned about his personality before accepting this job. Still, she found it hard to believe someone could be as bad as she'd been told. Actually, she'd found him darling in his own way.

"I'm not a real stranger..."

"Of course not. Genies must know a lot about the masters they materialize in front of."

"Now you're being sarcastic, Harry."

"Sorry. Believe it or not, you are the first genie in my life. Look, I'm at a loss. My sister drops her kid off for who knows how long. As you can plainly see, I'm not father material..."

"You will make a wonderful father some day." And she meant that, but his look said he didn't believe her.

"Yeah, sure I would if I ever..." He turned back to the fire. "It's not that cold in here." With that, he bent and shut off the beautiful blaze.

"Pity." She stood and walked toward him. Oh, dear. He'd started that backing up thing again as if he expected her to jump his bones. Well, that wouldn't be too horrible a thing—

Jeanie!

"Pity about the warmth, because the fire was beautiful. Anyway, you care a great deal about Leo even if you don't know what to do about it."

"So now you are a psychic, too?"

She laughed, although he may have been serious. "Nope. What I see is that you worry about him, but you are preoccupied with your business. If you had a child of your own, I'll bet you would be more aware. More in tune..."

"Isn't a mother a requirement to have a kid of one's own?"

"Why yes, but..."

His forehead wrinkled. "Listen, Jeanie, my having kids, not

having kids, not having a wife, is no concern of yours, nor do I want to discuss it. The topic is Leo and school. You make a good point about the shot record. So, what do you suggest?"

He'd asked her advice, but he looked off into space as if pondering what he'd just said.

He really is adorable, she thought as she said, "I guess home-schooling as Elizabeth had been doing." Elizabeth! Oh no! How'd *that* slip out? Her eyes widened as she forced herself to look at him.

Harrison didn't notice. Thank goodness. Maybe he was too busy thinking of a wife—

And her so affected by that thought—she'd let Leo's mother's real name slip out.

Chapter Six

Capricorn: Chill out. Don't be so straight-laced and serious. You are almost unapproachable—you lose out that way. Loosen up.

"Hey, kid, you may have a future as a chef," Harrison said, brushing his hand across Leo's forehead. He and Jeanie had come into the kitchen to find the table set, the salad chilling, and three glasses of milk all poured. *Milk? Can't win them all.*

She smiled at Leo. So why'd Harrison's heart jump?

"What's on the menu next?" Harrison asked.

Leo looked at Jeanie. "Didn't I hear you mention pizza the other day?"

She laughed. "Yep. I'm not certain if your uncle has the ingredients…"

"Might and might not. But what I do have is Domino's phone number."

"Ack!" she yelled. "There is nothing like homemade pizza."

Leo laughed and sat on the barstool near the counter. Zazu sat next to him.

Harrison ended up next to the monkey. "I like Domino's." He frowned. Leo guffawed.

Jeanie leaned near. "Not once you taste me… mine."

That wiped the smile off his face.

"So, what do you need, Chef Jeanie?"

"Okay." She sat opposite them and leaned on the counter. With eyes shut, she continued, "Water…"

"Hey! I've got that!"

Leo laughed.

Jeanie looked at Leo and rolled her eyes. "He's nuts, you know. And, sugar, salt, oil…"

"Olive?" Harrison asked. This was beginning to be fun. He couldn't remember having fun in a long time.

"Vegetable."

He looked at Leo. "Isn't an olive a vegetable?"

The kid shrugged.

"I thought you were a vegetarian, kid?"

Leo's eyes grew solemn. "That's only been since last week when Tabitha decided she needed to go to India."

Damn. Harrison wanted to bite off his tongue. Jeanie gave him a stern look, then turned to Leo.

"They are a fruit and their oil is much heavier than vegetable; tastes very different. Anyway, we're batting a thousand here. Okay, water, salt, sugar, oil; I'm guessing you do have vegetable?" She turned to Harrison.

"Got it."

"Good. Then I'd prefer wheat flour, but I doubt if…"

"You doubt right. The white evil stuff is all I have."

"We'll make a convert out of you yet." She pulled Leo into a hug. He didn't pull back. "So, sounds like we've got us a pizza in the makings… oops. Forgot the yeast." A concerned look crossed her eyes. "Of course you don't have yeast." Before he could answer, she stood, walked to Leo and put her arm around him. "Sorry, sweetie, it would've been fun but…"

Harrison got up and headed to the cabinet. Before Leo could say a word, he opened the door and pulled out a package. "Active dry yeast, Miss Health-food nut. I bake my own bread, with white floor."

Leo and Jeanie howled.

Leo took her hand and looked at her. "This is so much fun. Tabitha doesn't even know how to cook."

Jeanie looked at Harrison. "But she loves you, sweetie. And that sometimes is a whole heck of a lot better than knowing how to cook."

Harrison put his arm around the kid. "That's why they have Domino's Pizza, too."

*

Jeanie rolled up the sleeves of her top and took off the outer silken covering. Harry's gaze followed her every move. She smiled at him several times. Each time he shifted his gaze so fast, she thought he would get dizzy.

At least Leo was having a ball rolling the dough.

"Okay," she said, taking the spatula and swinging it around. "I'll probably settle into a carbohydrate-induced coma from this white flour." She reached out and touched a powdery spot of it on Leo's nose. He pulled away, laughing. "But, I'm willing to make a sacrifice as long as I get my topping of choice."

Harry pretended to be upset, shaking his arms wildly in the air. "Oh no! What's it going to be? Wait. Let us guess." He looked at Leo. "You first, kid."

Leo looked at Jeanie with his eyebrows wrinkled. "In lotsa ways you remind my of Tabitha, so I'm gonna say, bean sprouts…"

"Oooooooh." Harrison clutched at his chest, looked up to the ceiling. "Take me now before America's favorite food is desecrated!"

Leo's childish giggles warmed her heart.

She shook her head in mock disgust. "What's your guess, Mr. Junk-food junkie?"

Harry stopped his antics and leaned near her. He inhaled, paused. "Nice spicy perfume. So, I'm going with something spicy. So, am I correct?"

He and Leo leaned near.

"You didn't make a specific guess." She laughed.

"Okay. Red chili peppers. You look like the chili pepper type."

"Tuna," was all she could manage between laughs.

"Eeew!" Harry and Leo shouted.

Harrison watched Jeanie showing Leo how to flip the pizza

dough into the air—and not have it land on his black and white tile floor. Margaret had insisted that a bachelor's pad, as she'd put it, should have a black, white and chrome kitchen. He looked at the flour-covered disaster area and had to agree. But having a woman and kid here made the usually sparkling cleanliness of the room warm. Homey.

"If you do that any higher, the ceiling is going to be wearing it," he teased Leo. The kid howled.

It was so good to see the difference in the boy who'd stepped out of the cab yesterday. Somber. Never smiling. And so alone. When Elizabeth got back—

He looked at Jeanie, his eyes scrutinizing her. Wait a minute! What had she said before about Leo's mother. Did she call her Tabitha? Or Elizabeth? He shuddered. Man, he was going nuts here. How on earth could she know his sister's real name? The genie stuff had him starting to go wacko.

"Harry, turn on the oven to four hundred and twenty five."

He glanced at her. For a second he still pondered his question. "Sure."

"Get out the sauce, tuna, and mushrooms if you have any."

"Mushrooms?" he asked.

"Um. Leo decided he'd go with mushrooms on his third."

"No problem." He walked to the cabinet and bent down. The cans were neatly stacked. Soups to the left. Vegetables to the right. In the center, fruits. He grabbed a can of mushrooms, a can of tomato sauce, and turned. He'd forgotten the tuna.

Jeanie stood glaring at his cabinet.

"What?"

She shook her head. "Don't forget my tuna."

"I was going to get it…"

"Why's it taking so long? That place must be in alphabetical order."

He went to get up and bumped his head on the counter. "Ouch!"

Leo looked at Jeanie. "*T* is for tuna, Uncle Harry." They both howled.

Harrison grabbed the tuna and stood. "Funny. You two get to clean up for making fun of your host."

They laughed louder.

It was a wonderful sound in his kitchen.

When the pizza was pronounced done, Jeanie cut it into several uneven slices. Harrison watched, cringing that she didn't make them look so nice and even like they do in the pizza parlors. She'd caught him, he knew, and he figured she wanted to tease him about it but didn't.

Guess she got the point with having to clean up.

He smiled to himself, took a bite. "This isn't half bad."

"If you had whole wheat flour..."

"Yeah. Yeah. What do you say, kid? How is it?"

Leo rubbed sauce across his lip. "Great."

"Okay, she wins."

They all laughed and ate until the pizza was gone. Jeanie and Leo did clean up, but Harrison broke down and helped.

"Go get ready for bed, kid," he told Leo, who didn't argue.

On the way out, he grabbed Zazu. "Come on, buddy. 'Nite, Uncle Harry. You will come tuck me in, Jeanie. Won't you?"

She turned to him from cleaning the counter with Windex until it sparkled. "Sure, sweetie."

Harry looked at her, at the kid. What a great evening; but that's all it was. Reality sunk in as the night wore on. She had to leave, the kid would, hopefully, be gone in a few weeks, and he would get back to writing an advertisement for clothing that looked as if it had come from a used consignment shop.

That was Harrison Rainford's life.

"Coming?" Leo called from the spare bedroom.

"You first," he said to Jeanie.

She dumped the paper towel into the garbage can. "I thought we'd go together. You know, so we don't waste too much of his bedtime."

He looked at her, and without a thought walked to the doorway. "Sure."

On the way to the spare room, Harrison watched Jeanie's ponytail bounce across her back. When did she do that? He hadn't even noticed her gather it back into a ponytail. Obviously she did it before cooking.

With only a few feet between them, he calculated she might be a inch or so over the five feet he'd originally guessed before. She really was a nice person from what he could tell, but nice people were mass murders, too.

Not that he thought Jeanie was one.

Nope. He was a good judge of character. That's why he'd managed to hire such loyal employees. He'd had that gift since childhood when he could logically look at his parents—and know he'd never chose them if given the opportunity.

But he couldn't justify hiring a woman who thought she was a genie to take care of a kid. Not even his own kid. There actually seemed like more responsibility taking care of someone else's. If you made a mistake with one of your own, you could blame yourself.

He'd never be able to live with himself if he had used bad judgment with Elizabeth's son. The kid had had a rotten life as it was. No way would Harrison add to it.

Jeanie was kneeling at the side of the bed, telling Leo some story about Zazu being his buddy for life. The kid needed real friends. Not stuffed animals. He needed a real, stay-at-home mom, not some woo-woo mom who jetted off on a whim.

What he needed, Harrison couldn't give.

But, he reminded himself, he at least could give the kid a few weeks of normalcy.

And Jeanie Merriday didn't fit *that* bill.

★

Jeanie noticed Harrison out of the corner of her eyes. He stood in the doorway watching as she finished her bedtime story for Leo.

Sure, he was a bit old for stories, she admitted, but a child-like quality could be found in anyone. And she'd found it in Leo. He actually had a gaping hole in that part of his life.

Damn Tabitha.

"So," she continued, adding a bit of fantasy to real life since the child was eight, "when she arrived at Heathrow Airport, the man was waiting. He whisked her off in a black Rolls Royce..."

Through sleepy eyes, Leo looked at her. "That's a fancy car, right?"

She tucked his blankets beneath the mattress. "It certainly is. Big, black, and expensive. But when he took the woman to the mansion he lived in... she was never the same... again," she whispered as his eyes shut. Placing a kiss on her fingertip, she touched it to his forehead. "Nite, sweetie."

She shut her eyes and hummed a soft melody to make certain he traveled to a pleasant dream state. Mother had always done that for her, and she never had nightmares.

Least not in her dreams.

"Good night, kid," Harrison said from the doorway.

She turned, stood, and walked to the door.

He smiled. "He must have been exhausted."

As they walked out and Harry shut the door, she turned to him in the hallway. "Yes. You know, you really do look like Harrison Ford. Not that I've ever been so close to him, but your eyes..."

A flush chased up his neck to his cheeks. She'd embarrassed him without intending to. Her openness and honesty had always gotten her into trouble, but she never let that stop her from speaking her mind.

He yawned. She thought he'd forced it most likely to hurry her out. To go where?

"My eyes... look, we need to talk. Can you sit for a few minutes?" They'd made it into the living room where he waved toward the couch.

She sat in the chair opposite. If she sat next to him, she'd probably notice more than the color of his eyes. Right now, she needed her wits about her.

Because Harry was once again going to try to send her away.

Why did he have such a hard time believing in her?

He settled across from her. "Oh, can I get you something to drink?"

"I'm fine. The fire would be nice. It's getting chilly." She'd forgotten to put the top layer of her outfit back on after making the pizza.

He hesitated. Harry didn't want the setting to be romantic, she guessed. Well, he hadn't wished that as far as she could tell, but by the way his hands clenched and unclenched, he was nervous.

How unlike him.

"Sure." He stood, walked to the fireplace, and turned the knob once again, instantly sending flames of blue dancing through the logs. Before he went to sit down, he poured himself a glass of cola. When she looked at it, he set it on the coffee table in front of him.

"So, what do you want to talk about, Harry?"

He smiled at her, lifted his drink, and took a sip. "You don't beat around the bush, do you?"

"I don't have time. What is it?"

He couldn't look her in the eyes, she noticed. That had to be a good sign. He was going to try to get rid of her, she knew that much, but she also knew she couldn't let him. Her mind whizzed as she watched him and wondered what she could say to make this man trust her with caring for Leo. Wait. His wallet. At least she could stall for time. "Your wallet was delivered today." She'd almost forgotten it was in her pocket. "Here."

"Oh, yeah." He took it and looked down. "Well, then." His fingers shook as he reached in and pulled out a handful of bills. She noted a one hundred and two fifties amongst the pile.

"Here." He held the handful out toward her.

Oh, boy. That may have backfired. She didn't take it. "An afternoon at the zoo is hardly worth that much."

Harry shut his eye. "You know it's not only for that. Take it, Jeanie. Get yourself a place to stay, a job, some help."

"Harry, open your eyes."

They flew open as if he were embarrassed that she'd noticed. "Don't make this harder than it is. You know I can't let you stay…"

"So, who is going to take care of Leo. Teach him?"

"I will." He set the money on the table.

"Hm. I wonder why Leo says it's boring with you. That he only plays video games because there isn't anything else to do…"

"Look, Jeanie." His eyes darkened. He stood. "What I do with my nephew is no concern of yours…"

"Like if you want a wife and kids isn't?"

He hesitated. "Yes. That's exactly right. I… will manage. I always do."

She leaned back and tucked both feet under her. The comforting position had started when she was a child. Mother had said she was double-jointed, but as a kid she couldn't care less what the term was. She loved being able to bend, fold, and fit into tiny hiding places. Thank goodness for that because it all came in handy when she worked for The Great Santanloni and his magic show.

She looked around the room. The expensive leather furniture, the crystal chandelier, mirrored walls, and built-in bookshelf that had several leather-bound spines sticking out. Most likely first editions.

"Yes, you look as if you've managed quite well—financially."

"What's that supposed to mean?"

"Just that I've heard what Leo said. I see you living alone here, no pictures, Harry."

"I've got several lithographs and oils…"

"Pictures as in photographs. Of family. Of friends. Of… women." That last one was hard to get out. How would she feel if she had to sit here and look at a picture of some gorgeous blonde of Harry's? *Jeanie,* she ordered, *don't go there. You are here to help with the boy—and the man.*

But not in that way.

"So what if I don't have…" He finished off his drink. "Look, I don't need to be discussing my life with a total stranger…"

The little gasp sneaked out. She couldn't help it. When someone hurt her, she reacted without thinking.

"Sorry. Jeanie, you can see my point. I mean, you claim to be a genie, for crying out loud!

She unfolded from her comforting position, stood and walked to him. "Did you believe in Santa as a child, Harry?"

He gave her a look of disgust. "Of course, what does that have to do with…"

"The Easter bunny?"

"You're nuttier than I thought." He tried to move back, she leaned forward, purposely invading his private space to throw him off.

"Okay, Harry. Those myths have brightened the lives of millions of kids and some adults too. Maybe, though, someone so concrete sequential as you, can't see past believing in something like a man who would bring joy and presents to kids throughout the world."

"This is making no sense. Take the money and go." He stepped back. She stepped forward. "Stop doing that…"

It was then she pulled out the big guns.

With both hands, she grabbed at his shoulders, pulling him down to meet her gaze as close as she could with their height difference and said, "Do you believe in some higher power? Any kind? Any type?"

He didn't struggle to free himself, thank goodness. She'd managed to mesmerize him with her voice, softening, capturing his attention. It had taken years to learn to do that, but Santanloni had helped her learn. That way she could be more convincing in their act.

"Yes… I. There must be something, someone…"

"You see, Harry. You do believe in some things that you can't see, hear, smell or touch." She took his hand and guided his fingers across her arm. "You can touch me. Yet, you don't believe."

"I… you are a woman, of course, but a genie…"

"Make a wish."

He tried to pull away this time. Years of lifting her mom into a wheelchair came in handy, she thought as she pulled him back. "Make one, Harry. Make a wish. I dare you." Her breath flipped the hairs off his forehead she'd leaned so purposefully near.

"This is insane."

"Yes, perhaps. But isn't life insane in it's own ways? Make the wish. If I can't grant it you'll never see me again."

He shut his eyes. "This is crazy, Jeanie Merriday."

Big guns aimed, fire!

She kissed him.

It didn't last long enough though. Harry pulled back like a shot. He blinked frantically as if trying to pull himself from her spell. She smiled to herself. She wasn't a witch, for crying out loud.

But she'd sell her van and be homeless if he hadn't just wished for her to kiss him.

She pushed the strands of hair from his forehead. "That make you believe?"

Harrison glared at her a minute. Geez, he had to get himself together. She'd fooled him into that kiss, and, no matter how it made him feel, she was a nutcase.

"I believe you need to leave." He had to turn. Not look at her and see the pained look in her eyes. The sparkle had dulled with his words. "If you want, I can have a cab take you to Tulane Hospital or wherever you want. I think you need to be seen…"

She sighed. "I'm not crazy, Harry."

"I…" He couldn't think of an argument against her saying she was a genie. If he said so, she'd most likely point out that—each time he'd wished for something—it came true.

Coincidence, Harrison.

You believe in things like coincidence, not woo-woo stuff like genies. Leave that up to Elizabeth. Where was that woman so he could give her a piece of his mind? He sucked in a breath, blew it out slowly. That helped clear his thoughts. He looked at Jeanie, and once again thought of how like his sister she was.

That alone was a perfect reason to send her packing.

"I hope you are not, Jeanie. But I have to get on with this business of dealing with Leo being dropped off like some discarded luggage…"

"Is that what you think of me, Uncle Harry?"

Harrison and Jeanie swung around at the same time to see the kid standing in the doorway, rubbing his eyes.

"You two talk too loud." He yawned.

Harry went toward him. "Hey, kid. No. I don't think that. You're my favorite nephew…"

"I'm you're only nephew."

Harrison took him into his arms. "But if I had any others, you'd be my favorite. I'm not upset with you, kid. It's just that your mom doesn't give me any notice to plan for your visits…"

"And I know you like things just so since you are so straight-laced."

"What?"

Jeanie snickered.

"That's what mom says anyway. I'm not sure what it means except that you like to have your life all in order."

"That's true. Now how about heading back to bed so I can say goodnight to Jeanie?" He shook the boy's head and eased him around.

"Goodnight. Right?"

"That's generally what I say when someone is leaving." Harrison chuckled.

But Leo turned and stared at him. "Not *goodbye*. Promise?"

Oh, my. Harrison shook his head and knelt down in front of the boy. "I can't promise that…"

Leo pushed at him, sending him back on his heels and ran to Jeanie. She scooped him up, barely able to hold him. "If you send her away, I'll run away and find her..."

"You'd never do that, sweetie," she said.

"Yes I would!"

He'd grown defiant, and Harrison wasn't sure how to handle him. After a few silent choice words at his sister, he pushed himself up to stand. Maybe his height would give him some authority over these two. Genies. Running away.

How in the world could he complete the biggest advertising campaign of his career with these kinds of dilemmas plaguing him?

"Let her stay, Uncle Harry. Please?"

"Leo, I like Jeanie..." He noticed her eyes light up with that admission. "But, I don't know her that well. As an adult, I'm responsible to do what is right for you and that includes having a babysitter that I can trust..."

"Why can't you trust her? She brought me back safely today. She taught me some geography." He looked at Harrison's wallet on the coffee table. "She gave you back your wallet, and I bet she didn't steal anything. She..." Giant tears filled his eyes, and Harrison knew it was killing the boy not to cry. "She makes me smile. Oh, and she's a lot like my mom."

And that's exactly why I don't want her to stay.

Chapter Seven

Capricorn: What started out as your dull, ordinary week, turns into one of the most exciting weeks of your life. Enjoy. Don't be so stuffy.

Harrison was exhausted. Physically and emotionally. He'd never argued with Leo before, or any other kid for that matter. This entire situation was blowing up in his face and his organized world was crashing into a million pieces.

The one thing he knew was, he couldn't hurt Leo.

Jeanie had proved herself so far, and if she reminded Leo of his mother, that might help the kid get over her leaving him here. He shook his head, ran a hand through his hair, then caught his reflection in the mirror above the fireplace.

Another new wrinkle had formed.

As a man, he could care less if wrinkles formed, but this had to be his body's way of telling him that life stunk right now, and if he didn't do something about it, he'd be a prune by week's end. No clients would believe an ancient man could devise a campaign for teens, nor for anyone else except maybe some senior citizen's club.

He looked at both Leo and Jeanie, and knew what he had to do. "She can stay, temporarily..."

Leo hooted. Jeanie hugged him and set him down. With a kiss to his forehead, she patted him on the back before he ran out to his spare bedroom.

Harrison yelled, "Temporarily! Until I get a reference on her!"

She shook her head. "You know that's not possible."

Harrison looked at her, then the money on the table. She'd had the opportunity to take it and run. She'd had the chance to steal him blind when she watched Leo yesterday or when she had his wallet with all his credit cards inside. And, God forbid, she had the chance to kidnap the kid on more than one occasion.

She had proved herself in some ways.

Was he asking too much because of how he was? Stuffy. Straight-laced as Elizabeth had said?

Exhaustion had him collapse onto the table. He looked down and didn't budge. If it broke up into a heap of metal and glass—he guessed the world wouldn't end. He'd buy another table. Geez! The old Harrison would have sprung back up like a jack-in-the-box.

"Move yourself into the room downstairs next to Margaret's office. As soon as my sister gets back—and Lord only knows when that will be; no, he probably doesn't even know—I'll give you a month's severance pay and you'll be on your way. Understood?"

She smiled at him.

He nodded and forced a smile back. "Hey, what does a genie need money for anyway?"

She laughed. "When sent on a job, we have to eat, dress ourselves and..."

"Blend in."

Was that a grin?

"I'll get my stuff in the morning, Master. I'm too tired."

"Fine." Sure he'd heard her call him "Master" but he'd decided if he was going to lighten up while the kid was here, he'd go along with the whole shebang.

Maybe she was sent here by fate to brighten up his dull life.

It *had been* dull up until yesterday.

And he wasn't at all sure anymore if he liked it that way.

★

Midnight might be the bewitching hour for some, but when Harrison had tossed and turned a thousand times, he considered midnight the most horrendous hour of the day.

He looked at the clock to make sure he hadn't misread it. It'd only been a short time since he'd checked to make certain that Leo had indeed gone to sleep and then he'd said good night to Jeanie.

Well, he decided to force himself to relax. First he tightened the muscles of his feet, then relaxed them. They felt much looser. He did the same with all body parts, working his way to his face. This was working. He felt much more relaxed, although he'd never admit to his sister that he'd tried this routine. She must have told him about it years ago when she harped at him for being—the way he was.

He grabbed his pillow, tucked it under his arms, and shut his eyes. After a few seconds, he realized he was still awake.

Foolishly peaking out of one eye, he made sure the room was empty. Only moonbeams intruded. A soft snoring sound came from the hallway. Leo. At least Leo was enjoying a good night's sleep. Harrison looked up with both eyes to make sure no one was around.

Then, he again relaxed his entire body and quietly said, "Ummmmmmmmm."

★

After several days, and using one of Margaret's many connections, a distant cousin, Harrison found out that there was no criminal record to be found for a Jeanie Merriday. He started to relax.

She had been doing a great job with Leo. Harrison would find himself watching them together, playing a game, doing schoolwork, or one time even listening to saxophone music while their bodies were folded up in what she'd call a comfortable position. At his age, Leo was limber enough to keep up. The kid had shown Harrison some of the papers she'd graded for his schoolwork, and he'd a smile on his face most of the time. He actually looked forward to seeing them together.

Good. Fine. All was right with his world. He leaned forward, and jabbed a finger on the intercom button. "Margaret, is my meeting still at one tomorrow?"

Her disembodied voice came through with, "Wouldn't I tell you if it wasn't?"

He laughed. "*Next* year's Christmas bonus is in question now."

"Liar. Look, boss, the meeting is the same, and need I remind you that Mr. Renée will more than likely want a pitch of some kind for what you plan to do?"

"I was hoping you wouldn't remind me."

The door opened. Margaret came in, and set herself across from him, pad and pencil in hand. "That's my job, which you pay me so meagerly to do. So, what did you come up with?"

He groaned, looked out the window. Must have been Jeanie's version of recess for Leo. He stood at one end of the yard, balancing on one foot. She nearby, in the same position.

"Reminds me of egrets," Margaret said, following his gaze.

Harrison laughed. "I think you mean flamingos."

"Maybe, wait, no, reminds me of Tabitha."

Harrison winced. "Stick with the egrets."

"Whatever, boss. Nice to see the kid out and about."

"Yeah. So, back to business. I have no business right now, Margaret. What am I going to do?"

She looked at him with her motherly stare and stood. "Get out of here."

"What?"

"I said get out. Go somewhere. Take the kid and nanny. You need…"

"I need to work and get this campaign started."

"Duh, as my grandkids say." She stuck her pencil into the bun that she always wore tucked neatly behind her head. "You won't get it started sitting here, looking out the window, and thinking of her…"

"Who?"

Margaret slammed her hand across her forehead. "Duh again. You're in worse shape than I thought. Take them out somewhere—no, take her. Leo could stand to play some wrestling video after days of schooling. Go get a coffee and bignét with Jeanie. Then your mind will clear of the cobwebs she's wound in it, and you'll whip up a dynamite campaign so I don't have to stand in some horrendous unemployment line months before Christmas."

"Go easy on me, why don't you?"

"You don't need easy at your age. You need 'open your eyes and smell the coffee' reality, boss."

"Even men my age need some coddling..."

She howled. "Go!"

Harrison watched her leave and close the door behind her. He turned to the window and realized this was about the millionth time he'd been staring at Jeanie.

But that was because he was checking up on how Leo was doing.

He heard Margaret calling them. They looked at her and headed toward the side door. Great. She'd called them inside. Well, he could use a very strong cup of chicory coffee right about now.

*

"I can't believe you've never had chicory coffee before," Harrison said.

"I'm not a big coffee drinker, but this is great," Jeanie hurriedly added.

He looked into her cup. "No wonder. You don't know how to even drink it. What'd you use, ten sugars and fifty creams?"

She curled her lip at him. "I like it light and sweet. That's why I don't drink it much. Too many calories."

He leaned over, looked at her. "As if you need to..."

She took a napkin and wiped at his chin, straightened his tie. He knew he should have taken the thing off. After he'd agreed to let her stay, she'd never mentioned being a so-called genie in front of Leo or Margaret, but she did keep taking care of him.

It was driving him nuts.

Reminded him too much of Laura and the servants she insisted they hire. That is until Harrison found her telling her mother that she was marrying him for his money.

He took Jeanie's hand as she reached for a spoon, most likely to stir his coffee. "Even genies need a break. How about for the next, say..." he looked at his watch, "hour, we pretend you are merely a woman." *Merely!*

"Okay," she said.

He looked at her and knew he was squinting. "Okay, what?"

"Harry? I said it was okay. I'll pretend I'm not a genie for one hour."

The waiter picked that time to bring the bill. He got an earful, but the guy must have been a long-time pro. He didn't even blink when one of his customers said she wouldn't be a genie for an hour.

Geez, how Harrison loved the Big Easy.

He took the bill, shoved a ten on the table, and stood. Jeanie grabbed her purse. It was gigantic and black velvet with little stars on it. Hadn't Elizabeth... er... Tabitha had something similar? Who cares, he told himself. He wasn't going to think of her, compare her to Jeanie, or think of anything actually. He was freeing his thoughts for mindless enjoyment of the French Quarter—and the beautiful woman who Margaret so foolishly thought had captured his brain in her web.

He guided her up the walkway toward the Mississippi. "Never had chicory coffee. I find that hard to believe. How long have you been in the New Orleans area?" he asked.

She stopped suddenly, causing two guys from behind to bump into them. "Sorry," she said.

Harrison nodded at them and looked at her with what he knew was confusion. "Never mind. I'm not being suspicious. You've proven yourself as trustworthy. It was just a silly conversation." They started walking. "You don't need to answer..."

"I arrived two days before I met you."

It was his turn to stop. "That's only how long you've... I thought you lived here."

"I know I promised no genie stuff, Harry. But there never was a reason for me to come to New Orleans before."

"Okay. Halt the promise temporarily. Why exactly did you

come here?"

The afternoon sunlight sparkled in her eyes, so she reached up to shield them, making it easier to look at him. "I think I already told you that. To... help you with Leo."

"So, when he leaves, you would have left anyway?"

She hesitated. "I... no."

"No?"

"I also came for you, Harry."

He bend forward, took her hand from her eyes, and kissed her smack on the lips.

Why?

He had no idea.

Well, that wasn't exactly true. Having a beautiful woman stand there and tell him that she came here for him might have had something to do with it. And Jeanie was beautiful. Smart. Fun to be with. And perfect. All qualities that had him lean over and press his lips to hers.

Her lips were as soft as cotton candy. She didn't pull back, and for one terrifying second, he expected her to disappear in a puff of air.

But she remained and returned his kiss.

★

She shouldn't do that. Kiss her boss, her Master. This was not right. This was wrong. Genies didn't do that. *So what!*

Surely even a genie was allowed a moment of insanity, one bad judgment call.

He eased free and looked at her. "I... hungry?"

She chuckled. "We just stuffed ourselves on bignéts."

"I know," he said, "but, well, sugar things don't fill you up. Know what I can go for?"

She laughed. "I guess I could eat real food. What?"

"A gigantic oyster po-boy."

"Poor what?"

"Ohmigosh!" He grabbed her arm, spun her around and headed away from the water. "I can't believe you don't know what a po-boy is. They're like a giant hoagie."

"Hoag..."

"You're in worse shape than I thought. Grinder? Don't genie parents feed little genies?"

"I like..."

"I know. Tuna pizza. But you haven't lived until you've eaten a New Orleans po-boy. They come in beef—which I'm guessing you don't eat."

He'd led her back to Jackson Square where they crossed the street and hurried along toward the quaint buildings decorated with wrought iron, hanging plants, and painted signs. When he came to a gift shop, he froze.

"Hope you can hold off on food for one minute."

"Why?" She looked in the crowded window to see Mardi Gras masks of feathers and glass, T-shirts and several cookbooks.

"Wait here and you'll see."

She nodded and watched him hurry into the store. He never said anything about not looking. Normally she didn't mind her five-foot-one height, but when she had to strain to see over the half curtain in the window, she wished she were a bit taller.

He took something off the shelf, but she couldn't tell what. It looked black as far as she could tell, and he held it carefully as if it were glass.

A young boy came by, carrying an old wooden mailbox. A few feet past the store he set it down, put a tin plate on the sidewalk, and started to clap and tap dance. Jeanie laughed and hurried toward him.

"Could I borrow that for a second, sweetie?"

He hesitated, looked her over and nodded. "Bring it right back, lady."

"Thanks. I will." She ran back, set the box on the sidewalk in front of the store's window and looked over the half curtain, to see

Harrison holding up the most beautiful bottle she'd ever seen.

It wasn't a plain glass bottle. No, it was shaped like one that would hold expensive perfume. The sides had gems of sorts on it since they sparkled and winked at her even from this distance. He handed the clerk some money and watched her carefully as she set it into a box.

Jeanie jumped off, ran the box back to the boy, grabbed a buck from her pocket for him, and went back to the spot Harry had left her as he came out the door.

"Caught my eye." He handed her the box.

"Should I open it now?"

"Unless genies have X-ray vision." He laughed.

"No… genies… we don't."

It was glass in fact, but had a covering of silken material over it. The mouth was much wider than she could have seen from the angle outside. But it did wink and sparkle at her.

"Reminded me of the one that genie on the old television show used to come out of. She lived in it. Now you'll always have a place… besides a VW." He laughed.

She looked at him through blurry vision and forced a laugh. "Thanks."

"Look inside." He pointed as if she didn't know were the inside of the bottle was and held on to the top of the bottle with her. "Go ahead. It's a kick."

She bent her head as he held it in her direction and looked to see her reflection in the bottle. Apparently the glass reflected the light with the dark background. She swallowed and looked up to see him grinning like Leo.

"Jeanie in a bottle," he said. "Like the song."

"Thank you. It is a 'kick' as you say." But it felt as if she'd been kicked in her gut. His gesture hit her hard—in the heart. But she had to ignore those feelings. He was her master for crying out loud.

"Okay, detour's over. I'm starving." He placed his hand on her back and hurried her along.

She grabbed his arm to stop him and look at a horse drawn carriage sitting near the curb. "What a hoot! That horse is wearing a hat!"

He laughed. "Later I'll take you on a ride so you can see more of the French Quarter. Right now, your lesson is in fine New Orleans cuisine. You eat oysters?"

She curled her nose.

He rolled his eyes in mock disgust. "Shrimp?"

"Nope."

"I should have known."

He led her to a restaurant whose doors opened to the street. Several customers dinned on what had to be delicious delicacies by the aroma.

"Okay, veggies for you, oyster for me."

She laughed. "I'm much hungrier than I thought," she said as she pushed past him to the hostess. "Two. Non-smoking."

He came up behind and followed her and the hostess to the table. "I thought I was going to be able to do everything on my own. I wish, for one hour, that you'd let me be in charge."

She stood near her chair, waiting.

He grinned, pulled the chair back for her to sit.

"That's a girl."

Hours later, Jeanie sat on the bench in Jackson Square and looked out into the crowd. She and Harry had eaten wonderful, spicy food until stuffed. Rode the horse-drawn carriage for hours and learned about the history of New Orleans. It had been fabulous, educational and the best thing since po-boys, not to mention she was able to sit next to a gorgeous guy in the process. They even had their fortunes told by an old woman with raven hair, and nails two inches long.

She never mentioned Jeanie's secret.

If she were able to grant herself any wish in the world, it would be to have this afternoon with Harrison last forever.

But Jeanie Merriday couldn't successfully grant wishes—to anyone.

Chapter Eight

Capricorn: A sudden, incredible romance is beginning to give you second thoughts. Put your feelings on hold for the time being. Try not to worry about it—your insight will guarantee that you do the right thing. Hopefully.

"That was fun," Harrison said as he pulled into the driveway after his afternoon with Jeanie in the French Quarter. "I think we made it back just in time. Margaret would have my hide if I was late. Thursdays are Jazzercise night."

"You do Jazzercise?"

He looked at her. "Ha. Ha. Margaret's been doing it for years. I think she goes there to meet men, since her husband ran away with the neighbor five years ago."

"How sad." She unhooked her seatbelt after he stopped the car.

"Yeah. But she's a tough cookie, and if the guy ever came back into town, I'd buy front row seats to see her deal with him."

She poked him in the side. "You're horrible."

He pouted. "I thought after the fabulous time I just showed you, you'd have a different adjective to describe me."

"Nope." She laughed and shook her head. "I need to see if Leo completed his math." With that, she opened the door, hurried out, and headed up the walkway.

"Math. Math? All you can think of is adding and subtracting when I..." Whoa. He nearly said when I kissed you like that. The romantic, hypnotic atmosphere of the French Quarter must have been the reason he'd acted the way he did. He'd been there a million times with dates going all the way back to junior high school and right up until a few months ago with Laura.

But he couldn't ever remember having as much fun.

"Math indeed," he mumbled.

Once inside, he looked to see Jeanie, lying on the floor next to his nephew, scrutinizing Leo's math papers. The kid sat there following her finger along the page. Margaret looked up from her computer keyboard—and grinned.

Harrison curled his lip at her and readied to threaten one more Christmas bonus. Let's see, he thought, they'd be up to three years from now, but he figured that might sound like an empty warning. Margaret wasn't easy to fool, either. She was usually right. Sitting there grinning, she looked as if she knew some secret. He turned his gaze to Jeanie—and smiled to himself.

Darn, had Margaret been right about him and Jeanie?

Well, he wasn't going to discuss it with her. She was his employee for crying out loud. *Was that really it?* he asked himself as she watched Jeanie fold her legs under herself to be closer to Leo on the floor. They were a match, those two. Maybe because she was so much like Elizabeth/Tabitha. That might be why he didn't want to discuss her with Margaret. It was too scary.

A chill chased down his spine at that one. Sure he wanted the kid to love his mother, but if she didn't get her act together and stop putting this metaphysical stuff over his care, his upbringing, who knows what the boy would turn out like.

Jeanie laughed. Harrison pulled his thoughts to her and Leo. They were actually having fun while he learned some math. It dawned on him that he really didn't know if Leo and Elizabeth had fun together. He hadn't spent much time with them, business and all. Well, the kid was his sister's concern, not his. He'd show him what a normal life was like for the time he was here, and then have a long talk with his sister. Jeanie folded her legs back more, and rested her head in her palms—maybe normal was a bit of a stretch.

"So, boss, how'd it go?" Margaret whispered.

He looked at her and her foolish grin. "Go?"

"The date."

Harrison rolled his eyes and walked past her. Before he could get to his chair, she was fast behind. "Any messages for me, Margaret?"

"Wouldn't I give them to you if there were?"

"Yes, but..."

"No 'buts,' I'm the best secretary in all of New Orleans. But I have to get to my class soon, so how'd the date go?" She leaned near, glaring.

He slumped into his chair. "You look evil, Margaret."

She hooted and sat on the edge of his desk. "Good. Maybe you'll feel intimidated and spill your guts. Did y'all have a romantic date?"

He looked at her and shook his head. "It wasn't a date. Merely an afternoon in the French Quarter to clear my head..."

"From the cobwebs Miss Jeanie spun there..."

He sighed. "Anyone ever tell you that you are a busybody?"

"Plenty. Even you a few times. Regardless." She pushed up and headed to the door. She turned and paused, then leaned closer, her eyes squinted. "You kissed her. Didn't you?"

Harrison nearly choked.

She pulled back, laughed and turned. "Good for you, boss." With that she opened the door, turned and said, "I like her," walked through and shut the door.

Then, cackled.

Harrison leaned back in his chair, swiveled it around to face the window. Blue birds frolicked in the birdbath in the yard. He'd never noticed before, but the trees were a brilliant shade of green, reminded him of a trip he'd taken to Ireland, although here they were much more tropical looking. Flowers bloomed bright pink along the walls. Funny, he'd never noticed all the colors in his yard and that flowers even bloomed in the fall here.

He swung back around. There wasn't time in his life to ogle flowers and trees. He had an advertisement to write—and had no idea where to start.

But what he did know was that he wasn't going to be taking

Jeanie to the French Quarter, listening to Margaret's foolishness—and heaven forbid, kiss the babysitter—again.

He jammed the intercom button. "Margaret, get me the latest teen magazines please." She didn't answer. "Margaret?"

Static came across as if far away Jeanie said, "Um. I'm not very good at this." She increased the tone of her voice. "I'm not sure if you can hear me." She got louder. "Hello. Hello? Margaret's gone for the…"

Harrison covered his ears before suffering permanent damage. He got up and walked to the door. It was safer to talk to her face to face. He opened the door to see her leaning over the desk, Leo gone.

"I can hear you fine on that…" He pointed.

She let the button up and smiled. "Sorry. It's kinda like when I talk to someone who doesn't understand English. I keep getting louder as if that helps." She sat upright on the edge of Margaret's desk.

"That's common." He said and wanted to kick himself. He was allowing merely looking at her to cloud his mind.

What a mess he was in.

"Where's Leo?" At least talking about the kid would ground Harrison in reality.

"He did such a good job, I let him go upstairs to watch a little television."

So we are alone down here, was his first thought. Then, being the logical, okay, straight-laced guy that he was, he thought to send her upstairs or he'd never get any work done.

"You can go join him."

"Oh no. I'm not about to waste good brain cells on MTV. I've got better things to do with my time than watch them gyrate around singing the same three notes."

"You…" He had to swallow, not having any idea why that helped. But it gave him a momentary reprieve from staring and saying something stupid or kissing her again. Then being eternally sorry that he did or having darn Margaret guess again that he did. "You…"

He lost his train of thought. He smiled at her, biding his time, searching his brain. Nothing. So he figured he'd better focus on Leo instead. "Are those good kinds of shows for Leo to be watching?"

"He said his mom lets him..."

"Great. That's not exactly a vote for MTV."

"I think he'll be fine. Leo's a good kid. Knows right from wrong. He just likes the music. It's a good release for his brain, a mindless release I grant you. But he did extra work today while we were gone. Margaret said he wanted to impress me." She leaned near. "Isn't that cute?"

Like you. "Um. Adorable. Well, I have to get back to work..."

"Oh, right. Work. Okay, what kind of magazines did you want?"

"Never mind. I'll wait until Margaret..."

"I understand from her that you need to get going on this project. Let me help, Harry!"

Never. "No... I need to concentrate..."

"I'll be a statue."

"I thought you were a genie?" Oh man! He wasn't making any sense.

She gave him a pathetic smile. Make that: she smiled at him—pathetically.

"Let me run out and get the magazines, then we'll..."

"No. Really." He did need to start looking at what the kids were wearing nowadays though. The circles he traveled in didn't include nine- to nineteen-year-olds, so he didn't have a clue where to start on writing something that would appeal to them. No wonder he knew so little about Leo.

She grabbed her gigantic purse. "Teen magazines, you said. Any kind?"

"Yes, but..."

She touched his arm. Oh, no. This might be his undoing. He could feel it coming.

"It won't kill you to let me run to the store and save you time."

"No, it won't."

She looked at the watch she wore in a locket, now always hidden by her unusual necklace of dancing fairies. "Besides, it's long past the hour I promised not to mention being your genie. You wish magazines. I get you them."

"Can't you just *poof* them onto my desk?" He bit his tongue after that foolishness came out. Oh man he was in bad shape.

She looked into his eyes. "Is that what you want…"

"No! Of course I don't want…" He ran a hand through his hair. Frustrating, the woman was frustrating. "—you to do that. I shouldn't have even said that and encouraged your ruse."

"Ruse? Huh?" She shook her head. "Harry, Harry. Oh ye of little faith. You want store-bought magazines?" "Yes, any of the teen magazines…" he reached into his wallet and pulled out a hundred, "—that you can find. There is a little store two blocks down to the right."

"You don't have anything smaller?"

He looked at he bill in his hand. "No. Sorry. They'll have change."

She hesitated. Did she think he didn't trust her to bring back the change? Couldn't be. Then again, he had checked her out with the police. But he'd hired her on to watch Leo. Maybe genies knew all this anyway.

"I'm sure they will have change. I feel funny using such a large bill for a few magazines though." She turned and went to the door. "I'll be right back."

"Yeah." He sat on the edge of Margaret's desk. Oh great. By the looks of Jeanie's van, that must be all she owned in the world. He'd handed her a hundred-dollar bill without a thought. It must have looked so decadent to someone like her. He shut his eyes, leaned back.

Would this mess ever end?

"Aye!" he shouted and jumped up. Margaret's cactus minus a few spines glared at him.

"Why am I not surprised?"

★

Jeanie stumbled up the stairs to Harrison's house, the stack of magazines nearly falling to the ground. Who would have thought that teens even bought magazines? They seemed like the least likely people to read. Well, glancing at the top magazine about to fall, she decided they liked to look at the pictures.

At the top of the stairs, she paused. With her hands full, she couldn't get the door opened. So, she leaned down and pushed her nose against the doorbell. A wonderful chime filled the air. She looked through the beveled glass door to see Harry approaching.

Her heart fluttered.

It had to be because she'd been exerting herself, carrying this stack of magazines down the street. Sure. That was it. Genie's hearts couldn't flutter over their masters. Look what happened to "I Dream of Jeannie" every time she let her feelings get in the way. She made a mess. She'd told Harry she didn't own a television, and she didn't anymore. But she and her mother had spent hours watching their old one since Mother couldn't do much else.

"Let me take some of those," Harry said as he opened the door.

"I've got..." He'd already reached out.

"Thanks," she murmured when she wanted to throw the magazines onto the floor and kiss him again.

It had been nice today.

But that's not why she was here. "I'll put the rest on your desk." She hurried through Margaret's office and into his, hoping that the look in his eyes really was disappointment.

She *should have* come here as a mind reader.

Chapter Nine

Capricorn: A business project takes a new turn. Go with the flow—or the rushing current. Believe. Well, at least try to.

"Coffee?" Jeanie asked for what Harrison guessed was the millionth time. At least she'd stopped calling him "Master."

"I'm fine. Go ahead and see what Leo is up to."

She stretched like a feline, then scrunched up in the corner chair. How she managed to pull her legs up, or why, was beyond him. None of his clients could ever sit in that chair again without him picturing Jeanie contorted like this.

"What Leo's up to is snoring like a cougar. If in fact they snore."

"Snoring?" Harrison muttered as he flipped through one more page of the awful magazine. "What kinds of kids read this stuff?"

"Zillions of kids around the world according to the store clerk. You really are detached. And yes, Leo is snoring, Harry. He's been asleep for hours."

He looked up, blinked. The clock on his desk said midnight. "I had no idea how late it was. Go to bed."

She shook her head. "I'm a bit of a night owl. If you need anything, I'm here. Pay no attention to me. Work." With that she shut her eyes, and hummed softly. This time it was more of a tune, kinda Harry Krishna. He laughed to himself at the play on words.

He rubbed his eyes, yawned out, "I'm surprised genies even sleep."

She looked at him.

"Oops. Sorry. I know. Ye of little faith again."

"Yep." She shut her eyes. "Don't any of the wishes I've granted you count for anything?"

"I… coincidence."

"Harry. Harry. Fine. Your prerogative. But you know, the more you doubt me, the harder you make my job."

His eyes could barely stay open. "I wouldn't want you working too hard." If he had a nickel for every magazine he'd thumbed through a hundred or more times, he'd never have to worry about his employees again. The room had become rather hazy in his sleepy state. Even Jeanie had a glow around her. Man, if he didn't watch out, he'd think she really was some kind of, well—genie.

He couldn't remember ever being this tired. This beat. Of course, he hadn't worked this hard on an account in a long time. With the top-notch employees he had, he didn't need to. Most of his time was spent getting clients. He yawned so loudly, Jeanie looked at him and stopped humming.

"I… wouldn't want you to tax your genie brain." He rubbed his eyes. "All right. Me of little faith wishes…" He summoned every ounce of energy from his body and finished, "I wish I… was… tucked into my…"

"Bed" was the last word he remembered uttering. Seemed like awhile ago, too. He moved. Something sounded like sheets rustling. Sheets? In his office? He really was exhausted. Hallucinating sounds. He looked out of one eye with great trepidation. That's because he almost felt as if he were lying down. The room was dark. Jeanie must have shut off his office light—wait a second! A shadow of light came through the beveled window—he didn't have beveled windows like this in his office!

Both eyes flew open.

Dim shadows lightened the room enough to see his dresser, valet, and clothes neatly hung on it. This was his room and the last thing he remembered was wishing that he was tucked into his bed.

And darn it all if he weren't here, neatly tucked.

Another wish granted.

He looked down to see he still wore his clothes. Phew. Another sleepless night lay ahead, he knew it.

Only this time the tossing and turning would be caused by him trying to yank memories out of his head that might never be found. He had been tired. He had joked about wishing to be in bed.

He grabbed the sheet, pulled it over his head, and shut his eyes. For several minutes he lay there. It was hot. His eyes wouldn't stay shut. And, he needed air. With a shove, the sheet landed on the floor, yanked out of the "tucking" Jeanie obviously had performed.

Why couldn't he remember?

The mantel clock in the living room chimed one. Another wasted hour. He reminded himself that he needed sleep to be fresh and creative in the morning. Grabbing the pillow, he shoved it under his head and shut his eyes.

His eyelids flew open.

"This is ridiculous." He got up, shoved his feet in slippers neatly waiting for him bedside the bed. His nanny had often given him warm milk with a teaspoon of butter floating in it when he was a kid. Cholesterol overload, but right now he couldn't care less. If the L-tryptophans knocked him out, he'd go on a low-fat diet tomorrow. Too bad he didn't have a turkey he could throw in the oven. He could use a mega-dose right now.

On the way to the kitchen, he paused to listen to a soft snoring coming from the other end of the hallway. Leo must still have his adenoids. Man, he was tired. Couldn't even remember if his nephew ever had his adenoids out. Well, he'd drink his milk, head back to sleep, and awaken with energy to burn, forgetting all his problems. He shoved open the kitchen door.

"Oh!"

"Jeanie?" he called as the kitchen door swung back and forth on its hinges. When he grabbed the door, he opened it all the way to see Jeanie standing there, holding her nose. "Oh, great! Again? I'm sorry…"

She waved her hand. "Just a bump. I'm fine."

He ran to the refrigerator. "Let me get you some ice." The cubes stuck to his fingers as they melted. "Wait. Let me get a paper towel."

She stood waiting, her face reddened beneath her hand. "I'll just go splash cold— Ouch!"

"Sorry. Was that too hard?" Too hard? He'd nearly knocked her over, shoving the paper towel full of ice onto her face. "Sit down. I had no idea you were in here."

She looked at him over the wad of paper. "I hope not. I wouldn't want to think that you were trying to get rid of me..."

"No. No. It's just that..." He looked at her smiling. "Oh, I get it. You were joking." He blew out a breath. "I'm not running on all eight cylinders right now."

She moved the paper towel. Her nose was red, slightly swollen—looking adorable. Worse part was, he had to grab onto the counter to keep from kissing her adorable red nose.

"Cylinders?"

"An expression. Like in a car. I'm not. Forget it."

"No. I like to learn new things."

"I need some milk."

She chuckled. "By the look on your face, I'd say a Pinch scotch was more of what you need."

"Ha. Yeah. That was a good one." He sounded like an idiot. A moron.

Jeanie set the ice into the sink and threw the paper towel in the trash. She approached him.

He stepped back. Don't let her touch me. "Well, guess I'll be heading off..."

"Harry, you are acting odd."

He forced a chuckle—and that's exactly how it sounded—forced. "Maybe I'm sleepwalking." He raised his arms in front of him, shut his eyes. "You're a dream. You're a dream..."

She didn't touch him but said, "I don't know what is wrong with you. Sleepwalkers that I've seen don't shut their eyes."

His eyelids flew open as if on springs. "How many have you seen? Oh, right. Someone who has lived as long as you have..." He had to ramble on foolishly, or she might touch him.

At this rate, he'd need a gallon of milk and twenty pounds of butter.

"I took care of a child who walked..."

His mind cleared for a second. "You cared for other children?"

She shoved her hand into the folds of material of her T-shirt. But he could swear he saw them shaking as if Jeanie Merriday was nervous—hiding something.

For crying out loud, man, what do you think she is going to say? Since she really is a genie she'd never watched a kid in her life?

But that was what she wanted him to think.

"Yes, well, there was this couple in Bangladesh that had a little boy..." Her hands wrung the material.

With Herculean effort, he pulled his gaze from her shirt, turned. Then he opened the refrigerator door, grabbed the milk and butter and set it on the counter. "Bangladesh? Huh?"

She yawned. Maybe for real. Maybe as fake as her chuckle. "Yep. Their son walked in his sleep. Once I found him outside..."

"Why didn't your master just wish that his kid wouldn't walk in his sleep?" He turned to pour the milk into a mug he'd taken from the cabinet, then shut his eyes. What a jerk. He sounded like a real idiot, not to mention the fact that he was adding fuel to her crazy insistence that she was a genie. He added a spoonful of butter to the milk and stuck the mug in the microwave.

By the sounds of her footsteps she'd come closer. "Harry. Harry. The child never walked in his sleep again. If I told you it was because the father had wished it, you wouldn't believe me anyway. So, suffice it to say, some outside force interfered."

He turned around. So late at night her eyes took on a much deeper hue. So gem-like. She looked at him as if waiting for him to respond. "I... guess. Jeanie, I'm a reasonable, logical guy. Woo-woo isn't my strong point."

"These things often take time. Although, I will admit, I can't imagine a tougher nut to crack where masters are concerned." With that she walked to the door and turned. She wiggled her chin. Then, she walked out the door, softly saying, "Learn to lighten up, Harry."

The microwave binged. His heart jolted.

And he wondered if he really should lighten up. No doubt Margaret would agree with that suggestion.

★

Harrison swiveled around in his office chair, looking out the window. He'd have thought that a nap would sound tempting after the miserable night he'd had, but the milk had done the trick, or maybe it was Jeanie's words.

Either way, he managed a good four hours.

Now, all he needed was a stroke of genius to come up with a dynamite campaign. Well, Margaret had made him a pot of strong chicory coffee, which he now sipped, and his mind was cleared of any debris.

"Boss?" Margaret's voice interrupted his thoughts.

He swiveled back, poked the intercom button. "That's me."

"Well, you may not want to admit it. Mr. Renée is on line one. I'm guessing he wants a tidbit of info on your progress—although I couldn't pry a word out of him." She paused. "Nor did I tell him you looked like something the cat dragged in this morning. Long night?"

Harrison chuckled. "I'll handle Mr. Renée. You, on the other hand, are out of my league." He let the button go, but heard her laughing through the door. With a smile, he picked up the phone. "Hello, sir. I was just going to put in a call to you."

"That mean you have my campaign all ironed out, son?"

Harrison rolled his eyes. "Not completely."

"How's about a little hint of what's to come?"

Oh boy. Margaret was right as usual. Harrison ran his gaze over the many magazines he'd left in a heap on his desk. She wanted to tidy them up today, but he thought he'd try being more creative in a mess.

So much for "lightening up."

"Now..." He scanned the magazines, pushed all but one to the floor. "I don't want to spoil the effects, but I will tell you this much..." *What? What the heck could he tell him?*

A snippet of a redhead caught his eyes on the back cover of the one left. She had Jeanie's build, but there was something very jungle-like in the girl's eyes where Jeanie's had a more forest—fairies, nymphs-type—look in hers.

But there was a similarity in the two.

Man how he wished he could forget these useless magazines and come up with an ad.

"I don't have all day, son."

He could picture Mr. Renée, cigar in mouth, Stetson on head, feet on his desk and phone cradled on his shoulder. "I understand, sir. Well, the campaign will involve a girl—petite redhead..."

"Oooweee. I like 'em small. So far so good." He let out a nasty chuckle.

Harrison sat foreword, making a mental note never to let this guy set eyes on Jeanie. "She'll be in a jungle setting..."

"Jungle?"

"Yes, sir. Kids go for tropical settings, animals. You know..." He cleared his throat and spun around to buy time. Leo and Jeanie ran across the backyard, playing some kind of tag game. Her hair caught the morning sun, looking like filaments of copper. The backyard did have a tropical look to it.

Suddenly he pictured Jeanie in one of Mr. Renée's outfits. Skintight pants until the knees where they flared out into bell-bottoms. One of his floral tops, giant yellow ones would look fabulous against her fair skin.

"Son? You there?"

"Hm. Yeah." He leaned forward. "She'd be wearing white pants, your bellbottoms with a yellow floral shirt..."

"She? Oh, yeah. The redhead. I get it. Yep."

"Fine. Sure. You get the idea." Zazu perched amongst the Spanish moss hanging from the trees. "There'd be a giant monkey in it..."

"Monkey? I like the doll, but a monkey..."

"Don't monkey around when you could be hanging from her tree. Oh, there'd be several guys around her, hanging from trees, wearing your clothes. Jeans without shirts, et cetera."

Leo ran around Jeanie, laughing.

"They'd be laughing."

Harrison blinked himself back to his phone conversation. Mr. Renée hadn't said a word. "Sir?"

"Have your secretary set up an appointment, son. I want this expedited." With that he hung up before Harrison confessed—only blank sheets of papers scattered his desk.

He looked at Leo, Jeanie, and wonderful Zazu—and shouted, "Margaret!"

She ran in. "Shall I call 9-1-1?"

"No. Why?"

"I don't know. You screamed as if one of the boys had fallen out of one of your tropical, jungle trees that the kids go for nowadays and was eaten up by one of the animals they like so much. A monkey maybe."

Harrison glared at her.

"You think the best secretary in all of New Orleans doesn't know to listen in on her boss's conversation when he's about to lose a client?"

"You are good."

She howled, tapped her notebook. "Got it all right here." She gazed out the window. "But I most likely didn't have to write down the descriptions." She leaned near. "You devil."

When she had the decency to leave, he turned to see Jeanie bending to pick Leo up.

"Creamy, like a smoothie. Jungle tan—you'd burn your fingers on." A helpful breeze sent her hair dancing about. "The scent of a woman." He swiveled around to see the door open and paused.

"That it, boss?" Margaret called.

He felt his face flush. "What? I don't know what you're talking about." He could see her leaning over her desk, looking at him, her pen in hand—cat-eaten grin on her face.

"No? Well..." She pulled back out of sight. "You just described the little doll in your ad. How convenient that you have bay windows."

And a genie to grant my wishes, he thought.

Chapter Ten

Capricorn: A relationship changes courses. Get out while you can. Or at the very least, get yourself a good compass.

Jeanie looked out the window to see Harry pull in the driveway. "He's here, Margaret!" She scooted behind the drapes, leaned near the window.

"And?"

"I can't see too good. It's dark out."

Margaret came closer. "You need more practice at this spying stuff, sugar. Let me take a look." She leaned near Jeanie. "Smiling. He's smiling."

"Great!" They hurried away from the window, Margaret collapsing into her desk chair. Jeanie landed on the couch, tying to look nonchalant. "You're sure he was smiling?"

Margaret shook her head. "I know my Harry."

Jeanie laughed as the door swung open. She really did know her Harry. A smile covered his face, making that one little dimple to the side of his mouth visible. His eyes sparkled with joy even though the lighting wasn't very bright in the office.

She couldn't help smile, too.

"So, did the client like it?" Margaret asked.

"Guess." Harry sat on the edge of the couch. Jeanie straightened up, looked at Margaret who winked.

Harry glanced from one to the other. "What?"

Margaret pretended to busy herself with a few papers. Blank ones. "Oh, nothing, boss."

"Something is up with you two? Your 'nothings' always cause me concern."

She kept her head down. "You're always too worrisome, boss."

"I won't deny that, but always with good reason. Now what's going on? Don't try to deny it. I can feel it. Jeanie?"

Margaret set the papers to the side. "Don't harass the babysitter."

"Harass?"

Jeanie laughed.

He slid onto the couch and looked at her. Diamond-like sparkles winked at her from his chocolate eyes. The dimple deepened with his smile. An enticing—no, make that interrogating—kind of smile. It was going to be hard not to spill her guts with him this close. "It's just… we were waiting to see how things went…"

He turned toward Margaret who already had on her coat. "So, that's a crime?"

"No. I wondered why you were here so late. Isn't tonight ninety-nine cent movies near your condo?"

"Yep. Only thing is, my grandson got sent home with a detention today. Teachers. Don't they know boys will be boys? Why can't a kid wear his bathrobe and slippers over his gym clothes out of the locker room to get a laugh?"

Jeanie jumped up. Margaret had her coat on! She was getting ready to leave!

"He most likely deserved the detention," Harry said, getting up.

Margaret rolled her eyes. "I'm glad you're not his teacher."

"Too bad about your movie, Margaret," Jeanie said, "but now you can help us celebrate…"

"No can do. I've been waiting to see the new Adam Sandler flick. Grandkids got me hooked on him. He's a hoot. And, I've got myself a date."

"Oh." Jeanie looked at her. "Guess it will be just Leo and I to help Harry celebrate his success with Mr. Renée."

Margaret winked again. "Who do you think my date is?"

As she said that, Leo bounded down the stairs, wearing the new navy jeans and floral shirt Harry had gotten him from Mr. Renée. Far too big, far too baggy. But in style. He also had on a silver necklace with a monkey hanging off it, and she'd swear he had on a spicy cologne that smelled suspiciously like Harry.

Now what?

Harry looked at her and paused. "I… guess that we'll have to wait until tomorrow night…"

Margaret nearly yanked his arm out of his socket she pulled him so hard. "Can't. Shrimp jambalaya waits for no one. Jeanie and I slaved for hours making it along with my favorite avocado salad, oysters on the half shell, nice and salty ones, and, your favorite. Bread pudding with rum sauce. No way on God's green earth are you going to turn our fabulous meal into tomorrow's leftovers." She shuttered. "The thought of warming up jambalaya in a microwave!" She grabbed Jeanie's arm, too, pushing them toward the door. "Go. Eat." This time she winked at Harry. "Enjoy."

That last word came out very deviously.

*

Harrison watched Leo and Margaret walk out the door. Thank goodness she'd released her death-grip on his arm. Rubbing the soreness, he thought of how he still had work to do on his campaign and needed both hands. She was a winner, that Margaret.

Who did she think she was kidding?

Detention my foot, he thought.

He turned to see Jeanie paused as if frozen. The sparkle of her eye had dulled a bit. Most likely from Margaret and Leo's desertion.

Was it that painful for her to have to eat with him alone?

Was he really the stick-in-the-mud Margaret insinuated?

Well, he'd admit he was very different from Jeanie, but their being together shouldn't be painful. He had visions of the last time they were alone—in the French Quarter. *Painful? Whoa boy.* He may need a bottle of aspirin for dessert instead of bread pudding.

"Margaret!" He hurried to the door. Maybe he could convince her to stay. Tell her he needed her. Force her to work—this was Margaret he was talking about.

"I think they're gone."

He spun around to see Jeanie standing there. He'd expect her to be smiling, but her face was as blank as his mind. Maybe she was nervous, too.

Nervous?

No way. He wasn't going to admit that a woman who professed to be a genie. Harrison Rainford was a successful businessman and too old to let nerves affect him.

Jeanie stood silent as if waiting for him to take the lead. He ran a successful business, had for years, in addition to dealing with all types of people. He'd never felt this way—as if his insides skittered about like one of Leo's toys—with any woman before. And certainly not in his own house!

Laura had her faults, pompousness not withstanding, but he never felt nervous with Laura. Bored, yes, disgusted, a few times when she ordered servants about and, how could he forget, never as aroused as he was right now.

Jeanie moved closer to the couch sat down and proceeded to tie herself into knots—much as his insides felt. He turned to look at Margaret's desk. A safe haven until a soft umming sound had him look back.

Whoa boy.

She'd tucked her legs beneath the dress, if that's what it was, that she wore. It was long, narrow at the legs and deep purple—much as her eyes right now. The material had tiny mirrors sewn into it, casting reflections of colors onto her skin.

"Are you hungry?" she asked.

He glared at her, wondering how she managed the position, how her voice could come out so softly, yet as if verbal tentacles reached out and grabbed his thoughts.

"Hungry? I… yes." He'd been famished on the drive home. How could he have forgotten that?

She started to uncurl herself. "Then I'll fix your meal…"

"No!"

Her eyes blinked, then widened. "I don't understand."

He sucked in a breath of air that went clear to the base of his lungs and blew it out just as deeply. "Sorry. I didn't mean to startle you. I meant, well… you don't have to wait on me. You're Leo's babysitter. Or nanny if you prefer the term…"

"Harry. Harry." She laughed. "Seems I say that a lot."

He forced a smile, but his lips quivered as if he was posing for a picture and the darned photographer was taking his time. "Um." Brilliant comeback.

"Terms don't mean a thing. You can call me what you like. Whatever makes you comfortable."

"Harry, that's why I stopped calling you 'Master.' The term doesn't mean a thing. You know who you are…"

"Your master," he mumbled. *What?* he screeched in his mind. "I meant…"

Perhaps along with being a genie—thinking she was a genie—he corrected himself, she was clairvoyant, too.

She looked at him and smiled. "I know what you meant."

He tried to look over her head into thin air, but tonight she'd worn that little velvet headpiece—obviously to confuse him. Trying to look like a genie didn't *make* her a genie. He stepped back with that thought. "I really am hungry. What I meant before was, you don't need to wait on me since I hired you for Leo."

"I see."

And so did he as he met her glance. She'd firmed her lips and the color of her eyes looked as if some artist had diluted the paint too much. The brilliance was gone with his words.

"I didn't mean anything, Jeanie. It's just that I don't want you to feel as if you need to wait on me…"

She pushed a pointed nail into his chest.

"Ouch!"

"Sorry. But you had that one coming. I've told you I was sent here to help take care of Leo. You pay me, sure. If that makes you feel better, fine. But if my job, as I see it, involves taking care of you some, what's the harm?"

She stood on tiptoes and glared at him.

"I… ." He had no argument there. Actually, he was beginning to enjoy her company. Red flag! *She will be gone very soon when Elizabeth gets back. Don't start "enjoying" anything about Jeanie Merriday.*

But he looked at her and remembered the kiss.

★

Jeanie watched Harry's face. Normally she was an expert on reading people. Had been since her mother taught her so well as a child, then she learned more from Santanloni. No wonder she was chosen for this job. But this guy was a challenge to say the least. He looked as if he had lost his best friend and his puppy, and flunked kindergarten all at once. Hm. She'd have to let up on him a bit. "Tell you what. The meal is all done. Let's do 'Dutch treat' in the who-serves-who department." She offered her hand.

Reluctantly, she was certain, he reached out and shook. "Good idea. You do understand what I meant about not wanting you to wait…"

She shook vigorously and let his hand drop. "Give it up, Harrison! I got it. I understand. Beneath this ponytail is a brain."

"I'm certain you are intelligent."

She rolled her eyes. "If we don't go eat, the jambalaya will be a cake of dried rice, the dessert will be so soaked we'll both end up intoxicated, and Margaret will have Leo home." She leaned near, figuring she needed his full concentration. "You want to face her wrath?"

Finally he chuckled. "Nope. Let's go." He stepped aside, waved his hand, and let her pass.

Once in the kitchen, Harrison headed to the refrigerator. He looked inside to see the oysters gleaming on their plate. Oysters. Weren't they considered an aphrodisiac? Leave it to Margaret. He started to reach for them, then paused. Turning around, he smiled at Jeanie and shut the door—oysters neatly remaining in the frig.

Luckily she didn't notice as she opened the pot on the stove and leaned near. "Um. Margaret's a wonderful chef."

Harry came beside her. "The woman's a saint in my book." He turned toward Jeanie. "I'll deny that I said that to my death."

She laughed. "Make a wish and my mouth is silent." She turned to him and grinned.

He rolled his eyes, shook his head. "I can't believe I'm going to say this, but I wish you wouldn't tell Margaret."

She wiggled her chin. "Done."

"How can I be sure? Maybe over a cup of coffee tomorrow, you'll spill your guts..."

She put her finger to his lips. "Oh ye of little..."

He hadn't meant to do it, Harry told himself. But it was there, her finger that is, and his lips were so close, feeling so warm—he just had to kiss the tiny tip of her finger.

And wished that she wouldn't pull away.

Chapter Eleven

Capricorn: Look out below! Your life is about to take a downward spiral. You are not equipped. Then again, maybe you only think you aren't.

"Look, I was out of line, Jeanie. Forgive me," Harrison said after Jeanie took her finger from his lips.

Waving her hand, she turned away from him and headed to the stove. "We do need to keep this on a business like level. Let's eat. Oh, wait, we forgot the oysters..."

"No! I mean, it's getting late. Let's go straight to the main dish."

Harrison watched her ladle spoonfuls of jambalaya onto two dishes. She was right about keeping their relationship on a businesslike level. "I'll set the table." He turned to walk into the dinning room.

"I'm surprised Margaret didn't..."

"Oh great."

"What's the matter?" She set the dishes on the counter. "Harry?"

"In the dinning room."

Jeanie stuck her head in. "Oops."

"Margaret is on year four of losing her Christmas bonus." He looked to see his grandmother's Wedgwood china sparkling in the candlelit room. Two place settings. Two glasses already poured of what he assumed was his finest wine. Wait. This was Margaret's work. Make that champagne.

Jeanie laughed. "Earlier you said she was a saint."

"I got my heavenly souls and evil spirits mixed up. I meant 'devil.' I'll get the dishes..." She touched his arm.

"If you don't mind, I think I'll sit in the kitchen."

He looked at her and readied to argue that the table was already set, but he knew she was right and his arguing would only come from disappointment.

For a second, he'd looked forward to their dinner in here.

"I'll join you. No sense in dirtying the china. I noticed you already served on the everyday dishes anyway." He had a dishwasher, for crying out loud, but what he didn't have was a good reason why he didn't want to eat in here alone—while she remained in the kitchen.

He sighed as he followed her out. Life had gotten so complicated for a simple guy like himself ever since his fool sister had slipped out of town.

How long does it take to find one's soul anyway?

"I'll get the wine—champagne—that Margaret poured," he said, turning back. The devious secretary.

"Fine."

When he came into the kitchen, she'd seated herself on the counter, looking quite comfortable, balancing her dish on her lap. It didn't take a pot of jambalaya to fall on him to guess that she didn't want to share the table.

He handed her a glass, sat down, took a spoonful. Margaret didn't cook very often, but the few times she did, Harrison was duly impressed. "This is great."

"Um," she said with a forkful to her mouth.

Well, that was stimulating conversation. He felt more like a fool every minute. He needed a safe, non-sensual topic to discuss. After several bites, the palpable silence had him on edge. The quieter it was, the stupider he felt about earlier.

He wished they could find something to talk about.

"How long does it take to get back from the movies?"

Phew. At least *she* broke the silence. He chose to ignore that she had answered yet another of his wishes. "Let's see. Margaret likes to go across the river to a little restaurant I'm sure Leo would love, too. So, I'm guessing they'll be a few more hours."

"I've never been across the river."

He looked up. "I'd forgotten you haven't been around here long." Then why had it seemed as if she belonged here? "Well, you have to head north of here to get to one of the bridges that goes across the Mississippi."

She looked ready to jump off the counter. "Can I get you something else. More jambalaya?"

"Let me get it." He stood and took her dish. She settled back, leaning against the cabinet while he lifted the cover off the pot and took the ladle from the spoon rest. "Jeanie, Leo said you live in your…"

"Van."

He turned around, ladle in hand. "Do you?"

"Yes, Harry. I live in my van… for now."

"I thought it was only a story you'd made up to entertain him."

"It's not bad. Not entertaining though, I'm afraid. But I do have everything I need…"

"What about food?"

She laughed.

"Oh, right. You wiggle your chin, poof it, and dig in."

She shook her head. "I find an inexpensive restaurant. Besides, it had only been a few weeks that I lived in it until you hired me and gave me room and board."

"Oh, right."

She did jump down, took her dish to the sink then turned and took his, too.

"Why?"

"Why am I cleaning when you are quite capable of doing it…"

"No, Jeanie. Why do you live in your van?"

She turned around, paused, and leaned against the counter. For several minutes she remained silent. He guessed she debated whether to tell him the truth. Geez, he hoped she didn't love that lifestyle.

Sounded too much like something his sister would do.

"It's... what I can afford right now."

He glared at her. "You... can't get an apartment?" Now he wondered what her previous job had been. She hadn't acted like the type to throw her money away, except maybe on the fancy necklace that she always wore. He hadn't seen it on her the first time he knocked the door into her, but she had it on in the restaurant later. Looked like something from that little boutique down the street Tabitha loves.

"I... no, I can't. This is an expensive area and the down payments alone are more than I have in my savings account."

He pushed back his chair, the legs scraping the tile, as he stood. "There's nothing to be ashamed about..."

She straightened her shoulders. "I've always worked hard at every position I've ever had. I do an excellent job and I'm conscientious."

He smiled. "I know. That's why my being your 'master' is so difficult. I'm the first to admit that I'm a tough cookie to work with. You do, however, give it your best shot."

"True. I... will be able to afford my own place soon."

"So you're saving what I pay you?"

She nodded.

"Good. Look, if you need an advance..."

"We don't know how long Tabitha will be gone. I can't take an advance from you and then she comes back. My job will be over."

He ran his fingers through his hair. "True. I may be able to find a job for you in my company. That's it. I can hire you..."

"Did you sign your new contract?"

"Well, not yet. But it is close. He loved my last ideas."

"Then there is a chance it can all fall through." She waved a hand before he could interrupt. "Not that I want it to. I hope it goes perfectly. But I can't work for you, knowing you are in a tight spot with your business location."

"How did you..."

She grinned. "Saint Margaret and I have shared a cup of tea or two."

"Figures. Look, when my sister comes back, I can't let you go live in a van in some parking lot. I couldn't let anyone do that."

She noticed a protectiveness in his voice and thought it wasn't any wonder that all his employees loved him. Still, it would have been nice if he'd hadn't included anyone in his concerns about the van. She envied his relationship with his staff. Certainly Margaret treated him like one of her sons. But that wasn't the kind of relationship she wanted. "I'll be fine."

He walked to her and took her hand. "You never told me how you chose New Orleans and where you came from… and I don't mean a bottle."

She looked into the living room and saw the bottle he'd given her. While she stayed here caring for Leo, she'd set the bottle he'd bought her in the French Quarter on the mantel. Harry had said it was fine to do that, and she was thrilled to be able to see it each time she walked past. He more than likely expected her to disappear in a puff of smoke and live in the bottle. Well, that was for television, not real life—not even real genie life.

"I don't live in a bottle, Harry. If I did, I wouldn't need my van."

"I know. You need to blend in."

"That's the only way I can be of help. If not, people, such as yourself would never believe that they could change—have their wishes come true."

He tightened his hold and looked into her eyes. "I wish that I could… would… believe in you, Jeanie. I really do."

She met his gaze, wiggled her chin—and smiled.

★

Harrison bent, kissed her hand and looked into Jeanie's eyes. "You still haven't told me why you can't afford an apartment."

"My mother is older…"

He chuckled. "What? She's about four or five hundred?"

She smiled. "No, Harry. Mother isn't *that* old."

"I just thought… well, you know."

"Yes." She sighed. "I know that you are thinking that genies are ancient." She leaned near. "Do I look that old?"

"Absolutely not."

"Anyway… my mother needs a lot of care. Expensive care."

He watched as she spoke. Sadness filled her eyes along with concern and love. The love must be for her mother, but why the sadness? "Care?"

She pulled her hands free. "I told you, we have to blend in, live real lives. Mother… is in a convalescent home up in Baton Rouge."

"I see. Small world. That's where Leo and my sister lived before moving back here last year."

"Oh. Anyway, mom didn't have insurance, so we ended up selling our house to pay for her care. It's only her and I, so I figured I could live in my van until I got a job. Then I'll move near her and be all set…"

"So why come all this way? Why not look for a job in Baton Rouge."

She hesitated. He'd never gotten the feeling she purposefully lied to him, except the fabrication of being a genie. But right now, a look on her face said it was hard to tell him the real reason.

"I… you were here and I couldn't turn down my first master."

With that she turned and walked to the door.

Harrison debated about running after her; yanking her around and screaming that she stop this nonsense. If she didn't, he couldn't help her.

Instead, he watched her ponytail swing back and forth and wished that his sister would come back so that he could concentrate on Jeanie Merriday and getting her help.

Ring. Ring. Ring.

He grabbed the phone off the wall. "What?"

"Nice way to answer your phone, darling brother."

Chapter Twelve

Capricorn: Once again family problems interfere. Change your usual tactics. In the matter of love, a more difficult task awaits you. Oh boy.

"Where the heck *are* you, Elizabeth?" Harrison grabbed the phone so tightly, a pain shot down his arm. No great surprise by the way things were going. He merely ignored it, awaiting his sister's answer.

"It's Tabitha, Harry. I told you that I changed my…"

He held the phone out in front of him for a few seconds to gain what slight control was left of his temper. "Tabitha," he spit out. "Whatever you want to call yourself. Where are you?"

"Well, let me see. Some public gathering place. There are shops and locals and…"

Give me strength. "Tabitha, I mean what continent are you on!"

"India, darling. Still here. I've had the most mind-altering experience."

He'd like to alter her. "Wonderful. Your son…"

"How is Leo? Tell him I found him this fabulous outfit in Bombay…"

"He doesn't need clothes, Elizabeth…"

"Tabi…"

He gritted his teeth until they hurt. "Elizabeth," he pronounced loudly, "Leo needs a stable life, to get into school. He needs…"

"Don't profess to tell me what my kid needs, Harry. You don't exactly have any experience in that department. Leo and I do fine."

"Then get home and *do* with your kid!"

"I can't… yet. You'd never understand since you are so…"

"Straight-laced?"

"That'd about cover it."

"At least I care enough about Leo to see that he is taken care of, schooled..."

"I've taken care of him, Harry."

"How? By sending him here in a cab from the airport while you jet off..." He grabbed the phone tighter. The pain now numbed his arm.

"You have no idea how. Just believe me."

"Yeah. I'm going to believe you."

"Great."

He rolled his eyes. "I'm being sarcastic, Elizabeth."

"That's not like you..."

"I guess people change."

"That's what I'm telling you. I'm changing as we speak, and I need a bit more time to complete my metamorphosis..."

"Geez."

"Give Leo a big kiss for me..."

The line crackled. "Elizabeth?"

"I'm loosing you, Harry. Tell Leo I love him, please. I'll be home as soon as I can..."

"Oh no you don't! Don't you dare hang up on me. What about school, Elizabeth?"

"I'll call my friend, Lila, up in Baton Rouge and have her send you his records. I'll be moving to your area, so get him into..."

"How dare you leave me with all of this! I have a business to run. A giant contract hanging over my head." His vision blurred from anger. Good thing she was thousands of miles away or he'd... he didn't know what he'd do. But what he wanted to do was attack her verbally if nothing else. He knew that would have to do since he wasn't the physical type.

"You get yourself here, Tabitha. I can't be worrying about *your* kid..." Harrison heard a shuffling behind him and swung around to see a flash of navy. "Don't hang up, Elizabeth. Don't you dare." He dropped the phone and ran down the hall in time to see Leo run into his room.

Great. He'd never forgive his sister for this mess.

"Leo?" He tapped on the door. A faint sniffling came from inside. "Please, may I come in, kid?" Nothing. "I'm going to open the door because I really want to talk to you even though I'd normally not invade your privacy. It's important though."

Slowly, he opened the door to see Leo huddled on the bed, Zazu tucked under his arm. The kid looked much younger than his age.

"Hey, kid. Your mom is on the phone…"

Through teary eyes, Leo glared up at him. Harrison's heart twisted. Damn Elizabeth. "I know you must have heard part of my conversation, but that's the problem."

Leo stared, hugged the monkey tighter.

"You only heard part. That's called 'taking it out of context' and sometimes, as in this case, what you hear sounds bad. But that's not because it is, but because you didn't hear the entire conversation. Your mom said to say she loves you…"

"When's she coming back so you can get back to your business?"

Oh, my. "She said soon, but you know I've been doing my business all along. Isn't that right?"

He released his hold on Zazu and sat up. "I guess."

"You guess?" Harrison sat on the edge of the bed, wiped a tear from the kid's cheek. "Hey, do you think Margaret would let me get away with not doing my work?"

Leo cracked a slight smile. "There's Jeanie, too."

That there is, Harrison thought. "Yeah. She's been a godsend for you…"

"And you, too. You know what, Uncle Harry?"

"What, kid?"

"You seem kinda different since she came here. You both would make neat parents."

Whoa boy. He couldn't get into that with the kid. "Look, your mom is waiting to talk to you. Let's cut her some slack. I was kinda hard on her…" He touched the boy's arm. "But nothing to do with you. Adults sometimes say things out of anger that they really don't mean. You know you're my favorite nephew."

That caused his smile to widen. He poked at Harrison's arm. "I told you, I'm your only one."

Harrison ruffled Leo's hair. "And I told you, you'd be my favorite even if I had a zillion nephews!"

"You think she's still on the phone?"

If she values her life. "Of course. She called to talk to you and..." He tickled him under his arm. "You haven't said a word to her yet."

On the way to the kitchen, Harrison looked to see Jeanie sitting in her room within earshot.

"Hi, Tabitha," Leo's voice came down the hallway.

Harrison nodded at Jeanie and hurried to the kitchen.

"Sure... That's cool... Yeah... Oh, Uncle Harry got me the best nanny in the whole wide world. She's the smartest, prettiest, coolest person and can bend all sorts of ways."

Harrison leaned against the counter, stifling a moan when he added "best kisser" to his thoughts.

"Yep, Jeanie reminds me of you, Tabitha."

Harrison heard Leo laugh and shook his head to clear the cobwebs of daydreaming. "Don't hang up, Leo. Let me talk to her..."

"Yeah, I'll tell him..."

"Wait!" He grabbed the phone. "Elizabeth! Elizabeth!"

Leo looked at him and curled his lips. "She hung up, Uncle Harry."

He slammed down the phone so hard, Leo jumped. "Sorry, kid. It's just... I needed to talk to her. She didn't by chance leave a number..."

Leo gave him a you-know-Tabitha kind of look. "She said she'd call in a few days. I told her about Jeanie..."

"I heard." Great. He was back to square one. Not only didn't he know when his sister would come back to reclaim her kid, now he had to get him into some school which he knew nothing about doing. Or even the location to pick. What do kids eat in school?

Do eight-year-olds get homework? What kinds of supplies do they need? All this with the biggest contract deadline hanging over his head. He blew out so much air he felt dizzy.

Leo stood staring as if afraid to move.

Harrison took a deep breath and let it out slowly. "Got a minute?" He took the boy into his arms and held him.

The kid looked confused. "I'm kinda tired, but I guess."

He waved toward the living room, and let him go. Leo turned and headed in while Harrison followed. Leo sat on the floor, folding his legs like Jeanie. Reminds the kid of his mother. Great. Just great. Harrison shook his head and sat in his favorite leather chair. "By the way, how was the movie?" He had to get the kid's mind off that bit of phone conversation he'd heard.

"Margaret said it was one of Adam Sandler's best. I kinda liked *Happy Gilmore* better. She bought me the extra large popcorn though."

Harrison smiled. "With butter?"

"She says no one in their right mind eats movie popcorn without butter."

He laughed. "Sounds like Margaret. By the way, where'd she go?"

He shifted position, now bending much further than he could when Jeanie first arrived. Or appeared. He'd made progress in laughing more and in folding himself like origami. "She had to go meet someone for a drink with a guy who lives near her condo and makes enough money to afford her tastes."

Harry smiled.

"So she let me in and said she knew you'd be here cause your car was in the drive. She said you wouldn't go across the street without your car so if your car was here, you'd be."

"Sounds like Margaret," he repeated. Now to turn the conversation back to darling Elizabeth. "What else did your mom say?"

"Usual." He shrugged. "She said I should go to school around here, and we'd move soon."

"Soon?"

Leo's eyes grew solemn. Harrison didn't want to hurt the boy's feelings—make him feel unwanted. He knew all too well how that felt. It was enough that the kid's mother dropped him off like a piece of luggage. God, how he wished Leo hadn't heard him earlier. He never wanted to add to the hurt his sister had caused. "Well, that's great." He reached out and ruffled his hair again. "I'd love to have you near all the time."

Leo unfolded himself. "I figured."

Harrison didn't like that tone. The boy looked upset in his own way. Leo had never been one to show much emotion, until Jeanie had gotten him to smile. Where was she? He could use her help right now.

"You figured?"

"Yep. Then you don't have to worry about my mom sending me here unannounced. Cause if she did, you'd know were we live and how to send me back..."

Harrison jumped from his chair and grabbed Leo by the shoulders. "Hey, don't ever say things like that. I love to have you come spend time..."

"Uncle Harry, you don't have to do that. I know a lot. You don't have kids of your own, so why would you want me hanging around? You even had to hire Jeanie to watch me..."

"Leo, kid..." He had no idea what to say. The boy was too smart for him. Man, he didn't have any idea how to deal with kids. Jeanie was wrong. If he had his own—he'd be a basket case. A failure. Heaven forbid—an absent father like his own. He shut his eyes and wished she would come help....

"Your uncle told me the other day, he'd love to have kids, but he doesn't have a wife—yet."

Leo and Harrison swung around to see Jeanie, standing in the doorway. Harrison felt his mouth gap open and didn't care.

How in the world did she keep doing that?

Leo looked at Jeanie. "He did? Uncle Harry said that?"

She leaned down, kissed her fingertip and touched it to his forehead. "Of course, silly. He loves having you here, too. When's the last time you saw your Uncle Harry so… so…"

"Happy?" Harrison added.

"You do laugh a lot more than I remember. Course, I was littler last time Tabitha left me here."

Jeanie laughed. "I'll bet you still remember every detail, sweetie. You're smart as evidenced by the work you've been doing." She settled on the floor next to him.

"You really think so?"

"I do and so does Harry. Don't you?"

He felt her nudge his side. "Oh, yeah. I…" What had she said?

"So you think I'm smart, too, Uncle Harry?"

That was it! "Hey, kid, who else could beat Margaret at a World Championship Wrestling video game? Even her own grandkids can't."

Leo's childish laugh warmed Harrison's heart. The kid jumped up, kissed both he and Jeanie on the heads and ran out, saying he needed his sleep and tomorrow he'd work extra hard at his studies.

Harrison felt his eyes fill at the change in the boy from only a few weeks ago.

Whoever said kids were resilient was a genius.

*

"Thanks," Harry muttered as Jeanie leaned against the couch. She should get up, but she preferred the comfort of the floor. Besides, Harry had the softest plush carpets she'd ever sat on. Surprisingly enough, he remained on the floor instead of hopping up to his chair.

"I didn't do anything."

"You saved my… you saved Leo from being hurt. I didn't mean for him to hear me…"

She touched his arm. This time he didn't tense and pull away. Smiling to herself, she gave herself a mental pat on the back.

Harry *was* lightening up.

She'd accomplished one of her jobs.

"I know you didn't."

He sighed and leaned back, shoulder to shoulder with her.

"No, I didn't. Actually, I didn't know the kid had come home."

"I saw Margaret drive up just as the phone rang. I stayed to talk to her... then came upstairs as Leo ran down the hallway."

"Then you didn't hear?"

She nodded. "I heard as I came up the stairs."

"She makes me so angry sometimes. She's like a kid herself—always was."

"And that is so bad?"

"A kid raising a kid?"

"I guess it's not the best thing for Leo, but she loves him enough to make certain he is cared for by the best."

Harry turned to her. Before she could say a word, he leaned over, touched her beneath the chin, and pressed his lips to hers.

"Thank you," he said after pulling back.

She hadn't seen that one coming.

It took her unaware and unprepared. Still, it also took her to a height that rivaled riding on a magic carpet high above the earth.

Harry was her boss. And if he ever found out about her—his problems with Tabitha would pale in comparison.

Why couldn't things ever be simple for her? Why did she have to find herself here, with a man she thought of as more that her master, and not be able to do what *she* wanted to do?

How she wished she could grant herself a wish.

Because she knew exactly what it would be.

Chapter Thirteen

Capricorn: Your life is a mess. Clean it up.
Well, at least try.

Harrison inhaled Jeanie. Sweet. Mystical Jeanie. She turned out to be a great comfort to him as a pain throbbed in his temple. This entire night had been a headache-inducing heck of a time. All he could do was blame Margaret for starting the entire mess. Her fifth—or was it sixth—Christmas bonus was in question.

Jeanie pulled to the side and folded her legs beneath her. "Harry…"

"Why do you do that?"

"What?"

He looked at her legs. "Fold yourself up like that."

She glanced down. "I… never think about it. It's something I've done since I was a kid. Comforts me."

"You're lucky to have that. When I was kid, I never had anything to hold, like Zazu, and couldn't fold myself like a pretzel or find a secret place in our house to call my own." He looked out across the room but really didn't see anything. "Guess that's why I keep things inside. I don't know where to find comfort…" His eyes widened. He couldn't believe he'd actually said that. Confessing a major fault to his babysitter—no, right now he felt much closer to Jeanie than as her employer.

Maybe that's why he'd let it slip out.

She had a way, just her mere presence, of making him feel so at ease. So folded up into a comfortable position deep inside.

She unfolded herself and came near. "Here. Put your legs out straight."

"I'm not… I can't do what you do."

She chuckled. "Of course not. You're built way different…"

"*Viva la différence.*"

"Do you want me to teach you how to comfort yourself or not?"

"Sorry."

She took one leg and lifted it over the other. "Start like this and bend both until…" She sat back. "I have to show you because I have no idea how to explain it."

Harrison watched her, knew he could watch her all night, as she folded and unfolded her limbs. Each time she did, he'd note something different, new, about her.

Like she had a tiny dimple only in her right cheek.

And her legs were much longer than he'd guess for a woman of her height.

"Harry? Harry, I asked if you're going to try it?"

"Hm?" She sat there, folded, staring.

"Try it." She waved her hands across her lap.

"Oh, yeah. I'll give it a shot. But you know, I'm not as limber…" He tucked one leg successfully. "—as you seem to be." With a grunt, he got the other partly beneath him.

She laughed. "I guess you aren't."

"What?" He pushed until she heard his joint crack. "Geez. I must be getting old."

"Well, you don't look as bad as some of the five-hundred-year-olds I know…"

He looked at her with his eyes squinted. "You really do know people that old?"

"No, silly."

"Oh." He sighed.

"Only genies are that old." She laughed until she glanced at him. "Harry?"

"Hm?" He wanted to tell her that he believed her, but no way could he get those words out. Instead he mumbled, "Nothing."

★

"Margaret?" Harrison poked at the intercom for the fifth time. "Margaret!"

The door opened. "I'm guessing someone got up on the wrong side of the bed this morning," she said as she sashayed in, coffee in hand, and sat on the chair opposite his desk.

"Sorry. Thanks." He took the coffee and a long sip despite it being scalding hot the way he liked it. Margaret took good care of him—well, except when she interfered—like last night.

"You called?"

"I need the file on Mr. Renée so that I can get going on that. Tell Jolene that I'll have some things sent over to her today so that she can make up the sketches. Also, schedule a photo shoot. He wants it in Houston at his ranch, so work it out with his secretary."

Margaret leaned forward. He half expected her to feel his forehead for a fever.

"What?"

"Nothing." She jotted down a note on the pad that she always carried. "Anything else?"

"Yeah, did you have fun with Leo last night?"

He'd never known Margaret to blush. But a redness climbed up her neck onto her cheeks. Maybe this was a first because she finally felt guilty about interfering in his life—love life that is.

"We had a ball. You know, for all the junk that kid's been through he's a doll. Well mannered. Smart. Good taste in movies." She laughed.

"That he is. I didn't hear you come in with him last night."

"Dropped him off. I knew you were there…"

"Having a romantic evening with the babysitter?"

She rolled her eyes. "Don't make it sound so *B* movie-like. She's not some teeny bopper…"

"Margaret!"

"Oops. Forgot who I was talking to."

Harrison drank a huge sip of coffee, sputtered the hot liquid out, and glared at her. "You never forget a thing. Except maybe your place as my secretary..."

Margaret's head flew up.

He set his mug down, and said, "Sorry," as he ran his hand through his hair and shut his eyes. "Margaret, my life is a mess."

She set down her pad and smiled at him. "I'll forget that secretary comment. Night didn't go so well with Jeanie?"

He peaked at her through one eye.

"You've got to give me more to go on, boss."

He shut his eye again. "Dinner was wonderful, by the way."

"And? Afterward?"

"Is none of your business, although nothing happened." He opened his eyes, swiveled around. "More pink flowers have bloomed near the wall since yesterday.

"Yeah, flowers. Get back to the after dinner part."

"I'll take care of my love life from now on.

"Goody."

"I wouldn't think you'd back out of interfering so quickly."

"Ha! You think right. I said 'goody' meaning you consider your relationship with Jeanie as a love life."

He swung around so fast, his elbow knocked the coffee mug, splashing liquid across his papers. He stared at the documents turning brown through the process of osmosis, until a puddle formed beneath the stack.

With a sigh, he thought something like ruining a set of important papers shouldn't be totally unexpected anymore.

Margaret jumped up, grabbed tissues from the box on his desk, and started to wipe the papers. She paused, looked at him. "You're not going to freak out?"

"No, Margaret." He sighed. "I'm past freaking out. I've learned to control my freaking out. My life is a daily dose of problems."

She threw the soaked tissue into the trash basket. "And look at how well you are handling them."

He groaned.

"Really, Harry. I'm proud of you."

The only other time she'd called him that was when he'd broken off his engagement and thought his world had ended. Margaret tactlessly, yet lovingly, pointed out that Laura was a money-hungry pariah, then kissed him on his forehead and said, "Harry, she wasn't right for you, but someday you'll find someone who is."

"Proud isn't a word I'd use."

"Well I would. When's the last time you noticed flowers growing?"

He looked from the pile of brown papers to her. "What?"

"You noticed the flowers growing, Harry."

"So?"

"Oh, nothing. Seems like you're blowing everything out of proportion."

"Elizabeth called last night."

She sat on the edge of the desk. "Darn. No wonder all my hard work was for naught…"

"Margaret."

"Okay. Okay. I admit I did envision a wonderfully romantic evening for you two, but Tabitha, a.k.a. Elizabeth, wasn't in that vision." She leaned near. "What's she have to say?"

"It's what I said that caused the problem. You know how angry she makes me…"

"With good reason."

He smiled inside. "Still, it's getting harder to control my temper with her. I used to let her walk all over me and never say a word. Last night I let her have it…"

"That's my boy…"

"But Leo walked in to hear me say I can't be worrying about her… kid." It was hard to even get the words out. They made him sick to think of how they hurt Leo. He'd never want to do that.

"Did you explain to him that you were angry…"

"I tried. He seemed to understand, then Jeanie came in to save the day."

Margaret grinned like the Cheshire cat.

"That's not a very flattering look on you."

She howled. "So, all is well now that Jeanie helped settle things."

"Kinda of... I guess." He leaned back, set his feet on his desk. "I'm not sure of much anymore."

"Yes you are." She pushed at his feet, sending them off the end of the desk. "You've changed, boss. For the better I might add. Leo and Jeanie came into your life and you've... loosened up as the kids would say."

He groaned. "I want my old self back."

"Ha! Too late now, and why would you? You've finally taken a baby step toward being more carefree, more let-the-coffee-stain-the-papers-without-freaking-out, and... this is the best part, boss, happier." With that she slipped off the desk, walked to the door and opened it. Before she left, she turned back. "When's Tabitha coming back?"

"Soon."

"Darn."

Harrison stuck his hands behind his head, leaned back.

What'd she mean by that?

★

It seemed as if hours had passed while Harrison remained leaning back in his chair, thinking of why Margaret had said that. He decided he needed to get some work done. As he lifted his hands, he paused.

His legs were tucked underneath him.

"I'll be darned." Obviously the position was comfortable or he wouldn't have remained here (he leaned to look at the clock on his desk) for over an hour.

Unfolding one's self proved more difficult, he thought with a groan. Thirty-year-old joints don't do well folded for over an hour. He'd have to ask Jeanie about that—

"You can't go in there unannounced!" Margaret shouted.

The door swung open. Mr. Renée stood, Stetson on, boots gleaming black, and a scowl aimed directly at Harrison.

Despite the jolts of pain, he jumped up. “It’s all right, Margaret,” he said, reaching his hand out to the client.

He took it and pumped so hard, Harrison thought he’d break his hand. “Thought I’d drop in to see how things were going.” He glanced down at the coffee-soaked papers.

“Fine. Fine.” Harrison shoved the papers beneath a stack of clean ones as if the man wouldn’t notice. Pathetic. Now he was acting pathetic in front of a client.

And he blamed it all on Elizabeth/Tabitha, Jeanie, and, oh yeah, Margaret had her hand in all this, too.

“I’ve about got your campaign ready to send off to my art department. What say I have my secretary set up a meeting in… a week or two to show it all to you?” A few weeks and Elizabeth should be back. Leo would be back with her and—Jeanie would be gone.

Suddenly he thought he’d never be able to concentrate on a stupid campaign.

“Week?”

“Or two.” *Please don’t argue with me, you fool Texan. I don’t have the stomach or the time.*

“How’s about some coffee so I can think about it?”

“Certainly.” He pressed the buzzer.

“Cream or sugar?” Margaret said in disgust.

Harrison turned away from Mr. Renée and smiled. “Is that…?”

“Black,” he said, looking out the window. “Beautiful garden, Rainford. You some kind of horticulturist?”

Ha. He never knew the flowers bloomed in fall nor that there were so many shades of green until a few weeks ago. “No. No, sir. I have a yardman.”

“Too darn bad. Gardening can be therapeutic, ya know. Done some myself.”

Harrison made a mental note to have Margaret order him a truckload of bushes, flowers, and trees.

“Is that a fact?” He sat forward and wondered how he could get this guy to wait several weeks.

"Great. I see why you don't pay much attention to them flowers. With a little filly like that, you get an eyeful of pleasure."

"Sir?" He wasn't sure what the guy was talking about. Fillies? Had his mind slipped to horses?

Mr. Renée licked his lips and pointed to the window behind him. "That your woman, son? Cause if she ain't I'll take a hankering..."

Harrison swung around to see Jeanie, in her flamingo pose, the breeze billowing beneath her dress to reveal legs that never ended. An explosion ripped through his brain.

He swung back, ready to give the guy what for, then noticed the picture of Margaret's grandkids on his shelf.

Sucking in enough air to fill his lungs for hours, he told himself he needed this contract for the employees. "She's my nephew's..." He let the air out, slowly, deliberately as he gripped a pencil from his desk. "... nanny."

"Perfect."

"Sir?" He really didn't want to hear what was so perfect about it. Where was Margaret when he needed her?

"You got the contract, doubled if you can deliver it in two weeks..."

Harrison jumped up, pencil still in hand. He reached out to shake the man's hand. "Great. Great. No problem."

"I sure hope you won't see it as a problem cause you didn't let me finish. It all hinges on that little 'nanny.'"

"Sir?" Did this old coot mean he wanted Jeanie in exchange for a contract? He wished that wasn't the case or he'd have to throw the guy—contract and stupid Stetson—out in one swift loss of his business.

"I want her..."

"No way in..."

"Then the deal's off."

The pencil snapped.

Chapter Fourteen

Capricorn: A problem is cleared up with a well-intended family member. Make it last. On a more personal note, you will be put into some situation where you have to choose. Good luck. You'll need it.

Harrison glared at Mr. Renée, thinking that his future was going down the drain—and couldn't care less. What a nerve the man had, saying he wanted Jeanie!

"I guess then that the..." He wasn't certain if the man was still standing there since his vision had been blurred by red, by anger, by explosions in his mind. He aimed his words toward where he thought Mr. Renée stood. "The deal is... off."

"Son, maybe you need to think about this. At least ask the little babysitter."

"The 'little babysitter' has a name. Jeanie. *J, E, A, N, I, E.* That's only one *N.*"

Mr. Renée chuckled. "I may not sound educated, son, but I know how to spell Jeanie."

"I... well, if that's all..."

"I'm a reasonable man, son. Just ask her if she wants to model for the advertisement. If she says no, I'll..."

Harrison felt himself sinking. Thank goodness he landed in his chair. "Model?" he said much weaker than he would have liked.

Mr. Renée's laughter boomed to the ten-foot ceilings. "What in tarnation did you think I wanted her for... Lordy. You thought I... a man of my age. Son, she looks like a sweet thing but a bit too celestial for my down-home taste. Besides, I've been hitched to the same woman near forty years."

"Congratulations," Harrison muttered.

"Someday you'll be in these boots, son."

He looked at Harrison, directly into his eyes. Harrison shuddered as if the man could see into his soul.

"I expect that little filly will be celebratin' with *you* come forty years down the road." He chuckled. "Any fool worth his gold can see you've got it bad for her."

Harrison groaned.

Could this mess get any worse?

He looked up to see Margaret, leaning against the doorframe—grinning.

*

"So, Harry, wasn't that the client from Houston that I saw outside your office earlier today?" Jeanie asked later that night.

He looked up from his dish. She'd wanted to try out a recipe she'd seen on a Cajun cooking show, and he'd agree to let her fix it tonight. Margaret took Leo out for a hotdog, saying even a vegetarian needed to be allowed to cheat once in awhile. The kid couldn't have run out the door fast enough. So here she and Harry were—alone again. But after all her hard work, he only played with the meal and sipped at his cola. "Harry, was that the important client?"

"Mr. Renée."

"He certainly doesn't look French," she said then laughed.

He poked at a piece of tomato. "He's from Houston."

She leaned near, touched his hand. "I'm certain there are French people in Houston. What is wrong? You seem preoccupied."

Finally he let the food alone and looked at her. "He wants you to model for him."

She took her hand from his and touched his forehead. "Excuse me?"

"Mr. Renée. He wants you to model for the advertisement of his clothing. You do look young enough and would certainly fit in the clothes. Actually, you'd give them that 'sixties' kind of feel and scent."

"Scent? What is this, a scratch and sniff kind of ad?"

Harry's eyes widened. "I didn't mean… it's just that your scent reminds me of hippies…"

She touched his cheek. "Poor Harry. You are a mess tonight."

"What makes tonight any different from the rest of my life?"

"Oh, my." She couldn't think of much else to say for a moment. All she could think of was—Harry had noticed her scent.

He set his fork down, took a sip of cola—and then another. "So, will you do it?"

"Do it?"

"Model for him?"

She laughed so loudly, she snorted. "Sorry. I'm hardly model material. There have to be thousands of teens that would love the opportunity…"

"That's what I thought, but when Mr. Renée saw you, he wanted you." Harrison couldn't tell her what a fool he'd made of himself over that one. And Margaret, who was definitely going to lose her seventh Christmas bonus, had the audacity to say the client was always right. Especially in this case!

She said Mr. Renée was an astute man and could plainly see that Harry had it bad for Jeanie.

He looked up to see her staring at him. The kitchen light had a way of capturing the sparkle in her eyes, and making them brighter. It dawned on him that she didn't wear any lipstick or other makeup. But she had a complexion that was smooth, flawless on its own. Her lips were a natural coral color.

Nope. He couldn't tell Jeanie how he had to argue with Margaret that she was dead wrong—because his heart wasn't in it. And he knew Margaret and Mr. Renée were right.

Speaking of his heart, right now it felt as if it was in his throat as he looked at the woman, who he'd thought was a nut, and wanted to kiss her.

But he couldn't do that. Couldn't start what he wouldn't be able to finish. This was a golden opportunity for Jeanie. She could earn more money on this assignment than if she worked for Harrison for years.

He sighed.

"You could have enough money to buy a house, hire a sitter and have your mother move in with you." It took all the strength and honesty he had left in his body—after lying to Margaret about his feelings for Jeanie—to get that out.

She pulled away from him and stood. "Is that what you think I should do?"

"What I think doesn't matter."

"I see." *Doesn't matter,* she thought. So, Harry didn't care enough about her to ask her to stay here. He thought she should grab at the chance to make all the money she'd need—instead of remaining in some aspect of his life.

When that was all she really wanted.

She picked up her napkin, wiped at her lips, and looked down at him. "Is that your wish?"

Harrison couldn't speak. He even tried not to think of his answer in case it came out like a wish. He did want what was best for Jeanie, but would that be best for him? Would the money really be best for her?

Of course, he told himself. She lived in a darn van for crying out loud.

"I don't know what I wish anymore."

"Then, I'll be in my room when you decide. I hope you don't mind cleaning up—unless you want me to poof all the dishes clean."

"No… I'll." He looked at her heading out of the room. "Wait a minute!" He jumped up and ran after her. "You can't just walk away…"

"I can do what I want."

He didn't want to grab her. First, because she always felt so fragile and no way would he ever want to make a mark on her pale skin. Second, because he wouldn't be responsible for his actions—once he had her in his arms. "Please just listen to me."

At least she stopped.

He had no idea what he was going to say. "I… believe, Jeanie."

She turned around, slowly. "Harry?"

"I do. You've made me believe in hopes, in dreams, in things I can't explain through all the wishes you've granted to me."

A tear trickled down her cheek. "I'm glad, Harry."

"So you can't…" How could he tell her she couldn't take the biggest opportunity of her life because then she could leave him? "… walk away without letting me know what to tell Mr. Renée. You will have to go to Houston to do the job. But his offer is more than generous, Jeanie."

"It sounds as if you think I should take it."

He swallowed, deeply. "You'd be a fool not to." *Please say no. You'll have to go to Houston.*

"Then I guess it's settled. Tell Mr. Renée I'll… do it." With that she turned, walked to her room, taking the first step out of his life to a golden opportunity.

And he couldn't even feel happy for her.

★

Jeanie walked into her room, hoping against hope that Harry would follow her. Run after her. Tell her not to take the job that would solve all her needs.

She flopped onto the bed and wished he would be standing in the doorway when she looked back.

Through vision blurred by tears, she slowly turned. No one. That's when the sobbing came. It felt as if she'd released a long pent-up damn, flooding her face, her pillow with tears. How could she have been so wrong about Harry? She'd felt the connection, the chemistry between them from the first day. He'd felt it too, she could tell by his kiss, by his nervousness when around her.

None of that mattered now. She would do this stupid job, collect her paycheck and leave. Mamma will be so happy to hear about their financial problems being solved. In the mean time, she had to start packing.

But what about Leo? She couldn't up and leave him, he at least needed her even if Harry didn't. She grabbed a tissue, wiped at her eyes, and stood. Not that she had any desire to see Harry right now, but she needed to discuss Leo with him.

Hopefully Harry would ask her to stay on longer. Maybe Tabitha would need months of finding her soul. Then Jeanie would feel obligated to stay—for Leo's sake.

But would time change Harry's mind, his feelings for her?

Determined that Harry wasn't going to get rid of her so fast, she wiped her face a final time and went out to find him.

She walked down the hallway, half expecting to hear him taking care of business on the phone in his room. Most likely telling Mr. Renée of her decision. But the hallway was silent, Harry's door open. The room was empty.

In the kitchen she looked at the table, cleaned off and spotless. Harry was back to his old self. There wasn't even a trace of their meal, the meal she'd worked so hard to prepare to impress him. Sucking in a breath, she bit her lower lip to prevent the tears from returning.

Jeanie Merriday didn't cry over spilt milk.

When she turned the corner to the living room, she froze. Harry sat in his favorite chair, legs tucked beneath him, humming softly. She shut her eyes and smiled. But when she opened them, she noticed he held something in his hands. He'd wrapped whatever it was so tightly, she couldn't make it out—until he shifted.

Her bottle.

Harry cradled her bottle in his arms while he sat in the position she'd taught him to comfort himself. Could she have been wrong? Could Harry really care about her? Could he be feeling the same feelings for her that she felt for him?

The ones that made her want to run to him, pull him from his comfort zone, and say she wanted to spend the rest of her life married to him.

She grabbed onto the wall, shut her eyes once again, and wished she would make the right decision.

"Jeanie?"

Her eyes flew open. "I didn't mean to disturb you." She turned to leave.

"I almost expected to find you in here." He held out the bottle and chuckled. "You know, like in the television show when Jeannie would be sitting on those cushions in her bottle, pouting, upset about something. Oh, that's right. You don't own a television."

"Harry, look…" It was time. Time to tell him the truth and face the consequences. She'd never felt absolutely sure about all of this. With the way she felt about him now, she needed to be honest.

A relationship would never last unless based on love and honesty.

He unfolded his legs with a groan. "Gets easier each time, but, man, these old joints need some oil." He looked at her and smiled.

"The more you practice, the easier it will get. I need to talk to you, Harry."

"Me, too." He set the bottle on the coffee table. "You know, I couldn't bring myself to call Mr. Renée yet."

Her heart lightened. "You couldn't?"

"Not yet. Sorry."

"Don't be. Harry, I know it's a once in a lifetime opportunity but…"

"I don't want you to go."

Her eyes widened. "You… don't?"

He came closer. Her heartbeats thudded louder. She'd never been the nervous type, but right now, her hands shook, her mouth dried, and she could barely swallow.

"I know I'm being selfish, Jeanie, but I really don't want you to… leave."

He doesn't want me to leave! She could barely believe her ears. "Oh?"

"I… you'd have to move, and, well, Margaret would miss having you around to help her and Leo. Heck, Jeanie, Leo's been through enough comings and goings with my sister. He'd be awfully upset if you left."

She came closer and couldn't help herself. The urge to touch him was too strong. So, she slowly reached up her hands and cradled his cheeks. He didn't stiffen, pull back, but relaxed in her hold. "And what about you, Harry? You've given me all kinds of reasons why I should stay for the others, but…"

He leaned near, placed his lips on hers and whispered, "Stay for me, Jeanie. I want you to stay."

The kiss was the icing on the cake after that. But Jeanie loved icing! Sweet, buttery soft giant rose icing—like Harry's lips pressing against hers. Soft. Buttery soft. And he smelled so good. Not sweet, but a mixture of sweet and spice—a veritable aromatic delicacy.

"Oh, my," she murmured.

Her heart did a jig. No magic carpet ride could be as exhilarating as kissing Harry Rainford—and having him kiss her back.

He wanted her to stay!

Things couldn't get any better.

"Hello! Leo, baby! Darling brother, are you here?"

Harry froze, his lips still pressing against Jeanie's neck. Tabitha. He eased back, looked Jeanie in the eyes and said, "I wish she would go away."

Jeanie glared at him. "I…"

"Holy mackerel. What's going on here?" Tabitha asked as she floated into the room, her now-jet black hair swirling to her waistline.

"You could have called, Elizabeth." He released Jeanie, but kept his hand on her back. Before his sister could answer, though, Jeanie slid from his hold.

She looked nervous. Very unlike her. And her gaze fixed on Elizabeth in an almost angry stare.

Maybe she was about to poof Elizabeth back to Bombay.

Well, he had wished it. Foolishly he looked at his sister, about ready to say goodbye, but then he caught Jeanie with an almost pleading look aimed at Elizabeth.

His sister remained rooted on the spot.

"I like surprises, darling brother, and seeing the nanny in your arms was a doozie."

"How'd you know who she was…"

"Lucky guess."

"Don't you want to see Leo?" Harry picked up the bottle, walked to the mantel, and carefully set it back. Jeanie was going to stay, so the bottle needed to be back in its rightful place.

"Of course, I do. Where is he?" She flopped onto the sofa, the silken material of her dress cascading across the arm as she settled her legs over the side. He'd never noticed before, but Elizabeth didn't wear makeup either. Hm. How'd he ever miss that? Parts of her were very similar to Jeanie, but, he looked at her folding herself into position on the floor opposite the couch—and smiled.

She was very different than his sister. His Jeanie would never run off like Elizabeth or be untruthful as she so often was when sneaking off on one of her quests.

His Jeanie?

Wow. That actually felt good.

"Leo is out with Margaret for dinner… supper." He looked at Jeanie and smiled.

Tabitha scowled at him. "I hope she doesn't get the notion to feed him some junk. We are eating purifying…"

Harry couldn't take it any longer. "Hotdogs! Margaret took him for a nice fat, smothered-in-ketchup hotdog!"

Tabitha gasped.

Jeanie stifled a smile and said, "Harry, go easy…"

"No, I'm done with going easy. I've gone easy on Elizabeth…"

"Tabitha," she started to protest until he glared at her.

"Elizabeth. You've shirked responsibility all your life. You left me alone as a kid when I had no one. You married young to get away from our parents when you weren't in love. And all we had to do was stick together, Liz. Stick together."

She raised her chin. "I needed to find..."

Harry's face grew hot. He knew he'd explode if he didn't get the words out fast. "You had a child, for God's sake, and still never took responsibility. You've run off so many times, poor Leo thinks he's the cause. When, in fact, Elizabeth, you cause all your own problems."

She jumped up and stared at him, hands on her hips. "I'm not like you, Harrison. I don't lead an orderly life. Nor would I want to..."

Jeanie unfolded herself and stood. "I should leave. Excuse me..."

Elizabeth grabbed her arm. "No, you shouldn't. Jeanie is a prime example of my showing responsibility..."

Jeanie's eyes filled with fear. "No! Don't!"

Harrison ran forward. "Let her go! What is wrong with you, Elizabeth?"

"Nothing, other than the fact that I will prove to you once and for all that I am responsible—although not as orthodox as you..."

Jeanie pulled free. "Please don't, Tabitha."

Harry felt his forehead wrinkle. This was getting confusing. "What the hell does grabbing Jeanie have to do with anything? She doesn't need to stay here while we argue..."

"She needs to stay here..."

Jeanie gave a pleading look at Elizabeth. "Don't. Please."

Harrison blew out a frustrated breath. "You are not making any sense. Jeanie, go ahead. I'll see if I can talk to my sister alone..."

"Jeanie is my proof, Harrison." Elizabeth aimed a painful look at Jeanie. "I need her..."

Jeanie pushed past Elizabeth toward him. Looking directly into his eyes, she said, "I will tell him, Elizabeth."

Fear had him reach out and grab the mantel. Something in her look said he wasn't going to be pleased with all of this. What on earth did Jeanie have to do with his sister?

Tabitha waved her hand, looking like some kind of sorceress. "Be my guest."

"Someone better tell me what the heck is going on before Leo comes home."

"Leo is the reason I came here," Jeanie said.

"I know. You told me…"

She placed a finger to his lips. "I know what I told you. If you care at all about me, Harry, please just listen."

A feeling of dread settled in his gut.

"Tabitha sent me here to care for Leo…"

"Tabitha? How could she send a genie…"

Elizabeth stood with an amazed look on her face. "My God, Harrison, you believed her. She did it."

He looked from his sister who stood with her mouth open, to Jeanie—who stood with tears running down her cheeks.

"You are not a genie," he said, more softly than he'd like.

She shook her head. "But, Harry, listen…"

"My wishes. How…"

"She's a contortionist…"

Jeanie swung around. "Shut up, Tabitha!" She turned back to face him. "I worked for a magician, The Great Santanloni, for years because as a kid I could get into all kinds of tiny places."

He felt as if he'd been punched in the gut. "But you disappeared that first day…"

"Only into the bushes near the porch. I folded myself up, until you'd left."

"But you answered my other wishes—ones in my head."

With a solemn look, she said, "Most I guessed at, some were very obvious and fitting of the circumstances…"

"Like when I wished you kiss me."

Tabitha whistled.

Harry looked at her. "Shut up, Elizabeth."

She waved her hand. "Go ahead with your true confessions, Jeanie."

"When I found myself in bed…"

Tabitha's eyebrows rose.

"You were so sleepy you didn't remember me walking you to your room." She turned to his sister. "Where I tucked you in fully clothed and left." She looked at him. "Harry, please believe me when I say I never meant to lie to you…"

"You did lie though. You lied about coming here to care for Leo…"

"No!"

Elizabeth's face softened. "That part is true. I met Jeanie years ago in Europe. She was born in Baghdad where her father traveled on business. Jeanie needed money, and I knew she would be perfect for the… I hired her to care for…"

Jeanie interrupted, "She did hire me to come watch over Leo while she was gone. We'd met in London several years ago. I was a nanny until my mother got sick and we had to sell everything, even our house, and we moved to Louisiana because Mother had a friend here."

"Her mother's a neat lady, by the way. Very ethereal. No wonder Jeanie is such a doll."

Harry glared at his sister. "You hired her? You hired her to make sure Leo had someone to care for him while you were gone…"

"Not that I didn't trust you, Harrison. I knew you needed to run your business. I sent along a nanny to help both you and Leo…"

"So why the genie lie?"

Jeanie flinched. "That was for you…"

"You lied for *me*?"

"Tabitha felt I could help you—get back your life. The joy you'd lost when your engagement fell through…"

"To learn to lighten up and enjoy life, Harrison. I was worried about you after Laura and all that mess. You've never really enjoyed life."

"Until I met Jeanie." He slouched against the mantel, his hand brushing against the bottle.

"I tried to tell you a few times, but never could get it out. You'd changed so much since I first met you—I didn't have the heart to tell you the truth. I could see the joy growing in you each day and couldn't stop it. In the interim, Leo inadvertently was affected."

"He started to smile again," Harrison muttered, "and I see colors."

Tabitha wiped at her eyes.

Jeanie nodded.

"That's great for the kid." He grabbed the bottle. "So, you were going to keep lying to me—then go off on your merry way after my sister took Leo back?"

"It's not like that… but, yes."

He wanted to throw the bottle into the fireplace. Shatter it to bits much as his insides, his heart felt right now. But he looked up to see Jeanie; she looked sincere, but so had Laura when she told him she loved him—until he overheard her on the phone, saying how she was marrying Harrison Rainford for his money.

A woman's lie that broke his heart.

Jeanie had healed his heart—only to break it again.

He set the bottle back on the mantel. "Leo will be here soon." With that he turned and walked to the door, never looking back.

Never being able to see the woman he loved—as he walked out of her life.

*

"Margaret, bring me the file for the chicory coffee ad," Harrison ordered.

She opened the door, file in hand. "Here you go, boss."

He waved for her to set it down on the desk.

She turned to leave, but stopped. "I know you as much ordered me never to bring up Jeanie's name…"

His head swung up.

"But you are a mess without her, and I don't care if you fire me on the spot."

He couldn't deny it. She was right. These past few days since he'd walked out of his own house, leaving the woman he loved was unbearable. He was unbearable. "I'm sorry I snap at you so much."

"Remind me of a wounded lioness, boss. You're hurting, Harry. Do something about it."

She'd called him Harry again. A tiny warmth touched his heart, but that was all he could manage. "There is nothing to do. That's all, Margaret."

She walked back, leaned over his desk. "Turn around."

"What?"

Before he could tell her to go, she came behind his desk and swiveled his chair toward the window. "What the hell are you doing?"

"Tell me what you see."

"Then will you go?"

"Sure."

"My yard. Now leave."

She poked at his back. "Details."

"Trees, some bird in the bath. A vine on the wall."

She swung him around to look at him. "You've reverted back to your old self, Harry. No color in your life. She took it with her—and you let her." Before he could deny her truth, she walked out and closed the door.

Harry turned toward the yard, wishing to see Jeanie appear.

But there was nothing except the bird. He shut his eyes. Was Margaret right? Had he reverted to his old self? Seemed that way when he looked out the window. He'd made a wish, though. Suddenly he realized that it came from his heart. He truly believed for a second that she might poof into the backyard when he wished for her.

He jumped up and ran to the door. After opening it, he looked at Margaret.

She shoved a paper out toward him.

He looked to see a hotel's address on it. "Metairie?"

"She's staying out by the airport until she flies of to do that modeling job." She leaned near, capturing his gaze with hers.

"Unless she doesn't *need* that job to help her mother anymore."

He leaned over, kissed her on the cheek and said, "All your Christmas bonuses are reinstated," then he ran out the door.

The drive out to the airport was the longest in his life. What if Jeanie wasn't there? What if she'd already left for Houston? Oh, God, what would he do?

You'll board a plane for Houston, a voice said in his head.

That's right! He could figure out these things without "freaking out" as Margaret had put it. He'd jump on a flight, throw caution to the wind, and find the woman he loved. Stopping at a red light, he looked out to see palm trees swaying in the breeze, red, yellow and violet flowers dotting a nearby yard and the most beautiful pink plastic flamingo balancing itself near the palm.

The color was back.

Now all he had to do was get the woman back—to enjoy it all.

★

Jeanie hung up the phone and sat on the bed. She couldn't leave with saying goodbye to Leo. He cried in his eight-year-old way, and it broke her heart that she wouldn't be seeing him again. She'd told him Zazu would keep him company. He'd said he didn't need the monkey any longer. His mother was here for him. Elizabeth had promised she'd change.

Jeanie smiled to herself and grabbed her suitcase. There was no reason for her to stay. Her mother had been doing so well at the convalescent home, they'd moved her into the retirement village section. She loved it and had made so many friends, she couldn't imagine leaving. She'd been adamant that she didn't want to live with Jeanie, be a burden on her, and that she was truly happy with friends her own age. She even started reading Tarot cards for all of them.

So, Jeanie had canceled the modeling job with Mr. Renee's solemn promise that he wouldn't cancel the ad for Harrison. Now he'd be able to move his employees. She'd decided to head up to live near her mother, and get some kind of job nearby.

A knock on the door startled her. She walked close and looked out the peephole.

"Jeanie? I know you are still here. No one else drives a VW van like that."

Despite the pain in her heart, she smiled. "I'm here."

"Then open the door."

"I'm leaving, Harry. There's noting to discuss…"

"I wish you would open the door!"

She reached up and turned the knob. Before she could move, he shoved open the door, sending her sprawling across the bed.

"Oh darn! I'm sorry!" He ran to her and lifted her into a sitting position. "Your nose, it's…"

"*Déjà vu*."

Harrison looked at her and they howled. "I am sorry. Let me… get you some ice."

"I'm fine. But I was on my way out…"

"Where? Where are you going?"

She sat up with her legs over the side of the bed. "I have to start a new life somewhere. My mother doesn't want to live with me—so I turned down the modeling job. Your business won't be affected."

He took her hand into his. "Right now, I couldn't care less about the business, Mr. Renée, or anything—except you. Come back, Jeanie."

She looked at him, tears in her eyes. "To what, Harry?"

"To a man who's been a fool. A man who only today realized how good you are for him. A man who—loves you." He leaned over and kissed her.

Thank God she didn't pull away.

"But, Harry…" she said against his lips. "I lied to you…"

"And never will again. I know that. I realized it was for my own good. My sister loved me enough to help me—and you put color into my life, Jeanie."

"I want to… but Leo is gone. What would I do…?"

He kissed her cheek. "Well, I'm not going to give you a job in my company as I'd said."

She eased back, her eyebrows drawn together. "Oh. I'm afraid I need to work…"

"My wife can work if she wants, but I think staying home to raise our kids should come first. Course, being a carefree, open-minded sort of guy, I'll let her decide for herself."

Jeanie looked him in the eyes. "I love you, Har. Oh, and 'yes' to that wife business."

He pulled her closer and kissed her. "Just in case you don't like staying at my place—we'll keep your bottle on the mantel *forever*."

The End

Shear Magic

Chapter 1

He's going to explode!

Becky Chambers nearly slipped to the floor as she leaned forward on the wooden seat in the office of Frenandez, Greeson, and Dunn, Attorneys at Law. She knew she looked obvious, glaring at the man waving his copy of the will in front of poor Attorney Harold Greeson's face, but she didn't want to miss a thing—there was too much at stake.

The muscle twitching to the side of the man's left eyebrow held her attention, until she pulled free and settled on his face. He was no doubt handsome in his navy pinstripe suit and obviously starched white shirt, she'd give him that, but the flame red color speeding from his solid, squared jaw line over his lips, and up to his hairline, took away from his rugged appeal. Yes, he was handsome, and mad as hell—at her.

Geez, she'd have to be careful or risk losing everything. Everything she'd ever dreamed of.

"He *had* to be insane to write this will! My uncle would never have done this to me!" the man shouted.

Attorney Greeson paused. Becky wondered if he was working up his nerve to confront the man. That was her best guess as the lawyer peered over his Benjamin Franklin-type glasses.

"Please sit down, Mr. Lawson. Perhaps… I can explain…"

"Explain? Explain how or why my Uncle Nate left half of my land to…" The man turned and wagged a finger toward Becky. "Her?"

Whoa! At first she pulled back, then leaned forward. He didn't scare her, whoever he was. "Hey, wait a minute…" Becky straightened in her seat. "Look, buddy, I didn't ask for..." *Control yourself, Chambers. Good luck has never fallen into your lap before. Don't blow it!* She aimed a smile at him and clenched her teeth. Beneath the chair her foot ground into the carpet as if she was putting out a cigarette. The action did little to relieve her frustration. Geez, how she wanted to throttle this guy!

The man looked at her and said, "Sorry, ma'am. This... news... has taken me by surprise." Then, he leaned within inches of Attorney Greeson's face. So much for her wasted smile at his apology. "Please explain," he said.

Attorney Greeson cleared his throat. "Perhaps you'd like to sit down first, Slate?"

Slate? What the heck kind of name was that? Sounded like some kind of stone. She looked at the outraged guy and figured he was about as stiff as stone. Thinking better than to interrupt, Becky bit her lip, tasting tutti-frutti, her favorite flavor of lipstick. If she didn't clutch the arms of the chair, she'd be too tempted to pop this Slate Lawson, apology or not.

But she couldn't.

She had to behave. All she had to do was picture how her daddy, the last foster father she ever had, used to talk about one day buying a house for their family. His words had become a lifelong dream that floated too near right now to let it burst in a fit of anger. Besides, she'd had her share of run-ins with men like Slate Lawson in her life. Oh, he looked great—hell, handsome—but beneath the movie star face, Becky knew there was someone out of her league. By the looks of his clothes, he had money and that right there made them miles apart—one more reminder of which side of the tracks she grew up on.

She looked at the furious Slate Lawson and laughed to herself. A relationship with this guy was not even a consideration. She told herself to sit still if it killed her. It sure felt as if it would as she sat there, forcing herself out of character. This charade proved to be very similar to her days back in high school. She had a devil of a time with the many rules and regulations the teachers had. It went against her independent nature. Right now, watching Mr. Lawson seethe as the attorney read more of the will and having to be quiet was like being back in high school—where all of her natural free-spirited instincts were choked to death on a daily basis.

She felt smothered, but remained still.

"Well, er... where do I start?" Attorney Greeson floundered, although Becky knew the man must have all the answers below his balding white hair. He reminded her of a kindly old gentleman in his squirrel gray suit.

She looked at Slate in his spotless outfit. Physically, the suit fit him to perfection. But, she noted, there was something about him that made her want to see him in a more comfortable outfit. Jeans, maybe? Not that the suit wasn't his size, hugging broad, solid shoulders. No, he looked great in it, but she figured jeans and worn black cowboy boots would help to loosen him up a bit.

On second thought, the outfit wasn't the cause. Slate Lawson looked as if he were a stiff, conservative kind of guy. Yeah! Stiff was the operative word. He reminded her of a balloon which Grady, whom she'd become guardian to after rescuing him from foster care, once blew up. She'd hollered at him not to keep blowing or it'd pop. Well, the kid didn't listen and sure enough after a loud *bang*, tiny bits of balloon covered their kitchen.

This Lawson guy looked so perfect and acted so... full of hot air that she expected him to pop, too. *That's it,* she thought, snapping her fingers. He needed something to loosen him up or he'd pop. Here she was like a fish out of water acting like some Miss Goody Two-shoes right now, ready to explode herself. Well, this fish would control herself. She looked up. Mr. Lawson could do to swim upstream for a bit.

Slate glared back at her. She stifled her so-what's-your-problem grin and gripped the seat so as not to snap her fingers again. Taking a deep breath, the leathery smell of the books lining Attorney Greeson's office walls filled her nostrils. What a distinct scent. Heck, she'd never owned a hard cover book in her life, she thought, letting her breath out slowly. Oh, she loved escaping into a good book, but her purchases consisted of ones she'd gotten at the local used bookstore or borrowed from the library. Someday she'd treat herself to a real book, a hardcover romance from *The New York Times* Bestseller's List. Slate turned toward the lawyer. Finally she relaxed a bit.

"As you know, Slate, I've been your uncle's attorney for more years than I care to remember." He smiled at Becky. "Excuse me, Miss Chambers, I don't mean to ignore you, but it seems I need to make a few things clear to Mr. Lawson."

"Good luck," she mumbled, then caught Slate staring and said, "Fine. No problem, sir." Hm, interesting how green eyes can take on an ominous quality in the throws of anger, she thought. Guess she had mumbled a little too loudly. She'd have to control her impulses, okay, not an easy feat, but a necessary one.

"Well, Slate, several years ago, Nate came to me to modify his will. Yes, you were correct. Originally he had you as the sole heir to Valley Del Sol." He turned and smiled at Becky. "That is the name of your… well, the ranch. It is located about a half hour from here in the foothills of the Sacramento Mountains just outside of Chaparral, New Mexico."

She smiled back. "Thanks… thank you."

"Don't tell me you didn't even know my uncle owned a ranch?" Slate asked.

"Well, no. The subject never came up."

"Yeah, right. Give me a break."

She'd like to break something, like his neck. It took all of her control, although it was killing her not to spit some snide remark at him. The legal setting helped. It reminded her of why she was here. Why she had to control herself. Why she had to play the sweet, innocent—heck, the "dumb blonde"—routine. Fate had forced her into this position, just as it had forced rotten luck on her family life. She had to play along or allow fate to throw another stinking curve into hers and Grady's lives.

When someone like Becky grew up attending the school of "hard knocks," she learned to trust no one—especially a man like Slate and the inevitable Fate.

Slate gave a loud sigh and slipped his hands behind his head. She'd love to suggest he prop his feet on the highly polished mahogany desk to loosen up, but remained quiet as he kept them firmly planted on the floor.

"At the time your Uncle Nate came to me, he had a provision added to his will. I understand your dilemma, Slate..."

Slate snorted.

"However, I assure you, Mr. Lawson was of sound mind when he added the codicil..."

Slate smiled at her—at least he tried. She could see he forced it, but the effect was the same. Those full, soft lips, the dimples that formed... her darn heart skipped like a pebble across the river when he smiled toward her, even if it was forced, until he leaned closer and spoke. *Musk. The guy wears some brand of musk cologne.* Her favorite. What a waste of a great scent. She wasn't buying any sincerity in his damn smile. Not for a second.

"Just how well did you get to know my uncle?"

For a second, her hackles raised at the insinuation. She'd never used her body to get what she wanted, no matter how skimpy her outfits, and she was damn tired of being judged by others. Hadn't he ever heard not to judge a book by its cover?

Plus, he'd just insulted poor Nate! Her dream would have to wait as she defended her friend's memory. But before she could say something, she noticed a sadness in Slate's eyes. Hm. He missed the old man, too. That common bond eased her anger. She grabbed the chair arm and said, "Nate and I used to frequent the same coffee shop near the salon I worked in. He would come in every Tuesday for his usual black coffee, BLT, and raisin bran muffin..."

She paused, seeing the memories must have been painful for Slate, but he nodded as if telling her to continue. "There was a group of us, mostly older folks that became known as the Nooner Coffee Klatch." She chuckled, paused. "Mr. Lawson, I really had no idea what Nate was up to with his will."

He patted her hand and seemed to linger a little too long. Geez, Attorney Greeson kept the heat on too high in here. Heat? In April? She looked at her hand, no sign of a burn. Slate had touched her for emphasis and to appease her, but the effect was… er… nice. Obviously he was buying her "dumb blonde" act. That was good. Forcing a sigh to clear her head, she cursed the sweltering heat speeding along her arm. That was bad. *Don't betray me now body,* she thought. I need all my wits about me today, so I don't lose the biggest, and only, chance at my dream. And a chance for Grady to have a better life.

"Call me Slate."

Smiling, she rubbed the darn tingling from her skin then sat on her hand to ignore the reaction he'd caused. It didn't help. She still felt his touch, felt the heat, and her temples started to pound. Imagine a physical attraction to this guy? Lust sure is all that it's cracked up to be, she mused.

"So what is it you and my uncle had in common to talk about all those years?" Slate asked.

She sighed. "Lots, actually."

"I see. I wasn't able to spend much time with him since I'd been so busy… lately. I…"

Becky sensed that Slate regretted something. Maybe not spending more time with his uncle? She knew nothing would keep her from being with her family if she had one more opportunity.

"I didn't know he went there," Slate said. She felt sorry for him even though he'd been such a bear throughout this will reading.

Attorney Greeson looked from Becky to Slate. "If I may continue?"

Slate nodded toward the lawyer.

Becky squirmed, trying to ignore Slate's touch tickling into her although he'd taken back his hand. She shifted all of her weight onto her hand. Damn, no luck. Still felt the phantom touch. She knew she was too skinny and often embarrassed to buy her clothes in the teen's department. Maybe before she hit twenty-seven next year, she'd grow a better figure. Sitting here was getting harder and harder.

Could her dream be worth all this?

Daddy would say so, and all she had to do was picture Grady's freckle-filled face. The kid needed a home, a real one. Deserved it like any other kid in the world.

"According to the codicil, if you were not married by the time of Nate's death..." the lawyer said.

Slate jumped from his seat.

Becky leaned sideways. The guy looked as if he wanted to strangle someone and she wasn't taking any chances.

He ignored her and shouted, "That's what this is all about? Damn it! The same old thing. If I'm not married...?" Slate slammed his fist onto the desk so hard a photo, obviously Attorney Greeson's family by the resemblance of the kids, toppled over. "Sorry, Greeson. Damn, my rotten luck." He stood the photo up and looked toward the ceiling. His voice softened to an almost eerie tone, "How in the hell could you do this to me, Nate? Interfering even from the grave. You know damn well why I never married."

Becky watched as if her favorite soap opera had sucked her into the TV screen. Hm, no wife, no ranch. So, the handsome, albeit straight-laced, probably wealthy, and well, handsome, Slate Lawson was single. Oh geez, why was she even thinking about that? There'd be no way she could ever be attracted to him, or visa versa. Not that she'd ever wish bad luck on anyone, but it was interesting to see that the rich had problems, too. She'd been told a million times by her friend and hairdresser Wanda, owner of Wanda's Hair Works Salon, that money doesn't buy happiness, and now Becky could see her friend may have had a point.

But that wouldn't change the dream she'd had since childhood—the one her real mother made so difficult to obtain. She'd love to ask Slate why he hadn't married yet, but it wouldn't fit in with the character she was playing. The real Becky would have a million questions, but, thinking of Grady, she held them all back.

Attorney Lawson continued through repeated interruptions by Slate until Becky thought she'd scream. She tapped her nails on the chair, then worried Attorney Greeson would make her pay to repair the scratches she'd soon make.

Slate interrupted once again. "I don't need to hear anymore. So, what's my next step, Harold?"

"Step, Slate?"

"Legal step. What can I do to get my land? All of it." He looked at her as if she'd say, "Go ahead and keep it all, I don't want half of a ranch given to me for free."

Her heart slammed against her chest. *Do next?* Oh heck, he was going to cause trouble. It was getting hard to breathe. He was going to yank back the carrot Nate Lawson had dangled in front of her. The carrot that had been a dream come true, although she hated loosing a friend to earn it. All she ever wanted was a house—a house of her own. Wanda always said you couldn't substitute material wealth for a family. Becky knew that, but she had lived in enough apartments to know that she wanted to give owning her own house a shot.

After her foster parents had passed away, she'd adopted Grady, one of the kids they had been raising. And Grady deserved a real house, too. She knew how the kids had teased her as a child since, wherever they lived—and it was plenty of places—they usually could only afford a small apartment without room for guests or kids to sleep over. Plenty of time the kids would say it really wasn't her house anyway. Yep, she'd fight tooth and nail to change Grady's lifestyle so his childhood didn't mirror her own. She sucked in a huge breath.

"Excuse me, Mr. Lawson, but you mean *our* land," she interrupted, overlooking Slate squinting at her. She had to say something, it was like releasing steam from a pressure cooker. If she didn't get to vent, at least a little, she'd blow up and ruin her chance for sure. Although Slate's head had to be pounding with all the wrinkles that had formed in his forehead when he looked at her, she had to remind him and the lawyer why she was here.

"I'm afraid she is correct, Slate. The Valley Del Sol belongs to both of you as stated in the codicil. According to your uncle, whoever turns a profit from the ranch, not including your outside investments, in the next six months, er... or... marries, will become sole owner."

Becky knew a blood vessel had popped inside Slate's temple. She was certain she'd heard it. She forced a smile anyway.

★

Slate glared at the blonde sitting there smiling at him. Even with his vision blurred by anger, he could make out the purple and yellow vest, short—very short—black suit skirt that just cried out for a man to imagine where her long, long slender legs ended, and nylons—if that's what you called black things that looked like fishing nets—running over those long, slender legs. Her waist beneath the silver buckled belt had to be small enough for his fingers to meet if he wrapped his hands around her. If she didn't stop her annoying habit of tapping, tapping, her long red, and pink, and—oh hell, each nail was painted a different color—fingernails, he might not be responsible for his actions.

Damn, why was he even thinking about how she looked? Or her legs? Or wrapping his hands anywhere around her body? He ran his tongue across his dry mouth and wondered how he was going to undo the lasso tightening inside his gut. He had no interest in her other than getting her out of his life—and his ranch.

Damn, it was hot in here.

The woman was trouble—or was she? He decided to be rational. She could have proven difficult to reason with, but if he looked past his anger, she was actually very sweet. She had remained quiet and poised, although he thought he noted a flicker of determination in her eyes. Baby blue. The only color that described the soft, powdery color. But she sure as heck didn't dress like someone with baby-blue eyes.

He'd never seen quite that shade of iris before, but he'd imagine a delicate, ladylike female would have that color. Not that she acted like some brazen snippet of a woman, but her appearance, well, with the velvety dark eyebrows contrasting her long golden hair—dyed, he guessed, although he had no clue about women's hair coloring but assumed it was dyed. She didn't quite act as she looked. His boiling pulse cooled to a simmer. Her outfit said she was a certain type, yet, she had a rather demure personality. If anything, she confused him. And he wasn't often confused.

When he first saw her, he'd expected a fight—guessed she should have icy blue eyes like the ice of a glacier. She tapped her nails louder. He looked toward her in time to see her cross her legs. The skimpy skirt rose higher. Or maybe he should think of those eyes as *hot* blue because that's what he felt inside as he noticed how smooth the skin of her thigh looked beneath her nylons. He loosened his tie.

Damn Uncle Nate.

Slate caught himself smiling at her. Shoot, it would be a lot easier to be angry with her if she were some brazen female. "Since you work, and I assume live several miles from Chaparral, I'm guessing you wouldn't want to leave your family to move to the ranch."

Well, you're guessing wrong, she thought. She stood and turned toward the window, determined to hide the moistness that filled her eyes. She and Grady would leave their apartment in a second, and there'd be no one to even miss them. Heck, she didn't even own the furniture. She swallowed hard and forced her voice to steady. "I'll work something out."

Slate groaned. He knew it. Despite her sweetness, she was determined to take something she had no right to inherit. "Look, Miss Chambers..."

"Becky."

"Becky, the ranch is something... that should have been mine since the day I was born. Uncle Nate had inferred that I would own Valley Del Sol ever since I moved there from my family's ranch in Arizona after college. I'm his only living relative left, and I'd grown up learning everything possible about sheep from my father's hired hands." Judd, his father, the master rancher, the absent father, he thought, but didn't relish sharing that information with anyone. "I lived every weekend on that ranch when I went away to school." That flicker of sadness crossed his face again, but he sucked in a breath and obviously tried to hide it.

"I'd taken every course related to ranching and business in college and spent years making Nate's ranch more prosperous." It had never been the money he was after. He'd had plenty of it all his life, and when he sold his parent's ranch following his father's death, plenty more. There was more to it that drove him to ranching, and now, this Becky Chambers was going to try to take everything important in life to him away. "I have lived and breathed ranching... since I could walk."

Becky couldn't help herself as she looked at Slate. His story had her reminiscing about the last foster parents she'd lived with. For so many years, they'd had to move from place to place. Her father, the only one she'd ever called "Daddy," had to find work as a migrant worker. All the moving had kept them from having a house, a stable home to go to. And all those years a lack of money that had been part of their lives. All she had now from her past was Grady, whom she loved dearly, and Miss France, a doll her father had brought home for her birthday. At the time, she'd known it wasn't brand-new, but she loved it dearly—still kept it on her bed as a reminder of the last set of foster parents she had lived with. The only ones she actually loved. Before she could think logically, she said, "Slate is right, sir."

"Miss Chambers?" Attorney Greeson asked.

"I said he is... The ranch should be his." She reached for her black backpack. She wasn't going to sit around here any longer—dream or no dream. How could she rob Slate of his rightful heritage? She knew all too well how important a family was, along with where they lived. As she swung the backpack over her shoulder. It flipped opened. Lipsticks, chewing gum, nail polish, and more lipstick splattered across the floor. She bent to grab everything at the same time as Slate.

Leaning so close she could see her own reflection in his eyes. He whispered in a voice that nearly hypnotized her, "Thank you." He picked up a tube of lipstick, and his hand touched hers as she reached for it at the same time.

Slate was all too aware that he brushed Becky's hand. He leaned closer and got a whiff of some sweet sent. It reminded him of the seventies, of hippies, flower children. For a second, he forgot what he was going to say. For crying out loud, he was a grown man! He could handle any type of situation. He summoned up every trick he'd been taught in life and said, "I'll buy you out. Fair market value of the ranch, split in half..."

Geez, that had to be a bundle! "Sell my share?"

"Actually, Slate..." Attorney Greeson started.

He waved his hands to interrupt the lawyer. "I'm talking about a lot of money..."

"Just how much... No, it doesn't matter. Your uncle must have had a good reason to leave me part, but I can't take..."

"Excuse me, Miss Chambers. As I was saying..." Attorney Greeson started once more.

Slate waved at him again. "Just a second, Harold." He turned to Becky again and said, "What difference does it make? My uncle obviously wanted to reward you for something, so getting a chunk of money would do—unless you rather I contest the will, and you'll get nothing."

Becky's eyes widened. "Contest the will?" she whispered. Suddenly his threat had her on the defensive. Here she was ready to give it all to him, and now she had second thoughts. She couldn't let anger or emotions get her confused. What would Nate want? Even if Becky didn't agree with her old friend, she had to decide if she could ignore his wishes. He must have known what he was doing. She had to respect him and his wishes.

"I have every right to contest..."

"But, Slate..." the lawyer tried again.

Oh geez. Now what had she gotten herself into? Becky sat upright. She knew this was all too good to be true. No one had ever given her anything in her whole life, least of all a piece of property. Looking at Slate Lawson, in his wrinkle-free suit, and obviously from the swanky side of the tracks, she knew he was going to yank her dream away in one breath.

She glared toward him. He met her focus, emerald eyes boring into her. Maybe she should just take his offer and use it to buy a small house? But if that's what Nate had wanted, he would have left her only the money. Yeah, she had to do what her friend had wanted. Man, this was all so confusing. Her head started to throb when she mulled over, give up the ranch free and clear, take Slate's offer, or do what Nate must have wanted.

"No, Slate, I can't accept your offer." Damn, but she wanted to. Batting her darn eyelashes like some dainty cream puff, she turned toward the lawyer before Slate's smile had a chance to confuse her. Even if Slate had nearly convinced her with his sob story, Nate didn't want that. He must have known how hard Slate had worked, but Nate still wrote his will including Becky. "I'm sorry, Mr. Greeson. You seem to have something to say."

Slate stared at her as if she sat there naked. She watched him run his gaze from her legs to her eyes—and stop, and stare. She should have stayed focused on the portly attorney. Oh geez, there goes the temperature again. Becky wiped her forehead. Twenty-six had to be too young for hot flashes.

Attorney Greeson cleared his throat. "I'm certain, yes, certain, that Nate wanted you to have part of the ranch. He was rather specific in his will. The property is to be divided equally..."

Slate groaned.

"There can be no buy-out, and although it's admirable that you'd give up your share, Miss Chambers, I think you can see that's not what Nate had wanted. Slate, since you are more knowledgeable about sheep ranching…" Attorney Greeson smiled toward Becky. "No intention of insulting you, ma'am."

"I understand," she said over Slate's growl. She tried to think if anyone had ever called her "ma'am" before.

"Yes, Nate spelled out the terms quite clearly. Slate will continue raising the sheep and corn. However, if Miss Chambers has any interest… you will be required to instruct her—"

"Oh hell! Now I've got to teach a hairdresser how to raise sheep?"

She wanted to say, "Don't bust a gut, Mister," and then tell him what he could do with the fluffy creatures. Instead, she forced herself to say, "I really have no interest in sheep ranching," she said, then mumbled, "That is, at the moment." She gripped the seat of her chair until her fingers hurt. It helped to settle her temper though.

"There's a minor miracle," he mumbled.

"—or, she is free to do what she wants with her share of the property. Mr. Lawson apparently foresaw that fact and left a nice sum of money to you also, Miss Chambers, to invest in your property."

Becky sighed. She could see Nate with his wisps of silver hair sticking from beneath his brown Stetson. His encouragement had given her a reason to look forward to work—to save money for a house. She wasn't one to cry, but her throat tightened when it occurred to her that she no longer had anyone special to give her homemade coconut macadamia nut cookies to. And she'd even invented them. She could just take the money and run, but that'd be against Nate's will.

"I'm not done with this mess yet. Harold, what does it take to contest this thing? I mean, she's not even family! She's a hairdresser!"

"That does it, buddy!" Becky exploded and stood again. Apparently she hadn't had enough practice of controlling her temper. Good thing she never aspired to be an actress. Sure, she was risking losing everything by reverting back to her real self, but she'd learned at an early age to defend herself, or no one else would—and her actions just came naturally.

"Please sit down, Miss Chambers," the lawyer implored.

She looked at the pleading look in his eyes and sat. At least he'd gotten her temper to calm and let her slip back into her act. "I am so sorry, sir." She fanned herself with her hand.

"Actually..." an obviously nervous Attorney Greeson started, "...the specifics of how the land is to be divided is spelled out quite clearly in a... letter..." He fumbled around on the top of his desk until he held up a legal-looking paper. The white paper embossed with some official seal quivered in his hands.

Her heart twisted. Legal-looking papers always brought bad news for her.

"...right down to the Riparian Rights," Attorney Greeson finished.

Slate cursed and dropped into the chair next to her.

Riparian Rights? What the heck were they? Maybe something that said someone like Becky Chambers really couldn't inherit anything. Obviously Slate knew what Riparian Rights were, but no way was she going to look ignorant in front of him. A quick stop to the library on the way home would clear up whatever they were. Making a mental note to remember the term, Becky tried to look as if she understood.

Attorney Greeson leaned toward her. "Of course, you understand that Riparian Rights allow ownership of the banks of the lake, the soil under the water, and the use of the water to both of you, and we all know how coveted water is out here. Although it is difficult to cut a lake in half, that is, in fact, what has been proposed in Nate's will. I trust you will both oblige."

Becky nodded as if she understood what the heck he was talking about. There was a kindness about him that had her believing that she understood, but her mind was a mass of confusion. She owned part of a lake? She hadn't blown it?

"Is that it, Harold?" Slate stood and walked to the door.

Becky watched him grip the handle. She ran her hand along her throat. Why'd she get the feeling Slate Lawson wished her neck was the brass handle? Obviously she watched too much TV. A surge of adrenaline pumped through her at the thought of a challenge. And it seemed sharing this ranch with him was going to be a humdinger of a challenge.

"Well… there is one more thing," the lawyer said. He stood as if he needed to try to meet Slate's height, but the stocky man had about a foot to go to come eye to eye with Slate's six feet. But Attorney Greeson still tried to straighten his frame taller. Actually, he followed that gesture with a step backwards, away from Slate.

Oh boy, this has to be good. Becky stood. She needed the best view possible when Attorney Greeson laid the "one more thing" on Slate Lawson. Nothing could have made her day any better than it already was. She owned property—she'd never owned anything in her life besides her '88 Buick, and that she bought used. All the money she'd been saving for a down payment on a house wasn't nearly enough yet. But now she owned land and half of a lake! *Maybe dreams do come true.* Maybe someone upstairs was going to turn the tables in her favor. Maybe she'd paid her dues by living her past and now her life was going to take a different direction.

"The codicil stipulates that Ms. Rebecca Chambers, of Alamogordo, New Mexico, and her son, Mr. Grady Chambers, must occupy the residence on the ranch—the west wing of the…" He swallowed hard. "…the main house."

Whoa, boy. She'd been wrong. Her day had just gotten better.

Chapter 2

Becky felt her eyes widen as she stared at Slate. Yikes! His eyes were the size of half-dollars! He was not taking the news of sharing the house at Valley Del Sol very well.

"Nate had to be crazy!" Slate yelled.

No, not very well at all.

"Slate, please let me finish," Attorney Greeson said.

The lawyer was holding his own, except for the beads of sweat pouring down his forehead. Well, at least he only had to listen to Slate Lawson carry on a few more minutes—apparently she was going to be living with him. Well, in the same house anyway.

"Of course... er..." Attorney Greeson continued, "Hector and Rosa..." He turned toward Becky. "Hector Gonzales and his wife, Rosa, live there, too. She is the housekeeper, he's the foreman. According to Mr. Nate Lawson they will be allowed to remain employed at Valley Del Sol and to act as... er...."

Becky wondered how the lawyer could stand the beads of sweat tickling his reddened face as they must have been doing. She bet he couldn't wait until she and Slate left his office, at least then Attorney Greeson's blood pressure could return to normal and he could madly swipe at his face. As it was, he tactfully brushed a finger above his eyebrow as he spoke.

"Act as what, Greeson... Oh, hell..." Slates rolled his eyes toward the ceiling.

Becky gave Attorney Greeson a curious look.

"Chaperones? Chaperones. Chaperones! My Uncle wills us, total strangers, the same house and...." Slate interrupted then looked at her.

Well not exactly looked, more like stared at her boots and worked his way up to her skirt, top, and face... then to her feet again. With both hands, she pulled her skirt down and wished she had worn her ankle-length skirt—he ran his hand through his hair—or she should have worn her jeans.

He started to clear his throat, but she interrupted. "I agree with you, Mr. Lawson. This must be very difficult... and painful to accept." Pleased with her theatrics, she smiled.

He looked at her a second. A tenderness sparkled in his eyes. "Slate." He sucked in a breath. "Call me Slate."

Hm, there was a hint of graciousness in his tone. Something made her think that Slate had made a lousy first impression. His blow up about the will sure seemed justified, even if she stood to gain. Heck, she'd be spitting mad if she were in his polished boots. But now he had calmed enough so maybe this was his real personality. Obviously, he had a short fuse, but he didn't seem to hold a grudge. Of course, she'd always been a lousy judge of character. Her dating history, filled with losers, proved that. At least she'd learned to keep on her toes and be wary of men.

But for now she'd remember she could get more out of Slate with her acting the Good Two-Shoes thing than her usual spitfire self.

"You may be correct, Slate. I mean, the idea of someone like you and me... well, we are not exactly two peas in a pod." *Oh damn, what a dumb thing to say.* By the look of confusion on Slate's face, she knew he thought the same thing. She had to get him back on the subject. "Perhaps Nate did have a moment of temporary senility—to think we'd need chaperones." Geez, she better not plant the seed of doubt about Nate's mental instability in Slate's head! All she needed was for him to contest the will. "I do mean temporary. Other than this chaperone business, Nate was as sane as you and... well, he was perfectly sane."

Attorney Greeson stood. She knew he wanted them out of his office—now. She didn't blame him. "Well, if there aren't any questions..." he said.

"Questions? I've got... shoot, no point in haranguing you about it, Greeson." Slate turned toward the door. Putting on his black Stetson, he asked, "When are you planning to move in?"

"I... well...." Slate turned, and she looked into his eyes. "Tomorrow? Grady, too."

He tipped his hat toward her and left.

Becky slouched into the chair. "I'll be out of here in a minute, sir."

"No hurry, Miss Chambers. Take your time. I'm going to lunch."

She nodded toward Attorney Greeson's back. Lunch? The poor man—it was only ten in the morning.

Becky loved a hair-raising, wild, death-tempting roller coaster ride, and she always stayed on for at least three trips, but this morning, this ride, she'd never want to repeat. Her heart hurt from having her feelings yanked about. Elation, anger, noticing Slate Lawson's bod, and fear.

Fear, she didn't like.

Actually, she hated fearing anything, and she did fear losing her chance at happiness. Happiness right now would come in the form of a yellow clapboard house trimmed in creamy white, a picket fence, and a swing set for Grady. A new one, not something already used. Of course, Wanda would argue that owning part of a ranch wasn't going to bring Becky and Grady happiness. But she knew it would. It had to, and the only one standing in the way of her happiness was Slate Lawson.

She'd sidestep him at every turn.

★

Slate slammed shut the door of his black Chevy pick-up and jammed his foot on the pedal. The truck lurched out of Attorney Greeson's parking lot, nearly missing a red Blazer. He eased up his foot and nodded an apology to the woman scowling at him from the Blazer.

As he drove through Las Cruces, he shook his head. How could

Uncle Nate have done this to him? Slate's anger receded, leaving his heart to take the brunt of his emotions. It hurt. It hurt like hell to think his uncle had taken away something so important to him.

Sure he knew Uncle Nate had wanted him to marry; shoot, he'd only mentioned it a million times. How often did the old man suddenly have some gorgeous woman over for dinner, someone he'd met at the store, a rancher friend's daughter, or who knew where he dug them up? And Nate used to be so embarrassing, overtly encouraging any relationship Slate would start with some female. Having never married, Nate obviously only wanted what he thought would make his nephew happy. Slate smiled to himself.

Nate had meant well, sure, Slate knew that. But Nate hadn't grown up with his parents arguing daily. Nate didn't see the pain of his mother's face when his father had left her alone all day until dark. He didn't see his father put the care of the ranch above his wife's needs until she divorced him right after Slate left for college. And Nate hadn't seen his father work himself into an early grave at the age of fifty-nine, two years after his mother remarried a nine-to-five businessman in Albuquerque. But Slate saw it all, lived through it all—and unfortunately, inherited his father's workaholic tendencies.

He wasn't going to do that to any woman.

He passed under the wooden entrance of Valley Del Sol and stopped. Good thing he'd taken the day off. No way could he concentrate on his ranching. Stepping out of his truck, he leaned against the open door and looked at his property. The knot that had tightened his insides like a lasso when Attorney Greeson had read the codicil started to unravel. Slate usually wasn't a hothead, but he'd really lost it today. Damn, he'd never had such a painful shock before. Poor Becky must be afraid for her life having to move in with him.

He bent to grab a handful of sandy soil and breathed in. The earthen scent comforted him as if the land were part of him—actually, his entire life. This situation Uncle Nate had gotten him into was only temporary. Heck, what could a hairdresser know about a ranch? She'd run through her inheritance like the soil filtering through his fingers. Then she'd be gone, and he'd have Valley Del Sol to himself.

She seemed so sweet and, well, he couldn't put his finger on it, but he was certain that there was more to her than the first impression he'd gotten this morning. Years of good manners assured him that he'd treat her with the respect that any woman deserved, even if she was there to take what was so important to him. He regretted coming across as such a jerk.

All of this mess really wasn't her fault. He knew he couldn't be mean to such a sweet, blameless young woman, since he'd grown to be a trusting person—almost to a fault. Heck, he would even make sure Dave Palmer, one of his best ranch hands, kept a close eye on Becky so that she didn't destroy her side of the ranch. Of course, Slate wanted the ranch kept in good order so he wouldn't have a mess to fix up after she lost. Nothing to worry about where she was concerned. Yep. Nothing. She seemed so… delicate in a confusing sort of way.

But her appearance did bewilder him.

Those clothes didn't fit her personality. She looked… wildly sexy, yet she was so sweet, calm. Becky's long legs were so… luscious, yet she reminded him of the ladylike women he usually dated. How clearly he could picture her lips…. His pulse pounded in his veins, reminding him he'd have to ignore her appearance to make it through this. Yep, she was puzzling, and he had to share the ranch with her if that was Nate's wish.

He'd be agreeable. How long was six months anyway?

★

Becky shoved the last box into her car's trunk and collapsed against the bumper. All of hers and Grady's worldly possessions fit into her pink Buick. Renting a furnished apartment was handy, although she'd hated using someone else's furniture every minute. But it had been the best way to save money. Refusing to feel sorry for herself, she pulled up, walked to the front of the car, and paused.

"Well, kiddo, are you ready?" she asked.

Grady jumped into the tiny space she'd left vacant in the front seat. "Yep. Are we really moving to a ranch, Becks?"

She waved to the apartment house they'd lived in for the past three years and stepped into the car. "A big one, it sounds like. Buckle up, pumpkin. I understand there are sheep and horses…"

"Yippee!"

Becky laughed as the motor coughed, and she shut her eyes to wish them good luck in their new endeavor—she knew they'd need it. "Um, pumpkin, now you can't go running around that place as if we own it…"

"I thought we did, Becks."

"Well, technically only half, and only for six months…"

"Then where we gonna live afterwards?"

"I… we'll be fine, pumpkin. You don't have to worry about a thing. But I do want you to pay attention to this…" How could she get the kid to go along with her charade without promoting lying? Kids were so honest and spoke their minds. It'd be just like Grady to question why Becky was acting like such a weirdo in front of Slate. "…sometimes grownups act different, more polite in certain situations. Yeah, that's it. You might notice I'm like extra polite around Mr. Lawson. You be polite, too, like you always are. Okay?"

He leaned his head against the window. "'Kay."

Steering with one hand, she held the directions to the Valley Del Sol in the other, but that didn't seem safe so she held the paper toward Grady. "Grab this, kiddo, and hold it so I can see it better."

"Okay, Becks."

She followed the directions as sunlight reflected its brightness on White Sands National Monument while wave-like dunes of sand crept onto the road. Becky grabbed her silver sunglasses and shoved them on. The road turned south and her heart fluttered. She really was doing this. She really was putting her job on hold and moving to a ranch.

She really was crazy.

Occasionally she'd catch a worried look on Grady's face as she peeked at him from the side. The poor kid. He's too young to be thinking of things like where they're going to live. Grady shouldn't have a care in the world—nothing more than what toy to play with next. "Hey, let's sing something like we usually do when we drive. What'll it be?" Grady seemed nervous and it killed her. Not that she'd blame the little imp. He'd been through so much in his short six years of life that she'd vowed to protect him as much as she could. She started to sing, "If I had a..."

Grady looked silently out the window, the map to the ranch wrinkled on his lap. She pulled the car over to the shoulder and shoved the gear into Park. With one hand, she reached over and grabbed his little fist. He turned toward her. "Everything is going to be okay, kiddo. I know it's scary leaving the only home you remember..."

"How old was I when we moved there?" He nuzzled closer to Becky.

She swallowed back a tear, thinking of the rotten luck this little boy had had, losing both parents, but she wouldn't let herself dwell on that. She needed to ease his worries. "Let's see. You were still single..." That produced a slight chuckle. "And you hadn't graduated from college yet." The chuckle grew to a laugh and she tickled the soft spot under his arm that never failed to bring on hysterics.

"Okay, Becks, I'll... siiiiiing!"

"If I had a..." she started.

"Hambuuuuurger." He chuckled at their version of the song.

"I'd eat it in the morning."

"I'd eat leftovers in the evening."

"All over this kiiitchen." After a quick kiss to his forehead, she put the car back into Drive and headed off toward their future, singing merrily and relieved that he was so resilient. Before they had time to finish their song, a huge wooden sign appeared on the left. Valley Del Sol. She slowed her old Buick and turned without another thought.

Their chance at happiness stretched before them. Small red barns circled a large one like presents under a Christmas tree. Clusters of dull-green prickly pear cacti bloomed red and yellow flowers along the drive. Swells of mountain flanked the property with the land between so flat you could see for miles. Canyons gouged out the rock's sides like giant folds of material. And then she saw it. The house. Their house! Okay, half of their temporary house.

Her heart leapt.

"Why are we stopping her, Becks?" Grady leaned closer to the dashboard. "This some kinda hotel or what?"

"Or what." Becky mumbled. "Actually, kiddo, it's our house."

"Wow."

"I couldn't have put it any better." She brushed back the strands of yellow hair that often covered his left eye. She'd have to cut his hair soon. It reminded her she needed to call Wanda to tell her about this place.

"It really isn't a house, but a mason."

"Mansion," she corrected. "And out here they're called villas."

White adobe walls rambled on forever with arches at every turn. Huge logs jutted out from the angles in the red tile roof that glowed like a candy apple in the ever-present New Mexico sunlight. She licked tutti-frutti, grabbed Grady's hand and both stared out the window before she drove closer.

She could never have made up a dream like this.

Stopping in front of the main entrance, she tapped her nail on the steering wheel. Now what? She didn't even have a key. If she and Grady poked around here, someone might call the sheriff. She bent to get her denim bag off the floorboard. Certain she'd need proof that she and Grady really had lived here after the six months passed, she grabbed the disposable camera she'd gotten, bent on documenting every second. When she sat back up, she looked into the lens, turned toward the door and gasped. "Holy cow…" Slate

Lawson stood outside the window of her car, the center of her photo. She clicked the shutter anyway.

"Didn't mean to scare you, Becky." He looked at Grady and smiled.

"Oh… I'm all right," she managed as she shoved the camera onto the seat and rolled down the window. Biting her lip, she wanted to shout, *what the heck are you doing creeping up on us like that?* Temper, temper, she reminded herself. "This is Grady."

"Grady." Slate nodded.

"He's my best friend in the world."

Slate hesitated, then smiled. "Welcome, Grady."

"Howdy, Partner," Grady said, in what Becky guessed was his version of a John Wayne impersonation. Geez, she let the kid watch too much TV. Most kids his age wouldn't even know who "The Duke" was.

Slate laughed. "Well, I'm Slate Lawson, but you can call me Slate…"

"Becky doesn't let me call adults by their first name, sir."

She turned in time to catch the impressed looked on Slate's face. "Oh, she doesn't does she? That's a good idea. Well, what do you suggest you call me?"

Grady turned to Becky as if she held his answer. "Mr. Lawson?"

"Too formal for a ranch hand. How about just Mr. Slate?" Slate offered.

"A ranch hand, Mr. Slate? I'm really and truly gonna be one?" Grady asked, his eyes widened like saucers.

Slate chuckled. Rather warmly, Becky noticed.

"You didn't think you'd be just sitting around here? Nope. My men are ready to show you around whenever you're unpacked…"

Grady jumped from his seat. "Can I go now, Becks? Please? I've got to learn ranching. We only have six months…"

She held up her hand. "Easy, kiddo. First we have to unpack…"

Need any help with your luggage?" Slate asked.

Her cheeks warmed as she watched Slate crane his neck to look in the back seat of her car. Obviously he wondered where all their stuff was.

"That's very kind of you. We didn't bring that much… this trip." Grady started to interrupt, and she knew he was going to say something like they didn't have any more stuff, so she said, "Hold on, kiddo, if you want to see the rest of the place."

Slate had opened her door and reached for her hand while she had been turned toward Grady. Normally, she'd swat a man's hand away with a lecture of how she was quite capable of getting out without help, but she held her hand out—then wished she hadn't. His hand covered hers in a grasp, lightly, but it felt as if a beam of sun burned into her skin. She didn't know what surprised her more, his offer to help, or her darn body's reaction to him.

Ignoring her lustful thoughts, she eyed him for a second. Why was he being so nice? After yesterday, she wouldn't have been surprised if he made her sleep in the barn. Admitting she was a natural born skeptic, she decided she'd have to keep a close eye on Mr. Lawson.

"Shall I send Hector into town to get the rest of your things?"

"No!" Becky pulled free. "I mean, that is kind of you, but no need. We have what we need right here."

Slate looked as if she'd just spit at him. She guessed he wanted more of an explanation, but no way would she admit that Becky Chamber's worldly possessions fit into one carload. Not that she cared what he thought about her, but she'd do anything to spare the kid's feelings.

"Let me take that box, and I'll show you to the west wing. Is it all right if Hector unloads your car for you later?" he asked with a certain degree of caution.

Becky smiled, and this time it came naturally. Heck, she must have scared the poor man when she freaked out over him suggesting to send Hector to get the rest of her stuff. "Sure. That'd be fine."

She could see him look at an anxious Grady, who kept swinging his head back and forth to take in everything at once. "How about

I get Grady's share since he's a guest here? Dave Palmer, one of my best hands, will show Grady around." Slate pointed toward a man who looked like a cowboy out of some movie standing near the fence as if waiting for an order from the boss.

"Please, Becks," Grady said.

Becky could never resist the kid's innocence. Oh, she was strict when she had to be, but, luckily with a six-year-old, that wasn't too often. "Sure, kiddo. Thank you, Slate." Okay, the man just earned himself some brownie points for treating Grady so well.

Slate motioned for Dave, and after the preliminary introductions were over, he led an overly-excited Grady off toward some barns. Becky yelled out, "Be careful, kiddo. And no climbing or jumping or running. Stay close to Dave. And don't touch anything..."

Slate placed his hand on her arm. She turned, forcing herself not to stare at his hand. But, man, it was darn hard not to since she could feel him. "He'll be fine. Dave has three sons of his own."

She knew her cheeks had to be redder than the barns, but she managed a smile. Slate seemed to have a genuine concern for Grady. Maybe she misread the dear man yesterday, but she'd keep a wary eye on him anyway. With his looks, it wasn't going to be difficult.

Becky followed Slate through the giant wooden doors of the front of the villa. When she stepped down into the coolness of the tiled foyer, she gasped. Geez, she'd never been in a place like this. Her gasp actually echoed.

"Are you all right, Becky?"

"Yeah, er... yes, I'm fine. Seems the cool air took my breath for a second." She waved her hand in front of her face like some Southern belle with the "vapors."

The foyer led to a sunken living room whose ceiling curved into a dome. Sunlight filtered through leaded windows built into the center. Wondering how the windows didn't crash to the floor, she followed Slate down a hallway, cautiously looking up as she passed under the window.

"This section is the west wing. Are you certain you are all right?"

"Hm? Oh, yeah, yes, I'm fine." She pulled her gaze from the windows before he thought her some classless lunatic. "Sorry I forgot to mention Grady. I've been taking care of him since his foster parents died."

"I'm sure he'll enjoy it here. Of course, you can choose whichever room you like, but my favorite has always been the last one on the right. Grady could take the one next to yours. Becky? Is something on the floor?"

"Hm?" A flush zoomed up her cheeks as she realized she was bouncing her feet on the plush forest green carpet. "Oh, no. I just... where's this room you were talking about?" Heck, she'd never even walked in grass that was so soft.

"Here." Slate opened a door and moved to let her pass.

"Holy... cow!" She walked into a bedroom—if that's what you could call it—that actually had steps in it! Becky's toes wiggled inside her Reeboks as she noticed the bronze carpeting. She couldn't wait to fling her shoes off. Windows surrounded the room, overlooking the mountains in the distance. In the center, a bed—heck, a round bed—sat. The headboard was wooden and had a brown striped Navajo blanket draped across the top. The bed was so huge, one person could get lost in it—and two could.... Her cheeks burned hotter than the red chili peppers embossed in the tile floor. No wonder Slate liked this room.

He stepped down the three steps. "The view's spectacular, isn't it?"

"Um," she mumbled.

"That's why I love this room."

"So how come you don't stay here?" She followed him down the steps. The urge to run her fingers across every nook and cranny of the room had her clench her hands around her box. She would really look like some country bumpkin if she did that. He reached out to take her box. With a slight hesitation, she released it, and he set it on the floor.

"Funny, I never thought about that. I guess I'm just used to the room Uncle Nate gave me when I moved in here part-time years ago."

She couldn't stand it, so when Slate turned away, she quickly ran her finger across the dresser. The wood looked so expensive she thought it might actually feel different. Tapping her fingernail, she asked, "When was that?"

With a faraway look in his eyes, he said, "First time Uncle Nate had me come out to New Mexico for the summer, I was a few years older than Grady. Then, every summer like clockwork, I came until I graduated from college up in Albuquerque. Uncle Nate kept my room exactly the same. Since being in school so close, I would live here on the weekends and on campus during the week."

She wanted to ask if he shared that campus housing with anyone... like a female, but instead, she asked, "You didn't grow up in Chaparral?"

"No, Arizona."

Becky sank into a rust-colored leather chair. The coolness caressed her legs like a cloud. Running her hand across the buttery skin, she inhaled the tanned scent and asked, "Why'd you move?"

Slate paused. He turned toward the window. Darn, now she couldn't see his face, and she had so been enjoying watching him. It also ruined her being able to read his expressions.

"My family... I sold my father's ranch, and Uncle Nate was getting on in years."

Sold his father's ranch? That meant either his father had died, or Slate sold it out from under him. Yesterday she would have thought the latter, but now, she guessed his father had passed away. Dying to ask, she pushed herself up and walked toward a doorway past the bed. Slate wasn't volunteering any more info, so she held her questions—which wasn't easy. Ever since she could talk, she had asked questions. Either someone answered—or more than likely ignored her; but she had to revert to her acting role or Slate might say something she didn't want to hear.

"What's in here... oh geez, how many people do I have to share this with?"

Slate stepped next to her and laughed, his warm breath tickling her neck as he leaned against the bathroom door's frame. Her legs threatened to give way, so she pulled herself out of the line of his breath and walked into the beige marble bathroom with a mirrored ceiling.

"This bathroom's all yours; goes with this guest room. Grady has one on the other side of his room. Look, I need to check on the ranch hands. Why don't you unpack these boxes, I'll have Hector bring in the rest, and let's say in…" He pulled a gold pocket-watch from his brown suede vest. "…two hours, I'll show you around. Dave has the afternoon off to spend the time showing Grady around."

"Okay," she mumbled. Slate's behavior really warranted watching. And, her reaction really warranted a cold shower.

★

Becky never remembered taking a bath in the middle of the day, but she couldn't resist the sunken tub. Why on earth would anyone want their tub in the floor anyway? Shrugging the thought away, she stuck her toe into the warm bubbles and slid in. The fragrance of strawberries filled the air as the crystal chandelier above cast hundreds of rainbows on the transparent orbs. With her hand, she lifted a million bubbles and blew them into the air. "Cool!" It was going to be a piece of cake slipping in and out of her character charade.

She had plenty of time before Slate came to get her. Unpacking her stuff didn't take anywhere near two hours. Hector, a short golden-skinned man with a bushy mustache, had brought everything in while she started to undo the first two boxes. Politely speaking with a heavy Mexican accent, he offered to drive to Alamogordo to get the rest of her things. Not nearly as defensive as when Slate had offered his help, she was able to decline Hector's offer, this time making sense as she spoke. Poking a hole thorough the layers of bubbles with her toes, she imagined even the foreman owned more than her and Grady put together.

Over the years she'd learned to be frugal in her efforts to save for a house, but looking around the mirrored room, she was glad she had gone on a small shopping spree yesterday. Nate wouldn't have minded if she treated herself with some of the money he'd left her, and thank goodness, she bought some new clothes and boots for herself and Grady. Boots. Even though she'd always lived in the West, wherever her father's job took them since childhood, she'd never worn cowboy boots. Now she was the proud owner of five pairs—all different colors—and matching Western-style hats! It gave her a kick to see the smile on her Grady's face when she let him pick out his own "duds," as he'd called them. At the time she'd made another mental note to not let the kid watch so much TV.

A knock on the bathroom door scared her. Shielding herself with the flimsy bubbles, she called, "Grady?"

"It's me, Slate."

Slate! Geez! She looked at the clock embedded in the onyx horse's side on the counter. *Two hours flew by when she was in a sunken tub!* "Hold on. I'm almost ready," she lied.

"I'll be in the hallway. I didn't mean to come into your room, but I'd knocked several times and didn't hear you. I just wanted to make certain everything was...."

Yeah, yeah, yeah. Beat it, buster, so I can get dressed. "How very nice of you to be concerned. Everything is fine. I'll meet you in the hall." Clutching the disappearing bubbles, she leaned toward the door to hear Slate's footsteps click away. When the door to the hallway shut, she blew out a sigh, sending bubbles flying to the mirrored ceiling. Jumping out, she grabbed a towel and swiped off the bubbles.

Yanking on her new jeans, Becky leaned down to choose a pair of boots. While she rifled through the ones in the bottom of the closet, she found a tan shoebox. The size was too small for boots and she knew she hadn't bought any shoes lately. Opening the top, she paused. Miss France. A nostalgic tear burned her eyes as she looked at the chic looking doll dressed in a silver gown, navy cape, and black plastic heels.

Although she loved Miss France and gave her the name, hoping to someday visit Paris as a model, her heart wrenched. There were very few reminders of her last foster parents left, since they really didn't have much to begin with. She carefully set Miss France onto the bed, careful to smooth out any wrinkles of her navy cape. Then, she took several pictures of the room before finishing getting dressed. Grabbing her white boots, she shoved her feet in with excessive force.

She'd owned a white Stetson for years but rarely went anywhere suitable to wear it. Sticking it on her head, she pirouetted around in front of the mirror. It looked good with her boots. She only wished she'd had time to redo her nails.

Wanda had shown her a fabulous pattern of little daisies, one for each nail, which would look great with her new boots. Oh well, she had all her beauty equipment, that Wanda had gotten her wholesale, shoved in the back of the closet. She'd do her nails tomorrow. How great not to have to go to work! Luckily Wanda had helped her convince her boss to give her a leave of absence for the six months with a promise to photograph the area around the ranch. Heck, Wanda seemed more excited about this inheritance than Becky did! Laughing to the empty room, she headed to the door.

In the hallway, Slate sat on a wooden bench with his head resting back, eyes shut. Even half asleep he looked damn good. He'd stretched his legs out across the tile, but promptly stood when her door clicked shut. It dawned on her that she was now seeing him as she'd thought he'd be more comfortable—out of a stuffy suit. Much better, much better indeed.

"All set?" he asked.

"Yes." Becky followed Slate's gaze down to her feet. Had she missed something? Maybe her fly was open? Nonchalantly running her finger across her waist, she felt the zipper. Pulled up tight. What the heck was he looking at?

"Did Hector bring all of your things in?" Slate managed to ask, glaring at her. She looked different, and it wasn't just her new boots. Not a scratch had marred the new leather, and her jeans—tighter than the casing on a hotdog—looked great on her. It had to be the shirt. Instead of some wild color, she wore a white, thin blouse that, oh hell, you could see her bra, lacy and white, if you used your imagination.

Slate swallowed and forced his legs to move. He jammed his hands into his pockets to fight the urge to wrap his arm around her shoulder. If he touched her slender arm beneath the nearly transparent fabric, he couldn't guarantee his self-control. Damn, this was going to be a long six months.

Once outside, Slate shielded his eyes from the sun. Four planes zoomed above like giant eagles soaring through the clouds. He shook his head. "Noise scares my sheep. Those are the Sacramento Mountains, and behind the barn is the… our lake. My sheep graze in those fields, and beyond the foothills is an old gold mine…"

"Neat… I mean how interesting."

"And dangerous. Don't ever go out there. The timbers have been known to collapse."

An old mine! That sounded right up her alley, but she'd have to make sure Grady never went out there. How fascinating to explore an old mine. She grabbed a twig from a nearby bush and rolled it between her fingers. It was harder than she thought to control herself. "Certainly, Slate. I won't go there." *And if you buy that malarkey….*

The sun glistened on Slate's brown hair as he lifted his cowboy hat off long enough to run his hands through it. A tiny bead of sweat worked its way down his temple. Her fingers wiggled, she dropped the twig. The droplet crossed his smooth cheek. And she thought no one perspired in the dry desert.

"Thirsty?" Slate asked.

The bead glistened on his jaw. She swallowed hard. "What? Oh… thirsty. Yes, I am parched."

"Come on. I want you to meet Rosa. She's fixed us some iced tea. You do drink iced tea?"

"Certainly." Although a cold Coors would be better.

On the verandah, Rosa shook Becky's hand, welcoming her. With a smile, Rosa assured Becky that Hector and Dave were taking good care of Grady, whom the housekeeper said she'd already fed cookies and milk. The plump woman had the same accent as her husband Hector, but every sentence was followed by a hearty chuckle. A white apron covered her red flowered dress, and she wiped her hands across the apron several times, although Becky suspected they were as spotless as the yellow pottery that sat on the table.

Glazed dishes held cookies, and a glass pitcher with droplets of moisture sliding down the sides sat in the center of the table. Rosa poured the tea and fixed sugar and lemon in Slate's as if she knew exactly the way he liked it. Becky could see a maternal quality in Rosa as she silently pushed Slate's feet from the chair he chose to rest them on. He tipped his hat toward Rosa; she glared at him, causing him to nod and remove his hat at the table. Then, she chuckled and excused herself before leaving.

"She's very nice." Becky mixed three spoonfuls of sugar into her tea.

"Rosa had been with my uncle for years. Actually, I don't remember any other housekeeper here. Do you always use so much sugar?"

"I love sweet things." *Great, Chambers, you sound like a kid in a candy store.* She batted her eyelashes at him to hide her embarrassment, but it backfired. Slate's lips curved, and at any minute she expected him to lick his chops. Oh geez, he thought she was flirting with him! Fiddling with her spoon, she clanked it against the glass several times, then took such a huge drink, she choked.

"Are you all right?"

"Fine," she coughed out, fearful he would pat her on the back and her body would react to his large hands—large masculine hands that could massage her back and work their way down to her.... Ignoring the burning in her lungs, she took a small sip and looked out toward the mountains.

Six months at Valley Del Sol was going to be the longest six months of her life.

Through the corner of her eye she looked at Slate. Yep, the longest.

"So what do you plan to do with your share of my... our... property?" he asked.

Becky's glass froze at her lips. Well, at least his question managed to burst her bubble of lust. How could she tell him about the plan she had come up with during her restless night? It must have been about 3:30 a.m. when she had her brainstorm.

She could feel him watching her, waiting. Turning back, she smiled. He swished his tea with a spoon. He crossed and uncrossed his legs. His eyes bore holes into her larger than the holes in the cacti where the birds nested.

When he took a sip of tea, Becky proclaimed, "I am going to learn sheep ranching—from you."

Tea spouting from Slate's lips sprayed across her new white blouse that she'd splurged a bundle on.

Damn.

Chapter 3

Oh geez, he's choking!

Becky jumped up and slammed her hand against Slate's back. With each pound, he coughed louder, causing his face to turn an awful shade of red. Suddenly, he grabbed her hand and held it.

"Why?" His voice came out a gurgle as if the tea percolated in his windpipe. "You implied… No, you *said* you wouldn't want to ranch…"

"I need…" She refused to grovel and tell him that she needed the money. "I need something to do, and according to Nate I could learn to ranch. This is a sheep ranch…" Besides, that's not exactly what she had said, but she thought better than to argue with him right now.

Slate's reddened face instantly paled. "I *know* what he had said, but that doesn't mean you have to do it. I thought you'd spend your time here with Grady, you know, like a kind of vacation until your time is up."

He'd said "time is up" as if she were only her biding her time until he won the entire ranch. Okay, so that was the most logical scenario, but, damn it, she believed in long shots. There was always the possibility that she could win the whole shebang. She would have loved to point out that Nate must have thought it possible or he wouldn't have put her into this position. He was too nice of a man to humiliate Becky.

And, no one had ever been so nice to her so she couldn't think ill of him.

Once again, she swallowed the words that sat on the tip of her tongue and said, "I'm not the type to sit around not doing anything."

Oh, but she'd like to be. How she would love to lounge around here for six months, having Rosa wait on her hand and foot—but she couldn't. Her side of the ranch would lose money—and that she couldn't afford. "I've worked since I was fourteen…"

"I thought kids had to be sixteen to work."

"In some states they can work in agriculture, like picking tobacco or fruit, at a younger age." Slate looked interested in why she'd work so young, but she had no intention of telling him how much her family needed the money. She'd be damned if she would tell him that her father had made her quit school for a semester to work. The work wasn't as bad as avoiding the law when she knew she should have been in school. The family moved soon after they had enough money, and Becky pleaded with her father to let her go back to school.

She knew it had killed him to make her wear clothes that were too old and too small in order to save money, but she insisted it was no problem so he let her. It was a problem, though, when the kids teased her, and she got into many a fistfight over it. But she never told her father. The state never gave them enough money for all the kids they had taken in.

"Anyway, I would like to continue my side of the ranch as it is. I wrote out a few notes to go over." She slipped out from her jeans the ripped piece of magazine that she'd written on during the night. Wrinkled and torn on the top, it didn't look like something she could use to convince the stuffy cowboy of anything, much less teach her how to ranch. He readied to take it from her, but she pulled it back. "I use my own form of shorthand. I'll read it to you."

He leaned back in his chair, a drip of tea settled on his chin. Maybe the reason she couldn't help herself was because she'd been both a sister and mother to Grady. Whatever her rationale, she followed her impulse, reached over with her napkin, and touched at the droplet. *Whoops.* By the look on his face, her action had taken Slate by surprise, but damn it, his action had her nearly forgetting her list when he took her hand into his.

He paused for what seemed like eons and breathed so near her skin that she imagined he'd kissed her hand. As if he'd burned her with hot tea, she pulled back, collected her thoughts, and read. "First of all, I'd like to know where the boundaries of my property are. Then, I would like you to help me hire a staff of ranch hands to manage my share. Oh, I'll need to know where to buy supplies, and then, of course, I would like you to show me what I have to do to keep… to raise… my sheep."

She almost said to keep her sheep alive for the next six months until she could get her share of money and leave.

"We'll divide the property down the middle. Everything west of that Saguaro is yours; east is mine, unless you want Attorney Greeson to draw up some legal document called a partition. I don't see that it is necessary if we both agree to divide it in half right now—and keep to our sides." He stood. "But remember, Becky, the lake is in the middle—and I own half."

"Fine." No way did she want to become tangled in some legal mumbo jumbo. "And the ranch hands? Any go with my side?"

He shook his head, and let out such a loud sigh she felt the breeze from across the table. "I'll speak to the men."

"Oh, sure… I mean of course I want it to be voluntary."

"As for the sheep… are you certain about this? Ranching isn't something a… someone can learn overnight."

Obviously he was going to say a hairdresser—a woman yet, but at least he didn't out and out insult her. "I am a realistic person, Slate. I do not hope to accomplish the impossible. But I am interested…" Truthfully until yesterday, she had only cared about lambs that were broiled and topped with mint jelly. Not that she could afford to buy lamb though. "…and, eager to learn about sheep. I also thought that the more experienced my ranch hands are, the less I will have to learn."

He laughed. "And they'll run your share of the ranch into the ground if you don't keep on top of them."

Okay, that sounded doable. This was sounding as if she was going to be more of a supervisor than a rancher. No problem.

"The guys that work here are the best, Becky, but some also have lives outside Valley Del Sol and this isn't their top priority. Several live here in the bunkhouse, but those men are usually drifter sorts. When they don't like it on one ranch, they just move on to another."

She flinched. Like her father as a migrant worker although he only moved on for more work.

"Oh." Damn, she was counting on having a staff of ranch hands like the dedicated cowboys of the Ponderosa. She shook her head and decided she'd spend her off-time reading about ranching instead of watching television. Obviously this wasn't going to be like the Ponderosa. "Well, what shall we start with?"

He moved to the steps and said over his shoulder, "It's officially your ranch, Becky. You can start with whatever the hell you want to." Becky stared at Slate's back as spirals of dust spun from beneath his boots. She leaned back, looked at the land west of the Saguaro—and smiled.

⋆

"Okay, settle down, all of you!" While he waved his hand in the air to silence the ranch hands, Slate looked almost as upset as he had in Attorney Greeson's office. Slate had gathered the hands together in the bunkhouse to see who'd volunteer to work for Becky. She smiled to herself as she stood in the back of the room, watching as the now-familiar twitch above his left eyebrow started again. "I need some of you to work my side of the ranch, too," he said after everyone had shouted out that they'd switch to Becky's side.

"Shoot, Slate, your boots don't even match your hat like the pretty lady's do," one of the men shouted out.

Becky chuckled. Thank goodness she didn't turn beet red or she'd die. Having the men all volunteer made her feel welcomed, something she hadn't exactly gotten from Slate since her revelation that she did, in fact, plan to ranch.

"Hell, Buck, at least my boots don't have holes as wide as a cavern in them." Slate curled his lips, and Becky noted how adorable he looked—but thought better than to mention it right now.

"Excuse me, Slate. Perhaps I have a solution…" The men parted like the Red Sea as Becky made her way toward the front of the room. She had no idea ranch hands could flip their hats off so fast, but she smiled to each one as she passed.

Slate leaned against the wall. "Great."

"Let the lady have her say," Dave chimed in.

"She's gotten just about everything else around here already. Why the hell not?" Slate said.

Becky turned to the crowd. "First of all, I really appreciate all of you offering to help out. I had visions of Slate having to hog-tie you to make you change sides of the ranch."

They hooted and holler. A few whistled, but beneath the ruckus she could hear Slate groan. One called out, "Speakin' of visions, Missy Chambers, you're right up there with the angels."

"Thank you." She laughed. "Anyway, perhaps the only fair way to divide this group is in alphabetical order."

"Cripes," Slate mumbled.

Becky gave Slate one of her "dumb blonde" smiles that she'd gotten down to perfection lately. That thought was a bit daunting. "Thank you all for volunteering. I hope my side of Valley Del Sol remains as profitable as it has been. I'd like Nate to be looking down and smiling at us."

Slate pushed his Western hat back and glared. "Cripes again."

This time Becky smiled to herself and said, "So, I'll make a list of duties for each of you and post them." *As soon as I know what the heck they are,* she thought. Slate stepped forward, but she remembered one more thing. "Oh, excuse me, Slate. I forgot to mention that I think it is too confusing saying my side and your side, so I'm going to change the name of my ranch." She could see a look of dissatisfaction in Slate's eyes, and he didn't even have the decency to wait until she turned away to shake his head in obvious disgust.

"To what?" he said on a sigh.

"Sidewinder Valley."

For a brief moment she felt proud of herself. Slate looked rather surprised and impressed with her choice. She pulled herself straight and smiled to the crowd until Slate said, "Let's hope you never come upon one of those sidewinders, Missy Chambers."

She swallowed a retort and chastised herself for thinking of a name that Slate could make fun of. But that wasn't the worst of it. Damn, now he'd put the fear in her that she might run into a rattler while out on the ranch. She hated snakes, even the rubber ones Grady played with. Here she thought she was so clever thinking of a cute name, and now she had one more thing to worry about.

Oh geez, she'd also have to warn Grady to stay clear if he saw one. Several men yelled out they'd protect her from snakes, bringing her thoughts back to their offer in time to note an odd look covering Slate's face—as if he was a bit jealous. *How crazy,* she told herself. She really did watch too much television to think he'd be interested in her.

"All right. Show's over. Get back to work," Slate yelled.

She marveled at how he recovered so quickly from the upsetting news about the hands. He took right over, giving orders that the men followed without a word. With a sigh, she thought she should have paid more attention to how Wanda got her employees to do their jobs. Slate had the help off and running before Becky could contemplate what she should do next.

Well, she'd still do her damnedest not to let Nate and Grady down.

"You know how to ride, Becky?" Slate asked, coming up closer to her.

"Ride?"

He raised his eyebrows. "Horses. You can't exactly ride a pink Buick out on the ranges."

She looked down at her nails, gave a quick thought about what colors she'd do them next time, hoped she wouldn't break any, and said, "How funny, Slate," when she had all the instinct to say, "No kidding, buddy." Before she could finish, he took one hand into his.

"How do you get such tiny flowers on your nails?"

She should pull her hand away, she told herself. But she also told herself that wouldn't be in character with a sweet, shy thing. With Slate's touch near causing the poor daisies to wilt from his heat, she decided to be truthful with herself. It felt damn good having Slate hold her hand. *This is not good.* She eased away, gently. "They are tiny little decals, like stickers."

"Hm. Interesting."

Geez, she forgot what she was going to say next. *Pull yourself together, Chambers.* "Oh, and no, I don't have much experience riding." Unless you consider the merry-go-round past experiences.

"Much? So, that means you have some experience."

No, that means I'm not going to admit the truth.

"Good. I can refresh your memory for you to get around today. Tomorrow you'll have to have one of your hands show you more so you don't fall and get hurt." He tipped his hat forward then put one hand behind her back as he eased her to the door. "I'll have Dave saddle up Titus.

"Titus? As in that Greek giant?"

Slate laughed. "He's an older gelding, much less... spirited than some of the others."

"Still, I'd prefer a nice young female horse."

"No, you wouldn't. Mares can be more... temperamental. Titus will be best. You will ride him."

She readied to argue, but maybe he was right. He darn near made it sound like an order, which annoyed the heck out of her, but then again, she didn't think he'd want her falling off and suing him. So, against character, she merely nodded.

Slate looked at her as if she still didn't believe him. "My female guests always ride Titus."

Becky slowed her pace, walking a bit behind Slate so he couldn't see the faces she made at him that involved her tongue. His company? That was just his polite way of saying his dates. She rolled her eyes. Oh geez, why'd the thought of him having dates suddenly get her attention? *Stop it,* she told herself and curled her lips at the foolish thought. Keep to your side of the tracks. You've got more to worry about now then Slate's love life—like not loosing your life when Titus throws you clear across the desert. Becky walked faster to keep up with Slate. "Titus, huh?"

He chuckled. "He's a good horse and very used to different riders.

"But he sounds so… big…"

Slate laughed. "Titus is big, but gentle. You're not… worried. Are you?"

She stiffened. "Of course not. How silly."

Truth be told, Becky contemplated insisting on some miniature old nag that would be too tired to walk much faster than they were going right now, but decided if she was going to own half a ranch, she better not whine about riding a horse.

And she should especially not let Slate know the truth.

After all, he was in truth the enemy.

★

My legs are killing me, Becky whined to herself. After Titus was saddled and Slate had given Becky a quick lesson in horseback riding 101, they were off on a tour of the ranch. Not only did her legs hurt, but also she'd been holding the reins so tightly that she knew Slate would have to pry open her fingers soon. That would not go over well. She had to at least come across as competent or he might just contest the will as he'd threatened to do. He could probably accuse her of being incompetent to run a ranch, and he'd have a damn good case.

To add to her misery, her legs nearly stuck out straight to the sides since Titus was so big. Big? Well, if she didn't know he was a male, she'd think the horse was near term of a pregnancy. Of course, she'd have no way of knowing what a pregnant horse looked like, but Titus' belly swelled out to the sides so much that Becky wondered if he really was a she.

Slate had hauled up the open stirrups so Becky's feet would reach, but she couldn't grip her thighs onto the horse as Slate had taught her for her little refresher course. Instead, she pulled her feet into a jockey position and used her knees to apply pressure.

Slate must have chosen this horse on purpose!

Okay, old Titus was mild-mannered, but damn large. Titus did a quick sidestep of some sorts, taking Becky by surprise. She lurched forward, trying to grab onto the horny thing on the saddle that Slate had called a pommel, but it ended up in her gut. A whoosh of air flew from her mouth. She dropped her reins in the process. "Whoa!" she shouted as she slid forward and grabbed onto Titus' neck.

"Grab your reins, not the horse!" Slate rode near, catching the dangling leather and handed it to Becky. "Use your legs to hold on, not your hands. Remember, I said to hold both reins in one hand above the pommel."

Pommel, schmommel, she thought. And he knew damn well her legs were too short to use. He just wanted to discourage her from anything to do with ranching. "I've got it now," she out and out lied, along with saying a quick prayer that she'd make it back to the house alive. Poor Grady needed her.

"Come on," Slate called, riding off.

He looked like some television cowboy heading into the sunset, although the sun was to their backs. Still, his shoulders were straight, his waist narrow, and he would have fit into the Ponderosa, no problem. With his perfectly styled haircut no hair touched his collar, but damn if he didn't look sexy anyway.

A jet flew overhead, snapping Becky's attention back to trying to follow Slate and fearing Titus would bolt at the noise. But she didn't need to worry about that as he kept his gigantic hooves planted on the spot. Suddenly she couldn't remember what Slate had told her to do to get Titus moving again. Oh great. That's what she gets for ogling the guy. Oh well, she gave a try at nudging her left foot into Titus' side. He turned his head left. She repeated the same with the right. He turned his head right—and nibbled at her toes! "Yuck! Give me a break here, buddy." With both feet she pushed in, and his head went down, nearly sending her overboard.

"Use your knees, Becky," Slate called out. Damn, he would have to turn around and see her sitting frozen on an immovable Titus like some bronze statue. Well, at least her anger got her mind off Slate's body enough to remember how to get her horse to move.

Becky sucked in a breath, tucked her knees up and repeated Slate's instructions to herself. The horse cooperated. *You sit every other stride and hold every other stride,* she repeated like a mantra. Whatever the heck "stride" meant. She managed to remain in her saddle as she followed Slate.

"The sheep graze off to the west and those cornfields have to be irrigated on a regular basis or else you'll lose your entire crop," Slate said as he pointed out toward the range.

Oh damn, now she had to worry about watering corn, too. "No problem." It was taking every ounce of energy to keep from falling under Titus' hooves. Maybe the rain would take care of her corn. Yeah, that she didn't need to worry about. Well, then again, it was New Mexico. Darn. She made a mental note to check on the corn and rain with Dave.

Slate gave her a look as if he knew she'd never be able to accomplish all that she'd set out to do and clicked his tongue which had his horse speeding up a bit. Becky had to stifle her "giddy-up" and attempted a sound similar to Slate's, but hers came out too juicy, and Titus turned and gave Becky a stare as if to say, "What the heck are you trying to tell me?" So Becky whispered, "Please, move, Titus. There's a pound of sugar back at the house for you if you cooperate." With that, she pressed in her knees, and suddenly Titus took off after Slate, but thank goodness, not as fast.

Okay, I can do this, she thought. Heck, she and Wanda had been to a few horse races in their time. She summoned up a picture of the jockeys—gosh, she loved those colorful neon outfits they wore—so, remembering how they did it, she stood up in the stirrups. Titus obviously hadn't been to any of the same races. He did some weird maneuver that had Becky grabbing onto the pommel even though Slate had told her not to. The desert tilted as she found herself hanging off Titus' side. "Whoa, boy!"

"Becky! I thought you knew how to ride?"

Damn! Slate would take that moment to turn around. Before she knew it, he'd ridden up beside her, pushed her to a sitting position, and with what she'd consider an impolite smirk on his face, said, "On a Western saddle you have to stay seated…"

"I had all the intention of staying seated, but mild-mannered Titus apparently had other ideas."

He turned away for a second. She knew it was to laugh. Heck, his shoulders were shaking. When he turned back she saw why he made such a good ranch manager. Obviously, he could regain his control under any circumstance—even outright hysteria. "Titus is a well-trained Western style horse. You confused him when you stood up in the stirrups. Use your legs like I had told you."

"Use your legs like I had told you," she mumbled to herself while she flashed him her best "dumb blonde" smile. She was becoming quite a good ventriloquist lately. "How kind of you to offer such good advice." *Gag.*

Slate stopped near a large boulder and dismounted. He probably figured Becky needed to get down before she fell and cracked something important. "We'll go over a few things from here."

He offered his hand to Becky as she pulled Titus up to Slate's horse, Cloud Dancer, as if parallel parking. Good thing Slate held her hand as she got down. Her legs gave out, landing her face-to-chest with Slate. For a second he pulled her even closer. He seemed to stifle a laugh as she pulled herself away. "Sorry."

With a smirk, he said, "No problem. Your legs sore?"

"No," she lied. Well, it wasn't actually a lie. Her legs really weren't sore—they were burning in the throws of pain. And she couldn't even think about how raw the area above her knees probably was since that's where the saddle had rubbed.

"Have a seat." He motioned to a nearby rock and took out a few Thermos bottles, handing one to her. "Never go out onto the ranges without water." He leaned closer, looking at her face. "And sunblock." He gently tipped her hat forward to shade her face.

She nearly spilled her water at that little gesture. Man, he came up with some doozies that took her by surprise. She really had to keep on her toes around this cowboy. Not only to protect her share of the will, but herself, too. She was noticing far too many things about him, and he was doing far too many nice little gestures like that. "I won't."

What did he have up his sleeve?

Slate settled on an opposite rock and started to tell her all about the ranch, its history for the past hundred years, and how Billy "the Kid" Bonney played a leading role in the cattlemen staged Lincoln County War in the 1870s. Becky sat mesmerized and realized why Slate loved this place so much. It was brimming with history, scenery, and activity. "I have to get back to my side of the ranch tomorrow so you'll be on your own."

His words struck a vein of terror in her. Sitting on this rock, listening to the folklore of Valley Del Sol, Becky felt as if she belonged here. It was comforting to hear Slate go on so proudly, but the thought of him being on his side of the property all day had her worried. What the heck was she going to do? And, could her ranch hands handle everything? Would her sheep survive? Would Grady be safe around this place? "I'm certain I'll do fine."

He gave her a dubious look and said, "I'd take a few days to help you, but I've got a problem to deal with."

She wanted to scream, "What could be more important than helping a no-nothing like me?" but, instead, she said, "I understand," in the sweetest, most un-characteristic voice she could manage.

"Irrigation problem. Water's a premium out here." Slate wiped at his face with his neckerchief, making her realize just how hot it was out here. Funny how the heat hadn't bothered her in her preoccupation with listening to him.

Suddenly he looked too aware of their nearness. Oh geez, she had to say something fast. For some reason, she didn't want Slate ignoring her for the next six months. "I'm certain I'll manage without your help." With every ounce of gumption she possessed, she forced a laugh. "I am a one hundred percent rancher now."

Slate leaned near, and she thought he was going to—actually she had no idea what he was going to do, but she watched his every move like an air traffic controller staring at a monitor with two planes heading nose to nose. "It takes a hell of a lot more than just owning a ranch to be a rancher." He wiped the droplet of sweat from her temple. She nearly fell off her rock. Not that he'd used any force. Actually, his touch was so gentle she barely felt it, but he had taken her by surprise—and Becky Chambers didn't much like surprises. She needed to be in control of her life and everything that went along with it, even wiping her own temple.

Oh great. This deception was harder to keep up then she thought it would be. Normally she would have pushed away his hand and told him to mind his own business, but she had to say, "I'm certain you are right, Slate. I only meant I feel like a rancher."

Surprisingly, that comment brought a deep chuckle from Slate. He ran his finger across her palm. "No, you don't feel anything like a rancher. I've been around them all my life, and no way in hell do you feel like one. You're too… soft."

"I didn't mean…." She forced a smile and calmed herself. "All your life, huh? You can't be that old…" She'd pegged him to be in his late thirties.

He looked out toward the east at a stretch of land that went on for miles. "Sometimes the years have a way of sneaking up on us. Fooling us. Taking away… things, people." With that he stood, offered her a hand and led them towards the waiting horses.

Becky's attention at watching Slate and wondering just how old he actually was shifted gears after his revelation about life. Obviously there were some skeletons in the Lawson's closet, too. "Is there something I can do…"

He looked at her as if to say, "Yeah, go back to were you came from," but instead he shook his head—making Becky feel as if that dangling carrot from Uncle Nate had just been yanked further away. Slate had much more at stake here than a place to live. He really wasn't going to let her ever have one square foot of this ranch. She'd have to make sure she earned enough money for at least a down payment on a house, take it, and run at the end of the six months. *Damn, Chambers, you've got to keep on your toes. By the shape of things, this rancher is one smart cookie.* She looked up and pulled her hair from her face.

One delicious, smart cookie—who could ruin your dream.

With muscles already protesting, Becky gaped at mammoth Titus and knew she really was the veritable "fish out of water," thinking she belonged on this ranch.

⋆

After an unproductive week of work, worrying what Becky was doing on her side of the ranch, Slate rode Cloud Dancer up a knoll the following weekend. He slowed beside a giant Saguaro and looked down. It proved to be a good vantage point for observing Becky and her ranching skills. Well, he should say lack of skills. If he had a nickel for every time she nearly fell off her horse, he'd be able to fund an irrigation project by himself. Right now, she managed to stay in her saddle, but she looked lost. He knew she must be looking for Dave to see what her men were doing. After a long drink of water from his Thermos, he tipped his hat forward and clicked his tongue. Cloud Dancer headed toward Becky.

"Getting pretty warm today," he called. Sure it was a stupid thing to mention in the desert during June, but it was the first thing that had popped into his head when he got closer and looked at her.

She had on red boots, a red hat, and matching lipstick. He led his horse closer to see her nails. Red with tiny cacti on each one.

Becky tipped her Stetson backward and ran her palm across her forehead. Tiny beads of sweat sparkled on her cheeks. He remembered once seeing a shade of onyx similar to the whiteness of her skin at an art gallery in Santa Fe. The stone formed a woman holding a baby. Watching Becky now, he wondered what kind of substitute mother she was. Hell, where'd that thought come from? What did it matter to him? Still, what he observed of her and Grady, she did a damn good job.

Becky leaned forward, eyes squinting. Her forehead wrinkled and, he thought, *with that expression, she was a far cry from the statue.*

"Slate, what the heck is wrong with that sheep?"

"Damn!" Slate flew off his horse and ran toward the sheep Becky was pointing toward.

"What's wrong?" she shouted.

"She's in labor, and it looks difficult."

The ewe darted between greasewood bushes, stopping only to paw storms of dust with her hoof. Slate tried to catch her, but she would bleat at him and bolt toward the bushes.

"Grab that bag off the back of my horse!" he shouted.

Becky hurriedly dismounted, falling onto the ground. Ignoring the dust on her pants, she wrapped Titus' rein around a tree branch and ran to Cloud Dancer. The animal whinnied and moved as if he were going to bolt. "Stand still," Becky commanded. She grabbed at the black leather bag and untied it as fast as her trembling fingers could manage. A flicker of pain ran along her finger. She looked to see a nail broken on her ring finger—the cactus cut in half. Yanking the bag down, she ran toward Slate who now had a hold of the ewe. "Now what? Oh geez, Slate, she looks in pain."

"Grab her legs..."

"What?" She wanted to shout, "You've got to be kidding." But she really wanted to be able to manage her side of the ranch, and if tipping a ewe was part of it she'd try. Plus, the poor thing looked so miserable.

"We need to get her down. Grab her front legs, I'll get the back. On three, we'll tip her."

"Oh damn!" Becky bent to take the sheep's legs, but the animal pulled away. Once Becky grabbed one leg, the ewe yanked it free before she could get the other. Slate had a hold of her back legs. "She's not going to bite me, is she?"

"Keep away from her mouth. Just grab!"

"I'm trying. Look, lady, we're here to help. Now you can co-operate…" She grabbed one leg. "Or you can make it hard on all of—oh damn—us. Stop it!" she shouted enough to startle the sheep and finally was able to grab both legs.

"Three!" Slate shouted.

The ewe tipped onto her side with a thud. "Oh gosh!" Becky rubbed the ewe's head. "I'm sorry, take a deep breath or something. What should she do, Slate? Help her!"

"I'm trying." He flung the contents of the bag on the ground. "Hold her down!"

Becky leaned as much into the soft wool of the sheep's back as she could, hoping she wasn't hurting her. Slate had a pair of rubber gloves on and was doing things… she didn't even want to see. The ewe's bleating sounded pained. Becky felt sorry for the animal, so she leaned forward and whispered in her ear. The sheep seemed to calm until Slate would yank or pull at something. "Mary had a little lamb, little lamb, I forgot the rest, please stay still, Mary had a little lamb…." Becky sang into the ewe's ear over and over. Slate's arms strained as he tugged. His hat fell off and sweat ran down his temples. Becky leaned enough to keep holding the sheep and wipe the droplets that bothered his eyes.

"Thanks," he managed between grunts. "Look, Becky!"

"Yuck, no!" she shouted, but she leaned far enough to see a tiny head emerging. "Holy sheep!"

Slate managed a laugh between tugs. "It's a boy!" He quickly placed the wet newborn under its mother's nose. Becky stopped singing and stared.

"I'll be damned. I've never seen anything born before." She collapsed into a pile of brambles, not caring if they tangled her hair. The mother ewe lazily nuzzled the newborn. How lucky the animal was, although she could have been more excited. Becky would be flying high if she had just given birth.

"Oh hell!" Slate yelled, breaking the precious moment. "Sit up and start singing again. There's another one!"

Becky fought the greenness that she knew preceded her passing out. Sucking in the hot desert air, she sat up and sang into the ewe's ear. The mother stilled, her fluffy body going limp beneath Becky's hold. "Slate? What's wrong with her?" Becky nudged at the ewe. She wasn't even paying attention to the lamb. "Slate!" she screamed.

"Damn, damn!" Slate tugged as another life emerged.

He placed it near the worn mother. "Get me those towels!" Slate sat back on his heels and yanked off his stained gloves.

"Don't stop. You can't give up yet." Becky leaned forward. She didn't realize her fists pounded against Slate's chest until she felt his firm grasp on her wrists. As his hold pulled her from hysterics, she looked down.

"Stop it, Becky!" he commanded. With a softer tone, he eased his grip. "I tried, Beck. I tried." He pulled her tightly as she collapsed against his chest. Sobs shook her body. He murmured into her ear, pushing her hair from her face. "They'll be all right."

She leaned back and weakly slapped his chest. "Everyone deserves a mother..." Slates lips captured her words. Salty tears mingled with his taste. "Even sheep...." She kissed between sobs. He pulled tighter. "It's just that... a mother shouldn't leave her children."

"They're sheep. They'll be all right."

Becky pulled backward and looked into Slate's eyes. "They would have all died if you hadn't come along."

He pulled her tightly and decided not to agree, although it was true. "Becky...." Slate kissed her forehead. His chest muscles tensed as she spoke.

"I am not cut out for… this." Tears ran along her cheek, running black streaks down her cheeks.

"Becky, I'm sorry. I know you tried."

A guttural laugh came from her throat. "You don't need to be sorry. You haven't seen me working. It's a sure thing you'll get the ranch."

Suddenly that thought didn't sound too appealing to him. He pulled her close and leaned forward. She looked up in time for him to press his lips against hers. Thank goodness she didn't pull away—not only because he'd never force himself on a woman, but damn it all, if it didn't feel good to kiss Becky Chambers. "Just enjoy the ranch for the rest of the time."

"I can't…" She leaned forward and kissed him, and kissed him again. Annoying bleats broke the air.

"We have to get the lambs, Beck, although I don't want to stop." Slate wiped her tears with his neckerchief.

She knew she was covered in mud from the dust and tears. His boots and jeans were soaked in dust, too. "We're are a mess, Lawson."

He pulled her to stand. "Come on."

Slate balanced one lamb across her horse. "Now ride easy so this little guy doesn't fall off. I'll take the other and we'll cut across the fields."

Becky touched his hand. "What about…." She looked at the mother.

"I'll send one of your hands out to get her."

"Will he bury her?"

He paused as if he didn't want to explain it. "No, otherwise wild predators like a coyote will dig it up."

Becky sighed. She turned Titus with a gentle tug. "Slate, they need names."

"What? Oh, sure." He laughed. "Any suggestions?" He'd mounted Cloud Dancer, and they started down the path toward the shortcut.

Becky held the fluffy lamb that wiggled too much with one hand and the reins with the other. Just what she needed with her riding skills. "Is mine a boy or girl?"

"Girl," he called over his shoulder.

"Oh, so there's one of each. Okay, I never had a pet as a kid… so give me a few minutes."

He laughed. "Ride's gonna take longer than that…"

"Jack and Jill!" she shouted.

Slate's chuckle blended with the bleating of the lambs. "I love it!" He pulled to a stop and turned toward her. "Will you help me raise them?" he asked softly.

It wasn't often Becky Chambers was at a loss for words. But she managed a nod, looking at Slate through blurry vision.

Back in the barn, the two lambs pranced around, their fluffy coats white after Slate had cleaned them. "What an improvement, guys," Becky said.

Slate handed her a large milk bottle with a giant red rubber nipple. "Have a go at it."

Becky looked as if he held a snake. "I don't know what to do. I mean… what if I choke them?"

He laughed. "They'll drink so fast they won't have time to choke. Seriously, hold it high and pull it out every once in a while so their stomachs don't get filled with air."

She grabbed the bottle. "Oh great. A lamb with gas. Come here, Jack." She sucked in air for emphasis. "Look, um, nice and warm…" She turned toward Slate who stood watching and grinning. "What the heck's in this stuff?"

"Goat's milk."

"Geez, isn't that gonna confuse them? I mean sheep drinking goat's milk? Aren't they gonna be facing years of therapy…?"

He flung a handful of hay toward her. "Just feed them!"

Becky looked down into the trusting brown eyes of Jack as he guzzled and blubbered. Goat's milk covered his mouth, nose, and dripped from his chin onto her red boot. "Hey, careful, buddy."

After the two downed their meal in record time, they romped around Becky and Slate's feet. Still somewhat unsteady, the lambs would collapse into a bale of hay, then promptly stand and dance about. Becky's heart swelled with the pride she imagined how a parent felt—even if only a surrogate one. Watching Grady made her feel the same way.

Slate lifted up Jill—at least it looked like her. The lambs had similar coloring except Jill had a tiny beige spot on her forehead. He held her, cooing into her ear. Amazingly, she calmed as if mesmerized by Slate. Becky admitted to herself that he had the same effect on her. A wonderful tenderness contrasted with his rugged appearance. He was truly a caring person.

After the lambs were safely penned in the barn, Becky and Slate went into the house to clean up. During dinner, she told him she was giving up ranching, and he could take all the sheep to his side. Thank goodness he looked as if he genuinely felt bad and didn't rib her or say, "I told you so." Instead, he said, "Fine. Just enjoy your time here with Grady. Not everyone is cut out for ranching."

"No, that's true. But I am not throwing in the towel either."

He looked up from his fried chicken. "Meaning?"

Oh boy. Explaining this was going to test her acting abilities to the limits. She'd never mentioned that she had a contingency plan in case her "ranching" didn't pan out. But she did. So, she said, "I'm going to make my side of the property… a dude ranch."

He set his chicken down with deliberation. Then, he looked Becky in the eye. "What the hell are you talking about?" The fire burning in his eyes was a good indication that he didn't like her idea very much.

Swallowing the urge to yell that she could damn well do what she pleased with her side of the property, she summoned every ounce of "blondness" and said, "A dude ranch. With horses, a chuck wagon, and a bunkhouse. You know, one that city-folk can come to who have never…"

"I know damn well what a dude ranch is!"

"Oh good, that saves me from a detailed explanation," she continued, despite him glaring at her. "I think they'll love it out here. People who have never seen the desert or rode a horse can pretend... they can pretend they're in the Old West—or a John Wayne flick... er... movie!" She managed a giggle. "It is going to be such fun! I even get to keep the name, Sidewinder Valley; Sidewinder Valley Dude Ranch." Watching Slate speak with his lips clenched so tightly, she bit back a laugh.

Even when he was livid, he looked adorable.

"How the hell are you going to make a dude ranch?"

Becky nearly batted her eyelashes at Slate, but his glare kept her theatrics at a minimum. She smiled. "Do you mean physically?" Slate growled, but she continued, "Oh, well, I have enough money from your uncle to make some bunkhouses out of those barns to the west. They are on my side of the property, aren't they?"

Slate stared at her for a minute—a very long minute. "Yes." Hell, he couldn't think straight. Her plan threw him. He thought she was going to say she'd just live here until her six months was up. But a damned dude ranch! Well, now he knew she'd go through her inheritance quickly. What on earth did she know about running a dude ranch? He forced his blood pressure to calm with a few deep breaths.

Slate reminded himself that the rest of the six months would fly by, until he looked at Becky. She sat with her legs crossed at the knees, a spoon clicking on her lips, and her baby blue eyes glaring at him. Maybe if he hadn't secluded himself on this ranch, he would be a better judge of women. Now he was merely confused and angry at this whole damned situation that got worse every minute. She uncrossed her legs as if she knew how it'd affect him. He cursed at himself as flames tickled at him inside. This physical desire for sweet Becky had to stop.

He hadn't seen the dude ranch thing coming, and it infuriated him. Becky Chambers sure made a different first impression. Here he thought she'd be this sweet, quiet "roommate" until her time passed at Valley Del Sol, and then she'd leave. But now, confusion filled him. She sure didn't look like any businesswoman, so he'd guessed she would have been happy riding horses and basking in the sun. That'd teach him to judge a woman by her looks. Come to think of it, he didn't have much experience in that area. All the women he'd ever dated could have been clones. All just like models, tall and slender, and, oh shoot, all had been brunettes. No wonder he had such a hard time figuring out golden haired Becky.

"At least let me suggest a few investments with some of your money so you don't use it all on your… new idea," Slate said.

"Thank you. That is a good idea." Okay, so his suggestion insinuated that she'd blow all her money, but his idea wasn't a bad one. She'd never had anyone give her financial advice before.

He hated to see her throw away her inheritance, but his life had come to a standstill from the day the will was read. He couldn't concentrate on his ranching, and that ate away at him. If only he could turn time back a few weeks. Uncle Nate would still be alive, and things would be back to usual. Not an enviable life, but it was the life he'd grown comfortable with. It protected his heart, even though Uncle Nate had different ideas about Slate's life. He looked up at Becky nibbling on a chicken wing—not a care in the world.

No, if he could turn back time, he would never have met Becky Chambers.

Chapter 4

Becky shook Hank Wentworth's hand as if she pumped a well. "The ranch came out great, Hank. I can't wait for my first guests to arrive!" Over her shoulder, she looked for a sign of Slate. Once she saw the coast was clear, she danced circles around Hank.

"Great doing business with you, Becky. Now you let me know about the lake. Won't take but a few days to put the beach in."

She stopped dancing. The lake. The *beach*. Oh geez, she'd almost forgotten. Several times she'd been tempted to tell Hank to go ahead and make a beach on her side of the lake, but she remembered Slate's blowup on the first day she'd met him. Making a beach was permanent. Although she had every confidence that she'd succeed in winning the stipulations of the will, she hesitated on the lake issue. After all, Slate did own half of those rights, whatever they were. "I'll let you know. In the meantime, the guests will be busy enough."

"What'd you have in store?"

"I've hired several cowboys..."

Hank snickered.

"Well, I call them that. I mean they look so authentic and one even cooks real chuck wagon food! Something called blanket steaks, corned tomatoes, barbecue, and sourdough biscuits baked on the open fire. They'll teach riding, roping, and we'll have campfires..."

"Whoa! Sounds great, Becky. I wish you the best."

"Thanks." She followed Hank to his truck. "I will let you know about the beach." Wiping her brow, she smiled. "It would be nice for my guests to be able to take a dip now and then."

He nodded and shut the door. Becky laughed at his "Hanging

Hank" license plate as he drove off. She walked toward the lake. The sun glistened on the calm surface, blinding her vision. Yucca plants decorated the perimeter, spouting white flowers like a waterfall. Birds darted to the surface snatching a quick sip. She tried to figure out about where the halfway mark would be. Her guests could even do some boating. She made a mental note to check into the price of used canoes and rowboats.

Then she looked up.

Fluffy white bodies dotted the grazing fields across the other side. What little she knew of sheep, she knew they needed water. The lake's water. Slate would explode like a geyser if she interfered with his sheep.

But what could a little beach hurt?

★

"Are you crazy, Becky Chambers?" Slate's eyes enlarged like the day he'd learned of the codicil to Nate's will.

Becky swallowed and summoned the sweetest smile she could manage instead of hoisting the nearby living room lamp and flinging it at him. No, she wasn't crazy. She was a real businesswoman.

"Oh my, Slate. That beet color rising up your neck can't be too good for your blood pressure." She laughed.

Slate glared. "You can't touch the lake, Becky. I need it for irrigation for the corn and the sheep."

Sounds like you're "touching" the lake, buddy. Holding any sarcastic comments inside, she counted to ten and said, "But I thought I owned half of..."

"*That* is a temporary situation. In a few months you'll be..."

Had she been here only a few months? She couldn't even remember the color of her bedroom in her Alamogordo apartment. This was the first time she ever felt as if she had a real home. "I'll be what, Slate?" She hadn't meant for her voice to crack like that.

He looked at her with something close to a smile. Only his lips seemed to want to frown. "Look, I mean... I didn't put up any fuss over your plans..."

She decided against mentioning the iced tea on her new white blouse incident.

"I've been trying to be amicable about this situation, Becky."

"And I do appreciate it. Really I do. But my guests..."

"Guests." He huffed.

"As I was saying. They need some recreational activities, and it gets so hot here, I thought swimming is a must."

"Build a pool."

"A pool? I hadn't thought of that, and..."

"Good, then it's settled. No disturbance of the lake."

Oh geez, her "blondness" was slipping! Blood boiled inside her veins causing a searing pain to jab at her temples. The real Becky Chambers fought to get out of this stupid charade. Even counting to ten didn't help, heck, she could count to a million and her temper wouldn't cool off. A damned pool! "I never agreed to that. A pool is expensive. I mean, I do *own* half of the lake..."

"Temporarily."

If he'd yelled the word, it would have been much easier to argue about. But the soft, whispered tone, unmistakably chosen on purpose, caught her off guard, and as if Attorney Greeson sat on the couch behind Slate, the threat of contesting the will came loud and clear to Becky. No one ever accused her of missing the obvious.

He stepped so near, she could feel his breath on her cheek. She looked into his eyes as if he'd hypnotized her. "I'll check on the price of a... pool," she heard herself say. Holy crumb, how'd he managed that?

"Good." He brushed a few strands of hair from her forehead. "I'm sorry I lost my temper. It's just... this place means a lot to me."

That brick didn't have to hit her in the head either. From the day she had arrived, she could tell Slate loved Valley Del Sol. No, not just loved it—breathed it, lived it, actually, it bordered on an obsession. Anyone who spent so much time working his ranch when he probably had the money to hire a hand to ride his horse for him, was definitely driven. But what drove Slate Lawson? No one ever accused her of keeping her nose out of other's business either, so she asked, "Why is that, Slate?"

He stopped, probably not even aware of his finger lingering on her cheek.

She sure knew exactly where he touched. Her skin sizzled like one of Rosa's fried chimichangas. As if hot oil spilled through her veins, the heat scorched her insides, not unlike the pleasure one enjoys from an authentic Mexican meal. Hot and spicy. Oh damn, why couldn't she have inherited half the ranch with some old geezer? Someone she could think clearly around. Someone who didn't smell so good. She looked up. Geez, someone who had a big nose and no teeth.

He pulled his hand back and looked above Becky's head. As if seeing something that wasn't there, he said, "I love ranching. Guess I was born that way."

What a lie. She'd love to call him on it, but her darn body had her too preoccupied. Hot and spicy had her juices flowing. Nodding as if she accepted his explanation, she turned. "I'm... er... going to check on a few things for opening day."

Before she could make a clean getaway, Slate touched her shoulder. The slight pressure of his hand sent a warmth through her shirt. Oh geez, now even trying to lie could get tough. Turning around, she wiggled loose.

"When is it?" he asked.

"What?" How could a perfectly good mind turn to guacamole from merely looking into sparkling emerald eyes?

Slate laughed. "Your opening. When are your first... guests arriving?"

She squinted at him. "You're not planning any welcome booby-traps are you?"

His chuckle came from deep inside, all the way down to those rock hard abdominal muscles, just below the firm chest where the wisps of brown hair....

"Seriously, Becky, are you ready to open soon?"

"A week from tomorrow." She heaved a sigh as if a building was lifted from her shoulders. Hearing the words out loud made it real. Her dude ranch was opening soon. "Saturday!" she shouted.

Slate laughed and leaned forward. It couldn't have taken much thought, but when he planted the kiss—okay, a tiny peck on her forehead—she couldn't decide which made her feel like floating out of the room, her impending opening or the little kiss.

★

Becky read and reread her guest list over a hundred times. She'd made a great office space in the corner of her room, heck, there was enough room in the bedroom for a small family to live. Sitting near the desk, she looked at the list one more time.

The money she'd spent on advertising had paid off. She had a full house for opening day and figured word of mouth would take care of the rest. Wanda had relied on it for her business and did great. Counting on word of mouth made it a little easier to spend the precious money for the brochures and a few inexpensive newspaper ads. Thank goodness Wanda had connections all the way to New York. How many cousins could one woman have? She smiled to herself. It didn't matter, since Wanda willingly gave Becky her Christmas card list and addresses to send her brochures out. Five of the couples were coming thanks to Wanda.

The next two weeks were full, and she figured by the third week word from the other's would spread. A flutter in her stomach reminded her that she wasn't the nervous type—it had to be excitement. *That* she was full of.

"Señorita Beecky?"

A light tap sounded on her door. She loved the way Rosa called her "Beecky." She turned toward the door. "Come on in."

"A letter, how you say, registered, came for you. You have to sign speedy so mailman can go. He don't like waiting too long." She held out an official looking white envelope.

"Oh sure." Becky signed where Rosa pointed and took the envelope, handing Rosa the section to return to the impatient postman. "Thanks, Rosa." Before the door shut behind the housekeeper, Becky looked at the return address and her heart slammed into her chest.

What were the odds Attorney Greeson only wanted to wish her the best of luck for opening day? She cursed her shaking fingers as she ripped open the letter from Slate's lawyer. The words appeared wavy as her vision blurred with anger. She made out the words "partition" wherein both parties agree to divide the parcel in two. The word "suggest" became clear, followed by... "water not to be disturbed." The kindly old attorney wrote as tactfully as he could that it proved more difficult to cut the boundaries of a lake. If Becky could read between the lines she knew that he was suggesting she keep her hands off the lake.

Why the heck did lawyers have to call people "parties?" It wasn't any party getting this letter.

She slumped onto the rounded bed. Dealing with rejection had become second nature to her, but a new wound tore into her heart. A wound of deception. Slate couldn't have just taken her word that she'd wait on the lake issue—no, he had to make it legal, as if he didn't trust her. That's what hurt the most.

She'd never get away from that old pain of people judging her by her outward appearance.

Days ago she had decided she wouldn't touch the lake. She'd never do anything to hurt Slate. If only *he* had trusted her.

★

"Welcome!" Becky was having a ball on her opening day. At least her new business was a salve to sooth the hurt caused by Slate. As each car drove up and unloaded her guests, more tingles of excitement jolted her. Dave Palmer, her hired hand who drove to the airport in El Paso to pick up the guests, unloaded suitcases from the back of the old red Chevy van she'd gotten for a steal.

"Looks like your business is starting out well," Slate said.

Becky swung around to come face-to-nose with Slate's Appaloosa. Shielding her eyes from the sun, she looked up. "We have a full house this week."

Slate slid down and pulled his riding gloves off. Calluses covered his palms. Becky wondered why someone with the finances Slate obviously had, did any manual labor. Leather chaps covered his usual worn jeans, but she knew exactly what firm muscles hid beneath. His black Stetson hung at the right angle for the sun to glint on his straight white teeth. A smug little dimple threatened to form on both cheeks. He smelled like sweat, masculine and heady. Geez, he looked as if he'd rode off an old rerun of "Rawhide." She ran her tongue across her lips. The taste of lemon lipstick jolted her thoughts from Slate for a second. But only for a second.

He'd drawn a "line in the sand" between them with the recent letter from the attorney.

"I'm glad things are going well for you, Becky."

She caught his warm smile and knew he was trying to cover up what he'd done. "Thank you, Slate. Well, I need to join my guests at the welcome reception. Curley, that's my cook, has made a special punch, and I need to make sure everyone can drink tequila."

Slate laughed. He remained holding the rein of his horse.

"I guess you need to check on your sheep or something." She turned to see a crowd gathering near the tables.

"I imagine they'll survive while I ease my thirst."

She studied this man who fate, and Uncle Nate, had caused to become her rival. He wasn't a bad guy, actually, she admitted, Slate was a decent man. Still, they had a common goal and only one could win. With the water issue in the front of her mind, she decided that she better pretend all was well between them. If he could manage that letter from the attorney, what else was he capable of?

And her so close to succeeding once in her life.

"Thirsty are you?"

"Dry as the proverbial desert we live on." Slate heard himself speak but didn't know who was more surprised—him or Becky. Her blue eyes widened, and a smile formed across her—where they yellow?—lips. She tapped a fingernail on her tooth, and he leaned closer to see tiny cacti on the shiny canary surface.

"Come on." She grabbed his arm and pulled him toward the crowd.

The afternoon couldn't have gone better. Becky had a knack for remembering all the guests' names, and that was only one of her qualities that impressed Slate. She flitted around like a starving hummingbird, telling each guest all the details of the surrounding area. He smiled as she pointed out every Saguaro, prickly pear cactus, and the numerous wildflowers that grew around the patio near her bunkhouses. She'd done a damn good job making her dude ranch, and he allowed himself a feeling of pride. After all, what could it hurt to let her be happy for the remaining months of the will? He reminded himself that she'd enjoy her time here, run out of money, and close up her little ranch. It wouldn't take much to get the entire place back in order. His hands would love the new bunkhouses she'd had built for her guests.

He didn't blame her for their situation.

She giggled.

Nope, he couldn't blame her at all.

★

After Sidewinder Valley Dude Ranch had been in business for several weeks, Becky stood near the barn watching one of the hands taking a group of guests out on a horseback ride to the desert. Her feet hurt, her hands hurt—heck, her hair hurt—from working so hard to make everyone happy. But her business seemed to be succeeding. Only a few times did she catch one or two guests sitting around as if bored. After the group faded into the greasewood bushes behind the barn, she went in search of Dave.

"Hey, Dave," she called out as the ranch hand shoved a bale of hay into the corral.

"Ma'am."

She still couldn't get over being called "ma'am" or the way all the men, including Slate, tipped their hats toward her. It was so Western. "Look, Dave. There is something I'm going to ask you to do, and you can say no. Your Christmas bonus won't be affected."

He squinted at her from beneath his hat, but chuckled. "Okay, shoot." Leaning against the handle of the pitchfork, he stuck a piece of hay into his mouth.

"Well, I really don't know how to… I mean I did grow up around here, but not on a ranch, you see. So, my riding…"

"Why, Miss Chambers, you ain't saying you've never rode?"

"No, Dave." She leaned forward to whisper. "I'm saying I've been *on* a horse… but only since coming here. I'm not experienced by any means. My guests can't know that."

He slapped his hands and produced what Becky would call a guffaw.

"Would you teach me? You can refuse…"

"Come on, little lady." He gently took her elbow and guided her toward the barn.

Becky's heart soared at the thought. She was going to learn to ride a horse the right way. Wanda would drop her false teeth!

"Now let me see which one of these ladies will be the most gentle."

Becky shoved her hand into her pocket and pulled out a handful of sugar packets. She had come prepared. Too bad she hadn't been when she rode Titus. Up until now, she'd avoided riding but recently guests where beginning to notice.

Dave led a white horse, which looked extremely tall, out of the stall. Well, at least she'd look good. The horse matched her hat, and luckily she'd worn her white blouse with the silver bolo tie.

As Dave fiddled with a saddle, Becky leaned forward with a handful of the sugar. "I'll make a deal with you,…" She bent over to look under the horse's back end. "…girl. You treat me right—that is no roughhousing—and there'll be a lifetime of sugar in store for you." The horse's wet tongue lapped across her opened palm. "Oh yuck!"

"She's all set, ma'am."

Becky followed Dave outside, her legs wobbling ever so slightly. When she mounted what Dave called the gelding—but she decided to name Sugar—Becky felt like a real lady rancher. He held the checkrein and guided the horse around the large corral several times. Now her knuckles matched the horse.

Sugar whinnied, startling Becky, but she held tight so as not to miss a word of Dave's instructions. He led the horse around as if they were at the carnival. Excitement bubbled inside Becky. She wanted to snatch the reins from Dave, shout out loud, and tear out of the corral to ride into the desert.

After several more times around, Dave asked, "Ready to try by yourself?"

Ready? She nearly bounced off in excitement. The real Becky surged forth. There was no need for her "dumb blonde" routine now. "Let'r go, Davy!" *How cool*!

She gently pulled the rein while making the clucking sound Dave had instructed her to do. Sugar moved. She started a slow walk, and Becky's insides reeled like a kid on her first bike ride. "I'm doing it! Becky Chambers is riding a horse!"

"You're doing fine, ma'am. Now not too fast till you get the hang of it," he cautioned.

Becky gave Sugar a nudge with her heel. Wasn't that what they did in the movies? The horse must have seen the same flick. Sugar sprinted or whatever you called it when a horse went faster than a canter. "This is great!" Becky held the reins tightly and bounced along. The excitement had to parallel her first ride on the roller coaster at Six Flags.

Dave jumped out of the way as Sugar nearly missed his foot. He leapt onto the fence rail. Becky whooped and hollered when she passed. A few times she thought she'd end up at Dave's feet, but she learned to tilt to the other side. It wasn't much different from riding the back of a Harley.

"Yee ha!" She zoomed past a startled Dave. It was wonderful to be herself.

Sugar sped up.

Becky bounced past Dave as he tilted his hat toward her. "Eat your heart out, Annie Oakley!"

The horse made a quick turn to the left. "Whoa Nelly!" Becky shouted. Wind slapped at her face. The fresh country air of the barns stung her nose. She'd never had this much fun before. It felt as if someone had released her personality from the prison it had been locked in since meeting Slate. The horse galloped around the corral as if on a track. By now Dave had his hat off and whooped and hollered along with her, occasionally he shouted for her to hold tight and hang on.

"Geronimo!" she shouted, and flung her hat into the air. Wildness bubbled out of her like beer from a shaken can of Coors. Without a thought, she shoved her heels into the horse's sides. Sugar bolted as if stuck by a hot branding iron. Becky's hands slipped. She reached for the horse's neck, but it felt as if it had been covered in butter. Her hands slid off. Her new yellow boots flashed above her head as her body careened to the ground.

"Shoooooooot!"

Sandy soil broke her fall. She heard Dave yelling behind her, but needed to unscramble her brains before she could comprehend what just happened. Shutting her eyes, she sucked in a breath before opening them… to look upward.

Slate glared down at her from his perch on the fence.

Chapter 5

"Geez, I hope I have a concussion and this is a hallucination," Becky mumbled as she looked up at the vision of Slate careening toward her.

He leaned to within inches of her face as if to emphasize it was him. "Are you all right? Don't try to move. Should I get an ambulance? Where does it hurt? Anything fractured...?"

Becky squinted toward him. Her body could have been broken into tiny pieces and all she could think about was... he saw the *real* me. She eased herself to sit, although she had no idea her legs were capable of folding as they just had been. "I'm fine. It was just a little fall."

"Little? Becky, I thought you were going to, I mean, you could have broken something like your neck. Your arms and legs flew, well, it looked like...." He wrapped his arms around her as if she were made of glass. "That horse could have stepped.... Are you sure I shouldn't call a doctor?"

This was no time for her hormones to surge at Slate's embrace, fragile though it was. But they did darn it, and she consciously allowed them to send pleasure to her brain. It was either that or feel every muscle in her body screaming in pain. She'd better reassure Slate before he had the National Guard called out.

"I'm a little stiff, but..." She groaned against her will. "I don't think anything is broken—put me down!"

"I'm taking you into the house. Unless you have x-ray vision, how can you be so sure nothing is broken?"

"I can't, but maybe if I... Did that yucca just sway?" Suddenly a haze of green painted the desert setting, followed by a cloud of... It was too early for nighttime yet darkness snatched the scenery away.

"Beck? Becky?" Slate's voice seemed to come from a distance. Why didn't he get closer so she could hear? Was he chanting? No, that sounded like a female's voice.... Her eyelids fluttered, she peered out to see Rosa teetering back and forth, chanting something in Spanish, and that she was lying on the bed in her room. All Becky could recognize was an occasional "Oh *Dios*" and a few "Señorita Beekys. A cool cloth rubbed across her forehead, and she looked to see that Slate held it as he stood above her. A worried look covered his eyes.

"Hey, we thought we'd lost you." He smiled.

"Just a quick trip to Oz." She squinted toward him. "Is that you Uncle Henry?"

Slate shook his head. "I'm glad to see you've got your sense of humor back. I… never knew you had such a good one."

She shuddered beneath the mound of blankets he'd obviously covered her with. It all came flooding back.

Her charade was over.

"Look, Slate. I didn't mean to…"

His finger touched her lips. "Get some rest."

"I thought I was just conked out for awhile. I'm not tired." She strained to sit and collapsed like a crumpled rag doll.

"Oh *Dios*." Rosa made the sign of the cross, making Becky wonder if she wasn't hurt worst then she thought. Isn't that what Rosa said when she spoke of the dead?

"I'm really fine." She managed to sit with Slate's arm around her. Inhaling his heady scent, she sighed and looked around at the room she called home for some time now. A knot twisted inside her already sore gut. *I'm going to be thrown out on my keister by morning.*

"Rosa, would you please get Becky some iced tea?"

The housekeeper made one final sign of the cross and left.

Slate smiled. "She needed something to keep her busy. She was so worried, I'm not even sure what she was mumbling."

Becky laughed. Geez, her entire body hurt. "Rosa's a doll." But she wished she hadn't left. At least with Rosa in the room Slate might not bring up the subject of her deception.

"I've never seen you enjoy yourself like that, Becky."

Oh well, might as well get it over with. "How much did you see?"

"Let me think." He tapped a finger to his tooth exactly as she did. "Oh yeah, I came to the fence around the first 'yee ha.'"

"Oh geez." Becky tried to summon every logical thought from her mangled brain. Some electrical signals must have shorted, since she couldn't think of how to wiggle her way out of this,one. Slate glared at her. There seemed to be a sparkle in his eyes where she'd expected a flame of anger. "I can explain."

He sat next to her. Ordinarily her heart would have leapt into her throat at the thought of sitting on this Olympic-size bed with the handsome cowboy, but she'd been found out, and one thing Becky Chambers always did was fess up. Sucking in enough air for the entire explanation, she pushed past him and stood. "I thought if you knew the real me...."

His eyes narrowed. "Are you a convicted felon?"

"No! I'm..."

"A drug dealer?"

"Never! If you'd let me..."

He tilted his head. "Murderer?"

"Slate! How could you think...?"

"I don't, Becky, so why did you feel you needed to deceive me?"

Damn, how'd he manage to look so pitiful. He'd be so much easier to deal with if he were spitting' mad. He looked hurt mixed in with a bit, no, a lot of anger. "I thought..." She sucked in a needed breath. "I thought you'd contest the will."

"Why? What would give me just cause?"

She hated his use of a legal term. Maybe he was trying to confuse her. "If what you mean by 'just cause' is why did I act like a "dumb blonde,' then it's because, well, I didn't start out that way, but when you blew up like you did the day we met—it was either that or hurl one of Attorney Greeson's fancy knick-knacks at you." She couldn't tell him how she feared losing a chance at her dream.

The only thing she hated worse than admitting fear was… that she feared anything to begin with.

"I'm not exactly some socialite—and when you called me… you did call me a damned hairdresser…"

"Oh God, I'm sorry, Becky. I've always had a short fuse, but I never hold a grudge." He pulled her near. "I had no right to insult you like that. Uncle Nate had his reasons for… doing what he did. I'm sorry my temper got the best of me." He leaned so near, Becky saw her reflection in his eyes. This time, it didn't scare her. "You have every legal right to fulfill the terms of the will."

Legal right? He believed that? So he never had any intentions of contesting the will? He had her running scared and pretending to be Miss Goody-two-shoes for nothing. If he didn't look so adorable, she'd wallop him, but she didn't have a chance. Slate pulled her too near—near enough to look into her eyes and melt her flame-retardant socks. Her arms scrunched into his solid chest. Before she had time to breathe, his lips brushed across hers. "Can I kiss the *real* Becky Chambers?" he whispered.

"No," she murmured. He loosened enough so she could free her hands and wrap them around his neck. "*She'll* do the kissing."

She shoved his black Stetson to the floor, tilting her head so their lips met without any interference. She pulled back enough to look at him, give him a chance to run for it. The look of surprise in Slate's eyes immediately transformed into, hm, sensuality is the word that came to mind. He moaned. She kissed harder. His lips parted, she tickled his teeth with her tongue. Their tongues met, touching, feeling, dancing inside each other's mouth.

A warmth surging from her head to her toes masked every ounce of discomfort. Her heart beat a melodic rhythm as if Carly Simon sang "Anticipation" in her ear. When she ran her fingers through Slate's hair, his moan sent a jolt of giddiness throughout her, and she knew falling on her head had nothing to do with it.

"Um, lemon," he whispered.

She ran her tongue across her lips and nodded.

Slate took the lead this time, nuzzling behind Becky's ear. Strands of his hair danced about in her sigh. He placed his hands firmly at the small of her back. Perhaps he worried she might pass out again. She might. But it wouldn't be because Sugar had thrown her. When she inhaled, she shut her eyes to lock Slate's scent into her memory. The mixture of man, dust, and a hint of spicy cologne blended into his distinct fragrance. If she could bottle it, she'd make a fortune.

Slate whispered near her ear, "Are you okay?"

When the exciting tickle eased enough for her to comprehend what he'd asked, she mumbled, "Hell, yes." It felt so good to be herself, as if some door blew open and Becky Chambers flew out. No more pretending, no more sitting up straight as if a rod had been glued to her spine. Oh, it felt good, but not nearly as good as Slate's hands working their way up her back with the slightest of pressure.

It touched her that he worried about her even now. Genuine concern filled his eyes, and a tiny crease wrinkled into his forehead as if he had to access her condition for himself. She'd never felt that concern from a man before, and a feeling born of caring arose insider her. Not that she wasn't experienced. In the days of her wild youth, she'd let her body be used in hopes of finding someone who cared for her. *Her*, Becky Chambers. Not just a female body, until she wised-up and stayed celibate. But she'd never felt the consideration she longed for—until now.

Her body relaxed as if Slate had the power to turn off a switch that contracted her muscles. When her knees weakened, he tightened his hold, pulling her body tightly against him. She felt his heart beat against her. She felt his chest, firm and warm. She felt him press into her. Damn, every bit of Slate Lawson felt good.

With a gentle touch, he traced the frame of her face. Gliding his hand down her cheeks, beneath her chin, and up to her other cheek, he ignited a heat beneath her skin. She knew she glowed like a flame of fire.

"Do you need to sit?" he asked.

She looked at the Olympic-size bed. Even if her bones turned to mush, she couldn't admit it. If they sat, then they'd lie down, then.... He'd only learned of her deception, she needed to know he really accepted her for herself. The soft white comforter looked too tempting. Glancing at Slate, she could see the desire in his eyes. Not that she wouldn't want to but.... "I'm fine."

He followed her words with a kiss of acceptance. Her toes wiggled inside her socks, and she realized Slate must have removed her boots earlier. He kissed her again, and she rocked backwards. He caught her in a firm embrace.

"I think you need to lie down."

"But..." He silenced her words with a touch, the roughness of his skin hesitant against her lips. With his free hand, he brushed her hair behind her ears. Usually she didn't let anyone touch her hair, but... she'd make this exception. At the bed, he eased her down. Her heart sped so fast, she thought she would lose consciousness. Before she could expound on why they couldn't take their actions any further, Slate lifted the Navajo blanket that had fallen to the floor and covered her. He leaned over, placing a feather of a kiss on her forehead, then straightened.

Although she knew he should leave, she knew her eyes couldn't hide her confusion and wanting, so she turned toward the window.

"You rest. I'll see where Rosa is with that iced tea."

Turning back, she smiled. "Thanks, Slate."

He nodded, then headed toward the door. Without a word, he lifted the blouse and jeans she'd worn yesterday from the floor and carefully put them on the back of a chair. She wished she'd learned to be neater. Slate smiled one more time and walked out the door, obviously to get her a glass of that marvelous iced tea that seemed to solve the awkwardness of the situation for her.

Then a thought struck her. Did he give in too easy? Had his

anger evaporated too fast?

What was Slate Lawson up to?

No matter how good she felt right now, she wouldn't take her eyes off of him.

★

Slate shook his head. Sitting atop his horse, he watched Becky playing with some children in the corral. Obviously, she'd recovered from her fall the other day. Damn, he should be angry that she managed to deceive him, but he wasn't. Actually, he felt relieved that she wasn't like all the women of his past. She'd brought a change into his life—and he liked it.

He smiled when he looked at her. She had an area sectioned off for a petting zoo, but he wasn't sure for whom—her or the guest's kids. Each time a baby goat would prance about, Becky would squeal louder than the two girls, who looked about five years old, standing near her. Jack and Jill loved it too and played along. A calf nuzzled against Becky's leg, and she rubbed its head briskly as if it were a fluffy golden retriever. A tenderness touched him, knowing she must like kids, too.

But the thing that had him shake his head in wonder again, was her clothes. Ever since his accidental "discovery" of Becky, she'd taken to dressing more like, well, he guessed, herself. Today she wore boots redder than the tile roof. A vest matched the same color with a giant green chili pepper embossed on the back. Her shorts were denim, and he wondered if the kid's parents had any problems with the skimpy length. He certainly didn't as he noticed the creamy skin of her thighs. Only she could get away with an outfit like that.

He eased his horse closer to see her nails. An irresistible obsession with her fancy nails had taken hold of him. If he'd met her in a bar somewhere, he'd be polite enough but never ask for her number. Now he'd learned not to judge a book by its cover—or a Becky by her appearance.

He chuckled, looking at her nails. Alternating red and green.

Yep, her nail polish matched her outfit. He wondered how she didn't break them as she moved outside the corral with the kids and swung one of the girls in a circle as the child giggled in delight. Maybe her nails weren't real. That made more sense, but looking at her jumping over a rope the two kids held, he felt sure they were.

She sure as heck was real. No one could accuse Becky of being inhibited or hiding her feelings. The only thing he had to find out was—how determined to succeed was she?

Because no matter how things were going now, his ranch was still a stake.

Slate turned his horse and rode out toward the lake. The sun burned hot as usual, so he dismounted and undid his neckerchief. Bending to soak it in the water, he noticed a few of Becky's female guests sitting on boulders near a cluster of greasewood bushes. They looked bored. Wringing out the neckerchief, he wiped the back of his neck, forehead, and face, then tied it back on.

With a friendly wave, he stepped forward. "Ladies." He tipped his hat toward them.

They perked up and smiled. "Hello," said one in a pink outfit.

"Hi," purred the other.

"Too hot for you out here?" Slate asked.

The one in pink sighed. "It's really dry, so it's not too bad. We're just sitting here, doing nothing."

Doing nothing? A pang of worry stabbed at Slate's gut. If these guests were bored, what about all the others? Would word spread and ruin Becky's business? "Nothin' to do with all that goes on at the dude ranch?"

"Well we've done the tours, petted the animals, ate until our…" She giggled. "…our pants are getting snug."

He smiled. "It doesn't show. Well, I'll bet if you ask Ms. Chambers, she could find something for you to do. She's usually full of great ideas." He mounted his horse and tipped his hat. "Afternoon, ladies."

Slate pulled the rein to lead his horse out toward the fields to check on the ranch hands repairing the fencing. He should be glad to see Becky's business taking a downward spiral. That would mean he'd get the entire ranch—the ranch that should have been his all along. Exactly what he lived for.

So why did the thought send a lump to his gut the size of a desert boulder?

*

Later that day Rosa set a steaming bowl of rice between Becky and Slate. He handed Becky the spoon and wondered how he'd tell her about the conversation with her guests he had that afternoon. The thought to keep it to himself was tempting, but as he rode the trails to find the ranch hands today, he decided he couldn't keep it from her. She'd looked so happy playing with those kids and worked damn hard at her business. He always liked a fair fight. It wouldn't be right for him to keep the guest's concerns from her. In the end, when he got the ranch back, he'd feel like a heel.

"So, how's business?" he started with.

Becky spooned a mouthful of rice into her bluish lips. Anyone meeting her might think she lacked oxygen, but Slate knew it was just one of her many lipstick colors. He wondered if it tasted like blueberries and found his tongue running across his lips.

"Well." She swallowed a sip of tea. "The first week was a smash. Then..." She scooped a mouthful of rice, hurriedly chewed and continued, "...sorry, I'm starved. Anyway well, some of the women seem a little bored."

Slate let out a sigh.

"You all right?" she asked.

"Fine. Sorry for the interruption." But he wasn't sorry about her revelation. She'd saved him from breaking the news that might hurt her, and he didn't want to hurt Becky.

Looking at her chowing down on Rosa's chicken and rice as if she hadn't eaten in days, he smiled to himself. He watched the slender muscles of her neck as she swallowed. The skin of her face and neck had stayed exceptionally white for being in the sun so much lately. Guess her hat and, knowing Becky, an entire bottle of sunscreen did the trick. His glance ran along her arms, now a light golden color, to her slender fingers—fingers she used to massage the lotion into her skin. Fingers that could run lotion over his.... He forced his concentration on Becky rattling on about something—and not her fingers on his body.

"So, that's what I've decided to do. What'd ya think?" she asked.

Oh shoot. He couldn't say he'd been too busy ogling her body to pay attention. Women had this thing about men being interested in their minds. Although his attraction to Becky may have started out with the physical, once he got to know the real woman behind those wild outfits, he couldn't help himself. Her zest for life, her wittiness, and her feisty spirit absorbed his attention like the chicken gravy soaking into the roll she now dipped into the serving bowl. He wasn't sure he'd ever get used to some of her habits since he was so damned conservative.

He wouldn't mind trying though.

"Helloooo!" she called.

Slate laughed. "It's your business, Becky. I wouldn't want to interfere." Ah ha, great cover-up.

She leaned forward and squinted. "Hm, maybe you *want* my dude ranch to fail. After all, we've only got a few months until showdown."

He leaned within inches of her nose. "Slate Lawson always fights a fair fight." *Hell, one a few months left?*

She kissed the tip of his nose with her gravy-flavored lips. "Good. So do I."

Rosa cleared the table and served fried ice cream with honey drizzled on top as if a hive of bees had flown into the kitchen and spun the sweet web. Becky finished hers and half of Slate's. He couldn't refuse her as he watched her lick the sticky flavor from her blue nails.

"Care for an after-dinner drink, Becky?"

Surprised that Slate hadn't rushed off to work, she figured she'd choke down anything into her already full stomach just to spend more time with him. "Love one."

They settled in the living room. Slate poured crème de menthe liquor into fine crystal snifters. He watched Becky take stacks of magazines from the shelf and shove the rest back.

"Here." He handed her the snifter and after placing his on the carved pine coffee table, he rearranged the magazines.

She clucked her tongue.

"Something wrong?" he asked.

"Nope." She took a sip of the mint liquor. "Geez, this stuff will sure settle your stomach. It's as strong as minty mouthwash."

Slate moved to the sprawling leather couch across from her. He set his feet on the coffee table.

"Have you always been like that?" she asked.

He looked at her. "Like what?"

She pointed toward the magazines on the shelf.

"Oh, that. I've learned that neatness and organization can be a great asset when you're in business."

She reminded herself that she needed to look for next week's guest list. It had to be somewhere in her desk.

"Too much time can be spent looking for things," he continued.

Maybe in her search she'd find Wanda's Christmas card list so she could return it to her. "Is that right?"

"Yep."

"So, if I put things back were they belong, I'd have more time in the day?"

He grinned. "More time for important things."

"You're not talking about my soap operas are you?"

He laughed and looked at his watch. "I've got to run." Slugging down the last sip of liquor, he grabbed his hat from the table.

A wave of disappointment passed over her. She enjoyed the first night of Slate staying around after dinner. She rose and followed him toward the hall. As she paused by the west wing, he grabbed the front door handle. "Don't you ever get tired of working so much?"

He stopped and turned. "I'm used to it."

"But there's more to life... what's that about Jack being a dull boy? You're going to burn out before you're forty, Slate."

The door swayed in the cool night breeze as he let the handle go. "Becky, this place needs a lot of work and attention. Any business does. It's especially hard when you're the owner. You can see that with your own little business."

"Sure, but I have other interests, and I make time for myself. Yesterday I went to visit my friend, and guess what?"

"What?"

"When I came back, my ranch was still here! Then I watched my soap, 'All My Children.'"

"What's your point?"

"My *little business* was still there when I went outside again."

A solemn look covered his face. "It's different for me."

She stepped forward and took his hands in hers. "Why, Slate? Why is it so different? What is it that drives you..."

"This place is my life," he interrupted. With a kiss to her lips, he pulled free and turned. "There is nothing like owning your own land, Becky, nothing."

The door closed behind him.

"Yes, Slate, there's *me*."

Chapter 6

Becky leaned against the front door. Pressing her ear into the wood, she listened to the clicking of Slate's boots fad away. It had to be nearly ten o'clock. What drove him, sucked him out to the ranch as if he had no control? Why did he prefer working, instead of spending time with her?

A feeling of loneliness, something she hadn't felt in years, worked its way into her thoughts. She'd learned as a child to ignore how it felt to be alone. When her birth mother had left her for days with a full refrigerator and instructions to get herself to school on time, her eight-year-old mind trained itself not to care. Or so she tried to convince herself. It became a ritual. Her mother would buy her a "present" for no reason, then disappear for days. After about the fifth time her mother had left her for a week, she refused to cry herself to sleep anymore.

Instead, she started to play with her mother's makeup. She knew it would anger her mother, and that's obviously why she did it. What other recourse did a child have against an adult? Her mother had warned her not to call anyone, or someone from Social Services would yank her away. Terrified, Becky spent all of her free time cutting dolls' hair and making up their faces. She couldn't even play with any friends, or they might discover that she was alone and tell their parents. At least she'd gotten so good at applying makeup that it led to her profession and managing to graduate third in her class from the Oasis Academy.

Well, she didn't need to worry about being found alone. Her mother took care of that when she gave her up for adoption. The moment she watched her mother sign the adoption papers, she knew that she had never been wanted. In her years of foster care, she'd built a barrier around her heart so she'd never feel isolation again. Now, Slate's choosing the ranch over her caused a crack, a tiny fissure in that barrier.

The pain of loneliness returned.

Obviously she wasn't as important to him as his land. Now she understood why he'd lost his temper that day in Attorney Greeson's office. During the past months, she could see he was a hothead at times, but also caring, patient, and it still amazed her that he was so gracious about the terms of the will. Heck, he even helped with her dude ranch. She guessed Hector came over to see if she needed any help each day because Slate had sent him.

Oh, Slate was set in his ways, and obsessed with order, but that wasn't such a bad quality. He had a point about finding things. She'd do well to learn a little organization herself. He'd make a darn good instructor—a heck of a lot cuter than any she'd ever had in school, although a little stiff looking. Not that Slate didn't look fabulous in the same outfit each day, but his conservative taste stuck out like a thorn on a cactus.

She pushed away from the door. Looking toward the empty east wing, she knew Slate lived and breathed the ranch. He'd never be able to return the feelings of caring that grew each time she saw him. She looked around the opulent villa. The sparking white tile floors, the crystal knick-knacks in the hand carved curio cabinet. The beige carpeting beneath her feet that sunk like sand on a beach as she walked.

How could she compete with Valley Del Sol?

She couldn't.

Heading to her room, she decided she needed to get busy on improving her business. The idea she'd told Slate about at dinner, and knew he never heard a word of, started to fizz in her brain like ice cream in a soda.

Once inside her room, she shoved papers around on her desk until she found the phone book. The letter from Attorney Greeson about not touching the lake fell to the floor. Becky picked it up, held it to her chest and felt the stinging in her eyes. Then, she shoved it into the desk drawer.

Slate wasn't about to lose Valley Del Sol.

A niggling of mistrust formed when she looked at the damned paper. Shoving in back into a pile, a childish defiance caused her to shrug off the idea of straightening her desk. Grabbing a pen and paper, she started to mark down numbers of photographers, local clothing stores, and she jotted down Wanda's number so she wouldn't forget to call her for more beauty supplies.

If her idea didn't work, she'd never have a chance at winning *all* of Valley Del Sol.

★

Slate watched Becky shove another mouthful of *huevos rancheros* between her plum-colored lips the next morning. He wondered how the fruity taste mixed with the spicy eggs. Running his tongue across his lips he fought the urge to sample Becky's mouth.

"You wake up late today?" She asked as she ladled yet another spoonful of sugar into her coffee. "Alarm not go off?"

He knew she meant why wasn't he out on the range already. When he came into the kitchen earlier, even Rosa had raised her raven eyebrow at him after he'd said he would be around for breakfast today. After the soul-searching ride he'd taken on Cloud Dancer last night, he decided it might not kill him to let Hector get the ranch hands organized for one morning. After Becky had questioned him about spending too much time with the land, he needed to get away and think. Riding with the moon's glow as his only light had been a calming atmosphere in which to consider her words. *All work and no play makes Jack a dull boy*. He'd heard that saying before, but he'd convinced himself he wasn't bored with his life. When he had rounded the curve of the lake, it dawned on him that Uncle Nate must have agreed with Becky.

"No, I didn't set my alarm," he said.

She eyed him with her baby blues that matched her faded denim jacket. Beneath, he could see a hint of her transparent white blouse, but that was all. No lacy bra showed this time—but he knew it was there. Actually, she looked rather dressed up in a long skirt that sparkled with tiny round mirrors sewed along the front, and he couldn't help notice her cornflower colored boots before she had sat down.

Stirring a spoon around in the cup as if winding a rope around a yo-yo, she asked, "You didn't set your clock?"

He laughed and touched her hand. Her stirring stopped. "Nope. I thought I'd go into work late today."

Becky pulled her hand free and touched it against his forehead. "Just wanted to check if you have a fever."

He smiled. "Well, doc?"

"Cool as a cucumber. So what made you decide to sleep in?"

He wasn't ready to say, *you*, so he fibbed. "Just wanted a few extra hours of shut-eye." Watching her empty the pitcher of cream into her cup, he asked, "By the way, have you ever tried black coffee?" He needed to get the focus away from why he had joined her for breakfast.

"Yuck!"

"Yuck, because you've tried it before? Or yuck because you 'think' it wouldn't taste good?"

"If the good Lord meant for coffee to be drunk black, he wouldn't have made cream and sugar."

He watched her neck as she swallowed a huge gulp. A slender muscle bobbed ever so slightly beneath the creamy, unblemished skin. He wasn't sure if women had an Adam's apple, but if she had one, he knew she'd still look great. Easing the cup from her hand, he said, "Try it…"

Her golden hair flew about her shoulders as she shook her head.

"…for me."

"Oh geez." Strands of hair settled onto her collar, the ends of her long hair landed behind her shoulders like filaments of gold.

Not able to stop himself, he brushed the hairs she'd missed from her forehead. Beneath his fingertips, her skin felt softer than the fleece of a newborn lamb. Slowly he circled across her bronze eyebrows, the color much darker than her hair. She had a knack of curling them ever so slightly, as if the entire world amazed her.

Softly she murmured, "Okay."

He stood and got a white cup with a prickly pear cactus embossed on the sides from the cabinet. From the window he could see Rosa hanging wash on the line as he poured steaming black coffee into the cup. Walking toward Becky, he set the cup on the table and eased her to stand. Her eyes held a glassy stare as she followed his movements.

Holding her hand, he whispered, "Close your eyes."

As she obeyed, he held the cup near enough to her face, careful to keep the steam from burning her. "Savor the aroma."

She inhaled, a soft sigh escaping her lips each time she repeated the action. Her eyelids fluttered. He touched softly against the thin flesh. "Not yet. Tell me what you detect."

She cleared her throat as if needing to force the words to come. "It's strong, pungent… yet, um… it smells delicious."

"Rosa grinds fresh Colombian beans each morning." With his free hand, he brushed along the slender muscles of her neck. She moaned. "How does it make you feel?"

Her voice cracked as she managed, "The scent, spicy yet rich, makes me crave the naturalness of the beans…."

"Taste the scent before you taste the liquid."

She inhaled deeply.

He leaned forward, careful not to spill the hot liquid and nuzzled against her chin, down her neck, and behind her ear. She sighed. He moved upward, across her chin, rubbing his cheek into her skin warmed by the steam. His body burned inside hotter than the coffee Rosa insisted needed to be boiled to enhance the flavor. "What does it make you want?" he asked, pressing the words into her skin.

"Oh God…." she inhaled. "It makes me want… to taste… the

spicy, sharp flavor. It makes me want…." Becky realized the aroma heightening her senses wasn't coming from the coffee. His distinct scent—the one she'd love to bottle—confused her taste buds. "I want…" She opened her eyes to look into the sea green depths of his eyes. "I want you." Her lips found his as he held the cup to the side.

The taste of plum, fleshy and tangy, tickled his lips. She teased at his mouth with her tongue until he opened. She tasted of sugar, spoonfuls that she'd leveled into her cup. She tasted of spices, left hot and burning from the eggs. She tasted of Becky, plum today, banana tomorrow, maybe apple the following day. Each morning a new flavor, but the unmistakable taste of Becky could not be masked by the lipsticks.

He eased her back and blew his breath into the coffee. As he held the cup, like an aphrodisiac offering near her mouth, his voice came out a throaty whisper. "Taste."

Her lips parted. With the softest of gulps, sips of the coffee worked between her lips. "It tastes bitter," she murmured.

He leaned forward to lick an errant drop that remained near her bottom lip. Moving his mouth upward, he met hers and tasted the bitter flavor. Softly the sound of his lips taking hers, and hers responding with a need, touched his ears. The tone, hushed to the world outside their singular space, weakened his muscles. Fearing he'd drop the cup and burn her, he set it on the table.

He needed to touch her. He ran his hands along her neck, following the contours of her oval face. The delicate smoothness of her skin met with the harshness of his callused hands. He pulled back, but she reached up and as if inviting the roughness to return, she placed his hands on her cheeks.

"I don't want to scratch you," he whispered.

"I've got all sorts of creams and lotions…" She was a hairdresser, damn it—a hairdresser with no business getting involved with this wealthy rancher. A hairdresser bound to get hurt—and enjoying every minute.

Her soft laughter resonated against Slate's chest. His heart skipped as if in syncopation with her rhythm. He kissed her, reminding himself they had to stop—they were in the kitchen. He kissed her, knowing he wanted to make love to her on the carpet near the sink—hearing the back door open. He kissed her, falling for Becky Chambers then eased free as Rosa coughed so loudly, if he didn't know she did it to announce her presence, he'd have sent her to a pulmonary specialist.

"Oh *Dios*," Rosa mumbled as she set the empty clothesbasket on the floor. A flame of red surged from her neckline to her chubby cheeks, followed by a nervous chuckle.

Becky straightened herself and took a step to the side. "Hey, Rosa."

Feeling like a kid caught steeling Rosa's famous chocolate chip *bizcochitos* from the cookie jar, Slate shuffled his foot. "I was getting Becky to try coffee without sugar. She uses way too much. Have you seen all that she adds to her coffee, Rosa? And the amount of cream...."

Becky smiled at his rambling. How adorable to see a solid rock of a cowboy stammering like a kid—all to protect her reputation, to prevent Rosa from judging Becky poorly. No man had ever considered her feelings like that before in her life.

Rosa—sweet, sensible, knowing full well what had been going on Rosa—marched toward the table and proceeded to carry dishes to the sink. She leaned over her shoulder, and Becky saw a glint of mischief in the older woman's eyes as she asked, "Will you be eating lunch *in* today, Señor Lawson?"

Becky chuckled.

Slate yanked his Stetson from the chair top and shoved it on. He grabbed the doorknob and pulled. Turning, he said, "No, Rosa, we'll have lunch *on the verandah* today."

Becky grabbed the back of the chair. Rosa turned and their glances caught. Hysterical giggling, that only a female could produce, floated to the beams of the kitchen ceiling.

★

Becky handed Tim Howell, the photographer she came to meet, the bills after she carefully counted out enough to pay him an advance for film. She'd started a savings account with the money from Uncle Nate, and although it caused her to make frequent trips to the bank, she paid everyone in cash. That way, she figured, she'd spend less money. Wanda insisted Becky needed a checking account, but she knew if she could write out some flimsy piece of paper to everyone it wouldn't be like really spending. She knew she'd get a notice one day from the bank saying it was all gone. No more money. Paying cash, she felt the loss with each dollar she handed out, and her frugal nature always induced some kind of bartering.

"So, you'll be there at two this afternoon, Tim?"

"Yes, ma'am." He shoved the wad of bills into the old silver cash register, handed her a receipt, and nodded.

Wanda had given her Tim's number. The son of one of Wanda's regular customers, Becky trusted him. He had to be about five years younger than her, and at least they had struggling businesses in common.

"You'll be by Saturday to do the bride's makeup?" he asked.

She groaned inwardly. As if she had time to make up a bride when she had her ranch to concentrate on. But those were the terms she'd agreed to with Tim. He'd shoot pictures for her at discounted rates, and she'd come to his shop and make up his customers before he took their photographs. She was getting to be a darn good businesswoman. Dressing her guests in Western outfits, having Tim photograph them, and selling them the pictures had to work.

It was all she could come up with to win the ranch.

"I'll be here. Make sure she's got some kind of smock over her clothes." She grabbed her denim purse and turned toward the door. "Have her sitting in good light, not chewing gum, and face washed.

I'll be pressed for time." She turned to wave at a pale Tim, who seemed to be allowing her instructions to sink in. She laughed. "You'll learn the routine in no time."

Back in her room, Becky changed into her comfortable white shorts and a red halter-top. She shoved her denim bag, now housing a hand mirror, various combs, and other makeup items, over her shoulder. Hopefully, Dave had unloaded all the boxes from her van into the bunkhouse.

Grabbing her green hairstyling kit, she pulled open the door. The carpet felt softer than usual—or maybe her light mood made her feel as if she walked on air. Her brainstorm to save her business had her stomach knotted with butterflies colliding in excitement. She should be nervous it might not work, but since she wasn't the nervous type she let herself be ecstatic instead.

⋆

Slate jabbed his heels into Cloud Dancer's sides and pulled the rein toward the West. She galloped down the hillside toward the open range. He needed the openness to ride fast, to ride free, and to ride until his thoughts could clear. The scene with Becky in the kitchen this morning had his mind all confused. He could barely instruct the ranch hands about what fences needed mending or which sheep to move to what pasture today.

Inhaling the arid scents of the desert, a phantom aroma of coffee and plum nearly toppled him off Cloud Dancer's saddle. He'd never met anyone else like Becky, and suspected he would never meet another. If anyone had told him teaching someone to drink coffee black could be a sensuous experience, he'd have said that they were crazy. Easing the horse to a canter, he admitted to himself that other than actually making love, Becky and her coffee had to have been the most arousing act he'd ever experienced.

"Whoa." He pulled the horse to a stop and dismounted. Dropping the reins, he knew Cloud Dancer wouldn't venture far. A cluster of boulders sat off the path so he made his way over and sat on the smallest one. Welcome shade came from larger boulders above. Dust devils spun in the hot breezes, reminding Slate of the lack of rain they'd had. If he didn't have water rights on his property, the sheep and corn would be in bad shape. Thinking of his corn, he made a mental note to get the irrigation system repaired on the northern fields.

A pang of guilt stuck into his heart like the cactus spine he pulled from his leather boot. If he let Becky make her beach, her guests would have a lot more to do and he'd heard she couldn't afford to build a pool. Swimming and boating would have kept them busy, but it would have been the downfall of his side of the ranch. Is that what Becky wanted?

Leaning against the cool hardness, he shook his head. No, Becky wasn't the devious type. Oh, she'd succeeded in her little deception scheme of pretending to be a "dumb blonde," but he always suspected there was something more to Becky than what he saw and he really couldn't blame her. Guess she really couldn't keep her feisty self under total control though. Thank goodness. He laughed into the dusty air. She had to have been bursting at her skin-tight seams wanting to make comments, laugh hysterically, or put him in his place a few times.

It didn't make sense that she'd go to all that trouble just so he wouldn't judge her. Heck, if she really knew how he envied her wildness, her ability to be free, she'd have acted like herself from the first day they met. He wished she had. Then he wouldn't have missed a day of her real personality. Thinking of Becky caused an ambivalent feeling in his gut.

And he was scared to death.

He couldn't hurt her, and inevitably he would. With his past, he had no role model for loving someone. Shutting his eyes, he pictured his mother as he'd found her one night sitting alone in her room. At the age of seven, he had no idea parents should sleep in the same bedroom. He always thought his mother had her own room because she liked the frilly covers on her bed. It didn't take too many more years of growing up to realize his parent's marriage wasn't the best example for him.

That night she had a tear-stained face, and he'd believed her story that she'd just watched a sad movie on television until his father came back from working the ranch. Even two pillows from his bed couldn't shut out her shouts that she hated the ranch, hated living alone, and hated him, Hank Lawson, his father.

Slate had gravitated toward the ranch hands because his father didn't have time for his son either. Unfortunately, his actions backfired on him. The land grew to be Slate's life, his whole family—other than Uncle Nate—and it grew to be his future. He was exactly like his father. He'd never had a successful relationship himself.

Could his future ever hold more than the ranch?

Could he have a family, children to play with, enjoy the wonders of nature as the guests on Becky's ranch did?

Could he have Valley Del Sol *and* Becky Chambers, too?

He leaned back and shut his eyes. It seemed impossible.

★

Slate's eyes flew open at the sound of screaming. In the distance a spiral of dust indicated something was going on near the cornfields. Before he could see clearly, he grabbed Cloud Dancer's reins and mounted. Skillfully the horse rounded the boulders until she came to open range, and Slate sent her into a gallop.

Stalks of corn fell like tenpins before his eyes. Becky and Dave rode down the rows shouting at what looked like a guest on a runaway horse. Becky's damned guest, tearing up *his* corn!

"Yah!" he shouted and turned Cloud Dancer toward the west to head the woman off before she rode into the next row of corn.

Between the two sections, Slate pulled his horse to a stop. Headed toward him was the woman on a black gelding. "Pull the reins," he shouted. By the horrified look on her face, he knew she wasn't capable of stopping. Before she got hurt, he turned Cloud

Dancer and rode toward her. The second they were side by side he reached out and grabbed her reins, confident that his horse could stop.

The woman screamed into his ear as he reached for her.

"Catch her, Slate!" Becky shouted.

With a hold on her arm, he eased the woman to the ground where she collapsed.

Becky and Dave jumped from their horses. "Are you all right, Margaret?" Becky yelled. "Oh geez, what happened?" She knelt next to the woman who managed to sit.

Slate jumped down. "Is she hurt?"

"I'm fine," Margaret said. She gave a nervous laugh. "I'm so sorry…"

"Don't worry. At least you're all right. Can you stand?" Becky asked.

Embarrassed, Margaret stood and wiped at her purple Western outfit.

"Dave, take her back to the bunkhouse and see if she needs a doctor," Slate commanded.

"No, I really am fine," she said. "But I'd like to get back."

Dave helped the woman up on to his horse and rode away.

"Phew! That could have been a lot worse…" Becky's words were silenced by the fire in Slate's eyes. She started to continue until she looked behind him.

His corn lay flattened like wounded troops.

"I'm sorry, Slate…"

He lifted a broken stalk and threw it to the side. It landed like a javelin, piercing the ground. She winced. "Slate, look, I'll pay…"

"What the hell was she doing on that horse?"

Becky pulled back. "She was riding…"

"Riding? Who the hell taught her?"

"Actually, I had given her some instructions…"

His nostrils flared. "You?"

"Well, usually Dave does, but she was so eager to learn…"

He grabbed her arm. "Don't you know she could have gotten killed?"

"Don't be so dramatic. She's fine." Becky yanked her arm free. "No one said she could ride by herself yet anyway."

He glared at her. "Then you need to set some rules for your *guests*."

"I was going to..."

"Up until now, I've let you have free reign on your place. Let you play 'lady rancher'..."

She pushed at his chest. "What a minute? You *let* me..."

"This is no game. This is my life, and I'll be damned if you and your guests are going to tear up my ranch. *My* ranch!" He turned and grabbed the reins to his horse. Over his shoulder he said, "Keep them off my half, Becky, or you'll never make it to your six months."

She watched him ride off, wishing he'd disappear into the sunset—for good.

Chapter 7

"Now hold still," Becky cautioned Mrs. Weinburg. She stepped closer to the middle-aged woman to adjust her cowboy hat. "A Stetson should sit right about…"—she pulled it toward the back—"…here." She'd had a hard time concentrating the last week—since the massacred corn incident. She saw very little of Slate lately and knew he'd even slept out on the range a few nights. The damned land was so important to him. Of course, he had every right to be angry with her—but she had every legal right to be there.

"Yoo-hoo," Mrs. Weinburg called, pulling Becky's attention from her worries.

The woman laughed, revealing a mouthful of obviously capped teeth. She could afford it, Becky thought, knowing the guest's husband owned a chain of dry cleaning stores in upstate New York. Wanda's cousin from lower Manhattan had told her about their business. When she thought about it, she knew quite a lot about all her guests lately, since the ones from the previous weeks had recommended the new guests come to Sidewinder Valley. Thank goodness for word of mouth.

"Okay, Tim, get Mrs. Weinburg down for posterity," Becky said.

Tim clicked his camera while Mrs. Weinburg laughed, nearly knocking the cowgirl hat to the ground. Becky gave herself a mental pat on the back for matching the salmon hat to the woman's hair color, brassy though it was. She'd recommend a rinse when she did Mrs. Weinburg's next makeover.

"Too busy to wet your whistle?" the familiar voice asked.

Becky swung around to face Slate. He looked wonderful, holding a glass of tea dripping with crystal clear moisture. "My… whistle is rusted from all the darn…" She almost said "dust" but remembered the cloud surrounding the corn the other day. "…the darn dryness. Thanks." She took the glass and told Tim and Mrs. Weinburg to take five.

"Let's find some shade," Slate said, guiding her toward the verandah with a gentle pressure on her lower back.

Damp cotton clung to her skin, giving a heightened sensation from Slate's touch. He set his glass on the white wicker end table and motioned for Becky to sit on the swing under the ceiling fan. She readied to defend her ranch when he brought up the corn, but he said, "Looks like you've been fairly busy lately. About the corn incident."

"Yes?"

"Don't let anything like it happen again. You could ruin the entire place."

She bit her lip, but he was right. "I am sorry."

"Let's forget it ever happened."

He really *didn't* hold a grudge. It was nice being back to a pre-corn relationship. She took a long sip of sugarless iced tea. For the past few weeks, since the coffee incident, she'd taught herself not to scrunch up her face at the bitter flavor. Actually, she was developing a taste for it much as everyone says you had to develop a taste for scotch. Why anyone would force themselves to develop a taste for the bitter liquor, she had no idea, but peering at Slate from the corner of her eyes, she knew why *she* was drinking tea and coffee sugarless.

"Um, I've been working my little tushy off."

Slate gave her a leer. "I hope there's some left for me."

She pushed at his chest. He took her hand and laughed. "How the heck do you get such tiny flowers on your nails?"

She pulled free. "Uh-uh. Any cosmetologist worth her weight in henna doesn't tell trade secrets."

"I like seeing the things you do to your nails. It's so… so you."

Her slender shoulders shook as she laughed. The tiny cows on her sleeveless blouse seemed to jump over her pert breasts as if jumping over the moon. He'd love to be one of those cows. She looked adorable in her skimpy shorts, her wild tops, and her boots that always matched. Heck, her hat even matched her horse. Shoot, she was something else. He looked down at his usual shirt and jeans—he and Becky were so different.

Footsteps on the wooden porch took Slate's thoughts to the present. Hector came toward them.

"What's going on, Hector?"

"I need to run into town for some supplies. The sheep are near the northern part of the lake, near the border of the canyon. I won't have time to check on them 'til after dark."

"Don't worry about them. I'll ride out there."

"Bye, Hector," Becky called. She stretched her arms above her head. Slate thought the cows smiled.

"Hey, do you have time for a ride?" he asked.

"Well, I guess Tim can manage without me. I'm done with makeovers for today. He needs a few more shots of Mrs. Weinburg, so a ride sounds great. And Grady is off to a neighbor's ranch to play."

"I'll saddle up that white gelding you learned to..."

"I named her Sugar," she interrupted.

"Okay. Come on." Slate reached for Becky's hand and they walked toward the barn. She ran ahead into her bunkhouse to tell Tim to finish the photographs without her.

Cloud Dancer's hooves pounded the dusty trail as Slate and Becky rode side by side. She chattered on about her guests, Rosa's cooking, the hot sun, and something about a woman named Wanda and her false teeth. Becky found excitement in just about anything. He envied her that. "Right about there is where Nate's grandfather started this ranch," Slate said, pointing east.

"Wow. It sure has grown through the years."

They continued on, Slate giving her more history along with the tour. She'd come to learn how land could be so important to him, to anyone.

She herself felt a great deal of pride when she looked across the foothills at what could be hers.

At the base of a canyon, they dismounted and settled on some large boulders. Silence filled the air for several minutes while they each contemplated their own thoughts.

Slate turned to her. "I've always wondered why your family never came to see you."

Taken aback, she looked at him. "Grady is all I have. My mother never wanted me. My birth mother that is. Never knew my real father."

"Oh my God, Becky." He pulled her tightly. "Becky...."

She wanted to leave it at that, but couldn't. The words had started a cleansing of her past, and she had to continue. Slate needed to know.

"On my ninth birthday, she packed my suitcase and said we were going on vacation... to the mountains. I was so excited because she'd never taken me on a vacation. We lived in air force base housing; she was a sergeant working in the hospital lab. I even went to school on the base. I was so thrilled that she wanted to spend time with me."

Slate kissed her forehead. His chest muscles tensed as she spoke.

"But when... we pulled into the parking lot of some brick building, I knew. Even at nine I knew my mother never wanted me." She sobbed. "She signed the papers right in front of me."

He cursed. "How long before you were adopted, hon?"

The endearing term eased the past pain and the concern in his eyes gave her the strength to say, "Never. I grew up in three different foster homes. Passed from one to the other... like some used toy. Finally the last family turned out to be decent. They actually cared about me. I did my share of making trouble... but... only to get attention."

"Becky, I'm sorry."

A guttural laugh came from her throat. "You don't need to be sorry. I survived the years of loneliness, the years of getting into trouble, and the years of mothers not letting their kids play with me. Ignoring his curse, she said, "They never thought I'd amount to anything, Slate, but I'm a damned good hairdresser and…"

"A successful businesswoman," he finished.

Her heart swelled. He couldn't have made her happier if he'd given her a million dollars. Hearing him acknowledge that she had succeeded was worth a hell of a lot more. She leaned forward and kissed him, and kissed him again.

"Your nail… what happened to the little cactus?"

Becky looked at her hand. "Oh, I forgot. I broke that today."

He kissed her finger as if it were wounded. "How?"

"Playing with Grady and Jack and Jill."

"I'm sorry." He moved to her lips with his kisses.

"No big—there are fake ones to fix…." He kissed her wrist. "Course I prefer the real thing…"

"So do I."

He moved to her neck. As if her entire body had been shocked, a tingling surged through every crevasse. Slate eased her down without any hesitation on her part. Even her toes curled happily as she ran them across the buttery softness of the couch. With straining arms, he balanced himself above her. Bending, he nudged his tongue near her mouth.

Parting to welcome Slate, she allowed him to enter the waiting darkness. He tasted of coffee, rich and black. She'd grown fond of the flavor and licked at his tongue as he playfully darted it along her teeth. In the distance a plane flew overhead.

Beneath her cotton halter, her body begged for Slate's touch. Easing to the side, she pulled at his arms for him to lie next to her. Despite the hard rock surface, she felt as if she were lying on a cloud.

He nuzzled her neck and licked across her lips. "Um, fresh peaches. I'm so proud of you. You're doing a better job of keeping your guests under control, too."

She stiffened. Couldn't he forget the ranch for a few wonderful minutes?

Who cared about land when her body was burning up inside? She sure as heck didn't, and if Slate didn't put out her fire soon, the damned rock would melt beneath her.

"Also, with the water problems, keeping your guests from the lake is a help. Thanks for that. And my sheep thank you. I've only lost a few who strayed too far from the watering station and got dehydrated."

The sobering thought froze her. She pulled her hands from his arms. "You lost some?"

"Yep, and I can't afford to lose too many of my flock... especially after the corn incident."

She flinched.

"Ranching has a lot of barriers. Weather, predators, running a ranch takes plenty of..."

She knew he was talking, but she wasn't listening. Was he so preoccupied with this place that all he could think about *now* was corn and sheep?

Slate started to run his hand beneath her blouse. Gently, she took it and kissed his palm.

"I think we're on a one-way ride here, and we need to examine a few things before we take that final plunge," she said, although talking should be the last thing on their minds.

His eyes narrowed. "Don't you want me, Becky?"

Oh hell, leave it to a man to throw the blame on a woman. "Of course..." She pushed him to the side enough to sit. "Heck, what woman in her right mind wouldn't want a hunk like you." He looked adorable with red cheeks.

"I mean do *you*, Becky?"

"Yes... but I'm not sure *you* want *me*..."

"Hell, Becky, if I wanted you any more, I'd explode."

"That's just male hormones. I mean, Slate, we were getting darned close to... really *wanting* each other and you... you started talking about your *sheep*."

If she'd shot him with a rifle, he couldn't have looked more pained. Well, she was right about him being preoccupied with his sheep. Damn it. He was the one who brought up the fool ranch, not her.

Slate stood and looked down. Then he turned toward the horses. Becky wished she could have swallowed back her words."I didn't mean to hurt you," she said.

He waved her words with his hand. "You're right." He grabbed the reigns and mounted. "Come on."

For a minute she remained still. Truthfully, she didn't have the energy to move. The pain was too great. She at least expected a decent argument about how she was imagining things, blowing things out of proportion, heck, even saying she was lying would have been better.

He should have disputed her words that he wasn't preoccupied with his ranch.

He should have said she was more important. Picturing the sadness and anger in his eyes, she wished he had argued with her.

At least then there'd be a chance that she wasn't right.

Chapter 8

Slate shoved a pillow across his face. Blasted sun insisted on annoying him. He'd lain awake most of last night with thoughts of Becky's childhood, her survival, and how she flourished. But the major attack of insomnia came when he remembered how she stopped them from making love. She made the right decision, he knew it. The thing that bothered him most was—why didn't he see it for himself?

He couldn't deny that his feelings for Becky ran deep. He didn't want to just make love, he wanted to make love *to* her. An overwhelming desire to please her led his actions, yet he had to bring up the subject of the ranch. Throwing the pillow across the room he thought, an apple really *doesn't* fall far from the tree.

After a lingering shower, Slate headed to the kitchen. The sweet aroma confused him. Usually, he could name every course Rosa was serving by inhaling the tempting flavors before he got to the kitchen. What was she cooking for breakfast today?

When he reached the doorway, he stopped. The counters were covered in flour, or powder, or some white mixture. He wasn't sure what you'd cook with the eggs dripping from the counter to the brick floor. Even the bunch of dried red chili peppers hanging above the sink had been splattered by something beige and probably sticky.

"Surprise!" Becky beamed from beneath her flour-covered cheeks.

Oh God, she's killed Rosa, was his first thought. If she hadn't, the housekeeper would surely die when she got here and saw her kitchen. "Wow. This *is* a surprise." He collapsed into the chair she motioned toward before his legs gave out. "Has Rosa seen… ah…

been here yet?"

"Yep..."

"Is she all right?" He couldn't keep the frantic tone from his voice. Maybe Rosa would kill Becky... why didn't she if she'd already been there? "She has come *here*... into the kitchen and seen..."

"What the heck is wrong with you? Yes, she's been here, in the kitchen, before I got up, and left this note." She handed it to him with a flour-covered hand. "Here, maybe some caffeine will clear up that case of tongue-tie you seem to have." She poured steaming coffee into his white mug.

Confused, he took a sip and watched her above the mug's rim.

At the stove, she removed a pan, and flipped something onto a dish with a spatula. "She's in Albuquerque. Her sister is sick... stroke," she informed him.

Setting down the note, he asked, "Is she all right?"

"I don't know. It doesn't say." She motioned to the letter sticking to his hand. He read it and made a mental note to call Rosa at her sister's place to see if she was all right or if she needed anything. He'd try now, but she couldn't have had time to get there yet.

"Something smells good. What're you baking?"

She stuck a piece of what she'd taken out of the oven into her mouth and mumbled, "Cookies—coconut macadamia nut."

"For breakfast?" He took a slug of coffee.

She licked her finger. "Where's it written what time of day you can eat a cookie?" She handed him a box of corn flakes. "For those who are so fixated on—here." She grabbed a cookie and ate it.

"I'll try one."

Becky scooped up a cookie on the spatula and aimed it toward him.

"Looks great."

She sat and drank her black coffee. Leaning forward, she squinted. "Guess Hector wasn't around to tell the ranch hands what to do today." She paused as if waiting for Slate to jump from his seat.

Truthfully, he'd forgotten it was so late when he'd seen the kitchen; he tapped his foot on the floor. He wanted to stay… yet, he needed to leave. "They'll… manage."

A smile formed on her lips, and he knew she was surprised. He was proud of himself. Taking a bite of cookie, he readied to lie so he wouldn't hurt her feelings. She'd never struck him as the "homemaker" type. Heck, they were delicious. "These are great."

"Thanks."

"No, I mean it, they *are* great!"

She eyed him suspiciously. "Someone would think you doubted my culinary abilities."

He fumbled, "No, no. I mean…" She looked him in the eye. "Well, the decor had me in doubt."

Becky looked around. "I'll clean it all up. I do try to be neater, but it doesn't come easy for me."

He didn't doubt that. The cookies were great, but he felt like jumping up and cleaning around her. For someone who liked everything in its place, sitting in the mess proved difficult. He looked at the smudge of flour on the tip of her nose and his heart jolted. She looked adorable. Then he caught the scene behind her—a reminder of how different they were. Slate forced his thoughts to the cookies. After the last bite and final drop of coffee, he tipped his chair onto its back legs. "That was super. I'll take a shot at supper."

"Well, that'd be great, except it's the last night of my guest's visit so we always have our chuck wagon meal. Maybe you'd like to join us?"

"Sounds great. What time?"

"It starts about six. We have dancing around the campfire so it runs late." She smiled toward him and her heart fluttered like a teenager on a first date. "Can you dance?"

He laughed. "I can try."

She stood and took his dish. "More coffee?"

"I really should get…" He caught her looking at him. Her glare remained fixed on him as if she dared him to stay. Was he that obvious? "One more cup won't hurt."

Becky smiled to herself. Sitting back down, she took a drink of coffee. Above her mug, she noticed movement outside the window. "Who's that riding this way so fast?"

Slate stood to look out the window behind Becky. "Luke, one of my men."

"He looks upset…"

Slate pushed away from the table, sending splashes of coffee from his mug onto the floor, and ran to the back door.

Before Slate could ask what was wrong, Luke shouted, "Coyotes!"

Slate grabbed his hat. "Where?"

"Out near the northern part of the lake."

"I was supposed to…"

Luke gave Slate a knowing glare.

Slate cursed. "I told Hector I'd get the sheep… and forgot."

Because of her, he thought.

Turning for a second, he saw the look on Becky's face. She stood near the table ready to pour him another cup of coffee.

"Go ahead." Her eyes narrowed as if she questioned his motive, and she pulled the coffeepot away from his cup.

He shoved his hat on, stepped toward her. "Look, Coyotes can kill a lot of sheep…" He wouldn't go into how their nearly making love had gotten him so preoccupied.

She interrupted, "So what are you waiting for?"

He was waiting for her to say it was all right. He was waiting for her to say that she understood his need to leave. He was waiting for her to say she would not hold it against him—like he wished his mother had said to his father, even if only once.

But she stood silent, the coffeepot dangling from her hand.

Could she ever understand?

Running toward the door, he turned. "Don't you see? It's my fault, Becky. I was so damned preoccupied with… hell, I left them there to invite any predator." The door slammed behind him.

Preoccupied with us... with me. Becky sank into Slate's chair. She picked up the green-stripped linen napkin he'd just used and inhaled. His fragrance lingered. A sick feeling as if she'd eaten too many cookies settled in her stomach. It was her fault that Slate had forgotten the sheep. Luke hadn't said how serious the situation was, but she noticed the fear in Slate's eyes. He knew what could happen, and he'd blame her—and rightfully so—if the coyote killed any of his sheep.

Resting her head on the back of the chair she shut her eyes. Things were going along too well for her, and she finally had someone to make her special cookies for. No great surprise that it wouldn't last. She'd never had all this good luck; heck, she never had any good luck, so of course it would start going downhill fast.

Well, she brought it on herself for getting greedy. She should have lived on the ranch for the six months then bought herself a small house with the money from Nate. No, she had to have some harebrained idea that she could succeed at a business and that she could... be interested in someone from the swanky side of the track. She had no right having these feelings for Slate. She didn't belong here and the damned ranch seemed to be telling her so. She never should have sunk a penny into it.

Valley Del Sol was going to win him after all.

She'd have to concentrate on winning the terms of the will.

⋆

"Welcome, everyone!" Becky yelled above the chatter of her guests. Dave Palmer slammed a metal spoon against a pot. The crowd silenced. Laugher floated across the picnic tables like a ripple on the lake. "Thanks, Dave." Becky laughed. "It's been a tradition here, at Sidewinder Valley, to have our authentic Western meal on the last night of your stay."

Grady danced about in all the excitement. "Can I go play, Beck? Me and some of the guest's kids are going to pet the animals."

She'd gotten used to the little guy's independence around her.

It had to be good for him to build his character. She ran a hand through his hair. "Sure. Then make sure you come back and stay right here when it gets dark." She leaned to kiss his forehead.

He nodded and ran off.

In the foreground, the crowd blurred as she scanned the path behind the barn. No sign of Slate. With a quick peek at her watch, she ignored the hands claiming it was six-twenty and continued, "So, I hope ya'll are hungry. Cook's made another fabulous meal, and the only thing I ask is that you eat slowly and... keep coming back for more!"

Dave let out a whoop followed by the guests cheering and starting to line up to get their dishes.

"Is something wrong, ma'am?" Dave asked.

Becky pulled her gaze from her searching. "Oh, no, Dave. Go ahead and start. I'm not too hungry." She hated lying, but what was she going to say, "I'm waiting to see if I've been stood up"? She knew the imminent danger of the coyote had passed after seeing Luke around five o'clock. He'd said they had shot a large male, and he felt sure that had been the one a ranch hand had spotted earlier. Slate had enough help so he'd never have to leave his office if he didn't want to.

Walking toward the barn, she headed to the back where the sun cast a purple glow on the lake. The western sky threatened to swallow up the flaming ball into the horizon in a short time. Beneath the fading rays, she scanned the desert. No movement. Greasewood bushes stilled in the breezeless surroundings. Birds nested in the cactus, spending time with their loved ones.

She stood alone.

Behind, she could hear the laugher of the guests, the festive hum penetrating the still night air. Loneliness worked its way into her thoughts. She tried to fight the old emotion. Yet, waiting for Slate had unlocked the door to where she'd hidden her fears of solitude so long ago.

And it hurt.

Why had caring for someone always led to pain? First her mother, then Nate, and now—she sucked in a breath—Slate Lawson.

Even owning half a ranch wasn't as great as expected… maybe Wanda was right. Something was still missing in her life. Turning on her heels, she decided she was a fool to be standing there lamenting her bad luck and headed toward the guests.

Back at the campfire she grabbed a dish and let Cook heap piles of blanket steak, tomato rice, and corn on her dish. She was going to eat every last bite. Most of the guests stopped by to chat as Becky finished her meal. Nearly all had assured her they would return and were going to tell their friends about Sidewinder Valley. One woman inquired about purchasing the Western outfit that Becky had dressed her in for her photographs. As she discussed it, two other women with what Becky assumed was phenomenal hearing, joined in the conversation. They, too, wanted to buy the clothing, and other outfits.

Becky took a bite of steak and tapped the fork against her teeth. The women waited near her table, and at any second, she expected them to start licking their chops in anticipation. She thought of Wanda's customer, Lily, who had made the clothing for her at a reasonable price. Lily, a single parent, stayed home sewing to be with her four kids. She guessed Lily would love the business. Wanda's husband had given her the name of the owner of a Western shop where she was able to buy the various colored Stetsons at a good rate. This could be the break she needed to have her side of the ranch out-profit Slate's.

"Okay…." Becky said. Did the women hover closer or was it her imagination? "I think I can manage… but let me make a few phone calls. Uncharacteristically, the city women whooped louder than Dave did. Becky laughed. "Enjoy the dancing, and I'll get back to you in a few minutes. She looked at her watch, hoping Lily would be home. Her wrist froze in front of her face. Eight o'clock! Her preoccupation with the guests had caused her to forget, Slate was two hours late.

★

Slate shifted in his saddle. The soreness reminded him he'd been on Cloud Dancer for hours. A tip of the golden sun peeked from the horizon as if the earth was flat and the blazing light had fallen off the side. Darkness replaced its brilliance, and he needed to head back before Cloud Dancer wouldn't be able to see where she was going.

"Let's go, girl." He eased the reins and she started a trot along the dusty path. The northern section where the coyote had feasted on two of his sheep passed inspection. Grumbling in his stomach reminded him that him he hadn't eaten since breakfast. Searching the range had taken his mind off his hunger, but riding in the silence gave him nothing else to think about until he remembered—breakfast.

"Damn," he hollered out and jabbed Cloud Dancer's side. As if a photo appeared in his head, he saw Becky and the look of abandonment in her blue eyes. He didn't need to pull his pocket watch from his vest. The sun told him it was way past six.

The horse sent sprays of dust into the air as Slate pushed her to the limit. Maybe he'd make the dancing part. Maybe Becky would understand why he needed to be out here so long. Maybe she wouldn't.

Had he really needed to stay so much longer than the ranch hands? He knew he trusted each one of them, but some damned force kept him searching for more coyotes longer than he needed to. As he passed the fork in the path that led to the gold mine, he wondered if he'd stayed too long on purpose.

His gut knotted and this time he knew it wasn't from hunger. Maybe he feared caring for someone, for Becky, so much that he stood her up, knowing he'd anger her. He'd never been a coward, but he'd never allowed himself to feel this way about a woman—until now. Fear gripping his insides didn't come from worrying about her anger, but her pain.

Slowing Cloud Dancer to miss a pile of tumbleweed on the path, he knew he'd failed. Becky would be hurt because of him.

"Ya!" He sped his horse forward, rounding a curve to see the lake gleaming under the moonlit sky. A few more minutes and he'd be at the campsite. The sky near the barn glowed a bright amber so he knew the guests were still celebrating. But would Becky even talk to him?

Slate dismounted and made his way around a middle-aged couple dressed in white Western outfits including dust-covered white boots. He smiled to himself, thinking Buffalo Bill Cody would be turning over in his grave at the greenhorns. But, they sure seemed to be enjoying themselves as they danced along to the female singer impersonating Patsy Cline's "Crazy." "Hey, Dave, have you seen Becky?"

"Sure haven't seen her in a while, Slate. Last I know is she'd taken Grady up to the house to put him to bed." Dave nodded and guided a pretty young guest, dressed in a pink outfit that enhanced her auburn hair, toward the dance floor.

He was going crazy, Slate thought, as he walked into the house.

"Thanks, Lily!" Becky's voice bounced down the hallway.

Slate stood in the foyer, tempted to go down the west wing, but that was Becky's side of the house. He dropped his hat onto the table and waited. At least she wasn't in her room crying. Actually, was that a whoop?

Becky surged down the hallway, then stopped.

"Look, Beck, I'm sorry about..."

She waved his words with her hand. "No you don't. You're not gonna ruin my night *twice.* I'm too excited right now." She started past him. "And be quiet before you wake up Grady."

He touched her arm and nearly pulled back. Surely she felt the chemistry, too. "Will you share your excitement?" He ran his hand along her arm. Silky material covered her skin, but the softness came through as if her blouse were sleeveless.

She scrunched her apple-green lips to the side. "Darn you."

He'd never been much of a gambler, but he gave it a shot and leaned forward. If she didn't belt him yet, there was hope. Kissing her cheek, he smiled to himself at his accurate guess of her lipstick. The tangy scent pinched his nose.

She pushed free. "I have to go."

Pleased that her words came out breathless, he dropped his hands to his side. His gamble was paying off. "I said I was sorry…"

"I heard you. I heard you. But I really do have to go. Some of the ladies asked about buying the outfits I'd dressed them in…"

"By the way, I noticed how well you outfitted some young lady with auburn hair that Dave was dancing with."

She stepped back and looked at him. "You noticed?"

Her soft tone had his heart dancing. "Sure. I have a pretty good eye…"

"Oh puleez! Anyway, that was Nancy, and yes, I picked out her clothes. Besides selling the photographs, I'm going to be selling the outfits, too!"

He expected her to bubble over on Rosa's highly polished tiles. "That's great." She turned to leave. "Beck, is it too late for that attempt at a dance?"

She tapped her teeth with a green nail that looked as if it would glow in the dark. Taking her hand, he said, "I see you've replaced your broken nail…"

"Hey, that's the only artificial thing about me!"

He laughed and leaned near her ear, "I have no doubt."

She should pull back. After all, he'd stood her up. But the sheep were threatened. She should be furious and protect her heart. But he looked so pathetically cute. She should push past him and go, but she pulled him around, only giving him a second to grab his hat. "Come on."

★

Becky rambled on to the women about the details of buying their outfits. She assured them that she'd mail everything they wanted within a few weeks. It was going to be great business for Lily, and it wouldn't hurt Becky's income a bit. As they stampeded to share their excitement with their husbands, she turned. Slate sat at the picnic table, one arm resting on the table, his head nestled in his palm, his eyes shut.

Damn him. He looked adorable.

"Hey, sleepyhead," she whispered. "Go home and get some shuteye."

He straightened, but she could see fine wrinkles beneath his eyes. Amazing how a shadow of a beard could make a man look so sexy.

"Sorry. Ready for our dance?" he mumbled.

She shook her head. "A little thing like me can't hold you up."

"I'm fine." He stood and wobbled.

"You've had a long day… did you see any coyotes?"

He shook his head and she noticed a sadness dull his eyes. "I really want to dance," he said.

"Come on, Wild Bill. See if you could make it through one number." She yanked on his lapels and led him into the crowd. Maybe he'd remain standing for a short song. At least the music was slow.

She wished the band would switch to a faster number. Slate's heady scent—too masculine for this close stuff—clouded around her. Each time she tried to turn for a breath to cleanse her garbled mind, she'd touch his shoulder or chin or vest, and his scent, tonight blended with the earthen smell of a day's work on the ranch, hit her. Geez, this had to be the most sensuous aroma she'd ever inhaled.

As if that wasn't bad enough, he breathed too close to her ear. Not that it bothered her—well, it did if you considered hearing a soft sigh tickling your ear a disturbance. It disturbed her logical thoughts as hot and spicy surged to her new pistachio boots. The hardened leather prevented her toes from curling.

"This is nice," he murmured.

Nice? She was thinking more along the lines of—geez, this is baffling, amazing, heck, mesmerizing so she said, "Um."

He moaned, and she knew his little catnap had revived him. With the gentlest of pressure, he pressed against her. Yep, he'd been revived. He pushed back her hair and nuzzled behind her ear. The music faded as if in the distance. The crowd blurred. He ran kisses along her chin, lips, and temples, weakening her knees. He tightened his hold, thank goodness, or she'd have collapsed to the dusty dance floor.

"Becky, I really am sorry about tonight."

She didn't care that he was three hours late. "I thought you said you couldn't dance?"

He chuckled, sending a warm breath across her cheek. "I lost all track of time out looking for more coyotes...."

She couldn't care less. *What's a few hours*? "You missed dinner."

He ran his hand along her back, down her spine, landed on her bottom, pulling her closer. She *really* didn't care that he was three hours late. Heat burned through her jeans like a branding iron. He kissed her, and her heart galloped like Sugar let loose on the range.

"When I'm out on my land... it's like I forget everything else..."

Forget everything? She pulled loose. His wrinkled brow caught her attention before she slapped at his chest. "You were three hours late!"

"I know. I just said I was sorry."

"You said you... forgot about me." Beneath her hand, he tensed. She smacked him again.

"I didn't mean... Stop that!" He grabbed her hand. "I didn't forget about you... I got preoccupied with the ranch and..."

She freed her hand. "I know, Slate." Stepping back she said, "Unfortunately, I can't compete with this place." Her heart wrenched at the look in his eyes. A sadness replaced the fire of his anger. How she wished he'd stayed angry.

"I'll *always* be a rival to Valley Del Sol."

Chapter 9

The lead singer belted out "Always On My Mind," as Slate watched Becky walk away. He should go after her, but to do what? To say what? She was exactly right: Valley Del Sol stood between them, corralling his heart from loving Becky the way she deserved to be loved.

With her vibrancy for life, she needed someone who could keep up with her and be there to share her joys. Someone who wasn't so set in his ways. Someone who didn't alphabetize his books. Someone who didn't let his work come before the woman he cared about. She needed—someone else.

The couples dancing around him blurred as if in the background. Mumbling his excuses as he bumped into several dancers, he made his way toward the barn. The night air cooled his lungs, but nothing could ease the knot gripping him inside. Anger tightened the knot—anger at himself.

He'd done what he vowed never to do.

He had no right falling in love, or letting a woman fall in love with him. As if he'd been born with some defective gene passed to him from his father, obviously he wasn't capable of putting a woman above his land.

The damned land threatened to ruin his life.

"Why did you do this to me, Uncle Nate?" he asked to the starlight sky. His uncle had to have known that Slate wasn't capable of distancing himself from the ranch. He'd seen Slate work from sunup until the sky grew so dark some nights he'd unroll the sleeping bag he carried on the back of Cloud Dancer and spend the night out on the range. And Uncle Nate had seen how Slate grew so set in his ways that he didn't have room for a relationship. Yet the old man persisted, even after death.

Slate turned into the barn. A sleepy Jack peered at him from behind a set of dark eyelashes. Standing and stretching, the little guy let out a bleat that annoyed his sister, but she snuggled into a pile of hay and slept.

"Hey, buddy, did I wake you?" He lifted the lamb and carried him to the bench. Sitting with him on his lap, he relived the scene with Becky and as if she stood in front of him, he could hear her accusations clear as the cloudless night.

Warmth spread through him deep to his core, inhaling an aura of her musky scent. He pictured her apple-green lips frowning. A dullness had clouded the sparkle in her eyes. And Becky did have the most sparkling eyes he'd ever seen. They glowed as if she'd sprinkled some of the glitter that dotted many of her outfits into them. And because of the pain he'd caused, the glitter had dimmed.

Jack nuzzled his arm. Slate ran his hand across the fluff of wool, scratching behind the lamb's ear. "Someone'd think you were a puppy."

Jack let out a sound of agreement.

Slate chuckled. "Hey, you're getting pretty heavy." He shifted his legs beneath the lamb's weight, proud of how well the twins did without their mother. He and Becky had done a great job taking care of them.

This must be how a parent feels. He thought of his father and wondered if Hank Lawson had ever been proud of him. It didn't seem likely since he hadn't been around enough to spend time with his son. They never shared a secret, spent a night on the range together, or did any of the things the other kids did with their dads. If it wasn't for the ranch hands, Slate might never have learned how to mend a fence, shear a sheep, or ride a horse.

A sadness tugged at his heart, thinking of the years of loneliness. He noticed a pile of ropes hanging on the wall. Lasso competitions and roping had brought him joy as a kid. There had been little wall space left in his room for all the blue ribbons he'd won.

Walking toward Jill, he settled Jack near his sister and took one of lassos from the hook on the wall. Memories flooded back with the twisted strands of hemp beneath his fingers. He spun it around, roping the edge of Jack and Jill's pen several times. Lifting it off, he stopped. Something was burned into the leather end, but years of wear made it near impossible to read. He held it under the light and squinted.

"I'll be damned."

Although it wasn't clear, he made out what looked like the initials "HL." This had to have belonged to his father. He leaned against the wall, wondering how he'd gotten it. Each competition his mother always made sure to attend, but he never saw his father. He'd been told since he could walk not to touch his father's favorite lasso. Maybe it got mixed up in his things when he sold his parent's ranch, but he'd been meticulous about packing.

He straightened and grasped the rope until his knuckles whitened. "Did you give it to me, Dad?" Was this his father's way of showing he cared but wasn't capable of being the kind of father Slate had wanted? Did he replace his lasso with Slate's years ago for him to use to compete? Shoot, he hoped so.

Sucking in a breath, he knew it was time to stop blaming his father for how he behaved. He needed to take responsibility for himself. His father chose the lifestyle he was capable of, and now he needed to choose his. Sending the lasso over the hook, he knew what to do.

★

Becky stuck her toe through the clouds of bubbles in the tub. She had two days free until the next batch of guests arrived. With no need to hurry, she soaked herself in the lilac-scented foam, letting the warmth drug her muscles into tranquility. If only her heart could enjoy the luxury—but she couldn't forget her dance with Slate last night. Her heart sagged under the weight of her thoughts.

He'd held her with a protective grasp that she'd ached for since childhood. Her earliest memories were to have a father, a protector, until she grew to adolescence. Needs changed, and she looked at boys with renewed interest. Instead of meeting someone who wanted to take her dancing and to the local fast-food hangout, she only met boys who wanted to get her into the back seat of their cars, and the term protection took on a different meaning.

But last night when Slate wrapped his arms around her and pressed his callused palms into her back, she felt something new. She excited him, but he eased up his hold before she could feel as if he merely used her body for his own needs.

When she left him last night, she walked to the lake to think. On the way back, she went to ease her sadness with a visit to Jack and Jill. Slate had beaten her to it. For a while, she'd stood and watched him nuzzling Jack. She loved those darn sheep, but she envied them Slate's attention. Before he caught her watching, she had left.

"Geez, now he's ruining my bath!" She stood and grabbed a towel. Once dry, she wrapped it around herself and headed to find some clothing. No need for anything fancy today. She grabbed a faded pair of cutoff jeans and her favorite T-shirt that Wanda had given her that said, "Hairdressers, Shear Magic," in gold across the chest and had a huge pair of sparkling scissors on the back.

Her stomach growled, so, *since* Rosa *was still in Albuquerque*, she went to the kitchen to fix herself something. In the kitchen doorway, she stopped. The table held flowers in the center—red wildflowers in a crystal vase. Two settings of china, not the everyday earthenware Rosa used, sat on crimson linen place mats. Her breath caught when she looked toward the stove.

Slate stood with his back to her, a spatula waving in the air to the peppy beat blaring from the radio. At least it looked like Slate's wide shoulders, narrow waist, and to-die-for derrière.

But Slate Lawson gyrating to music?

She cleared her throat.

He wiggled his bottom. The spatula waved near his face. Obviously, a microphone.

She cleared her throat again and took a step forward.

His feet shuffled on the beige tile floor, sliding as if on ice. With the "microphone" near his mouth, he wailed along with Hank Williams Jr., who'd apparently met a woman with a cold, cold heart.

She mumbled, "Hello…." Walking near enough to see the muscles of his back strain beneath his brown plaid shirt, she sucked in a breath and ignored the hot and spicy feelings tingling to her toes. "Slate?"

He swung around, the spatula flew in the air, landing smack against her cheek.

"Ouch!"

"Oh shoot, Beck…." He grabbed her shoulders and rubbed his hand against her face. "Are you all right? Heck, I'm sorry. I was just…"

"I'm fine, Hank. I was enjoying the entertainment." How adorable scarlet looked beneath the shadow of a he-man cowboy's beard.

Slate ran his finger along her temple, pushing strands of hair from her eyes. He leaned forward and kissed the spot where the spatula had smacked her. "Sure you're all right?"

She nodded, and he kissed her lips. Without the slightest hesitation, he pulled her close, running his hands along her spine. Beneath her shirt heat singed her skin. She peaked from behind his shoulder to see if she'd backed up into the stove. It stood a good foot away. Hm, what a way to start her day.

"Becky, about last night…."

He kissed her lips and eased back enough to look at her chest. With his fingers, he traced the words on her shirt. "Shear magic, hm. I love it."

He moved his hands to her waist. "You do make me believe in magic, Beck."

Thank goodness his firm grip held her or she'd stumble to the floor like Jill trying out her first steps. "How?"

"Just being you, your gusto for life.... I'm sorry about last night, the dance and.... I'm taking today off."

"Holy Houdini!" She grabbed his shoulders and shook. "Where's Slate Lawson? What have you done with him?"

He laughed. "I'm serious. I gave instructions to the ranch hands to do their work without me. Your magical trance has come over me, and I'm... no, *we're* going to do whatever you want to today."

Becky's heart jolted. A whole day together! Worry didn't come easy to her, but for a second, she thought of last night. She looked into Slate's eyes and saw the caring, the sincerity, and the magnetism that pulled her in to his life. A flutter of her heart said she had to see if she could trust him to keep his word.

"Whatever I want, hm?" She tapped a nail to her tooth. "Well, let me think." If she chose leaving the ranch, she'd never know if she could trust Slate. No, she had to think of something to do around there so he'd be tempted to check on the hands, or the corn, or the sheep.

"We could take a hot-air balloon ride," he suggested.

"Oh, I've never been on one... but we'd have to go... where?"

"There's some in Las Cruces."

"Nope. The air's too dusty today." She hoped he wouldn't look out the window at the crisp, clear sky.

"How about shopping in Juárez?"

"Oh geez, I haven't done that in years." But they'd have to leave the area. She should have kept the excitement out of her voice.

"Okay, then shopping it is..."

"No it isn't. I... er... the peso's too inflated."

Slate curved his eyebrow. "The peso is..."

"Never mind. I've always wanted to explore the canyons on the western part of the property."

"Glider canyon?"

She nodded.

"Best view of the hang gliders from there, but you wouldn't

rather go shopping—my treat?"

"Nope."

"Okay, it's your choice."

He sounded confused, but she couldn't explain that she was testing him. She knew Slate was as honest as he was gorgeous, but honesty didn't drive him to live and breathe the ranch. If she was going to lose her heart to this cowboy, she needed to protect herself—no one else would.

"I've made breakfast. Come here." Slate led her to the table with a gentle pressure on her back. He pulled out the chair as she sank onto the wooden surface.

"You know, normally I'd fuss about how I'm capable of sitting by myself," she said.

He chuckled. "I don't doubt it." At the refrigerator, he pulled out two frosted bowls embossed with roses. Setting one in front of her and the other at his place he turned toward the counter.

"Hi," Grady said, standing in the doorway, rubbing his eyes.

"Hey, partner." Slate nodded and Becky went to him.

"Sleep okay?" she asked after kissing his cheek.

"Beck, I'm too old for that." He wiped it off.

Slate leaned near her ear. "I'm not."

She pushed at his chest. "Let's get you some breakfast."

"Then can I go with Dave to do chores?"

Becky looked at Slate who nodded. "Sure, kiddo. But first you have to eat."

Slate continued on as if some chef in a five star restaurant. Grady ate in seconds, asked for permission to leave and after a fast kiss to his cheek, despite his annoyance, the kid was gone.

The sweetened scent of strawberries mixed with the distinct aroma of banana. She looked at the bowl, wondering how he managed to half the berries so each looked like a little heart. They swam amongst the circular bananas in the opaque white liquid that had to be heavy cream. The contents and both bowls probably cost more than she'd spend on a week's grocery bill. There was a lot to be said about having money. She'd argue all night with Wanda about it—living here was proof—and a reminder that she didn't belong.

Steaming coffee splattered into her cup as Slate poured. He set the pot between them on a tile coaster with a Saguaro cactus embossed on top. Next to the coffee pot he set a dish of scrambled eggs with chips of bacon nestled amongst the yellow hills and valleys. Before he sat down, he leaned against the counter, counted to ten, and flipped the toaster knob, sending two slices popping into the air to land on the plate in his extended hand.

Becky laughed. "Nice catch."

Slate tipped his imaginary hat toward her.

The food was delicious, the music blaring from the radio Western, and the company magical. Although she ate too much, Becky had never enjoyed a meal more.

"Go put something on to hike around in the canyons. I'll clean," he said.

"I have to change my favorite shirt?"

Slate eased her from the chair and brushed his hands against the letters of her T-shirt. "Uh-uh, just your shorts and boots. The rocks can get slippery so wear long jeans and sneakers." He cupped his hand beneath her breast.

She moaned.

He mumbled against her cheek, "Keep on Shear Magic."

★

Becky's legs punished her for her choice. With every step across the boulders, each muscle contracted with an I-told-you-to-exercise-years-ago nagging. Why couldn't she have chosen a nice hot air balloon ride and be floating amongst the clouds right now... Because then Slate would be out of range of Valley Del Sol.

Gouges in the rock walls provided steps up the sides of the canyon. She followed Slate, enjoying the outdoor scenery and the view of Slate's rear end. Faded jeans clung to his legs, defining the muscles of his thighs with each step. He'd kept his boots on, although he made her put on sneakers. Sure-footed, he climbed across the rocks, over the dirt path as if he had spikes in his worn boots.

He shed his vest, tucked it into his backpack, and rolled his shirtsleeves above his elbows. His skin gleamed a tawny color with fine hairs lightened by the sun running along his forearms. Frequently he'd turn as if to offer a hand, but she could read his hesitation—he knew she'd swat his help away. He was getting to know her very well. Heck, she could maneuver through this canyon with the best of them, despite the searing pains in her legs. Slate slowed when she slipped and looked over his shoulder each time, but continued on. Yep, he really had her number, and her heart. Occasionally when he'd look past her—toward the ranch—her heart would slow until he turned ahead and continued on.

Maybe she imagined he'd looked past her. Maybe he was enjoying the enchanting scenery as much as her. Maybe his heart leapt with excitement each time she smiled at him as hers did when he smiled at her. Oh God, she was falling hard for this cowboy. She stole a second to stop and look across the wide-open desert. It looked like the postcards her guests sent to friends back East. No man could ever manage to build something so spectacular as nature. In the distance, flocks of white bodies dotted the drab arid scene. Her heat sank. Could she compete with all that?

"Ready for a rest?" he asked, turning around.

Her breath caught as the sun gleamed on his sweat-beaded forehead, and sparkled in his deep green eyes that picked up a touch of hazel when he wore brown. "You're the leader." *Please let him stop,* her legs begged.

"Let's head to those rocks near the water."

She followed his pointing to a pool of water formed in a basin of stone. A small waterfall trickled from above, sending what had to be cold mountain water from natural springs. It looked like a mirage to her weary eyes.

Slate crossed an opening in the rocks. He turned and waited. It wasn't as if they were mountain climbing and she could fall into the space, but he waited with his hands at his sides as if ready to catch her. She jumped across. The soles of her sneakers had been good to prevent slipping, but this time the rubber stopped her from sliding to stabilize herself. She grabbed out, catching Slate's shirt. The sound of ripping fabric echoed across the canyon.

"Oh geez!" She felt him grab her shoulder, but like Lucy and Desi, her other foot knocked into his, and they stumbled across the rocks.

"Shoot!" Freezing water splashed around them. Slate reached out to cushion Becky's head from hitting the rocks, but he couldn't stop her from submerging. He yanked her head up.

A scream gurgled from her mouth. "Damn, that's cold!" She coughed out the water.

Slate patted her back as if that would help. When she caught her breath, he looked at her lying next to him in the clear water. Golden strands of hair, darkened by the wetness, clung to her cheeks. Glistening beads of wetness dotted her nose, cheeks, and lips like diamonds on a queen's tiara. Following the moisture dripping off her pointy chin, he gazed at her submerged form. *Oh hell.* The white fabric of her shirt turned transparent in the water. Brownish circles appeared on her braless chest, one each beneath the "h" and "g" of Shear Magic.

Despite the freezing water, his jeans tightened.

"I'm sorry, Slate," she managed through chattering teeth.

He wasn't.

The clear water masked the texture of the cinnamon rocks below. They looked smooth but when he tried to stand, his foot slipped as if on ice, and he slid back with a splash.

"You must be freezing."

"Nope, too numb."

"Well we need to get out of here before you get a cold."

She leaned against the rock. How nice to have a man care. "Any suggestions?" But she really didn't want him to think of any because they'd have to go back to the ranch now that they were wet.

"Here..." He moved to the side and braced his arm against the wall of rocks. "On three, lean against me until you get your footing."

She glared at him.

"One, two...."

Becky pushed against him. Her shoulders rose above water level, then her waist. She reached to hold onto his shoulder. With a firm hold he grabbed her to a standing position, but she moved too fast and bolted forward, landing on her back across his chest. He looked at "Shear Magic," inches away from his face—and moaned.

When their gazes met, he paused with her body teasing him so near. He pulled her forward. Their lips met, kissing the coldness away. Slate wrapped his arms around her shoulders, easing her shivering body forward. Nuzzling beneath the soaked hair on her neck, he mumbled, "You are cold."

"Not anymore." She ran kisses along his temple, licking the drips of water in-between.

The water warmed like a Jacuzzi with the nearness of her body. Clothing sticking to wet skin provided a sensual effect to her hands running along his spine. Chills followed the same path as her touch, and they didn't come from the mountain spring.

Who said cold water eased an arousal?

He'd need a glacier to slide along the canyon floor to thaw his. Her breath warmed his cheek. He turned to kiss her. A faint taste of cherry clung to her wet lips. She shivered under his hold.

"I've got to get you dry." Determined to stand, he eased her forward and jammed his foot into the rocks. Pain seared up his ankle, but he managed to stand and pull Becky up. Grabbing a branch of a nearby bush, he stepped out and pulled her from the water.

The sun warmed their soaked bodies as Slate embraced her. Hot currents of air blanketed them, and beneath his hold he could feel the cold discomfort ease from her.

"Let's sit here and drip off a few minutes."

"Really? We don't have to leave?"

"Not unless you want to."

She shook her head, so he guided her to a pile of rocks where she yanked off her wet sneakers and socks. He undid the balls of wool and laid them across a rock.

"Won't take too long to dry in this heat." He yanked off his shirt, and before he smoothed it out next to her socks, he examined the tear. Damn, his favorite brown plaid shirt.

Shear Magic clung to her pert breasts as if she'd stripped off her top to dry along with his. He sucked in a breath as she leaned against the rocks like a sunbather in the Caribbean. She stretched her arms above her head to fan out her hair along the rock. She wasn't tall, but laying there, her legs looked so long—shoot, deliciously long. He turned toward the freezing spring water. Hell, he'd have to dive in again if she kept this up.

He peeked over his shoulder.

She wiggled on the hard surface as the jeans that had clung to her like skin when dry now hugged her so tightly he thought he could make out a birthmark above her knee. He swung back around. The sun must be causing him to hallucinate. Forcing himself to turn toward her laying like a mermaid, he said, "Want to head back? You don't look too comfortable."

Her voice came out a throaty whisper as if she'd been dozing. "No! No… I'm fine." She patted the rock. "Stretch out and let the sun dry you," she murmured, softly. Hell, invitingly.

Laying next to her with the sun burning his skin, he knew the torture cowboys endured in the Old West when left to bake in the sun tied to poles with strips of rawhide. A breeze blew a hint of musk toward him. The water couldn't wash off her distinct Becky scent. Either the sun dried his pants in nanoseconds or her nearness was too much for his hormones. He shifted to loosen the tightness in his jeans. "Want me to hike down to the truck and get a blanket…"

Her eyes were shut, her cherry lips puffed softly. Slate reached his arm toward her head. With a soft moan, she lifted her head, landing on his chest with a sigh. He leaned back, holding Becky as if the seclusion of the canyon melted away their differences. Nothing interfered right now, nothing.

He could stay here forever, holding the woman who warmed his heart hotter than the ball of heat glaring at them from the sky.

★

Becky's nose burned. Her eyelids fluttered against the brightness. Hardness pressed into her spine, but her head rested on a firmness that felt solid and soft at the same time. She forced her eyes open to come face to face with Slate. He hadn't rushed them back to the house.

"Hey, sleepyhead."

She wiggled free. "Did I conk off?" She struggled to sit.

He sat up. "Let's just say you'd give a lumber mill a run for their money."

Heat surged up her cheeks. "Damn. I snore?"

"No one ever had the nerve to tell you before?"

She raised an eyebrow. "Everything sounds louder in the echo of this canyon." Standing, she stretched her shirt out. "Hey, the front is all dry."

He frowned. "I see."

"Look, I'm sorry about that dip we took…"

He stood and touched her lips. "I'm not."

Pushing against his chest, her hands froze. Hot skin burned beneath her touch. Geez, why hadn't he kept his shirt on? As if she had no control, she ran her hands in circles around his nipples, nestled between curls of chestnut hair.

He moaned, took her fingers, and kissed them. Pleasure radiated throughout her. She cupped his cheeks with her hands. "This has been fun." She kissed him full on the lips and realized he'd passed her test today.

"Um." He ran kisses from her lips along her neck.

Looking down the canyon behind them, she said, "We didn't

get too far did we?"

He grinned.

She swatted his chest. "I mean on our hike."

"We've got plenty of daylight left. Unless you're too uncomfortable in those clothes."

She pulled at her jeans, wiggling her narrow hips as if doing a little dance. The entire morning had felt as if she and Slate were the only two in the world. It had been wonderful spending time without him being preoccupied with the ranch. Yanking her stiff T-shirt from her chest, she decided to ignore the discomfort—nothing could ruin this day. She really *could* trust him. "I'm fine."

"Hey, look." Slate pointed to the other side of the water where his navy backpack sat on the rock near the space where they'd jumped over. "Hungry?"

"Now that you mention it."

"Wait here." He worked his way around the rocky ledge, careful not to slip into the water again.

Becky sat on the rocks and pulled her knees to her chest. How different Slate was away from the ranch. Except for him smoothing her socks and his shirt out on the rocks—neater than Rosa herself—he didn't seem to mind not having everything in order. She wondered what he'd do if he saw how his hair had dried with a tiny cowlick in the back. He looked adorable.

Of course, she was prejudiced.

As he stepped across the rocks, she teased him amid laughter that he might fall again. He threatened to get her if he did. She dared him, he chuckled. Even his laughter came out more natural as if the freezing water had relieved him of some burden that had kept him restrained.

"For Madame." He spread a sun-yellow tablecloth out on the surface of a flat rock. "Gouda cheese, crispy French bread, Rosa's chopped jalapeños, and a wonderful dry Bordeaux. Luckily, unbroken."

The meal progressed as if Becky and Slate had stumbled into

one of her soap operas. Everything was perfect. They laughed, they ate, they drank the wine after various toasts, and they kissed until she tasted the spicy peppers on his lips. Yes, everything was perfect—and she wanted to make love to him. She was ready.

Slate leaned forward and kissed her. A faint noise touched her ears. Geez, he had powerful kisses. She reached to pull him closer.

"Did you hear that?" He stood so fast the wine bottle toppled, shattering on the rocks.

"Hear what?"

"A howl," he whispered. His eyes widened as if that would improve his hearing.

"It's probably…"

"Shh!" He waved her silent.

Annoyed at his treating her like a kid, she bent to pick up the broken glass and stick it into a bag. Another howl, much louder this time, pierced the air causing her to jump and a sliver of glass sliced her finger.

"Damn it!" He yanked the backpack over his shoulder, turned, and started down the rocks.

She looked up speechless. Her usual response would have been, "Hey, buddy, didn't you forget something?" But the pain ripping into her heart drained any sense of humor she had left. There was nothing funny about having the damned Valley Del Sol ruin her day.

Nothing funny. And nothing she could do about it, yet again.

Chapter 10

Becky wiped her cut finger with a clean napkin as she watched Slate starting down the dirt path of the canyon. Coyote's howls broke the distant air. She shoved the remaining glass into the sandwich bag and stood.

"Becky?" Slate turned around and looked at her making her way down the canyon. He climbed toward her. "What're you doing?"

She wanted to fling the sandwich bag at him. What did it look like she was doing? Sunbathing? "I'm coming."

He neared enough to reach out toward her. "What's taking so long…?"

"Ouch!" She pulled free of his hand even though her pride hurt more than the little cut did.

He took her hand gently. "What happened, Becky? You're bleeding…"

"No kidding." She pushed past him. "I'm fine."

His boots clicked on the rocks as he neared. "Wait a minute, Beck…"

"I thought you were in a hurry?"

He grabbed her arm and swung her around. "I didn't know you were hurt."

"And if I wasn't, it would have been all right to leave me up there…"

Damn the sadness that filled his eyes. He couldn't have forced it if he wanted to. She could see the wrinkles in his forehead, the worry in his face.

"No, it wouldn't have been all right. I'm sorry. I heard the howls and…." He pulled her near and spoke against her forehead. Warm breaths soothed her skin. "Can I plead temporary insanity?"

She contemplated pushing him over the large boulders behind them. "Temporary?"

He chuckled. "Let me see your finger." He touched her gently, as if she were made of glass. "How'd this happen?"

She glared at him.

"Shoot. The wine bottle?"

When she nodded, he kissed her finger below the cut. "I'm sorry."

"I'll live. Come on. I know you need to check on your sheep."

This time he wrapped his arm around her shoulder until they neared the truck. Slate paused by the passenger door.

"I can manage," she said, knowing it killed him that she wouldn't let him hold the door open for her. Okay, it was a low blow to get back at him for leaving her, but it gave her a second of satisfaction—then she felt like a creep.

They rode silently back to Valley Del Sol. With every bump the truck sped over, she knew he worried about his sheep. He slowed the truck in front of the door and waited as Becky hurried out. Before she could say goodbye, a cloud of dust swallowed the truck in its wake. Did he wave goodbye, or had she imagined it?

★

Driving through the dust devils, Slate leaned forward to see through his clouded vision. A sick feeling knotted the pit of his stomach when he thought of leaving Becky in the canyon. Sure, it was a minor cut, but he'd rushed down the canyon so fast, he didn't even know about it. She could have slipped on the rocks… his heart wrenched. Coyotes' howling filled his ears. The windows were shut, so he knew he imagined the haunting, teasing wails. But he wasn't imagining that he'd put the needs of his ranch over Becky. He'd like to believe he had no control over himself, but did he?

The thought of monthly financial reports always stayed in a

corner of his mind.

His foot jammed the brake. He jumped out and headed into the barn. Nearly knocking over a startled Luke, he shouted, "Saddle up! Coyotes out by Glider Canyon."

"You saw them?" Luke yanked a saddle from the ledge.

Slate worked on saddling Cloud Dancer, then headed out of the barn. Over his shoulder he shouted, "Heard them!"

The Appaloosa galloped over the desert floor as if flying on air. Slate scanned the base of the mountains for any signs of coyote. Everything blurred with the speed he rode, so he slowed Cloud Dancer and pulled out his binoculars. Horse's hoof beats thudded behind as Luke and three other ranch hands approached.

"See anything?" Luke yelled.

The binoculars dropped to his lap. "Damn it! This way…." Slate sped off toward the bodies of his sheep.

★

After changing her damp clothes, checking on Grady, and redoing her cherry lipstick, Becky was well into her third soap opera, but she might as well have been staring at a blank screen. Her mind wandered to the morning, the kiss with Slate in the spring pool, their wonderful lunch… and how he'd left her. Slamming the TV's power off with her remote control, she stood and looked out the window. Tomorrow a new batch of guests would arrive. Thank goodness. Wanda would tell her she was bored with nothing to do. Money couldn't buy happiness.

"Oh hush, Wanda!" she said to the empty room. Looking at the mountains flanking the property, hummingbirds darting at the red liquid Rosa always kept in the feeder, and turning to take in the spectacular room she'd lived in the past few months, she said, "Who wouldn't be happy with all this?"

But all the beauty and opulence were lonely without someone to share it with—someone special.

At her desk, she riffled through a stack of papers, making sure no bills got missed. She prided herself in paying her debts on time. Too bad she couldn't pride herself on neatness like Slate. Oh well, when she had enough money, she'd hire a bookkeeper. So why bother to be neat now?

The financial report from Walter Payton, the CPA hired to keep track of both Becky's and Slate's earnings sat on a pile. She shoved it aside with a groan. She still had time to catch up or it'd be back to working eighty-hour weeks at Wanda's salon to save for her house.

Attorney Greeson's letterhead caught her eye. Lifting the paper from the stack, her heart slowed. She'd forgotten about that damned letter… or she'd purposely forced it into her unconsciousness. If she were the emotional type, tears would be flowing, but instead, her heart hurt when she read it. Why had Slate been so underhanded? Why not just ask her to leave the lake alone? Legal stuff bothered her. She'd been involved in too many "systems" since childhood and hated seeing formal papers like this. If only he had talked to her about it, she could have told him she had no intentions of touching the lake until things were settled about the ranch.

Her heart clenched.

Time was passing and soon her fate would be decided. Hope should have overpowered her, but instead, a tightness gripped her chest. What would happen if she lost the ranch? It seemed as if she'd been there her entire life. It was a perfect home for Grady with Rosa and Hector helping to watch him. It seemed as if she belonged, and had proved to be a great businesswoman. It also seemed as if she couldn't win this gamble.

She'd either lose the ranch and her home, or she'd win—and hurt Slate.

Looking at the azure sky through the window, she asked, "What the hell did you have in mind, Nate Lawson?"

A feeling as if she wanted to crawl out of her skin came over her. Geez, she was bored. Although cool air hummed from the ceiling vents, she felt smothered. It wasn't any fun being alone in a beautiful villa like this. But… she still wanted her own house and would do whatever it took to get it.

Grabbing her yellow Stetson to match her boots and daffodil-covered shorts, she slung her denim purse over her shoulder and headed outside with no idea where she was going. After playing with the calf and goats in the corral with Grady until he became more interested in running off with a neighbor boy, she went into the barn. Jack and Jill romped around, running in and out through the opening in their pen. They gave her a friendly "baa" but busied themselves with each other.

Handing her horse some sugar, she said, "I'll remember that, you two." She grabbed her saddle and, with a groan, shoved it atop Sugar as Dave had showed her.

Once outside, she aimed the horse toward the eastern part of the property. She had no desire to run into a coyote… or Slate. Greasewood bushes dotted the sandy soil as tumbleweeds skidded across the path she'd chosen. The sun beat down on her and she realized she'd forgotten her sunscreen. Tipping her hat forward, she'd at least protect her face from burning. The hat impeded her vision, so she decided to let Sugar be the guide. Maybe the horse could find something interesting for her to do.

No Trespassing. Keep Out. Danger.

Becky read and reread each weathered sign posted a few feet in front of her, then dismounted and tied Sugar's reins on a nearby fence post.

A niggling of excitement started at her toes, and even in the stiff leather boots she felt it work its way up to her abdomen. She had to get a closer look. Geez, it felt as if she'd traveled back to the Old West! When she mounted the fence to jump over the side, she froze. As if Slate stood directly in front of her, she could hear him commanding, "Don't ever go out there. The timbers have been known to collapse."

A fighter jet from nearby Holloman Air Force Base buzzed above, yanking the vision of Slate from her and back to reality. She looked at the dim shadow cast by the tree Sugar stood under and laughed. "Not just any shadow, a talking Slate shadow." Rubbing her forehead and ignoring her conscience, she said, "Maybe I have sunstroke." Digging around in her denim bag, which hung from the saddle, she found a penlight. She jumped over the fence and headed for the opening to the old gold mine.

★

Slate pulled the saddle off a tired Cloud Dancer. "Water her down, Luke."

"Sure thing, Slate." Luke took the horse and turned toward the trough.

Slate shook his head. "Thanks." He turned toward the house. "We need to have the men start some controlled campfires to keep the coyotes away. But, Luke, be real careful. It's so dry out there any spark could cause a fire to spread."

"That reminds me, Slate. The corn's been taking some awful hits lately."

He'd been so preoccupied with things lately—with Becky lately—he'd forgotten to get the irrigation system upgraded. "We losing some of it?"

Luke paused. His eyes darkened. "My guess is about a quarter..."

"Damn it! Send some of the men out with buckets, at least try to soak down what's closest to the lake." He hated working his men so hard, but without water, the corn would all dry up to withered stalks. "I'm gonna change, then I'll meet them out in the fields." The shirt had dried stiff in the sunlight and his jeans chafed his thighs. After a fast shower he'd change and head out again. Walking into the kitchen he inhaled the faint scent of Becky and decided changing could wait a few minutes.

"Becky!" He walked toward the hallway to the west wing. "Hey, Beck. You awake?" Silence filled the hallway so he headed down to knock on her door. "How's your finger..."

The door was open. Obviously she wasn't in her room or anywhere else or she'd have answered.

Unless she was still angry about this morning.

Shaking his head, he admitted she had every right to be. Hurrying to his room, he took a fast shower and threw on dry jeans and a blue denim shirt. Rolling the sleeves above his elbows as he ran toward the kitchen, he decided he needed to talk to Becky before he went to help water the corn.

There wasn't a note on the table—it was a long shot anyway. Becky wasn't the type to write a note. He smiled at her independence, but a worry nagged at him. Her ranch was empty until tomorrow and all of her hands had taken the day off. One of his hands had told him that Grady was spending time at a neighbors. Outside the kitchen, her van sat in the driveway and the petting animals lazed in the corral. Inside the barn he noticed that Sugar's stall was empty.

Becky must be out riding, but he couldn't see her anywhere along the paths. He didn't like the idea that she might be out alone. Stillness covered the flat desert for several miles, and the snowy gelding would stand out clearly amongst the browns of the earth. If she didn't stay on one of the paths that she should have, that meant....

"Oh hell, what are you up to now?"

He didn't have time to go searching the rest of the property. There was too much damn work to do. Maybe she'd ride back any second. He ran out of the barn and walked toward the path on the western side. Hoof prints dotted the dusty path, but he was no expert at telling if they were freshly made. One set looked much deeper than the rest, as if the wind had blown the top of the others smooth.

Slate ran back and got his binoculars from his saddle in the barn. He scanned the area but saw no movement except the desert breezes chasing tumbleweeds across deserted trails. When he turned to the right, he saw a car stirring up dust as it approached the house. Dave Palmer's red Chevy. He let out a sigh of relief. He and Becky must have gone into town for supplies. Of course, she usually used her van but....

Hell, his corn needed tending to.

He ran back to the barn and saddled Cloud Dancer. Leading her out, he yelled at Dave, "Tell Becky I'll be back in a few hours."

"Haven't seen her, Slate," Dave shouted.

Slate yanked the reins, snapping Cloud Dancer's head back. "She's not with you?" A stupid question since Dave just said he hadn't seen her, but he was fresh out of making sense when Becky Chambers was concerned.

"Nope." Dave grabbed a box from the car and came toward the barn.

Slate cursed and turned his horse toward the west. Tipping his hat toward Dave, he clucked his tongue. Cloud Dancer started forward.

"Slate, maybe I did see something!" Dave shouted.

"Whoa!" He turned toward Dave.

"It was pretty far away, but heck... No she wouldn't go out there..."

"Where?" He didn't mean to sound so gruff with Dave, but worry and anger had him on edge.

"Looked like something white, maybe a horse, maybe a stray ewe... hell, it was too far away to tell..."

"Where, Dave?"

"She knows better than to go out there... even tells all the guests to stay clear of..."

"Where? Oh hell...." Slate shouted over his shoulder, "Do me a favor and get word to Luke that I'll be gone for a few hours."

"Females!" Cloud Dancer snorted as he yanked the reins. "Don't *you* give me any trouble, girl."

The ride to the old gold mine seemed to take hours, although he knew it wasn't that long. His pulse sped with each gust of wind that knocked into his face. She had to have gone out there. Damn it! He'd warned her about the old mine the first day she arrived. Maybe there was no way to trust Becky Chambers. She'd do whatever she wanted no matter what he or anyone else said. She was too damn independent and wild.

And that's what he loved most about her.

He'd fallen for her the day she'd whooped it up on Sugar and fell because of her recklessness. That's when the real Becky showed herself and stole his heart. Hell, he envied her independence. How often, lately, he wished he could be free of the ranch, free to do as he pleased—without the guilt.

Pushing Cloud Dancer harder, he looked to see he'd taken a wrong turn. Cursing into the dusty air, he yanked the reins and headed down the right trail. At least he hoped it was the right one. It had been years since he'd ridden this section of the property. He could still remember Uncle Nate yelling at him for going out there when he was about eleven. He warned him that it was old and any day the timbers could collapse. Since the air force practiced maneuvers over that area, the fighter jets could cause a tremor of the earth to rock the timbers loose. He hadn't believed such a thing was possible and thought Uncle Nate had made it all up to scare him. Now he really hoped that Uncle Nate had.

Looking to the sky, he whispered, "Watch over her, Nate."

Chapter 11

Sugar stood in the shade of the tree near the "No Trespassing" sign. Slate shut his eyes and sighed. At least he'd found her. The sun beating down on his uncovered arms didn't match the heat boiling his blood. When he got Becky he'd....

He'd say a silent prayer of thanks... and hold her, and kiss her flavored lips.

After jumping off Cloud Dancer, he grabbed a flashlight from his saddlebag, scaled the fence, and ran toward the opening. He told himself to control his temper. It wasn't easy lately, actually; since meeting Becky his patience had been tested to the maximum. It seemed he only lost control when something or someone he loved was threatened.

The opening looked almost as it had nineteen years ago when he came there as a kid. Pausing for a second, he noticed more growth around the old tracks on the ground, and several beams had cracks in their centers. Maybe they were like that years ago, but an uneasiness filled his gut. In the distance, fighter jets roared across the cloudless sky. Slate knew they'd eventually be overhead. If the cracks in the beams were recent....

"Becky!" he shouted into the opening. Pebbles cascaded from the ceiling hit him in the face. Fool! He could start the timbers to collapse with his shouts. Clattering stones hit the ground as he tipped his Stetson back to clean it off. Shining the light along the tracks, he walked inside. His steps came cautiously with the reminder Becky was somewhere in the old mine.

Dampness stung his nose so he pulled his neckerchief over his nose and mouth. He tried to stifle a cough and walked as if crossing a thinly frozen lake. His boots clicked on the metal tracks. Spider webs tormented his face, dangling from the stone ceiling. Ripping them away with his free hand, he made his way further inside.

He aimed the flashlight forward. No sign of life lay ahead. Maybe Becky hadn't come inside. Maybe she was just exploring outside around the area. Maybe there was still gold in the old mine, too. Yeah, right. That was as absurd a thought as inquisitive Becky not entering the old mine was.

"Becky." His whisper echoed against the solid walls. Water trickled down cracks green with mold. The tracks split into a fork. "Damn it. Now what?" He knew if he took the wrong turn he could be searching for hours, or worse yet—get lost. What good would that do Becky?

Stopping, he decided he needed to think like her. Hell, what a chore. Which would she choose? He had no idea, so he decided to pick one—and then follow the other.

As he stepped along the track to the right, a clang sounded. "Becky?" No answer. Running his hand along the wall, he stopped and shone the light on the rocks. A spot of red. Oh god. Was she hurt or—no, he couldn't think like that. He brushed his fingers across the spot and held his hand out. With the light aimed downward, he rubbed his fingers together, it didn't feel sticky. Not that he'd know what blood should smell like, but he still leaned forward and inhaled. Mustiness, pungent and stale stung his nostrils, but something else mixed with it. Something, tangy, sweet. "Cherry!" He didn't mean to shout, but how in the hell.... He aimed the light further ahead on the wall.

"I'll be damned. You're one heck of a girl, Becky Chambers." Dotted along the rocks, as if a Boy Scout had passed this way with a paintbrush, were splotches of cherry lipstick. He knew choosing the opposite path that he thought Becky would pick would pay off. Hurrying along, he stumbled across loose rails, pushing against damp rocks for support. Another clang, followed by a curse—a wonderful, female curse—filled the belly of the mine.

Slate followed the sound until he saw a haze of yellow in a faint light. Leaning against the wall, his heart flipped. If he hadn't rested against the rocks, he'd have collapsed to the floor as his tense muscles relaxed like wax dripping from a candle.

Becky pounded against the rock wall with some metal object in one hand. In the other was her tiny penlight flashlight.

"Find anything?" he asked.

She swung around and screamed.

A rumble sounded in the distance. Then a crash—followed by silence.

"Oh hell!" He grabbed Becky's arm and pulled her down the path he'd come.

"Wait! Didn't you see what I found?"

"Who cares. This place could collapse any second!"

"Don't be so dramatic, Slate. This mine has been standing for years. Some little scream isn't going to… ouch!"

He hadn't realized how tightly he'd held her. If he could have, he'd pull so near they'd be one. His heart couldn't take the juggling of emotions. Anger. Worry. Relief. Caring. Caring about Becky, who'd managed to break free of his hold.

"You scared me!" She swatted his chest. "What are you supposed to be, some bandit?" She rubbed her arm. "Geez, Lawson. You've probably bruised my skin."

He wanted to bruise her bottom, but he apologized instead. "Do you know how worried I was?"

"No. I didn't know you were even back from your coyote search."

The blow was low and it hurt. "I had to go… Becky…?"

She waved away his words in the dim light. "I know. I know." Rubbing her arm as if to emphasis the bruise, she asked, "Did you see any?"

He shook his head.

"So, you cut our day short for nothing…"

"Only seven dead sheep."

If he'd knocked her to the damp floor he couldn't have stunned her more. She realized he had come looking for her taking the time away from his work. Things were getting too confusing. "I'm sorry. And you didn't see the coyote? Which means…"

"I'll lose more."

He didn't play fair when it came to emotions. Suddenly complaining about her cut finger and boredom made her feel like a jerk. A selfish jerk. "There must be things you can do…"

"I've got men on guard. Come on, this isn't the time to discuss it…" He looked around. "…or the place."

"It is a bit nippy in here."

He pulled her close and warmth flooded her body. "Come on." Gently he nudged her forward.

"Wait! Look what I found, Slate." She opened her fist. Slate shone the light onto her palm. The stones sparkled in the faint beam. "Gold," she whispered. "Gold! You're rich, Slate."

He laughed. "Money's never brought me happiness."

"Okay, so you've got plenty, but it's true. Look! I mean, there's a lot more in the rock where I was digging. I found this metal cup-like thing and when the light hit the rock wall I started to pound. The gold fell…"

He silenced her with his lips. "Fool's gold."

She pushed at his chest. "I'm not a fool…"

"I didn't say *you* were, Beck. But that rock you're holding is. This place was tapped out years ago. The only gold-colored stones you'd find in here now are called 'fool's gold.' It does look the same, but it's copper or iron pyrite."

She shut her hand. Heat burned up her neck and she knew if he shined the light on her face she'd glow redder than Rudolph's nose, even in the darkened mine. What a fool she was. He made her feel so dumb.

He leaned forward and kissed her hot cheek. "Let's get out of here." He took her arm and she yanked free.

"I can manage. I made it this far, alone."

He smiled in the dimness. "Hey, that was clever of you to mark the walls with your lipstick so you could find your way out."

She pulled her shoulders straight. "Yes it was."

Slate led the way through narrow rocks where only one person at a time could fit. Becky followed behind, steamed at her stupidity with the gold, steamed at her selfishness about this morning, and steamed at Slate for coming to rescue her. She would have been fine. The entrance to the mine lay ahead a few feet.

He grabbed her arm so fast she nearly fell.

"What the heck..."

"Shh!"

"Don't tell me to..."

He lifted her over his shoulder as if she were a sack of feed.

"What the heck are you doing? Put me down!" She pounded his back. She'd have kicked her feet but a boot in his groin didn't seem necessary. She sure as heck didn't want to injure anything important.

"Stop that and be quiet," Slate whispered.

Her hands slowed at his tone. Something was wrong. He didn't just get the urge to fondle her rear end as if she were some damsel in distress and he a knight in shining armor.

"Put me down, Slate."

Before he could reply, he bolted forward with Becky flopping against his shoulder. "Shit, we can't get past!" he yelled. Without another word, he dropped her to the ground, pushing her behind him.

"What the heck..." A whirring sound broke the air. "What's that..."

Her eyes widened as Slate grabbed a stick from near the entrance and moved in slow motion toward the venomous rattlesnake, a few feet away from where Becky stood. Oh geez, he could get bitten. A sick feeling welled in her stomach. She couldn't watch Slate get hurt—or worse. Scanning the area she looked for another stick. If the snake made a move toward him, she'd wallop it. Before she had time to move, Slate stepped closer.

"No! Slate don't...."

With a flick of the stick, he sent the unsuspecting snake flying into the air. The sunlight caught the rattler in a series of spasms like the letter "S" until it landed behind the hill near the entrance.

The stick clattered to the ground. "Ready?"

Sure she was ready—if she could get her boots to come unglued from the sand. Swallowing, she said, "Yes." She'd never heard her own voice come out so weakly. Of course, she'd never watched someone she loved come so close to being hurt. With a sigh she prodded behind Slate toward the horses. Living at Valley Del Sol had been one interesting endeavor after another.

Sugar followed Cloud Dancer along the path as if she, too, didn't want the responsibility of the lead. Becky sure as heck didn't. Geez, she'd lived in New Mexico all her life and never ran across a rattlesnake before. Of course, when you spent most of your time working in a salon or watching soap operas, there was little chance of running into one. Wanda could name a few rattlers that she worked on in the shop, but the worst they were capable of was annoying gossip. Heaving a sigh, she relaxed her tight fist on the reins and comforted herself staring at Slate's back.

And what a back it was. He'd pulled the sleeves of his shirt down to protect his tawny skin from more sun she suspected. The material strained against his upper torso as if his skin had turned blue denim. Her gaze traveled down to his waist. With every gallop of Cloud Dancer's hooves, Slate's bottom lifted off the saddle. Despite the movement, she could make out the firm muscles of his bottom. He wore his jeans snug, thank goodness, and the fabric of each cheek had lightened in obvious wear.

"Doing all right?" he asked.

She pulled her gaze from his derrière, and smiled. "Fine."

"Thirsty?"

She'd been too preoccupied ogling Slate's body to pay attention to her own. "Actually, I am."

"Whoa." He dismounted Cloud Dancer and rifled around in the saddlebag. "I guess you didn't bring any water on your little trek?"

"I thought I'd get a sip at the local mirage." She tried to lighten the mood, but he was right. She shouldn't have gone riding in the arid desert without bringing some water. He had a way of making her feel like he was so much smarter.

When he held a plastic water bottle out to her, she could see the worry in his eyes. Although his accusation made her feel dumb, the concern in his eyes felt good. She'd never remembered seeing that in anyone's, let alone a man's, eyes before. The closest she'd come was Wanda wrinkling her already wrinkled forehead when she worried about Becky.

She took the bottle. "Thanks." The warm water tasted as good as a sip of Dom Perignon—not that she'd ever had any, but she had a good imagination. She had been thirsty, and no matter what Slate had handed her, the concern for her made every sip taste delicious. "And thank you for coming to find me—although I would have been all right."

"I couldn't have waited to see." He realized he hadn't thought of anything else since learning Becky had gone off alone. And it felt good.

Before she could comment, Slate rode forward. As they rounded the barns, a wild-eyed Luke came running out. Slate galloped ahead. "What's wrong?"

"Damned corn—it's on fire!"

Slate spun Cloud Dancer around. Over his shoulder he shouted, "Go inside. I'll be home later."

Becky saw the worry in his eyes. "I'm coming, too."

"You stay here!"

"No! I want to help..."

Slate waved at her. "We don't need..."

Luke mounted his horse. "Half the men are exhausted, Slate. We could use all the help we can..."

He growled. "All right, but stay near me!"

He'd shouted the words, but they touched her heart as if he'd whispered tantalizing declarations in her ear. Just try to keep her away.

Flames leapt from the rows of corn like hundreds of birthday candles in the fields. Only there was nothing to celebrate as Slate watched his crops blacken into stalks of ashes. He could see there was no hope for the section beyond the irrigation piping. The crew had the faucets turned full blast causing a geyser of mist to swirl in the warm breeze above the corn.

He leapt off his horse and ran forward. "Leave that section. Get some water on those!" he shouted and pointed. Six men ran forward. He started to follow and caught Becky in his peripheral vision. "Come on!"

She ran toward him. Fear deepened the shade of her eyes. He grabbed her hand and pulled her toward the water tanks. "Grab a bucket and wet your hair!"

"What?"

"Sparks. If the wind picks up, they'll be all over us."

She did as he commanded then joined the men in a bucket brigade. Her hat had fallen to the ground so she left it. Water splashed across her shirt and shorts as the buckets passed along the line. The last man threw the water onto the nearest stalks. When Slate gave the signal, they moved down the line. Her wet hair clung to her face, but when she saw a crackling spark fly past her, she was thankful for Slate's foresight.

Her arms cried out in pain as the buckets seemed to get heavier and heavier. Several times Slate had tried to get her to leave the line and wait on the side, but she needed to help. If he hadn't taken the day off to be with her…

She had to help.

Smoldering steam wafted to the sky as the last of the flames succumbed to the water. Slate called off the bucket brigade and sent half of the men back to the ranch. One of the newer hands admitted to leaving a few ashes burning by mistake. Becky had never seen such exhausted workers before. Exhausted and dedicated. She had stayed out of guilt, but she could see these men would have done anything for Slate. His crew certainly appreciated their boss and he didn't hold the error against the new hand.

It dawned on her that they weren't surprised to see him in the middle of the line with everyone else. She guessed this wasn't the first time Slate had dirtied his hands along with the workers. He'd obviously worked hand in hand with them all the time—no wonder he had calluses. They'd followed his orders without a word, and worked like a team of trained horses.

Her heart swelled with pride for the exhausted soul heading toward her. Wrinkles formed below Slates eyes and his lips tightened across his mouth. His shoulders slumped forward as if he'd lost his best friend. Smudges of soot dotted his cheeks. She reached up and whisked her finger across the stubble of beard.

"You look exhausted," she said.

He forced a tired smile and bent to pick her muddied hat from the ground. "I'll replace this."

She frowned at her canary Western hat. "I've got others."

He laughed. "Yellow looks good with your hair." He brushed the strands that had stuck to her cheeks behind her ear. His touch warmed her skin as if lit by the fiery stalks. With his arms around her shoulder, he leaned his weight into her body as they walked toward the horses.

It didn't matter that he had a good fifty, maybe seventy, pounds on her—she'd hold up the man she cared so deeply about with the surge of adrenaline that pumped through her.

After they mounted the horses, they worked their way toward the barns. Slate dismounted and helped Becky down without any protests from her. Dave Palmer ran toward them.

"I'll water 'em down, ma'am," he said.

Becky didn't have the energy to refuse. Slate nodded a thanks to Dave and resting on Becky's shoulder again, walked toward the house.

When they entered the kitchen the spicy flavor of Rosa's cooking filled the air. "Oh *Dios!*" she shouted, looking at them. They had to be a mess. She busied about, taking Slate's hat from his hand and neckerchief from his neck like a harried mother who they were sure glad to see had come back home.

"A fire got half the corn, Rosa," he said.

Becky flinched at the childlike tone. He looked like a rugged cowboy covered in soot and wet clothing, but when Rosa wiped his cheeks with her wrinkle-free apron a tear stung her eyes. He really loved this place. She wasn't the sentimental type, but the housekeeper's action reminded her of her motherless past. Rosa bustled around her, fussing with the twigs that had entwined in her hair. She picked them out and shooed both her and Slate out of the kitchen for a hot soaking in the tub. Becky looked at Slate, who winked at her. He looked so sexy with his smudged face.

Geez, she wished there was a water shortage and they had to share the sunken tub. That had to be why it was so huge.

"Go, Missy Beecky. And don't drop those sooty clothes on my clean floor."

Slate chucked. Becky punched him in the back as she followed him to the living room. Careful not to touch anything, she made her way down the hallway to the west wing.

★

Slate watched Becky playing with her fork. They'd both cleaned up and, although exhausted, come for dinner. Thank goodness Grady had been asleep through it all. Thoughts of the day churned in his head. Pride for putting Becky first, anger for the lost corn, and fear—fear that he might loose his land.

"I haven't the energy to chew," Becky whispered, eyeing Rosa who busied herself near the stove.

He smiled. "If you think that fire was deadly today, you don't want to refuse Rosa's cooking." He smiled and shoved a forkful of Spanish rice into his mouth. In his exhausted state, his muscles worked slowly, sensuous. His tongue seemed to glide in slow motion across his lips after a few forkfuls.

Hot and spicy worked its way through her system, and she hadn't taken a bite yet.

Rosa served hot corn muffins and refilled their iced tea at the speed of the hummingbirds that drank daily from her feeders.

"Shoot, Rosa. I was so exhausted I forgot to ask. How is your sister?"

She wiped her hands on her apron. Becky noticed she'd changed from the one she used to wipe Slate's face. "Much better. She's home now and her husband has hired a woman to come cook."

"That's good. Does she need anything?"

Becky knew he'd give Rosa money for her sister, but she also knew the proud woman would refuse. Money really didn't matter to him.

"She be all right." Rosa brought two crystal goblets of vanilla ice cream out of the freezer. The kitchen air frosted the glasses as she set them on the counter and poured emerald crème de menthe over the tops. With a squirt of whipped cream and a cherry on top, she handed them each a tempting sundae.

Becky's mouth was tired. Her arms were tired. Even her eyes were tired as she eyed the dessert. "It looks scrumptious, Rosa."

The housekeeper smiled. Becky had to finish the sundae. She couldn't hurt Rosa's feelings no matter how little energy she had. Slate smiled, looking over his spoonful. She knew he felt the same way and she guessed he appreciated her concern for Rosa. The housekeeper had been like a surrogate mother to both of them.

"That was great, Rosa." Slate licked the last minty liquid from his spoon.

"Go rest in the living room." Rosa ordered them out of the kitchen, saying goodnight. Hector had gotten a cold in Albuquerque, and she wanted to get him to bed early.

In the living room, Becky collapsed into the buttery soft sofa. Slate put on a Reba McEntire CD and settled next to her. He wrapped his arm around her and sighed. The day had started out so well. Now it seemed like ages since they'd frolicked in the freezing spring water.

"About today… I'm sorry about your sheep and corn…"

"That's the risks of ranching. So many things could go wrong."

"But two things in one day?"

He chuckled. "Hey, you should be glad. Walt's due here next week and your balance sheet will put mine to shame."

She knew he was kidding, and maybe it was her exhaustion clouding her thoughts. But that comment hurt. How could he think she was so shallow that she'd be glad about his loss? Did he really think of her as a money-grubbing hairdresser who'd revel at his misfortune?

She pulled free and looked into his tired eyes. This time the tears stung her eyes and she let them.

"Is that what you really think of me?" She shoved free of his arm and jumped up despite his attempt to stand. Surprising herself with the strength to shove him back down, she pulled her shoulders high.

"I may be a *damned* hairdresser, Slate, but…."

"I didn't mean…."

"Then what did you mean?"

His hesitation gave her the answer.

"You do think I only want the ranch like some conniving—all you see is the package, not what's inside me. You're just like all the rest. I thought you were… different. You know, I've argued with Wanda when she said men judge a book by its cover. But now… she's right." She choked back a sob and cursed inside.

"I don't judge you by your looks. You are sexy…"

How many times had boys told her she was sexy? How many times had they whispered how pretty she was? And how many times did they try to use her "pretty, sexy" body for their own pleasure? Slate was no different. She turned to leave.

"Wait, Becky. That was a compliment."

"No, Slate. Telling a woman she is thoughtful, caring, or smart is a compliment. Saying she dresses wild and sexy is like saying she's looking for action. Action—sex, plain and simple, no feelings involved."

His eyes narrowed. "So why *do* you dress that way?"

She could hear the annoyance in his voice. "It's my business."

"Not if you know it drives men crazy as if you enjoy teasing them…"

She slapped at his chest. "I can dress any way I damned well want to!"

"Of course you can, but… hell, you're confusing me."

"You made yourself clear accusing me of teasing you…"

"I didn't say that! But now that you mention it, yeah. The way you look does turn me on. Is that so wrong?"

If he'd said just being herself turned him on, she'd jump into his arms in a second. But he only saw her outward appearance. She glared at him. "I started dressing… this way—when the second foster family turned me into Social Services because their "real" son was getting all hot and bothered. The sad part was, Timmy and I started out as friends. I learned then I couldn't trust boys… males. I decided it was always going to be only me—unless I could find someone to…" Her voice came out a whisper, "…to look past the clothing and love *me*."

He placed his arms around her.

She ignored the feelings surging throughout her body and pulled free.

"Maybe you *do* only want the ranch," he accused, a hurt look on his face.

"You're entitled to your opinion." She turned to leave—hoping he'd say something, hoping he'd say he didn't mean that, hoping he'd stop her. There had to be trust of a man loving her, not the package she came in. Once again, she had to protect her heart—no one else would. Not even the man she loved.

No, he only tended to break it.

Chapter 12

"Becky, wait!" Slate couldn't stop her. "I didn't mean that..." He'd never seen Becky get teary eyed before. She had been so bubbly, full of life—so strong—it surprised him to see her suffering show. He guessed she didn't want him to notice. "I'm sorry, Becky," he said as she headed down the hallway out of range of his voice.

Slate grabbed his hat from the coffee table and headed outdoors. The starlit sky twinkled above him as he walked to the verandah. Dropping into the swing, he leaned back. A cool breeze took the heat of the day, sending a chill through him. He didn't care if he froze out there, he needed to sit and think. Think about what had happened—what was going to happen.

An ache tightened his gut when he thought about hurting Becky. He had no intention of causing her pain, but obviously he had. Cursing her past and the way she'd had to fight for herself since being a kid, he thought of what she'd said about her clothing. Here she was trying to be loved for herself, and he'd fallen right into the trap judging her by her outward appearance since the day he met her.

Remembering his first impression of her in the black leather skirt and fishnet hose, he agreed, she did look inviting. That's what had confused him when she acted sugary sweet and like some "dumb blonde." Sure she turned him on physically at first, but now, now was different. Becky could wear a potato sack and his heart would flutter like a butterfly when she came near. Of course, she could even wear nothing and... well, she *was* beautiful. Her smooth skin invited his touch. Pert little breasts outlined beneath the skimpy tops she wore begged to be caressed. Hell, there was nothing wrong with physical attractiveness, unless that was all there was. But there was more.

He'd fallen for her carefree attitude, her love of life, how she cared for Grady, and how she enjoyed even the littlest thing like rubbing a calf's head as if he were her long-lost puppy. He loved everything about her—everything he wasn't.

Then why did he let her go tonight without telling her?

He looked across the yard. Moonbeams over the dessert painted an eerie picture. The barns sat silent, not even a "baa" or "neigh" could be heard. In the distance, he knew five ranch hands protected his flocks by camping out where the coyotes had been. A sickness welled inside at the thought of his massacred sheep. The loss was going to cost him.

Fear gripped his insides like a tight lasso. Could he really lose all this? Pulling his gaze from the darkness, he realized his mind had wandered to the ranch. Again. Valley Del Sol not only intruded into his actions, but his thoughts, too. Was that why he didn't stop Becky tonight? Could he have subconsciously wanted her to leave so he wouldn't have to face loving her? But, damn it, he did. He loved Becky Chambers—but these emotions were new to him. Of all the women he'd known, no one had ever caused him to question his love of his land.

He looked up. Was all of this worth loosing Becky?

What if he'd lost the ranch to her? It'd never been a reality, until lately. In the beginning, he would have contested the will if he thought there was the slightest chance that he'd lose Valley Del Sol. It was all he had. His only family had been Rosa, Hector, and the ranch hands for so long, he felt as if he couldn't have a life without them.

Leaning back, he realized how similar he and Becky were. Not in their behavior, but in their pasts. She'd lost her mother; he grew up with parents physically present, but he never really had a family either. That's why he turned to loving the ranch, but Becky… what drove her to want this place?

When she'd fallen from Sugar and confessed her deception

because she thought he'd contest the will, she never explained why that worried her. He knew now that she didn't just want money. She would have taken a settlement if that were the case—he could have managed something despite the terms of the codicil. He would have given her some of his money. But she didn't want that. He'd gotten so preoccupied... heck, he enjoyed every day with Becky, he'd nearly forgotten—six months wasn't forever.

Soon a decision would be made for him.

He jumped from the swing. He couldn't lose everything. He couldn't.

★

Becky stood in the cool water allowing water pellets to sting her skin. She needed something to revive her after the restless night. Crying herself to sleep had ended years ago when she moved in with the first foster family. As a child, she vowed she'd never do that again. But last night the old habit surfaced. This time the pain was different, deeper. Being hurt by someone she loved tore at her heart, knowing he didn't feel the same. If he did, he'd have stopped her from leaving and said that he loved her for being herself.

"Maybe I do watch too many soap operas." Her words gurgled in the shower streaming onto her face. Wanda had told her that a long time ago. She'd accused her of not being realistic, of fantasizing in some make-believe world that money would bring her happiness. All she wanted was a house of her own. Now, it looked as if her dear friend was right. Happiness only works on TV. In real life, happiness was going to cost her Slate.

She shoved off the faucet and dried herself with the mauve towel Rosa always hung fresh in her bathroom. Shimmying into her red lacy panties, she decided she'd better perk up for her guests. If she didn't show them a good time, her business would suffer. She'd lose the ranch. Finishing dressing, she grabbed her hat and headed to the kitchen.

"Morning, Rosa," Becky said as she entered the kitchen. She

looked on Slate's chair—no black Stetson. The familiar sight meant they'd share breakfast together before heading off for work.

Obviously, he'd already left.

Rosa's dark eyebrows rose as she stared at Becky. "No more sheep found dead last night."

"Good."

Rosa served a dish full of oatmeal sprinkled with brown sugar. "Grady went with one of the hands into town."

"Fine. He loves it there." But she couldn't help her stomach knot at the loss of the other sheep. She lifted her spoon and knew she'd never be able to swallow the cereal with her mouth so dry and her appetite nil. Playing with the spoon, she asked, "How is Hector today?"

Wrong question. Rosa's eyes darkened and she mumbled something in Spanish that Becky guessed was a curse.

"He just like Señor Lawson. No can stay home, even when sick."

"Did he go out with Slate?"

"*Sí.*" Rosa shook her head. Dark curls jumped about her round face.

Becky took a sip of fresh orange juice and forced a spoonful of cereal down. The hot sweetness tasted good, but her appetite hadn't come back. Slate's absence hurt—and it made her angry to admit that.

"Rosa...." Maybe now was a good time to pump the protective housekeeper for more information about Slate. Her anger at Hector might let a few things slip. "Does Hector always work as hard as Slate?"

"No one works harder than Señor Lawson."

"I noticed that when we went to put out the fire yesterday. He gets right in there with his men."

Rosa started to wash the dishes. Over her shoulder she said, "Always has."

"He was a good worker as a kid?"

"Not just good, he... he loves this ranch."

Geez, she *knew* that. What she wanted to learn was, why? She took another spoonful. If Rosa noticed her not eating she might get upset and not keep talking. "But he didn't live here all his life."

"No, since Señor Nate..." Soap bubbles dripped off her elbow into the sink as she made the sign of the cross. "...took sick. He saved Valley Del Sol."

Becky's ears perked up over the Spanish radio station Rosa always listened to. "How so?"

Rosa hesitated. Oh geez, was that the end of her info gathering?

"Señor Slate knows about business. He showed Señor Nate how to invest his money and to improve the irrigation system. Things got better when he come here."

So Nate needed Slate's help. Why wasn't he grateful enough to leave his nephew the ranch—no strings attached? Of course she appreciated the codicil, but it still puzzled her.

"You finished, Missy Beecky?"

She looked to see Rosa standing above her wiping her hands on her apron. "Yes, thanks." The housekeeper frowned. "I'm not very hungry. Sorry, Rosa. It was delicious." Becky stood and took her peach colored cowgirl hat from the back of the chair. "I need to go. Thanks again." At the door she paused. "Did Slate say he'd be back for lunch?"

"He took it with him."

Her heart sank. Back to old times.

She put on her hat and went outside. "Morning, Dave." She waved to the ranch hand as she neared the corral. He gave her a rundown on the arrival times of the guests and headed out to the airport in El Paso.

Becky walked out behind the barns. Morning sunlight glistened on the lake. She headed down the path near her side of the water. Bending down she cupped the cool liquid, letting it fall back through open fingers. This is where her beach should be.

She stood and surveyed the area. To the right a cluster of trees would provide an excellent shade spot. Hank Wentworth said he could build some bathing houses along the walkway so the guests wouldn't have to go back and forth to the bunkhouse to change. He'd add a section behind them for racks to store canoes. She slumped onto a large boulder. Darn Slate and his attorney. Her dude ranch would be complete—it'd be perfect, if she had access to the lake.

Ambivalence churned in her stomach. Looking out across the land she wondered if she would ever own it. Could she ever own it? Could she follow through with the terms of the codicil and take it away from Slate? Last night, she'd have done it in a heartbeat. Today… when she looked for his hat and it wasn't there… damn.

If only she knew what Uncle Nate had in mind when he redid his will. Maybe her old friend was getting senile. She thought about how spry he had been, how he discussed world events like a newscaster, and how his sunken green eyes lit up when she served him her chocolate macadamia nut cookies. There hadn't been anything wrong with Nate Lawson's mind.

Becky looked at her watch. Two more hours before Dave would be back. She ran to get her denim purse.

After a fast goodbye to Rosa, she said she'd be back in a few hours. Dave had given her a copy of his car key if she ever needed to leave the ranch while he had her van.

She needed to leave now.

★

"No, ma'am, I don't have an appointment with Attorney Greeson, but…" Becky tried to keep the frustration out of her voice, but how many times did she have to tell the silver-blue haired receptionist the same thing?

"Well, I don't see…" The woman ran a nimble finger up and down the appointment book as if looking at it for the hundredth time would have changed something. "No. He doesn't have any time. Court is in…"

The office door opened. Becky and the receptionist turned at the same time. Thankfully, Attorney Greeson stepped out before Becky tightened the woman's red, white, and blue scarf around her turkey-like neck.

He looked at Becky and hesitated. "Good morning, Miss Chambers." Looking past her, he asked, "Do you have an appointment with me today?"

If she heard that phrase one more time…. "No…" Her bangs tickled her forehead as she blew air from her lips. "I was hoping you could see me for a few minutes."

"Are you alone?"

She smiled. Poor man probably didn't want a repeat of the scene with her and Slate. "Yes." He ushered her toward the door despite the sounds of protests from Miss "Blue hair."

Inside his office, Becky rattled a volley of questions about the will.

"Now, I can't give you any information like that, Miss Chambers." Attorney Greeson leaned back. He'd gained some weight since April by the looks of his straining vest buttons.

"I know about attorney-client confidentiality. All I want to know is, did Nate give you a *reason* for changing his will?"

He leaned forward and gave her a fatherly stare. He knew the answer, and she knew—he wasn't going to say.

"You have been receiving reports from Mr. Payton, I assume?"

"Yeah." Did he have to remind her about that? The last results were closer, but Slate still had an edge. "Thanks for your time." She stood and turned.

"The final results will be ready… soon. How are things going?" he asked.

"Fine." She slung her denim bag over her shoulder and though of how it had spilled the first time she was there. A tightness gripped her inside when she remembered Slate saying she had no right to *his* land. Had he been pretending to have feelings for her all along? Was he really ruthless and ready to do anything to keep his land? Shaking off the chill running along her spine, she walked to the door.

"I'm sorry I couldn't have been more helpful. Give my regards to Slate. Also to Rosa and Hector."

"Our chaperones," she said.

He smiled.

"Why did Nate think we'd need chaperones?"

He shook his head and clucked his tongue as if she were a naughty child. "I need to go to court now. Good day, Miss Chambers."

Becky flopped into the driver's seat of Dave's car. Chaperones. She'd forgotten all about that part of the session. Why would Uncle Nate think... did he think she and Slate—could Uncle Nate have *wanted* them to fall in love?

He had to have known what opposites they were. On the other hand, Nate was an intelligent man. Hm. She shoved her foot on the gas pedal, nearly running over a startled Miss "Blue Hair" as she crossed the parking lot toward the mailbox.

Back at Sidewinder Valley, Becky greeted the guests, then Dave and Grady showed them to the bunkhouse. Along with the other ranch hands they'd followed the same routine for months. This group was much younger than most, which pleased Becky. She'd worried her Dude ranch had been turning into a haven for the elderly like some resort in the Catskills. Watching the last couple gather their suitcases, she leaned against the tree.

"Looks like a great group," Slate said.

Swinging around, she bumped into Slate's chest. "Oh, yeah. Average age is about thirty."

"Youngest group yet. Thirsty?"

She'd just finished one of Rosa's tumblers full of iced tea before Dave got back from the airport. "Parched," she lied.

"I'll get us some tea and meet you on the verandah. You do have time, don't you?"

She nodded, knowing she'd have dropped whatever she was doing. Stunned that Slate had appeared in the middle of the day, she forced her legs to move and walked toward the verandah.

Dropping down into the swing, she tried to calm her excited heart.

"Here." Slate stood holding a glass of iced tea toward her.

"Thanks." She forced a sip.

Slate sat next to her, his thigh brushing against hers. The ceiling fan spun cool air toward them, but her leg warmed with his touch. She inhaled the dust covering his shirt. Dying to ask what he was doing back at the house, she held her inquisitiveness. This way, she could assume he wanted to see her.

"Have a full house this week?"

"Um," she said after taking another sip. "No room in the inn for the next few weeks."

"Great."

He leaned back, placing his arm around her shoulder as if it were the most natural thing in the world. It *felt* natural, wonderful, but did he really mean what he'd just said?

"Rosa said you didn't finish your breakfast." He laughed. "You know how she is about that."

"I wasn't too hungry." She couldn't tell him that his absence took her appetite away. He ran a finger in circles on her bare arm. Tingly sensations spiraled through her skin. Occasionally he'd stop and pull her tighter.

"Aren't you going to ask why I came back?" he asked.

"You were thirsty?" Geez, she was dying to know.

"With the gallons of water Rosa packs for me everyday?"

He pulled his hand free and cupped her chin with both hands. She couldn't care less why he came back, just that he did. Leaning forward, he brushed her lips with his. "I missed you."

Her heart somersaulted.

It wasn't often that she was rendered speechless, but once again, Slate had that affect on her.

"Can Dave settle your group for you?"

"Well, I've already welcomed them. I guess he and Grady can keep them busy for a while. Why?"

"Let's do something."

She glared at him. "Is everything all right?"

"Yes. Everything is fine. I just want to get away for a few hours..." He smiled. "Not like the canyon incident."

"What about your sheep?"

"Luke can handle it. We've gotten two coyotes. Hopefully that's all there are."

Dark circles formed beneath his eyes. Worry lines, as Wanda would call them, creased into his forehead. He looked worn out. Maybe he did need to get away.

"Where do you want to go?"

"Pinenotch?"

She sat upright. "Pinenotch? That's at least an hour's drive. Besides what would we do up there?"

"I don't know, Becky. Just get away...." He stared forward, toward the eastern section of the property. "Just get away."

"I'm not sure I can do that to Dave." She paused. Maybe Slate was trying to distance himself from the ranch. Maybe he decided he needed to know if he could forget Valley Del Sol for one day. She had to let him try. Looking at him, her heart fluttered like Rosa's hummingbirds. She wanted to hold him and erase the dark circles from his handsome face.

She had to know if he could forget Valley Del Sol.

"I'll go talk to him and see if he can keep and eye on Grady, too."

"I'll be waiting."

She could feel Slate's glare following her until she turned into the barn. Leaning against Sugar's stall, she shut her eyes.

Please let him forget that this place exists, if only for today.

Chapter 13

Becky marveled at the change in scenery as Slate drove them through the mountain tunnel. The ride along the mountain's ridge provided a panoramic view of the desert below—the desert where Valley Del Sol was left in a cloud of dust. Cacti dotted the mountainsides, snaking their shallow roots into the tiniest bit of dirt encrusted in the rocks. When the darkness of the tunnel lightened, she exclaimed, "Wow!"

She'd never been to Vermont, but seeing the evergreens waving in the mountain winds, the deep crevasses dotted with Aspen, and green grass carpeting the roadside, she imagined this is what it had to look like. Pinenotch had the closest ski resort to where they lived, but like she once told Wanda, if God had meant for her to ski, he'd have fanned her toes out like snowshoes.

"Ever been up here?" Slate asked as he maneuvered the truck around a curve. A squirrel darted before the tires, but he skillfully wove around the little guy.

"The foster family that I lived with in my last year of high school took me here… once." Slate's shoulders tensed. A warmth flowed inside her at his uneasiness about her past. Maybe he really did care for her. She looked down at her "baggiest" pair of jeans and Shear Magic T-shirt. Today she'd dressed in the most conservative clothes she could find in her entire wardrobe. Even her nails sparkled a pale pink—each finger the same shade. "They came to ski; I watched."

"Never been skiing?"

"I like my bones they way they are."

"Someday I'll teach you. If you learn how to fall correctly, you'll do fine."

"See? Why do I need to learn a sport where you have to *fall* correctly? No thanks."

He chuckled as they turned up a winding driveway. At the top sat a huge building with a giant carved wooden bear guarding the entrance. The whitewashed building had to have been at least a hundred years old. Red paint trimmed each window, and above the entryway a stained-glass octagonal window sparkled rainbow colors in the sunlight.

"We come here for lunch?" she asked.

Slate pulled into a parking space and turned toward her. "Are you hungry now?"

"Not yet, but what else are we doing here?"

He smiled and placed a kiss on her cheek. "Do you like surprises?"

"Sure."

He held her by the shoulders. "Do you trust me?"

For a moment she thought about how he'd raced down the canyon leaving her bleeding. Okay, it was a minor cut, but he didn't know he'd left her there at first. Then again, the sheep were being threatened. "Of course I trust you." Her muscles relaxed as if the words had a calming effect on her body. She did trust him.

"Then come on."

Before she could unlatch the door, Slate stood outside, waiting. Wrapping his arms around her shoulder, he guided her into the Pinenotch Inn and straight to the front desk.

Becky's jaw dropped, but she held any words of protest as Slate asked for the Lawson reservation. Reservation? He'd planned to come here? He'd planned to *stay* here? Hm, she mused. What else had he planned?

Taking the plastic card from the pretty young desk clerk, who Becky thought was going to take off in flight if she batted her eyelashes at Slate any faster, he whispered into Becky's ear, "Surprise."

She should be furious at him for not asking if she wanted to come to a hotel in the middle of the day. But hot and spicy surged throughout her dissipating any chance of anger. She wanted to.

Slate stuck the plastic card in the door until the green light flashed. The handle clicked, and he stepped aside to let her in first.

"Wow!" The room was nearly the size of the mausoleum she lived in at Valley Del Sol. Beige walls surrounded the furniture, matching the alternating stripes on the green satin couch and chairs. The windows were small, above eye level, and Slate walked over to roll both of them open. A gust of mountain air chilled the room, followed by the chatter of guests passing below.

He flung his Stetson onto a mahogany coffee table nearly knocking over a bottle of wine chilling in a frosted silver holder and turned toward her. "Beck… the reason I brought you here…"

Heck, she *knew* the reason he brought her here, and looking at the serious look on the face of the man she'd fallen in love with, she would bet her last dime on it.

And she was *ready* since she knew he cared about her.

He came forward and motioned to the couch.

The couch? Okay, whatever….

"Thirsty?"

"A little."

He snapped the cork with a pop and poured the clear sparking liquid into two crystal flutes. She noticed the label, Dom Perignon. Wanda would say she lacked class calling the expensive champagne wine. Running her tongue across her lips, she couldn't care less what it was called—she was too excited waiting for her first taste.

Slate settled next to her on the couch and sipped at his drink. "I haven't been to this place since Uncle Nate died. We used to come here skiing."

"Nate skied?" She sat forward and rubbed her nose where the champagne tickled.

Slate chuckled. "A few years ago. He was darn good."

Leaning back, she guessed he was remembering times spent with his uncle. She, too, missed the older man, although sometimes it seemed as if he was in the room with them. With a week left on the ranch situation, she'd though about him more and more lately.

"Have you figured out why Nate rewrote his will the way he had?"

Slate tensed. Maybe he didn't want to discuss the ranch. She had to force the inevitable thoughts down several times herself. This time next week she'd be moving out. Slate would own Valley Del Sol. She'd have to wake up from her dream. Feeling the warmth throughout her body when she looked at him, she decided she wasn't going to think about that now.

She'd enjoy every second of today and lock the special memories into a corner of her mind.

He shook his head. "Nate knew how much the ranch meant to me…"

Controlling her impulses never came easy so she interrupted, "Why does it mean so much to you Slate?"

His forehead wrinkled as if she'd asked him if he believed in UFO's. A sadness masked the sparkle of his eyes. Running his hand through his hair, she could guess it was difficult for him to explain.

She took his hand and kissed it. "Forget it. I'm sorry I asked."

His gaze met hers. "No, it's time you knew."

Becky's hand tensed. That didn't sound good. Why couldn't she have kept her mouth shut? Since the day Nate Lawson's will was read, she was learning what it meant to worry.

He took a slug of the expensive champagne. "It's time we got this over with."

How many times had she heard that before? Each time the social worker was going to yank her out of one foster home, she'd say those words, and the pain in Becky's heart would deepen. Now Slate was going to break her heart in two. She looked at him running his finger around the top of the glass. Why'd he bring her all the way up here to "get it over with?"

"You know I grew up an only child on a ranch in Arizona. I

spent my youth listening to my parents fight."

The pain in her heart deepened, but this time it was *for* Slate, not *because* of him.

"I always thought my father didn't like me. He never did any of the father and son things my friends did. I gravitated to the ranch hands who taught me a lot about ranching. The land became a substitute for my family..."

"What about your mother?"

He looked at her as if she'd intruded on his thoughts. As if living through the past in his mind, his voice came out a monotone. "She took me to functions, but she didn't participate. My father... spent less time with her than with me." He sighed. "She distanced herself from him after years of complaining that he ignored her. They didn't even share a bedroom."

She, Slate, and Jack and Jill were all like orphans.

He chuckled. "I thought that was normal until my first sleep-over at a friend's house. After substituting the land for my parent's attention, I found some happiness. Only it backfired on me." He turned toward her. "I turned into my father."

She wanted to argue, but he was partly right. He did put the ranch above everything else, but partly he was wrong, too. Seeing the man she loved in such pain she had to try to help. "No, Slate, you didn't. Sure you kept up with your responsibilities toward the ranch, but look at how many days you came back for lunch lately? And what about going to Glider Canyon..."

He moaned.

"No." She touched his arm. "You made an effort. People can't change overnight. And how about now..."

A sparkle ignited in the depths of his eyes. "That's why I brought you here..."

"To explain your past?"

"Partly..." He took her hand, kissed it. "...but mostly for this." He set his goblet down and reached into his pocket.

What the heck did he have? Maybe he found some real gold on

the land? Maybe he'd worked something out so she could spend more time at the ranch? Maybe. *Holy Shit!*

Slate handed her a black velvet jeweler's box with gold engraved script across the top. Hanson's Fine Jewelers.

"Open it."

She'd only seen boxes like that in her soap operas. Forcing her foolish thoughts inside, she took a breath and let it out slowly, causing strands of hair to dance across Slate's forehead as he leaned near. Holding the box in one hand, she snaked her other hand to her thigh—and pinched. Geez, it hurt! She wasn't dreaming.

"Don't you want to open it?" He sounded like a wounded kid.

"Yeah, yeah, give me a second...." With a flip of the top, a flash of brilliant light twinkled at her. "This isn't a friendship ring, is it?" Her voice shook uncharacteristically, but no way could she strengthen her words. It'd take too much air, since looking at the pear-shaped diamond, surrounded with tiny round ones, had knocked the wind out of her.

Slate smiled. "Well, I do consider you my *friend*, but...." His breath tickled her lips before they touched. "I'd like you to be my wife, too."

Becky never thought this day would come. As a kid, she dreamed of having someone to marry, but she gave that up after gravitating to only losers. She'd focused on a dream of owning a house instead. It had seemed as if no one was ever going to love her for herself—until now.

"Becky? Will you marry me?"

She swung her arms around his neck, knocking both goblets to the spotless beige carpet. Inside her fist, she clenched the jeweler's box. "Yeah! Yes! Sure, why the heck not?"

Slate laughed as he pried the box from her hand, and she smiled as the self-assured cowboy shakily placed the diamond ring on her finger.

The box thudded to the puddle of Dom Perignon, but she didn't care as he pulled her tightly, and placed hungry kisses along her neck, chin, and lips. He pushed her hair from her face, callused skin scratching her softness.

"I'm sorry, my hands are so rough..."

She touched his lips with her finger. "Wait." From her denim bag she pulled out a tube of lotion and squirted some into his hands.

Slate moaned as Becky ran her fingers, covered in creamy white lotion, across his palms. She'd made him lie back as she straddled his legs and squirted the coolness onto each hand. Like magical wands, her fingers danced in the frothy cream, melting the hardness of his skin. Beneath her body a hardness tightened his jeans.

The coconut-scent intoxicated him as the cool lotion boiled with her touch.

He moaned.

She rubbed.

He shut his eyes, allowing a heightened awareness of the tactical sensations to bombard his brain.

She rubbed harder.

He struggled to control his arousal as her breathy sighs nearly knocked all control from his power. Yanking his hands from her seductive ways, he clasped her arms and pulled her toward him. "God, I want you."

She couldn't argue with that statement. Hot and spicy burned to her toes. Now that she knew Slate's past caused his obsession with the land, she felt a kindred spirit between them. Both had a lousy childhood, only he was lucky enough to have the money to substitute the land for his family—yet he hadn't been happy. Wanda would be proud to hear her admit, money didn't buy happiness.

No one had ever wanted her for herself until now. And she had every intention of giving, all that she had. "Let me make love to you, Slate."

He gave her a questioning look.

She nodded. "Now."

After easing from beneath her, he lay her back on the cool satin couch. Tracing each letter of Shear Magic until she thought she'd scream when he circled the second "a," he lifted the shirt over her head. Before she could catch her breath, he unclasped the front hook of her saffron bra. He whisked his lips gently across her taut nipples. "Does that feel good?"

She murmured, "Um."

No one had ever taken the time to ask if he pleased her. No one had cared how she felt as long as they got what they wanted. No one had ever made her feel so good.

"Yes… yes." Words wouldn't flow as his tongue brushed across one nipple, then the other.

Outside a bird chirped in the mountain pines. Becky's heart fluttered like the bird's wings propelling it away from the inn as the melodic sound grew faint. The chatter of guests dimmed. Her heartbeat pounded too loudly to hear anything else. Surely Slate could hear her heart since it thundered inside her chest.

He paused to remove his shirt. She ran her hands wildly across the tufts of curls on his chest before the shirt landed on the floor. A deep sigh escaped his lips.

Skin, warm and damp, pressed against her breasts as he bent forward. She touched the straining muscles of his arms as he held his weight from her. A protective feeling flowed from his strength; she felt it beneath her hands.

Her mind clouded in the fragrance of cologne, dust, and man. A heady feeling, as if she grew intoxicated, his scent had hėr inhaling deeper and deeper—her mind getting lighter and lighter.

Slate's arms stiffened, but he held tight unless he crush his weight into Becky's slight frame. She pushed against him to sit and silenced his questioning protest with her kisses as she guided him to lie backward. Ignoring her naked chest, she grabbed the tube of lotion and squirted circles of cream onto his shoulders, down his arm, and very, very low on his abdomen.

"Shoot… that's cold, but hell… that's great."

Skillfully, she massaged the lotion into his skin amid their moans of pleasure. "Told you I was a dammed good hairdresser," she said with a wicked smile.

Paralyzed by Becky's touch, he remained beneath her on the couch, but inside, currents of excitement ignited every nerve down to his toenails. The more she rubbed, and squirted, the more he inhaled and savored the coconut scent as if he basked on a Caribbean beach—but the heat burning his body didn't come from the sun.

She'd managed to work her magical fingers to his lower back, pressing her warm chest against him. If he didn't do something soon, he'd explode beneath her skilled hands. She unsnapped his jeans. He eased free and lifted his hips. She shimmied his pants and jockey shorts to his ankles, he slid her yellow panties down and smiled to himself. *I'll be damned, she really is a blonde.*

Becky hadn't come into this relationship inexperienced, but she felt the newness, the giving, which she'd never felt before. He eased into her with a gentleness that wrapped her in the warmth of wanting, the warmth of caring, the warmth of love. The room behind him blurred as she could make out nothing but his emerald eyes loving her. She could hear nothing but his breaths driving hot air against her. She felt the thundering of his heart against her chest, pulsing in perfect rhythm with her own like two instruments tuned to the same rhythm.

It was exhilarating, this first time, she thought.

They reached the summit of their desires simultaneously, clutching one another in a shudder of passion.

"I love you," she whispered.

"Let's get married this weekend." His words rushed out as if he'd no time to think. "We'll get our blood tests done this afternoon...."

Her heart sank. They'd have to go into town for blood tests. She'd envisioned a night of lovemaking at the enchanting inn. Well, maybe Slate wanted to save more for their honeymoon.

"We'll keep it a secret and surprise everyone. Grady will love it, and I can't wait to see Rosa's face when she learns Missy Beecky is my wife!" He held up her hand. "You won't be able to wear this ring..."

Her hand froze.

"Only for a few days. But I want it near you. We'll stop in town and get a gold necklace so you can wear it near your heart."

As a child, she had dressed her Barbie dolls in frilly white gowns carefully applying her mother's makeup to their plastic faces. Someday, she had thought, she'd dress herself like the lifeless dolls for her wedding. If they married so fast, she wouldn't have time to fulfill that dream. The thought was disappointing, but she'd never been used to fancy shindigs anyway. He seemed so excited, like a kid on Christmas Eve... excited and in a hurry. How cute. Looking into the depths of Slate's eyes, she wondered if all the frill of a fancy wedding was necessary. Of course it wasn't, as long as two people loved each other—she bit hard on her raspberry-flavored lips.

He'd never said the words.

Chapter 14

"Ouch!" Becky gave the laboratory technician a scowl as he drained blood from her arm into a tube.

"Sorry, lady."

"Sure you are." He'd caught her off guard when he stuck her since her mind had been preoccupied. On the trip back from Pinenotch a nagging ate away at her although she tried her damnedest to ignore it. Why was Slate in such a hurry to marry? And why... hadn't he said he loved her?

"I said fold your arm up," the technician said.

She frowned at him. "Keep your shirt on, buddy."

"Here." He stuck a bandage on her arm with what she considered excessive force.

Pushing to stand, she turned. "When will those results be ready?"

"Usual."

She blew out a sigh. "And that is?"

"Three days."

Three days and she'd be Mrs. Slate Lawson. Her heart didn't flutter—and it should have.

Slate sat in the waiting room, his shirt still rolled above his elbow. "You survive?"

"Barely. That guy was a vampire."

He laughed as he guided her to the door.

"Did you know it takes three days for the results?" she asked.

He frowned. "Yeah. Damn it. Wish we didn't have to wait."

Why Slate? She wanted to ask what the hurry was, but worried it'd be bad news. Her superstitious streak wouldn't allow her to ask. Maybe he'd call it off if she did. Of course, that was ridiculous thinking, but she'd learned never to press her luck. Look where she'd gotten on the wave of golden luck since hearing Nate Lawson's will! Besides, she loved Slate and reminded herself that she trusted him.

Before they left town, Slate took her to Hanson's jewelry store and purchased a thin gold chain. He slid the diamond from her hand, kissed her finger, and threaded the ring onto the necklace. As if performing some sensual ritual, he leaned forward, clasped the chain behind her neck, and whispered, "Don't take it off."

She had no intentions of taking it off.

On the way home, Slate sang along with Hank Williams Jr. on the truck's radio. Obviously he needed a spatula to carry a tune. As they rounded the curve of the front drive, Becky asked, "Can't we at least tell Rosa?"

"No!" He turned. "No, let's keep it secret."

"Okay." Had he overreacted or was she getting the jitters?

He leaned to kiss her. "I'm going to check on things. See you tonight."

She opened the door, but he touched her hand. "Remember, our secret."

Over at the bunkhouse, Dave had Grady and the guests all occupied, and it was a good thing. Becky had a hard time forcing her friendliness with all that weighed on her thoughts. This should be the most exciting time of her life, and she *was* thrilled to be marring the man she loved, but something was missing. Maybe Slate was worried about her keeping her ranch? That was it! He didn't know how to tell her she had to close it. How sweet that he didn't want to hurt her feelings.

She looked up to see a couple ride by. Her business had been fun, but she'd give it up in a heartbeat for love. She'd never admit that to Wanda, but now she knew having a house was not the same as having a *home*.

She wanted a home with Slate and a family. Brothers and sisters for Grady. Funny how a lifelong dream could change.

Becky forced herself to mingle with the guests at dinner. Slate wasn't back yet, so she laughed at unfunny jokes, ate a bowlful of chili, and smiled at the compliments on her ranch. Three ladies had already ordered several Western outfits, and Tim wasn't due to take their photographs until tomorrow. Their arrangement had worked out fine, but now she guessed she'd continue doing the bride's makeup for him, along with her customers at Wanda's salon. Hopefully she could get her old chair by the window back.

She excused herself when she noticed Slate ride into the corral.

"Hi." He switched the checkrein to his other hand and dismounted to kiss her cheek. "How are things going?"

"Fine. The sheep all…?"

"No more coyote attacks." Lifting the saddle from Cloud Dancer, he leaned forward and kissed her.

A warmth touched her heart at his little gesture. It took so little for her to get pleasure from Slate. God, she loved him.

For supper, Rosa fixed a huge meal of some spicy casserole with chicken being the only identifiable ingredient Becky could name. She made small talk with Slate and they ended the evening with a glass of sherry on the verandah.

Exhausted from the exciting day, she leaned against his arm and yawned.

"Is it the company?" he asked.

She poked his ribs. "No, silly."

He stroked her cheek and brushed a few hairs from her forehead. "Go ahead and rest."

Becky inhaled the scent she knew would make her a fortune if she could bottle it, and shut her eyes. The feminists could have their independence—she'd take a protective man any day.

★

Sunlight forced her eyelids to flutter. She yanked a pillow over her face to ignore the intrusion. A pillow? Looking around, she saw her room but had no idea how she got there. The last she remembered was resting against Slate's chest on the verandah. Yesterday had been quite a day.

After a leisurely shower, she dressed in black shorts and a yellow flowered T-shirt. Amazingly, she was choosing more conservative outfits lately. Refusing to wear pink nail polish with yellow, she took out her makeup kit. Each nail glowed like fool's gold as she tried to match the color with the flowers of her shirt. It amused her how Slate was so infatuated with her nails; painting them was more fun lately. Leaning back, she could almost feel his lips tasting each finger. Oh geez, she'd never get to work if she kept daydreaming. Slamming shut the case, she gave each nail an extra blow and headed toward the kitchen.

"Good morning, Rosa!" Becky said.

The housekeeper gave her a curious look. How she wished she could share her news with her. But she would keep her word to Slate—a marriage could only survive on trust.

Rosa handed her a dish of bacon and eggs.

"Slate leave already?"

"*Sí*. He left before I arrive today."

Hm, hope nothing was wrong. He'd said all was fine with his sheep yesterday. Oh well, in two days they'd be married. No sense worrying. She shoveled in the eggs and grabbed the bacon. On the way out, she ate both slices. "See you later, Rosa."

The housekeeper nodded as she cleaned up the dishes.

Becky met Dave in the bunkhouse and went over the plans for the day. Tim was due in a few minutes. Grady had found some friends among the guests to keep him busy. She headed to the cactus display where they did most of their photography.

After fixing Mrs. Marshall's lavender cowgirl hat for the hundredth time, Becky sighed. "It really shows your eyes off better if you keep it set back a little."

"You're the expert," Mrs. Marshall said as she pulled the hat forward.

"We're all set, Tim." She gave up and let him start taking pictures.

While he clicked the camera, she sat on a folding chair to watch.

"Phone call for you, Missy Beecky."

She turned to see Rosa coming toward her.

"Oh, thanks. I'll be right in." Hopefully nothing had gone wrong with the hat orders. This was the youngest group of guests so far and the most demanding. If they didn't get the outfits they'd ordered before the end of the week, she worried they'd cancel. And if and when the time came, she wanted to go out of business on a positive note. The thought saddened her.

Cool air wafted against her warm skin as she entered the kitchen. Through the window she could see Rosa hanging clothes. Lifting the receiver off the counter, she said, "Hello."

"Attorney Greeson would like to see you today, Miss Chambers."

Becky recognized Miss Blue Hair's whiny voice. "I don't *have* an appointment." That was mean, but the woman had it coming to her.

The receptionist breathed loudly into the phone. "Is one o'clock all right with you?"

Mentally scanning the day's schedule she said, "Sure." After a curt goodbye, she hung up the phone. Attorney Greeson must have some papers for her to sign to finalize the will—and lose Sidewinder Valley. He didn't need to rub it in—she knew the terms all along.

Slate didn't make it back for lunch, so Becky ate the chicken sandwich Rosa had left on the table while she called Lily to check on her orders. She couldn't find Rosa, so she took the van and left for town. No telling what Miss Blue Hair would do if she was late for her appointment.

The distinct odor, she remembered so well from her first visit, filled the attorney's office. Not as gut-wrenching a smell as the dentist's office, but definitely memorable as she inhaled the scent of leather from the hundreds of bound books lining the shelves.

Attorney Greeson shuffled some papers and lifted a folder from a pile. "How have you been, Miss Chambers?"

She wanted to say ecstatically, *I'm getting married this weekend,* but she said, "Fine."

"I guess you would be fine." His glasses bounced on the bridge of his nose as he chuckled. Becky thought the buttons of his paisley vest might pop at any second.

What the heck was he talking about? Maybe he knew about her wedding! Maybe the whole ranch sensed her excitement. Heck, the whole world! They had to have noticed she walked on air. Fondling her ring beneath her shirt, she looked at his puzzled expression. "And why would I be fine?"

"Well, six months ago you seemed overwhelmed to inherit part of the ranch..." He coughed and cleared his throat.

"Of course I was, but now that, well, I'll adjust to..."

He laughed. "It shouldn't be difficult to adjust to owning all of Valley Del Sol!"

"No, I guess.... What?"

He laid out some papers before her. Long legal-size sheets. Her heart galloped faster than Sugar. Nothing good ever came into her life when someone presented her with legal documents. Well, except for meeting Slate. The words blurred as his pudgy finger pointed to her name.

"If you sign here, I'll have Miss Whitherspoon..."

"That's her name?" she mumbled.

He looked at her curiously; she didn't blame him. She sounded like some moron and her voice shook. Becky Chambers never had trouble controlling her voice until the last six months.

He cleared his throat again as if the gesture would make Becky understand what he was saying. "Yes, Miss Whitherspoon can then draw up the deed to Valley Del Sol in your name."

She'd only fainted once in her life—until now. Attorney Greeson looked fuzzy, then green, then....

A sickly floral scent tickled her nose. Becky coughed and waved her hand in front of her face. Opening her eyes she gasped. Miss Witherspoon's hair *was* blue when you saw her so close. She was rubbing some powerfully stinking—unless you liked funeral arrangements—cloth across Becky's forehead.

"Shall I call a doctor, Miss Chambers?"

"Are you sick?"

The woman scowled at her. "*You* passed out and nearly scared Attorney Greeson to death. Are you pregnant or something?"

Becky swatted away the wet cloth the woman brushed across her forehead. "Or something." She pushed to sit, refusing to give into the woozy feeling in her head. Lately, she wasn't dealing too well with shocking information.

"I want to talk to Attorney Greeson, alone." She pushed to stand on wobbly legs.

"He has another appointment in…" She looked at her mother-of-pearl watch.

"I'll only be a minute." She swayed and grabbed the door handle despite Miss Blue Hair's protests.

Attorney Greeson looked up over his glasses. "Feeling better…"

"Did *he* know?"

"I beg your pardon…"

"Did Slate know I inherited the ranch?"

"Certainly."

"When?"

He ran a pudgy hand through his white hair.

"When did you tell him?" The poor attorney cringed at her tone.

"I believe it was Monday… I… I can have Miss Whitherspoon check the appointment book…"

Becky spun around. She hadn't meant for the door to slam so loudly or for Miss Whitherspoon to shriek so shrilly.

★

Becky shoved jeans, shirts, and jackets into the box. Sitting on top, she fiddled with the tape until the box remained shut. Her hands shook with anger, but she managed to pack since she didn't bring that much with her to begin with. After she was done here, she'd pack Grady's things and fetch him from the nearby ranch where he'd gone with his friends.

In the back of the closet sat the little shoebox. Gingerly she lifted the lid to take out Miss France. Hugging the doll to her chest, she thought of the father who'd give in to her, but couldn't forget the mother who didn't. She murmured, "Why, mama? Why did you give me up?" How could someone give up something they are supposed to love? Running her finger across the strawberry-blonde hair of the doll, she wondered if her mother really had given her up so she could have a better life. Maybe she wasn't capable of being a mother. Although it took her mother nine years to realize that, it had to be hard for her. Becky now knew what she had to do.

After giving Dave instructions to entertain the guests the rest of the day, she told Rosa she had a headache and gave her a sealed note for Slate. In it she'd explained that she knew of his deception, and he could have the ranch. She ran to the refuge of her room and locked the door, certain Slate would come once he read the note. Hopefully she'd be gone by then.

Valley Del Sol could have him. And visa versa.

Slate had asked her to marry him knowing full well that he'd lost the ranch. He couldn't live without his precious land, and was willing to stoop so low as to marry a hairdresser to get it. Only she was no longer a damned hairdresser, but a businesswoman. A damned successful one, too. She wouldn't marry someone she couldn't trust.

She'd drive under the wooden gates of this place and never look back. Six months ago she would have been devastated, thinking she was destined to cut hair the rest of her life and live in someone else's apartment using someone else's furniture. She'd had a small amount of money left from Uncle Nate, and the investment Slate had recommended had nearly tripled. She'd buy a small piece of property and start a new ranch. She'd have her own house—a house, not a home.

Tears streamed down her face. Funny how losing Valley Del Sol didn't mean a thing anymore. But losing Slate.... She cursed herself and shoved three pairs of boots into another box.

"He can have his damned raaaanch." She grabbed her makeup kit, breaking a golden nail. "No wonder he didn't want me to tell anyone about our engagement." Touching the ring on her neck, she yanked. The sparking diamond landed on the floor.

It still glistened despite her blurry vision.

Lifting it carefully as if the rock were glass, she held it to her lips. "I love you, Slate Lawson." Carefully, she set it on the bedside stand.

Going to her desk, she shoved papers into her briefcase. The letter from Attorney Greeson caught her eye. She lifted it, then ripped it into tiny shreds, letting the pieces flutter to the wastebasket. "No wonder he didn't want me to make a beach. He never had any intentions of letting me own this place. He would have done anything... anything! The low-lying cheat."

Wincing at the pain in her heart, she pushed the rest of the papers into the box with a swipe of her hands. She knew she could never take what he'd loved so dearly away. The ranch belonged to him. She'd give up her dreams for the man she loved as her mother had given her up for a better life. It didn't hurt any less, but she'd do it.

A thundering, barreling sound struck her ears. Clouds of dust covered the mountain view outside her window. Huge yellow tractors followed by several dump trucks passed by. Ignoring the racket, she yanked the tape from its holder to close the box.

Hank Wentworth's truck drove by.

"What the..." Becky walked to the window. That had to be a truck that looked like his. Through a clearing in the dust she read the license plate, "Hanging Hank." No one else could have the same plate. What was he doing here? With all the ruckus, she better make sure Grady wasn't around any of the trucks.

Becky wiped her eyes and grabbed her red hat from the bed. Running out the door, she realized she had on yellow boots. What did it matter what she looked like? She'd be leaving in a few hours.

Passing the barn, she stopped. Below the hill, bulldozers pushed greasewood bushes, boulders, and tumbleweeds into piles while a tractor scooped up remnants of the desert into a waiting dump truck. Another truck stood by laden with white sparking sand.

Beach sand.

She touched her broken nail to her tooth.

"Shoot. You ruined my surprise, Beck!"

She spun around in time to see Slate dismounting from Cloud Dancer.

"What's wrong?" he called and ran toward her. His voice cracked, and his eyes widened as if Becky stood there bleeding from every orifice.

Again, he'd rendered her speechless.

"Becky!" He shook her as if that'd make her talk. "Becky, are you all right?"

"Noooo! Yes… your *surprise*?" She'd never, ever, cried in front of anyone—least of all a crew of construction workers—but she wasn't herself. Emotions mixed with accusations, mixed with anger, mixed with… oh hell, love. "I love you, Slate." She sniffled and wiped the back of her hand across her nose.

"I know, Beck. I love you too…"

She yanked off her red hat and walloped him across the chest. "You *love* me?" Swinging the hat like a mad woman, she crinkled it into a mess with each strike against his hardened muscles.

Slate stood still.

"You love me, and I love yoooou!" she yelled and walloped him again.

He nodded, but didn't grab her hand. She stopped. A muscle twitched at the base of his lip. He hesitated, then lowered his eyes, "Yes, Beck. I love you and you love me." She thought his hands readied to grab her mangled hat. "And tomorrow… we're going to be married… aren't we?"

She sniffled again and nodded.

He smiled. "Right here on *your* beach."

She flung the hat into the air. Like a wounded cardinal, it fluttered in the breeze, landing in the dump truck. She looked at him.

He pulled her near as the hum of the tractor drowned out their laughter. "I've realized we can have both Valley Del Sol and Sidewinder Valley."

She waved her hands around what would be her beach. "This is why you wanted to keep it a secret?"

"Well... I lied." He took a step back. "Everyone knew. Dave was supposed to take you to town today so you wouldn't hear all this ruckus, but Rosa told him you had a headache. Even Grady knew, and to keep him from spilling the beans, we shipped him off to the neighbors. Are you all right?"

She nodded.

"This was the only chance Hank had to get his crew here. I wanted it done for—we were going to have our sunrise wedding service here to christen your beach. Rosa's going to be furious. She's been working for days preparing things to surprise you." He laughed and kissed her. "Maybe she'll be happy to cater our first born's christening."

First born. She wished Slate's baby grew inside her now... well, there *was* a chance....

"I'm sorry I ruined everything," she muttered.

"I guess I'll get used to your impetuous free-spirit." He ran his hand along her neck and paused. "There'll never be a dull moment in the Lawson home."

She pulled free. "I'll be right back." He called something as she ran back to the house and grabbed the diamond from the bedside stand. Passing through the kitchen, she spun around a startled Rosa. "I'm getting married tomorrow!"

"Oh *Dios*! I know!"

"Where's that note I..." She grabbed it from the counter and ripped it, sending pieces flying into the air.

Rosa scowled, then chuckled at Becky. "I'll clean. You go."

Slate remained where she'd left him with the same confused look on his face.

"Here." She handed him the ring. "Put it on me again, please."

He did.

"Slate, I met with Attorney Greeson yesterday…"

"Guess old Uncle Nate knew what he was doing after all."

She waved his interruption away. "Let me finish. He said I won the ranch, that you knew, and I… I'm so sorry… I though you only wanted to marry me for… the ranch."

Until the day she died, she'd never forget the pained look in his eyes.

If she could snatch back her words, she'd have done it in a second. Since she couldn't, she settled for a comforting hug. "It was hard for me to learn to trust, Slate. I've never had anyone in my life *to* trust…"

"You can always trust me, Becky. I love you."

"I know. There's nothing more important than loving someone. I… guess our parent's loved us in the best ways they knew how." She swatted his chest. "Why didn't you tell me you loved me in the mountains…"

"Shoot, I didn't?"

"Uh-uh."

He nuzzled her neck. "Guess you had me all discombobulated with your lotion and…."

"Oh."

Blushing was something else she'd never done until coming to Valley Del Sol—*their home*—where her life had changed through the sheer magic of falling in love with conservative Slate Lawson.

The End

After serving in the Air Force as a registered nurse, Lori Avocato decided to give up her nursing career to write fiction. She has sold six contemporary romances and one children's book (children's book under the pen name, Lori Lane).

Lori lives in New England with her husband, her two boys and their little dogs, Kirby and Spanky, Shih Tzu/poodle mixes. She's the past president of the Connecticut Chapter of Romance Writers and has served on the Board of Directors for four years. She is still an active member of the Romance Writers of America and attends various conferences throughout the year.

She is also a member of Sisters in Crime and Mystery Writers of America along with several RWA chapters. Lori writes full time with the focus of her work running from humorous contemporary stories, often with medical professional characters, to military romances. She currently has a novel with a female fighter pilot heroine, and has also begun a humorous crime solving series of a burned out nurse who becomes a medical fraud insurance investigator.

Lori loves the idea of romances having happy endings in which characters overcome great odds—often at great emotional prices. These books, she feels, in today's world can help women see that there is always that proverbial light at the end of the tunnel—or they can just be a great entertaining read.

Lori has won numerous writing contests throughout her career and teaches fiction writing in several Adult Education programs. One of her novels, *The Prince's Bride*, is a finalist in the Arizona Author's Associations published fiction category. You can visit Lori's website at *www.loriavocato.com*

We hope you enjoyed this book.

Other titles from Metropolis Ink

Fiction

Zarathustra / Walter Stewart

Point of Honor / Douglas de Bono

Cold Logic / C. J. R. Casewit

Laylek's Song / Timothy VanSlyke

The Logan Factor / Vincent Scuro

The Reckoning / John McLain

Roma / Helen Duberstein

Time Suspended / Lori Avocato

The Day of the Nefilim / D. L. Major

A Change of Heart / Jermaine Watkins

Non-fiction

God Makes Sex Great!
Dr. Renier Holtzhausen & Professor Hennie Stander

How to Promote Your Home Business
John McLain

For information about these and other titles,
visit our web site at *www.metropolisink.com*.

METROPOLIS INK

Printed in the United States
983200001B